THE RED JOURNAL

Deb Elkink

Rolled Scroll Press
Elkwater, Alberta

Copyright © 2019 Deb Elkink. All rights reserved.

Scripture quotations from The Authorized (King James) Version. Rights in the Authorized Version in the United Kingdom are vested in the Crown. Reproduced by permission of the Crown's patentee, Cambridge University Press.

Paperback ISBN: 978-1-9990904-0-1

No part of this publication may be reproduced or transmitted in any form or by any means, electronic or mechanical, including photography, recording, or any information storage and retrieval system without the prior written consent from the publisher and author, except in the instance of quotes for reviews. No part of this book may be uploaded without the permission of the publisher and author, nor be otherwise circulated in any form of binding or cover other than that in which it is originally published.

This is a work of fiction and any resemblance to persons, living or dead, or places, actual events, or locales is purely coincidental. The characters and names are products of the author's imagination and used fictitiously.

The publisher and author acknowledge the trademark status and trademark ownership of all trademarks, service marks, and word marks mentioned in this book.

Welcome to
THE MOSAIC COLLECTION

We are sisters, a beautiful mosaic united by the love of God through the blood of Christ.

Beginning August 2019, The Mosaic Collection will release one book each month for the next twelve months, exploring our theme, Family by His Design, and sharing stories that feature diverse, God-designed families. All are contemporary stories ranging from mystery and women's fiction to comedic and literary fiction. We hope you'll join our Mosaic family as we explore together what truly defines a family.

If you're like us, loneliness and suffering have touched your life in ways you never imagined; but Dear One, while you may feel alone in your suffering - whatever it is - you are never alone!

Subscribe to Grace & Glory, the official newsletter of The Mosaic Collection, to receive monthly encouragement from Mosaic authors, as well as timely updates about events, new releases, and giveaways.

Learn more about The Mosaic Collection at
www.mosaiccollectionbooks.com

Join our Reader Community, too!
www.facebook.com/groups/TheMosaicCollection

Books in THE MOSAIC COLLECTION

When Mountains Sing by Stacy Monson
Unbound by Eleanor Bertin
The Red Journal by Deb Elkink
A Beautiful Mess by Brenda S. Anderson
Hope is Born: A Mosaic Christmas Anthology

Coming soon: novels by Lorna Seilstad, Janice L. Dick, Angela D. Meyer, Sara Davison, Johnnie Alexander, Regina Rudd Merrick, and Hannah R. Conway

Learn more at www.mosaiccollectionbooks.com/books

Praise for
THE RED JOURNAL

Deb Elkink writes stories of ordinary people placed in archetypal situations that explore both their real, in-the-moment frustrations and discoveries while reflecting universal questions about human life.

— TERRY OLSON, Director of Arts & Cultural Affairs for Orange County, Florida

In The Red Journal, *Deb Elkink takes readers on a journey along the often painful and circuitous pathway to understanding oneself. A remarkable wordsmith, Elkink weaves a vivid portrayal of the quest of two strikingly different women seeking to infuse meaning and purpose into their lives. The discovery of a very real treasure pales next to the revelation that the greatest treasure of all may lie in finding a place to belong. In coming home.*

— SARA DAVISON, award-winning author of The Seven Trilogy and The Night Guardians Series

A tour de force of characterization. Two women, their lives so disparate, and yet so intertwined, their journeys so diverse. All tied together with a tangled mystery that in the end reveals truth and brings clarity. An exploration through time and levels of meaning.

— DONNA FLETCHER CROW, The Monastery Murders

Believable characters, plot twists, rising tension, social relevance, and a soupçon of coincidence combine to make The Red Journal *a hearty feast for the ravenous reader.*

— RON HUGHES, FellowPilgrim.org

Just finished the book. It's wonderful! Once I got started I couldn't stop reading.

— SUSIE MUNRO, reader

Just finished reading The Red Journal! *Wow! "Word ballet" is how I would describe the many beautiful phrases. Characters, time periods, and events play "peek-a-boo" and keep one interested to see what's next! Then . . . the surprise!*

— CHRISTA VILJOEN, reader

Deb Elkink is an energetic Christian who holds God's Word with conviction and theological integrity. She is an excellent writer with perspicuity. Her passion leads her to speak with giftedness to women.

— DR. GRANT C. RICHISON, Advancing Native Missions, Verse-by-Verse Commentary

The Red Journal *is a simmering pot of characters and plot elements, rich with symbolism. Take off the cover and savor the story.*

— WAYNE STAHRE, author and owner, The Habitation of Chimham Publishing

The Red Journal*'s restless characters made me restless, too, drawing me to follow the emerging main character all the way home. Elkink does not dumb down logic, symbolism, or theology for her readers. As satisfying as a bowl of homemade soup and as thought-provoking as a George MacDonald novel.*

— LORENDA HARDER, artist and poet

Which of us has not, at one time or another, longed to be back home, when all we want is a place of rest, a safe refuge, a sheltered harbor from all that threatens to overwhelm us? The Red Journal *evokes a common experience, rich with imagery of place, travel, food, smells—but most of all, longing. Elkink writes for those who are in need of hope, of restoration, and of comfort: It is possible to go home and to find rest.*

— MARJ MILLER, reader

The Red Journal is an entertaining read, with characters varied and interesting. Their interactions shed light on universal themes including family values, friendship, compassion, and a longing for home.

— ELMA (MARTENS) SCHEMENAUER, author

Elkink leads the reader along a magical journey of distant childhood memories that surface during the historic house tour with North Dakota as the backdrop.

— PAT SLAVIN, reader

I liked Libby from the first page. Her vulnerability invites my trust, as she recognizes "running away . . . won't deliver [her] from the restlessness in her soul." Fragments of memory, aromas, and tastes keep swirling and beckon me to join Libby as she searches for an understanding of what Chesterton calls "holy home-sickness." Deb Elkink's unpredictable, realistic characters exasperate and delight me by turns.

— PAT GERBRANDT, author

Libby N. Walker is mourning the recent death of her grandmother and wants to buy a bungalow. Sybil Tansey is Libby's only friend and wants to free her from her grief and celibate lifestyle through far-flung, spiritually exotic vacations. The tangled threads of these women's lives are deftly woven into a picturesque tapestry, without a lost or loose thread.

— ROBERT WHITE, award-winning journalist, author, and playwright

In her search for home, Libby embodies our collective desire to know and to be known. While an earthly father is a gift she never knew, she has forever been deeply loved—and cherished—by her Heavenly Father. Elkink masterfully reveals the heart of God for His children through Libby's journey to find home.

— CAMRY CRIST, reader

"My grandmother," I said in a low tone, "would have said that we were all in exile, and that no earthly house could cure the holy home-sickness that forbids us rest."
(G.K. Chesterton, Manalive)

The promise of entering his rest still stands.
(The writer of Hebrews)

THE LAIRD ESTATE

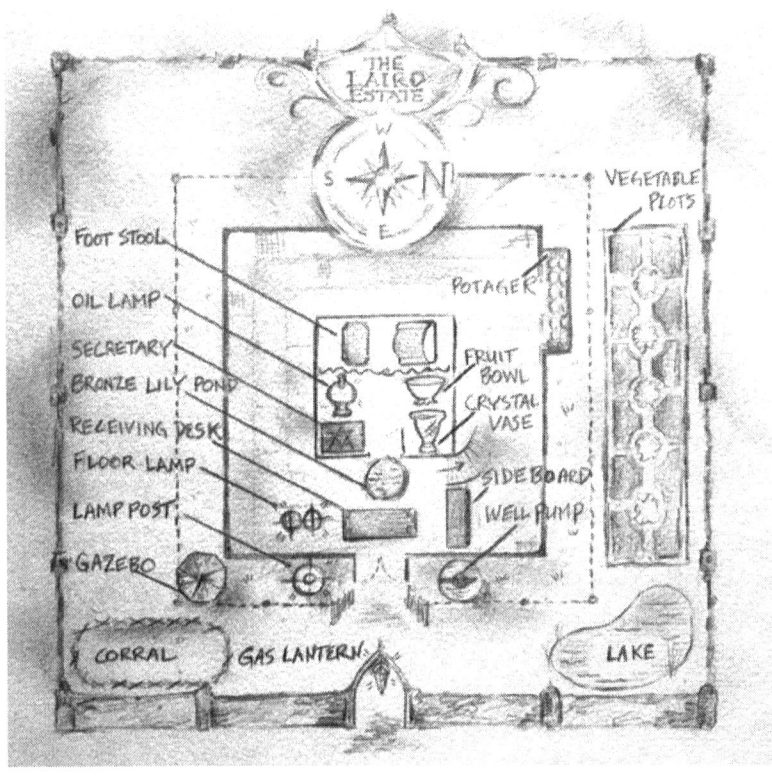

Sketch by Lorenda Harder | www.lorendaharder.com

CHAPTER ONE

Today

Libby N. Walker scrunches her eyes against the morning sunshine shattered through spring oak leaves. The splinters of light stab her retinas, so she tips her chin down into the shadows and runs her fingers over the deep ridges of the closest tree's thick, corky bark. She can't hear the wind whispering to her, although the limbs sway far above, because her friend Sybil insists on reading the posted placards aloud and providing running commentary.

"This stand of bur oak is more than two hundred years old. It says here it functioned as an above-ground graveyard for several Plains tribal leaders." Sybil's shock of beaded, teal-blue hair extensions bounces with her bobbing head, her eyes intense—she's wearing her amethyst contacts today. "Burial trees, they called them. Apparently the Sioux sewed their dead into buffalo shrouds and tied them into the crook of a branch a man's height up, out of the reach of predators."

Libby shudders. But, after all, maybe it's better than six feet under. "Let's get going," she says.

"Are you kidding? I didn't come all the way from the Cities to bypass a cultural opportunity like this. You can almost feel the warrior spirits still walking here." Sybil has already pontificated about the indigenous people's rites of passage from this world to the next, their prayers to the Great Spirit, the sanctity of the entire process. "It reminds me of the Tibetan sky burial. Isn't death fascinating?"

Libby shrugs one shoulder. Fascinating isn't the word she'd

use. The scent of death still lingers here—or maybe it's wafting back to her from the more recent past. She glances at her phone. "Will we make it for the mansion museum tour?" Their destination must still be two hours away.

"What's the rush? In a few minutes, the interpretive center is offering an acorn cake baking workshop. Right up your alley."

In spite of her inner angst, Libby's mouth waters. Frying breakfast over the open fire in front of the teepee does sound appealing. They hadn't factored in the length of the impromptu detour before leaving the motel in Grand Forks, but surely they have time to eat.

"I'd love that." Libby lets herself smile—can't stop it, in fact, when Sybil grabs her hand and pulls her along. Might as well make the best of the situation.

Back inside Sybil's Prius half an hour later, stomachs full as they hum southward on the I-29 once again, Libby rests her head against the passenger side window. She yawns, bone weary from her restless night or possibly from anxiety over all the death talk. But, in all honesty, Sybil's ghoulish curiosity isn't much stranger than her own unspoken mission. After all, she's come to the hinterlands of North Dakota on this road trip to dig up her grandmother.

Not literally, of course. For six months now Gram's been safely interred in a cemetery back in Minneapolis, just blocks from their shared apartment, although she's been calling to Libby just the same. Running away for a couple of days to tour historical sites won't deliver Libby from the restlessness in her soul that's been bubbling up again of late, but how will she find peace in this life unless she follows Gram's hints from beyond the grave? Maybe, if she does, she'll sort out the fragments of her childhood somehow linked to the Laird Mansion Museum—shards that gouge her heart.

Libby swivels her head towards Sybil, who is tapping the steering wheel to her playlist, the rhythm discernible despite her earbuds. Their overnight foray to an adjacent state won't placate Sybil for long. As far as Libby's let on, she's here only as a compromise to her friend's never-ending demands for company on her pilgrimages to what she refers to as "sacred destinations" around the world—a monastery in Japan, a mountaintop in Africa, a mosque in Istanbul.

As if Libby has the funds for such exorbitant excursions! She puffs air through her nostrils. Of course she'd love to go along, but her priorities are different than Sybil's. Even so, the timing for this weekend's imposed expedition is perfect, what with the mess of Libby's personal life right now. It gives her a break from the banker, the boss, the broken old woman—*especially* the specter of that broken old woman tormenting her for the past three weeks.

Libby fingers the antique gold band tethered by a long chain to her neck, slips the tip of her pointer into it, runs her thumb along its rough surface. It's become a habit already. She can almost feel Gram's soothing warmth resting in its crevices, and she tightens her fist around the ring. This is something real to hold on to, something to believe in.

She bunches her sweater up behind her neck, tilts the seat back, and relaxes. Maybe she can catch a nap. Indeed, she slides into a soft slumber, where she's young again and it's long ago—before she moved in with Gram, even—and she's about to learn a secret she mustn't tell. This isn't a new impression. For nearly five decades she's failed to reconstruct the details and has almost given up trying. But sometimes in the torpor of half-sleep, like now, Libby relives more of that particular memory through the mists of semi-consciousness.

In her reveries she's five years old and waking up in a bed not her own, sure someone's called her name. Moonlight lies in a ribbon down floral wallpaper and across matching bedding that blooms with forget-me-nots. In her far-away dreaming, as at the end of a tunnel, the young, long-ago Libby whispers for her mommy in the strange house but doesn't hear the usual sounds of retching in the bathroom or drunken lurching against furniture.

Libby watches herself in the dreamscape climb down from the stately bed, floorboards squeaky as a trapped mouse in the corner of their shabby kitchen back home, and still Mommy doesn't come. But from deep below surges the familiar, fierce rhythm of her voice. Creeping down the darkened hallway of the enormous house, the phantom Libby reaches her hand high to slide it along the polished wooden railing as she descends the stairs to the main floor. The carpeted steps tickle—*one, two, three, four, five*—all the way to the bottom. She pads down a hallway and stops by a water fountain set into the wall at just the right height to sip and dribble.

What is that glow? It shimmers around the edges of a floor-length curtain hanging wall to wall inside a larger room. Curious, the little-girl Libby edges closer. She hears breathing behind the curtain—shallow, slow snuffles like the neighbor's dog makes when it snoozes before it jumps up, fangs bared, snarling and snapping. Her tummy somersaults. She grips the heavy fabric—she can feel its twisted texture still, in her waking-dream so many years later—and begins tugging to unveil the source of that muted light.

And then her mother's strident shrieking pierces the night.

Libby's memory slams shut as full consciousness jolts her back to the here-and-now car ride, the flat grassland rushing by the window and Sybil still immersed in her music. Libby is clutching her shirt, the cotton sticking to her damp palms. Had she conjured up the childhood scenario after all?

But there's something too substantial and perturbing about it to blame mere imagination. It has to be real.

CHAPTER TWO

Three weeks ago

Libby inhaled the fresh newsprint fumes from Friday's *Star Tribune* spread open on the café table. Pedestrians passed by outside—university students lugging backpacks, a hipster in a sloppy vintage jacket surely too thin in the April chill. Twin toddlers each held one hand of a hoary-headed gentleman, the trio waddling towards the playground. Captivated, Libby leaned into the window and followed their progress until they turned the corner.

Then a spark of early evening sunlight flickered off a shopping cart piled high with ratty blankets, pushed by a bag lady in a crocheted cap of leftover yarns.

Libby's mouth went dry.

The grizzled crone stopped and stooped, thrust her chin forward. She squinted into the interior of the café, her gaze spearing Libby's cup then drifting upwards to Libby's eyes. The old woman's crusty, cracked lips cast a silent spell. In a trick of angles and light, Libby's own face reflected back at her from the pane, superimposed onto the bag lady's and morphing—the upturned corners of Libby's eyes in an instant dragging, her dark tresses now frizzled, velvety complexion sallow and pocked and crêpey with wrinkles.

Libby forced herself to sip but choked on her coffee.

By the time she grabbed her napkin, the woman had moved on, but the weird illusion of face layered onto face wasn't so easily dismissed. How on earth had that happened? Libby touched the glass, the outside temperature penetrating her body through her fingertips and grounding her again in physical reality. She drew in a long, slow breath and blew it out through pursed lips to untie the sudden knot in her stomach.

She flipped to the realty section, ink smearing her thumb as she skimmed the columns, most of the listings familiar already if only on paper. Nothing new in her price range had come onto the Minneapolis housing market lately but, still distracted, she circled a few addresses of older residences in the Longfellow area.

Sybil was late. She must have seen Libby locking up the card shop across the street from her own shop, but maybe her last client of the day at Amulets needed her aura read or something. Libby checked the obituaries—a body had been found in the squatters' camp below the Tenth Avenue Bridge—and then browsed a foods article. Spring mushrooms were coming into season, and she jotted down the ingredients for creamy wild morel soup, mentally checking the contents of her fridge. Mentally suppressing the image of that bag lady.

"Tibet!"

Libby jolted, her mug clattering on the tabletop.

"Sybil, don't sneak up on me like that." She mopped at the drops soaking into the newspaper, but Sybil was hardly sneaking. Never stealthy, she'd burst voice first into the coffee shop with typical drama.

"Tibet would be perfect. Check this." Sybil thrust her electronic tablet into Libby's hands and sang out her order across the room to the boy behind the counter: "Super-large unsweetened ginger chai tea soy latte to go, no foam, and make sure it's extra hot." She plopped down facing Libby, her fickle hair today a sandy brown and most of it tucked into a felted turban. She pointed at her tablet in Libby's hands. "Well? What do you think of Tibet?"

The video displayed a shaven monk in saffron and maroon robes chanting a mantra. With a stick he rapped a metal bowl and, as the ringing swelled, several patrons turned in their chairs to find the source of the offense. Libby fumbled for the volume button and pushed the device back across the table. Too bad she couldn't turn Sybil's voice down.

"We could fly to Lhasa," Sybil said, "maybe take in Kathmandu along the way." She had that gleam in her eye again.

"Sounds like your type of fun, not mine."

Sybil huffed. "Fun? It's a business write-off." She waited a beat and then grinned at her worn-out, ever-ready excuse. "But seriously, I do want to make it another buying trip. I think I can get hold of some wild caterpillar fungus for treating asthma, straight from the suppliers."

"And you can't order it?" Everything was available online, after all.

"Not the real goods. Anyway, you haven't lived until you've shopped in a traditional Asian market. Such as, for shoes." Sybil hauled her foot up, thumping her heel onto the tabletop, and showed off one curly-toed emerald slipper—brought back from Thailand last winter, Libby supposed, along with her baggy silk wrap pants. Sybil was dressing in theme again. "This is your chance to see the world, girlfriend."

"My chance this month." Libby curled her own toes. Would Sybil never give up on that same old subject?

Sybil whacked her hand onto the table, setting Libby's cup rattling again. "So you'd consider coming along, then, if I found the right destination?"

"You know I can't afford to travel."

"You only think you can't afford it because you don't know what you're missing." Sybil plucked a brochure from her purse and waved it under Libby's nose as if the scent of it would change the realities of her financial situation.

"Don't bother tantalizing me with promotional material." Libby crossed her arms.

Despite the rebuff, Sybil dropped more glossy pamphlets on top of Libby's newspaper before dashing up to the counter to collect her fancy drink.

"Now, Libby, be reasonable." Sybil returned to the table and removed the lid of the cup, added three packets of sugar substitute, and stirred. Her right cheek dimpled. "This is our chance to bond in a sacred setting."

"We can bond over a bowl of soup at home." Maybe her sternness would fend off the boisterous laugh bound to come next.

But it was no use. Sybil's huge hoop earrings flapped as she tossed back her head—almost knocking the cap off the guy sitting behind her—and rolled out a throaty howl with mouth so wide her molars glistened.

When she'd regained control of herself, she waggled a finger at Libby, bangles jangling. "Soup. You'd slip some red meat in there just to get even, wouldn't you?" Sybil slurped her drink, reached for more sweetener. "There's no trusting you."

Libby pictured mixing bits of raw lamb in with the lentils and couldn't help but chuckle. Making Sybil laugh, even unintentionally, held its own reward, and Libby's shoulders loosened.

Slouching back, she let Sybil go on about Tibet's yak butter and the grandeur of the Himalayas and the possibility of catching a glimpse of the exiled Dalai Lama if they added India to the itinerary. Libby liked the way Sybil's lips, constantly moving, also constantly smiled. For all her flakiness, hadn't Sybil been the one pursuing friendship—introducing herself personally that first day Libby stopped at her shop for an allergy cure, surprising Libby with thoughtful gifts, even sitting with Libby at the funeral home? Sure, Sybil had refused to view the body, but that was understandable.

"I tell you, Libby, what you need to cheer you up is a good vacation."

"Right." Libby straightened her back, on guard again. "And how am I ever going to save enough for a down payment if I blow it all on a trip?"

"You've lived half a century without worrying about a down payment on a house. Why start now?"

Libby forced her jaw to slacken—not, of course, over the reference to her ten-year seniority but over her younger friend's ongoing refusal to recognize normal fiscal responsibility. A continuing problem arose because of the difference between their budgets, if in fact Sybil observed any sort of budget at all. She spent money as though her resources were endless, and she expected Libby to keep up with her.

"We've had this discussion before." Libby began a fuller rebuttal, but Sybil hijacked her.

"It's an investment in your mental health. I'm only thinking about you."

Libby sniffed. "Right, so your concern has nothing to do with needing a travel partner."

"We could pick up a sexy beast along the way for you so—"

"Oh, I get it." The picture forming in her mind was tickling her funny bone. "You want me wearing a bikini in Bali as fifty-year-old bait for your own gigolo fishing." Libby, smothering a giggle, pressed her chest out, preening in mock vanity.

Sybil laughed. "Point taken, although again you underestimate your assets. However, I'm going to keep looking until I find a vaycay spot irresistible to you." She gathered the leaflets together and jammed them into Libby's bag. "At least take these home and read them. Live a little." As if Libby's life didn't count. "Got to run. Oh, and Iggy agreed to hit up the new Nepalese restaurant for an early supper. Want to join us?"

Libby chewed the inside of her cheek. She wouldn't mind the company, and payday was coming up. Cash flow itself wasn't an issue, but the bottom line on her bank statement would soon be under scrutiny. Before Sybil could insist on treating her to the meal, Libby made her decision.

"Thanks, but I think I'll head back home while there's still plenty of light."

Sybil shrugged. "Your loss." She stirred more stevia into her latte. "You're ever the homebody."

But it wasn't just that Libby preferred domesticity over socializing. Today she wanted to stretch her legs instead of catching the bus and, though only a brisk half-hour stroll, walking alone in her neighborhood was risky at twilight. She wasn't afraid, exactly—simply cautious. Several times lately she'd sensed somebody following her. She wrapped her scarf twice around her neck and pulled on her gloves against the capricious spring weather of the Twin Cities awaiting her outside the café window.

"See you Monday, Sybil."

Not far from her apartment block, Libby stumbled into a cluster of homeless people. They were a mixed batch, some elderly and others teens, shivering as though they'd recently returned from more temperate climes. Annually, around the time of the first snowfall, they diminished in number, hopping a Greyhound if they hadn't blown all their unemployment compensation on drugs and alcohol, or maybe hitching a ride south with a farmer hauling cattle to feedlots in Texas or hay to drought-stricken New Mexico. But spring saw their reunion with those who'd stayed to brave the winter. On the streets and out in the open Libby didn't always notice the sour odor of unwashed flesh of the vagrants drifting by as she waited at the station, or standing too close to her as she fumbled in her purse for her transit card. But today their collective pungency pierced the city-rank fumes.

Libby passed a fellow wearing a stained, reeking parka and then stepped around a collection of unrolled sleeping bags, tufts of stuffing visible through the rips. The plaintive cry of piping wove its way through the ragtag group towards Libby. She slowed as she approached a young man, flute hovering at his lips, and fully stopped in front of his empty plastic cup until the soft, reedy wailing finished.

"You like my song?" His mouth stretched in a crooked smile.

"Very much. Where did you learn to play?"

"My grandfather. This was his flute." He held it out for Libby. She hefted its weight and admired the carving before handing it back. She had no grandfather to talk about. "He courted my grandma with it, long ago on the rez." Libby hid a wince. The reservation. So life hadn't been easy for him, and yet he made such beautiful music in spite of it—or maybe because of it. The boy kicked one shoe against the other.

"It's a lovely instrument." Libby burrowed into her purse for spare cash. "Where are you staying? I mean, have you got somewhere to keep warm and fed?" His mother must worry about him. Or his grandmother.

"I just been hanging out around here. Shelter's full, but I got a friend with a place."

His eyes flickered towards the "crack stacks"—the tawdry monstrosity dominating Riverside's skyline. Sure, the city was making improvements but not quickly enough for Libby's tastes. She really needed to move out of the area.

"Thanks for the buck, lady." The musician gave her a thumbs-up.

She nodded and then continued on past the unfortunate lot trapped in a life fraught with dangers. At least she had a sure place to lay her head, not a burned-out flophouse or a cardboard carton in a cold alley fetid with the stench of urine. Her suite was overstocked with household belongings she was in the process of clearing away. Tomorrow she'd again face the ongoing task of dealing with a lifetime of Gram's possessions, packing them for donation or discard into the same type of boxes that sheltered these pitiable souls.

Possessions weren't people, but the irony didn't escape her.

On Saturday evening, Libby sat cross-legged on the floor of her apartment, an open garbage bag to her left, a box marked "Goodwill" on her right, and an ache in her chest. Sorting through Gram's stuff was taking a long time, what with her sniffing at hankies and snooping through letters and peering into canisters that might still hold her grandmother's essence. Libby had been dusting around the doilies and trinkets for half a year, a job Gram had managed in spite of failing eyesight right up until she died. Last weekend, Libby finally got serious and committed herself to a deadline. She'd never liked the kitsch, even at age not-quite-nine when she first came to live here, but every item was so familiar that tossing anything out was akin to throwing away a part of Gram herself.

Jagged pain slashed at her. It wasn't that she'd expected her grandmother to live forever; after all, grandmothers had heart attacks all the time. Just not *her* grandmother and not *that* heart attack. But as Gram used to say, all's well that ends well, and her life had been so well lived that, despite the sting of mourning, Libby couldn't ignore Gram's enduring bequest of cheer.

Gram's verve still infused the apartment. Mismatched garage-sale cushions overwhelmed the floral couch, and the coffee table sported a tasseled lamp, a never-used ashtray, and an aquamarine ceramic vase. The windowsills housed Gram's bottle collection, and colorful greeting cards collaging the walls dated back a lifetime, many brought home by Libby herself from overstock at Hearsay Card and Gift Boutique. Their sentiments reinforced the philosophy of this household: *The best things in life are free* and *Walk a mile in my moccasins* and—Gram's favorite—*One day at a time.*

Libby picked up the plaster figurine of a dove with a chipped beak and a crack in the wing where glue, now hard and yellowed, had oozed out. How many other broken objects had Gram mended on account of Libby's youthful disregard?

A shout sounded at the end of the corridor outside, followed by the pounding of running feet. Libby went still. Sure enough, a moment later bedlam broke loose as the hooligans from the tenement thundered into the hallway in an explosion of multilingual cursing. Libby leapt up to shoot the second bolt. But through her peephole she saw Zinnia poke her shiny face out of her apartment across the hall, barely missed by a swinging fist. Libby yanked her own door open.

"Get out of here, you thugs!" She lunged for Zinnia and pulled her into the safety of her own flat. A knife glinted, and Libby caught a whiff of booze.

"Mmm, it's the hot mama," one of the boys said, and another wolf-whistled at her.

"Show a little respect." Libby narrowed her eyes at them. She had to be older than some of their mothers.

"I'll show you respect." The gang leader licked his lips and stepped closer, but a yelp from one of the others drew all the ruffians back into the scuffle. They had tumbled out of earshot and back on upstairs by the time Zinnia sat on Libby's sofa, her great chest heaving and her ebony face beaded with sweat.

"Where are the cops when you need them?" Libby asked, though the thought of their flashing lights roused childhood angst. "I hate this place."

"What would Babette say about your ungratefulness?" Zinnia shook her head, setting her jowls to wobbling.

"Gram wouldn't have blamed me." Would she? Libby scratched at the glue on the plaster dove still in her hand. "It's a matter of safety. Hygiene, too. The plumbing in this place stinks, literally. Gram always imagined better things in store for our family." Of course, Libby was the only one left in the family now.

At first this subsidized residence was all her grandmother could afford, but when Libby started to contribute income and they had no excuse to stay any longer, the option to move lost its appeal, and Libby acquiesced to dear Gram's languor.

"But Babette never complained. She was the one taught me about that." Zinnia's eyes grew glossy. "I used to grumble something terrible, back before I knew her."

Libby stood firm. "There's a difference between complaining and admitting facts."

"Well, this block is all we got to call home, I suppose."

"Home?" Libby couldn't keep the sarcasm out of her voice. "No amount of lace and knick-knacks could ever make accommodations like this homey."

The building Libby returned to every evening was a nondescript, eight-story structure with a crumbling brick façade, splintered trim, and a few surveillance cameras that blinked dispassionately at the hostility playing out every night in the street below. Inside, the shabby foyer flooring hadn't been replaced since she'd moved in, and graffiti obscured the original paint color. Sure, pockets of community existed. Zinnia had been a true-blue neighbor, for example. But, for the most part, the thin walls seeped tenant anguish from one unit to the next—fretful children whining, the slap of flesh on flesh.

"So you moving or what?" Zinnia took in the bags and boxes littering the sitting room.

"These are all Gram's things but, yeah, I'm considering it, now that she's gone."

"You could do worse than this place."

Libby rubbed her chin. "I don't think so." Of course, one

thing was indeed worse than living in such a dump, but homelessness was an irrational fear. She'd squirreled away sufficient money to cover an increase in rent if not yet a down payment. Meanwhile, Sybil had been badgering her to lease a condominium in her plush complex way out near Arden Hills so they could plan exotic trips together. But Libby wasn't that rich, and she had other goals anyway.

"As for you, Zinnia," she continued, "you should rethink your refusal to apply to the Haven." Libby would never have placed Gram in the assisted living facility just down the street, but Zinnia didn't have the luxury of kin to care for her.

The old gal stared down at her hands—beefy mitts creased pink in palms accustomed to hard, honest labor. Then she rolled her eyes at Libby and asked, "Why'd I want to be stuck with all them toothless droolers?"

"As if your own teeth are real." At Libby's retort, Zinnia's face split in a monumental smile, revealing dazzling dentures she cleaned with household bleach, which Libby knew because she'd caught her at it once. "I'd come visit you," she promised Zinnia yet again.

"I know. Babette raised you right, you two always going on down to the Haven with your pots of soup for them poor beggars."

Libby agreed. She'd been taught well. Gram's insistence even into her nineties on trekking over to the geriatric center had resulted in a short human-interest story in the paper a few years ago. The clipping—with a grainy, colored photo of Gram holding onto Libby's elbow as they passed through the automatic glass doors of the nursing home—hung framed on the wall above the couch for all to admire. Libby read its caption to herself now: "Nonagenarian Babette N. Walker and Granddaughter Libby

Volunteer at the Cedar-Riverside Haven." The picture showed off Libby's high cheekbones but hid the few freckles sprinkling her skin during the summer. Her face tipped in tenderness towards the top of Gram's flossy head.

When Gram had first seen the photo in the *Tribune*, her eyes filled with tears and she remarked about how tall Libby stood next to her own bent frame, and how black her granddaughter's long hair was. Not the blue-black of a raven's wing, Gram had said, but the rich brownish black of a buffalo's underbelly.

What would her grandmother have known of buffalo, anyway?

That photo was taken the last time they made it over to the seniors' home together. Libby swiped at her eye.

"I miss her, too." Zinnia floundered to her feet to deliberate over the news clipping with Libby. "But we got to go on." Her eyebrows lifted when she spotted the plaster dove Libby held. "You're not throwing that out now, are you?"

Libby handed it over. One person's trash was another's treasure. Her neighbor clumped back to the door through the maze on the floor and left, cradling the cheap ornament as if it were an authentic Hummel. It was destined to join the rest of the clutter on her kitchenette counter, one less bit Libby had to dispose of herself. She reached for a battered tin tray full of pins and pens and pieces of a jigsaw puzzle.

By midnight Libby had progressed to the kitchen, sleep eluding her. She tackled the appliance cupboard and mulled over Zinnia's earlier suggestion that she lacked appreciation.

"Practice an attitude of gratitude, child," Gram intoned every school-day morning as she sent Libby off with her bag lunch and a kiss on the forehead. And Gram gave her a chance to exercise the virtue on the weekends, letting her tag along on her housekeeping job in a wealthier section of town and paying her a few dollars for her efforts. Maybe that's how Libby cooked up the idea of buying a house in the first place and began pestering her grandmother.

"We can't pay for a house, little one," Gram would say. "We're apartment renters, not homeowners."

"Una in fifth grade lives in a real house."

"Una has a daddy to help pay the bills."

Libby upended a drawer into the trash, tapping out the crumbs. At about that age her undefined longing first took shape. She began noticing real estate lawn signs and memorizing phone numbers posted at the supermarket beside photos of likely looking homes for sale by owner. By her teens, she was poring over library books and architectural magazines for something she couldn't quite put her finger on—the courtyard of a Spanish hacienda, the colonnade of a French abbey. But through the passing of the years, as her energy was spent in caring for Gram, so was the wishful thinking of her youth, lost in the growing up until she'd almost forgotten she was looking for anything at all.

However, now that she'd fulfilled her obligations and paid her dues to family, such as it was, perhaps the time had come to find a home of her own—to redeem the deposit of a childhood fantasy Gram in her poverty could never quite grasp.

Libby's favorite walking route took her along the west bank of the Mississippi, south towards the falls, and into a residential area congested with mature trees of unfurling leaf. It consumed the better part of three hours but was the perfect break from her sorting and, more, from the hollowness of her apartment on a Sunday afternoon.

No one she knew personally lived in Longfellow, but she'd tramped through it in every season—when summer birds sang from oak limbs, and frost turned weeping willows into cascading crystal, and maples carpeted her path in gem tones. The fresh spring green today revived her. She strode into and out of the shadows, down one block and then another, catching herself counting her steps one through ten in a rhythm that, since she was a girl, had attended all she did. Maybe she was keeping time to a sing-song memory: *Step on a crack and you'll break your mother's back* or *Once upon a time in a land far, far away . . .*

Libby had her usual destination in mind, a house that had first caught her eye from the passenger side of a dirty bus window back in the early seventies as she accompanied Gram to work one morning. During her painful teens in the eighties, Libby kept an eye on that house, and all through the nineties and on into the new millennium. Now she again slowed her pace in front of Seven Canaan Lane, her pulse racing.

The Craftsman-style cottage, less pretentious than some bungalows in the area, incorporated the requisite low-pitched and gabled roofline, small-paned casement windows, and tapering stone porch supports. But the exterior design was never what had charmed her most.

What charmed Libby was the family living inside.

The first time she noticed the house, she was enchanted by the swing set in the front yard, and soon by a shiny bicycle propped up against the ash tree. She began to wait fervently along the bus route, watching for the evidence of family like Gram might watch her soaps. Later, she'd take the same bus when she wasn't going anywhere in particular, or amble past the house at her own pace as though she weren't a nosy outsider who didn't belong.

She watched a mother and father raise a daughter about her own age in that house—a blonde youngster chasing her puppy down the street, then parking her first car at the curb, then festooning the front yard with white netting for her bridal reception. The senior couple grayed, and they made room on the veranda for the stroller of a visiting grandchild. One day a moving van parked in the driveway, and daughter, husband, and offspring took up residence—three generations living under one roof, father siring daughter birthing sons.

Libby had never known a father figure herself. Gram didn't talk much about that, but she must have registered Libby's pining after the house on Canaan Lane every time she took her along, until Babette was too worn out to render her housekeeping services any longer. Libby went on with her fiction, though, fabricating an elaborate story surrounding the family—how the mommy in a checkered apron would help the blonde girl with homework every day before dinner, and how the daddy would shrug off his jacket and enfold his daughter in his safe arms when he arrived home from the office. Oh, Libby envied her that daddy! Sometimes she whispered, so that Gram couldn't hear, supplications to some imaginary father. Even now, after life had tarnished her outlook and the blonde girl had grown middle-aged hips, Libby kept up the story and still made excuses to walk past the bungalow. She'd never come face to face with even one member of the multigenerational family, but the obsession hadn't abated. That family embodied her ideal of peaceful hominess.

This afternoon she allowed her eyes to slide sideways as she passed by. Although the flutter of the curtains made her heart stutter, she just kept walking.

She stopped by the market on the way home to pick up a few groceries, sticking the latest edition of the local real estate flyer into her grocery sack. She didn't expect any new listing of interest, though. Despite frittering time away on the Internet since Gram's passing, Libby was no further ahead in finding a potential house to purchase, even with all the foreclosures. Hoping she could afford something along the lines of Seven Canaan Lane was ridiculous, at least in her current financial position. But maybe she should contact that realtor Sybil talked about last week. Perhaps the time had come to take decisive action rather than just gripe, as Zinnia had pointed out, about how much she detested her apartment—time to finally put her money where her mouth was, as Gram might have said. Yes, she'd place the call as soon as she got home from her walk.

As dusk crept up behind her, Libby lengthened her stride for the last few blocks to outdistance potential stalkers. Even so, the freaky reflection she'd seen in the café window two days earlier hovered at the fringes of her mind, keeping up with her brisk pace.

CHAPTER THREE

Three weeks ago

Sybil Tansey stretched out on the leather sofa in her lakeside Arden Hills condo after an evening session on her yoga mat. An open bag of kale chips and a probiotic smoothie sat within reach while she clicked through the TV channels. The weekend had been a success. That is, she'd gotten her fill of Iggy and then sent him back to his wife and kid as though she was putting a pet out for the night. Not a tame tabby cat, though. No, Ignatius, "the fiery one" according to Google, kept her fuse lit, all right. The meaning of life was found in the pursuit of love, after all.

Or was she missing something?

The unsolicited question rankled. That was the problem with Sunday—the so-called "day of rest." Too much free time.

A travel show blazed across the widescreen and Sybil hit the "back" button so she could catch the beginning of a documentary about Canada's old-growth forests on Vancouver Island. Why, she'd walked that very coastal rainforest during her fledgling solo trip a dozen years ago. The trip that had been funded with the wad of guilt cash she scored from her dad, who'd just paid bail for one of her brothers and was susceptible to her carping about making it even.

"I'm your baby girl, right, Daddy?" She'd mumbled it around a lump of his favorite licorice gum and then blew a bubble to waft the smell his way.

"At least you finished college." He grimaced. "That useless brother of yours couldn't even make it out of high school."

"A getaway would do me good, but I haven't been able to save much at the diner." She let a tear well up in her eye.

"They don't pay you what you're worth," he said. But then he didn't know how much she earned in tips. He took out his checkbook. "What's a trip to Canada cost?"

Her father was such an easy touch, and she deserved to be rewarded. She wasn't the one in jail. Or, like her sisters, saddling Dad and his new wife with a mess of snotty-nosed grandkids.

Sybil had needed pampering after a gruesome breakup back then, in her mid-twenties. She'd learned from that guy how clingy and hard to shake men can be. On top of that, Mom had recently given in to the cancer, and her remaining female relatives—all in an Irish fluster—began hounding her to get a mammogram. She'd had moments of fear at the beginning, sure. But she expelled the idea of sickness from her mind, took Dad's money, and engaged in a little travel therapy instead.

Now, in front of the TV, Sybil slurped her strawberry shake spiked with a jigger of rum. Hair of the dog, so to speak. A slight headache still plagued her after last night's marathon of margaritas. She raised the volume to drown out her discomfort and sweep her back into her first globetrotting adventure.

Leaving the metropolis of Minneapolis for west coast wilderness after she dumped the sticky boyfriend had been a great escape from her troubles, if only for the few days she was gone. The trip turned out to be life altering in several respects. First, she made the commitment to stay away from anything carcinogenic. She followed that up by formulating a business plan for her own holistic health enterprise underwritten, of course, by said father and resulting in her opening Amulets Alternative Apothecary.

And the vacation allowed her to flee the scene of Mom's capitulation, too. Sybil had taken her turn sitting vigil in the living room while her mother fought against the passing, feebler each day, each hour, thrashing in the sweaty sheets until the stillness overtook her. At the moment Sybil raised the back of the hospice bed to reduce the gurgling rattle, Mom came to for the first time in days. She turned her head so their noses almost met and opened her eyes a final time. Sybil could have fallen into their infinite depths of love. But she recoiled instead.

Back then, Sybil still thought of death and love as opposites.

She cried alone for a week after the wake, leaving her father to his own private grief. The mingled fragrance of roses and baby's breath filled the house then, and even today turned her stomach and churned her emotions. Yet what floral arrangement had she sent to Libby for her grandmother's memorial service but an extravagant casket spray of long-stemmed reds pillowed in baby's breath?

Sybil's confusion had been mostly cleared away by that first ever international vacation, when she experienced the transcendence of nature in its raw state. That in turn led to the shift in her perception towards the new consciousness she now embraced—the swab she used against the cold sweat of self-doubt that chilled her at the most unexpected moments. The idea of spirituality had been foreign to her, but she was remade during that trip. She went from quivering sorrow to jubilation, from purposelessness to passion.

She'd driven through miles of magical island mists and then booked into a ritzy resort right on the Pacific Ocean. Not yet considering vegetarianism in any of its forms, she ate a plateful of pan-seared oysters.

Saliva spurted into her mouth now at the gustatory memory.

The spa therapy room of the hotel had been decorated with Haida tribal masks, the linens were satiny on her skin, and one wall opened so immediately onto the rocky coastline that briny spray spattered the deck a few feet away. The aesthetician scrubbed Sybil with mineral salts and kelp and then wrapped her in mud and organic seaweed like a piece of sushi. Sybil watched the sun setting in the ocean, almost sizzling in the snuffing. In the dusk the rollers kept breaking and the surf kept pounding in and swishing out, pounding in and swishing out—the heartbeat of the living planet.

The next morning Sybil had walked beside a salmon-spawning stream tangled with grasses and reeds and berry-laden bushes. Thousand-year-old trees closed above her, their bark wrinkled with the deep furrows of centuries, their branches sleeved in draping velvet.

"This forest is the source of the totem poles carved by coastal aboriginals—Salish and Sitka, Tlingit and Nootka," the TV commentator said as the woodland cathedral filled the screen and muffled drums thumped out the pulse of the universe within Sybil. She sat up on the couch to strain closer, carried back in time. "Fallen trunks molder in the undergrowth, ferns and vines and spongy mosses feeding off the decay." His description and the televised images took her back to the natural sanctuary, everything veiled in a moist haze of living green so luminous it shone as though giving off light itself.

The primordial beauty had overwhelmed Sybil back then. She'd worshipped for the first time ever. She actually knelt in the dense silence of the forest and bowed her head to its hymn—the plink of a dewdrop on a waxy leaf, the far-off cough of a raven.

This spontaneous bending of knee and opening of soul completely wiped out all thoughts of her mom's demise and her dad's emotional distance. How could a girl not worship when Mother Nature shouted out her presence like that?

And the god-like Canadian hiker she'd met at the bar later was pretty easy to worship in the sanctuary of her suite, as well. He was older, experienced, the perfect surrogate for an absentee father—with benefits to boot. Her spine tingled at the recollection. She marked the date as her psychic birth.

"That was the beginning," she murmured to herself. That trip introduced her to a whole range of destinations she began exploring one by one, every excursion bringing her closer to her center, to self-awareness.

She dipped into the bag for another chip as the show wound down. Libby needed this dynamic shift, too—this reformation or, rather, transformation. And, by Jove, Sybil was doing all in her power to release it in her. The first thing her friend needed was to be shaken loose from her short-sighted insistence on blowing her money on a house when renting would free her up to discover all Sybil had to teach her.

Besides, Sybil could use a touring companion.

While she was thinking of it, she snatched up her phone and sent Libby a quick text: *Want to go to the Amazon Jungle with me?* In all probability she'd ignore the message. And cheapskate Libby didn't have a data plan, so there was no use sending her a link.

But one of these days Sybil would break through Libby's resistance to travel. Then the fun would begin.

Back in her topsy-turvy kitchen after her walk, Libby moved a carton of rusty sieves, vegetable peelers, and ladles from the countertop then pulled out the soup pot, Gram's most precious legacy. The well-seasoned, cast-iron, eight-quart kettle with the thick wire handle had been purchased at Dayton's by Gram's mother—Libby's great-grandmother—when Babette was a baby, so Libby had been told. It'd produced the soups Gram grew up on, and in that same vessel Gram conceived the chowders and bisques of Libby's own childhood. Of course, it took Libby a long while to appreciate her birthright. No ten-year-old comprehends what goes into making a nourishing meal, only that she doesn't care for onions. No thirteen-year-old recognizes the difference between turnips and rutabagas.

By the time Libby recovered in her early twenties from the consequences of her gastronomic rebellion and discerned the value of a hearty bowl of soup, Gram was showing her age. It wasn't until she realized she wouldn't have Gram forever that Libby began to badger her in earnest for the recipes stored in her grandmother's lapsing memory. If Babette had forgotten recipes in her head, it didn't matter much to her hands because she cooked by heart and palate—a pinch of this and twist of that, each batch with its own character.

"The soups I make on my own are always thin, watery," Libby once groused to Gram of her initial attempts in the kitchen. "How are yours so rich and delicious?"

"Well, the trick is this," Gram said in her dear, quavering voice. "You just keep putting stuff in until it tastes right. Practice makes perfect, you know."

It was a typical soup-making episode, Gram directing Libby

from her chair in the kitchen despite having become increasingly muddled with age. "Start with your basic stock," Gram instructed in her measured cadence as she sat at the table and tried to chop a carrot, nicking a finger in the process. She didn't mean the boxed, grocery-store version or even bouillon cubes, both banned from her pantry although a concession Libby sometimes made these days.

"Okay, water and what?" Libby's stomach had rumbled. "We don't have any meat or bones."

"Nothing?" Gram tilted her head.

"Well, there's this dry rind of bacon . . ."

That got Gram nodding. "Perfect. I believe there's half a cabbage left at the back of the icebox. Trim off the moldy bits." A few cloves of garlic, a bundle of thyme and bay leaf, and a handful of dried beans later, they'd feasted.

"How did you learn to make soup out of nothing?" Libby had known Gram's answer before she gave it.

"Same as everyone who didn't have a garden in the dirty thirties. We scrounged. Waste makes want, after all. Didn't I ever tell you about Redpath and the hobo jungles?"

Of course she had, many times. But Libby never tired of the way the skin around Gram's eyes crinkled as she related the escapades of Redpath during the Great Depression, when throngs of hungry men for hire rode the rails across the continent, meeting around campfires close to the train tracks to toss a stolen potato into the pot or add a rabbit snared along the way. Redpath was a mythic figure throughout Libby's upbringing, a wandering vagabond who'd passed through Gram's life long ago to leave her with a baby—Libby's mother, Elsa N. Walker—but no legal name change.

There'd been no legal name change in the family of Walker women as far back as Libby had been told, four generations now including hers. She, her mother, her grandmother, and her great-grandmother all went by this same surname—same middle initial, too—and the history behind the name and the initial was unknown, or at least unspoken.

Once Gram hinted Redpath had been violent, had blackened her eye in a drunken rage. Maybe that was why, when Libby left home after graduation to move in with her high-school boyfriend and then returned to the apartment abandoned and beaten, Gram nursed her through the miscarriage with mugs of steaming soup and stories of hardship, told with empathy and a humor that lessened Libby's own woes.

This evening, alone in the apartment, Libby placed the heavy kettle on the back burner and turned the heat on medium until the butter sizzled. She sautéed slivered onion, carrots, and celery without browning them and then blended in a dusting of flour, a pinch of salt, and a bit of water, letting the concoction thicken. To retain the delicacy of the milk she added next, she skipped heavy seasoning. Hot milk was a natural sedative, and she was inventing this soup for Zinnia, who was suffering from insomnia after yesterday's upset with the hoodlums and whose usual diet consisted of instant noodles and canned tuna or whatever she happened to find at Dollar Tree. But Libby had a treat for her. When she'd stopped at the market on her walk, she picked up a *crottin* of creamy garlic-herb Gournay. Libby buried her nose in the brown paper bag before melting the cheese into the pot and stirring while the soup made its way back to a simmer.

During her organizing efforts of the past months, Libby had

been hoping to come across a cache of Gram's recipes. For all Babette's collecting of paraphernalia, Libby hadn't unearthed anything besides the cookbooks she herself had brought in. Otherwise, so far she'd found only a few notes scribbled on scraps of paper and the odd page torn from the back of a women's magazine with artsy pictures of steaming soups served in scooped-out pumpkin shells or crusty loaves of sourdough. And so, when she wasn't designing soup as therapy for others, Libby experimented for herself, trying to recapture the long-forgotten flavor of Gram's signature recipe—the one that eased the pain of bruised knee or broken heart. Or was she was trying to recapture the presence of Babette herself?

"Gram," she'd asked once again as they were planning Thanksgiving dinner last fall, "what was the name of the soup you used to make when I was young? Scotch Broth?"

"I don't know." Gram's eyes were vacant and her brows puckered as though she suspected it was Libby who'd lost her memory.

"The one with shreds of meat and veggies. The one you made when I had chickenpox. Remember?"

Gram didn't remember, even when Libby determined to jostle her taste buds out of forgetfulness by preparing the same basic soup every day for two weeks. Libby recorded each variation as if in a science lab—beef brisket and marjoram, or pork hocks with sage, or mutton and tarragon, and then combinations of them. At last her penny-pinching nature reasserted itself and she left the butchers alone.

Gram had never registered recognition.

Libby lifted a spoonful of her milky soup-in-progress but found it not quite to her liking, so she finished it off with a scraping of nutmeg for both its savor and its sedative effect. Perhaps it would lull Zinnia into sleep, and herself as well. Her concentration had been off lately and she wanted to be sharp for a first-time meeting at noon tomorrow with the realtor.

Before delivering a bowlful across the hall, Libby opened the *Tribune* to the notice she'd circled at breakfast. It wasn't a possible house for sale this time but an ad about a soup seminar taught by an international chef whose name rang a bell with Libby. A seminar would be expensive, for sure. But Sybil was nagging her to break out of her rut, and the spontaneous idea appealed. Libby hadn't taken a course of any sort in years, not since the customer service training required when she was first hired at Hearsay. Still, something was missing from her life—just as from her soup—and maybe her balanced diet as well as her predictable routine needed spicing up.

Paige Paulsson, guide and historian for the Laird Mansion Museum over in Kirkton, anticipated her first tour of the season coming up in just three weeks.

The baby kicked the inside of her ribcage as she sat, otherwise alone on this Sunday evening, with her legs splayed across the warped planks of the North Dakota farmhouse. She reached for a file of academic research from one of the piles surrounding her and then massaged her abdomen as the round nub of Baby's heel rubbed up into her palm. His living quarters were getting cramped, and his arrival loomed.

Why was it called the "arrival," anyway? Baby was present to her already—and to Danny, as well. He expressed delight in the way her abdomen, snuggled up close against his back in bed, bulged with their son's squirming and stretching. Last night Danny kissed her white tummy and cooed, "Come out, little one." He was rushing it. She longed to hold Baby in her arms as well, but there was way too much to do before she went into labor if she hoped to meet the cutoff for submitting her Master's thesis.

Paige opened her file and scanned the text, her eyes alighting here and there on scrawled margin notes while her mind meandered over the bedtime discussion.

"I've been waiting for twenty-seven years to have a family," Danny had said, as though he'd dreamed of fatherhood since his own birth. "I wish you were on mat leave already."

"Not with the tourist season starting in the middle of May."

"You should stay off your feet. You've got enough going on." He patted her belly. "Mom and Dad think you're overdoing it, too."

"You're ganging up on me." She was only half joking. Her in-laws lived three miles up the gravel road, and sometimes Paige felt outnumbered. "I know you all mean well, but my job isn't the problem." In fact, Paige's job offered her the only chance for completing her graduate studies before she gave birth. Leading tours and maintaining the archives provided complete access to the museum's informational trove.

She'd rolled over close to Danny's chest, his arm draping Baby, but her internal dialogue wasn't so easily hushed, and sleep eluded her. So she was already at the books when Danny came downstairs this morning on his way to the tractor.

"Stop working so hard." He'd kissed the top of her head.

"Easy for you to say. You're not the one with the deadline." Which was silly in light of his time constraints to finish seeding.

Danny had raised his eyebrows. "Only trying to help." He went to the kitchen to pour his coffee.

"I'm a grouch, I know." After all, he was just trying to protect and provide for his emerging family, even if Baby's timing hadn't been intentional. When her at-home pregnancy test read positive eleven months after their winter wedding, Danny whooped, but she thought his optimism misplaced.

"A grouch, yes," Danny replied, re-entering the living room, "but a cute, smart one. Want a cup?"

Paige shook her head. "It's just that all along I planned to supplement the farm income, and here I am only starting to draft my thesis." She sighed. "My supervisory committee is already leaning on me to apply for the Ph.D. program. The faster I get a lecturing position, the better for our savings plan."

Danny crouched down on the floor beside her, his face even with hers. "Stop worrying. We're going to have a bumper crop this year." As if he had any control over the weather. Paige brushed the sleep out of her eyes. Well, the last thing she wanted was to dampen his joy with her remaining reserve about the pregnancy. But, gosh, she'd studied too hard to be stymied so close to completion.

Still, sitting on the floor this evening in all her glorious plumpness, most of Paige's initial hesitance had faded away. Maybe her doctorate, her dream of professorship, would have to wait after all. However, nothing would prevent her from getting her Master's wrapped up by early June, in just over a month. And she needed time to paint and ready the nursery. Could she stay on target?

Paige had full access to UND's library in Grand Forks; most

books in the tottering tower propped against her couch were already overdue. But the university was more than an hour away from the farm, and even its library didn't give her the primary sources she needed at this juncture. The important documents—the handwritten papers—were conserved in the mansion museum with more, she suspected, yet to be found in nooks and crannies around the place. Hadn't the restoration in the seventies uncovered a whole set of accounting ledgers stored behind a papered-over door? And a while back, before her time, the astonished cleaning crew found a roll of long-missing blueprints stashed in a cubbyhole in the paneled hallway, which sprang open under the pressure of polishing rags.

"A secret cubbyhole, for goodness's sake." She said it aloud to Baby.

But the most promising resource available to Paige was her contact with other archival historians within the museum association, and quitting her job now would jeopardize that link.

She'd chosen her current area of investigation more out of convenience—a steppingstone to her academic pursuit—than out of genuine inquisitiveness regarding the founder of Kirkton. She lit upon the history of Moses David Melchizedek Laird, known to all as MDM, almost by accident and declared him her thesis subject out of sheer expediency. Her cursory interest had increasingly gelled the more she learned about him.

She surveyed the mess of papers spread around her on the floor. Delving into the life of the town's forefather had consumed her bit by bit. The Laird family history was now officially and indisputably her dedicated obsession, the swelling body of research kicking and squirming its way into life as surely as her child was doing—MDM and Baby wrestling within for her complete attention.

Paige twitched a cushion off the sofa and wedged it behind her for relief from her backache. The sun had set already, and Danny wasn't in from the fields yet. The stew in the oven gave off a spicy tang. She was always famished these days.

On a typical Sunday pre-thesis, she'd have spent the evening curled up on the couch with Danny, a good novel, and a bar of rich, dark chocolate. She used to read for pleasure—mysteries and fantasies and theological allegories by Dorothy Sayers and George MacDonald, C.S. Lewis and G.K. Chesterton. But there wasn't time for recreational reading any longer, every spare minute these days expended on educational texts.

So instead she'd been reading histories on the settling of the Great Plains, biographies on North Dakota's empire builders, and narratives of the interactions between homesteaders and indigenous Native Americans. She'd uncovered memoirs and missives and medical reports on smallpox epidemics, dispatches written by traders plying the Red River of the North, and economic opinions on the bartering system. She'd sorted through birth records and church records and records of the floods still threatening the area a hundred and thirty years after MDM came south across the Canada-U.S. border to fulfill his vision. And, of course, she'd almost memorized the catalogue of the Laird Mansion collection: sepia clippings from the *Kirkton Crier*, circa 1891; correspondence from a presbytery up in Manitoba's Red River Settlement, part of the peacemaking initiative at Kildonan; eyewitness accounts of the first Northern Pacific train to pull into town; bills of lading for furs and beef and wheat shipped from MDM's company; invoices for furniture from Winnipeg's wholesale district and for jewelry from Gerber's in Saint Paul.

It was exhausting.

"It is simply *exhausting*," she reiterated aloud to Baby. After all, he couldn't read her thoughts.

She chirped out a laugh. Of course he couldn't read her thoughts and, if he could, wouldn't understand her vocabulary anyway. Yet talking to him somehow cleared her mind and comforted her heart. "All this work and something is still missing from my research in spite of my endless reading. I just can't hear MDM's voice, no matter how hard I listen."

Baby nudged her as if in empathy.

Paige was obligated in the name of scholarship to act as a faithful scribe for MDM, to pass his story along to others. But all she'd found of a truly personal nature was the original, black-edged card signed *Father*, written by the Reverend Uriah Laird from the Red River Settlement to his son in 1882 while the young man was in Minnesota at university, telling of the death of MDM's mother caught in the crossfire of an interracial skirmish while she made house calls upon ailing neighbors. Oh, and Father Laird had sent the trinket from his wife's childhood, too, now on public display in the mansion. It was an enameled brooch shaped like a thistle, its bud set in sentimental Victorian fashion with the first "milk tooth" of MDM's mother. Her actual tooth!

"*Your* first tooth will go under a pillow for the fairy," Paige promised Baby. She hugged herself—hugged Baby—then settled back in to contemplating her research.

Besides the mourning card and a desultory smattering of domestic exchanges—MDM's instructions to the housekeeper or his responses to invitations from townsfolk asking him to dinner—Paige hadn't been able to dig up any writing of an intimate nature. That is, the published literature lacked history on the private life of the man, and the collected papers stored in the archives had a hole perforated right through them in this regard. She found the paucity of documentation peculiar.

Which was why—Paige blinked as Danny's truck lights finally glimmered through the living room window—she was so pleased to have made contact this past week with the curator of the museum up across the border in Manitoba. He promised to fax copies of several extant letters MDM had written to his father early in the establishment of Kirkton, halfway between Winnipeg and Grand Forks. Maybe this would be her breakthrough, the missing evidence she needed to help her discover who MDM really was.

CHAPTER FOUR

Today

Libby fiddles with the chain around her neck. She's waiting beside Sybil on the third-story terrace as the rest of the tour group behind them catches up, climbing the fire stairs clinging to the exterior wall of the Laird Mansion Museum. An Australian couple and a teacher with his class of junior-high students push their way onto the crowded platform.

"I'm picking up on stellar energies here," Sybil says to Libby. The tour guide standing near them is still catching her breath, but not in silence—there's never silence when Sybil is around. "Aren't you glad we made the trip after all?"

Sybil doesn't pause long enough to let Libby answer, instead turning to the teacher. "I'm sure this place must be haunted." She winks at him and reaches out a crystal-studded fingernail to poke at his shirt button. One of his students glowers and nudges her classmate, and Libby remembers being infatuated with her eighth-grade teacher, too.

Is she glad they made the trip? She's not sure yet.

She tugs the elastic from her ponytail and tosses her long hair free for the wind to comb. Gripping the wrought-iron railing and leaning into the freshening gusts still crisp with the late spring melt-off, she stretches towards the sun for a bit of warmth. In spite of her qualms about being here, something in her resonates with the barren countryside, the bleak sweep of the greening prairie that meets the shimmer of the flooding river on the horizon. Clouds spill their shadows onto the tabletop of the fields and draw her attention upwards into their billowing whiteness.

Usually Libby avoids looking up, not simply because the inner-city skyline back in Minneapolis obscures her view but because the sight of the heavens still fills her with blissful awe that gives way to vague bewilderment. Throughout childhood her schoolmates would find shapes of bunnies or lambs during recess where she could see only a snowy, flowing beard and bushy brows—a picture that brought with it a rush of comfort. Even now every cloudy silhouette morphs into the foggy lines of an ancient, kindly man beckoning her from his massive chair to come closer. But until this past Friday, the image has always dissolved to the echoes of a distant voice somehow related to the man, to the moment of standing before him. That female voice is shrill and raging, and the mere thought of it sets her teeth on edge.

Two nights ago, Libby's memory clarified enough to convince her that the Laird Mansion Museum is more to her than an impersonal historical site far off the beaten path. And this morning's waking-dream tied her more firmly to this new conviction. It also heightened her anxious foreboding.

Libby crushes a lilac floret between her fingers. She'd plucked it from a shrub growing beside the rust-eaten gate and tucked it into her jean pocket as she and Sybil first entered the yard. She holds the bruised petals up to her nose to inhale the incense as if it might overpower the lingering stench of the city's homelessness that's been permeating her senses in a new way over the past three weeks. It's not just the mustiness of a transient's sleeping bag laid out on the sidewalk she's trying to displace, or the foul vapors rising off a drunk begging for change. It's the picture in her mind of that bag lady shuffling along in front of the bistro window and glaring straight into Libby's being. And now Libby's life is collapsing around her and she's facing homelessness herself.

Yet here she is, wasting money on a road trip to satisfy Sybil's need for excitement.

No, in fairness Libby can't blame it all on Sybil this time. When the motel's alarm clock buzzed this morning after she'd finally fallen asleep again, she could have insisted they turn around for the city in Sybil's Prius instead of driving on to the museum. Besides, she'd agreed to come of her own free will, a concession to get Sybil off her back about tagging along on one of her more glamorous vacations.

But Libby has a feeling about this mansion. She licks her lips and the cool wind blows them dry. Her intuition might turn out to be whimsy, the nervous hope that's kick-started her circular thinking again. For example, at odd moments of the day she finds herself counting—*one, two, three, four, five*—all the way to ten before she begins again at one. She's been chewing her breakfast bagel ten times before swallowing, brushing her hair with strokes grouped in tens, tapping her pen to that elusive, ten-word rhythm: *Step on a crack and you'll break your mother's back . . . Once upon a time in a land far, far away . . .*

Does she want her mother's back to break? Is there ever a happy ending?

She blinks rapidly at the bizarre thoughts, and her stomach does another flip-flop. Maybe she's snapping under all the recent stress, or maybe it's the old woman's hex jinxing her. She could use Gram's solace about now. She could use a dose of Gram's sure faith and settled trust in something good beyond all the mayhem and unfinished tales.

Libby drops the lilac blossom for the wind to carry away. The museum grounds are spread out in an organized grid of walls and fences and boundaries softened by the new growth of the flower gardens. Even from this height the flames of red petunias and poppies and phlox steady her vertigo and, for the moment, her apprehension. Then a door slams deep within the mansion and the slightest shudder trembles through her palms via the metal railing.

Or is the shudder coming from inside her soul?

CHAPTER FIVE

About three weeks ago

The espresso machine hissed out Libby's caramel latte macchiato. She carried it to the table and sat down just as the door of the café opened. A lean man with silvering temples entered, and Libby nodded at his wave, recognizing Clive Clifton from the headshot on the realtor's card Sybil had given her. She took a demure sip of her latte as if she weren't a bundle of nerves about starting her house search in earnest.

They sat across the table from one another with knees too close for Libby and made small talk about the impending nurses' strike and the weather, about the bits of rotting snow the April showers hadn't yet washed away. As Libby was about to broach the subject of the real estate market, Clive launched into his pitch—but not regarding houses for sale.

"Sybil wasn't exaggerating when she described you, 'built like a model with a Mona Lisa smile and eyes full of the dickens.'" He fondled his chin with his left hand, too obviously ringless. Libby shifted in her seat and took a nibble of her grilled panini. Why had Sybil been discussing her physical appearance when Libby agreed only to a preliminary meeting about available properties? And where was Sybil, anyway?

Refusing to acknowledge his flattery, Libby said, "I'm looking for an older home, something modest."

"Sybil told me one of the condos in her development would be perfect for you to lease." Clive opened his binder and scraped his chair even closer to her side. "This is a fairly new, one-bedroom unit cozy enough for two." His hand bumped hers.

Libby pulled her elbows in close to her sides. "No, I mean I want to buy a single-family house, with a yard and a tree, in an established neighborhood. I don't want another apartment but rather a house along this line." She handed him a photograph of her beloved Arts and Crafts cottage with the Canaan Lane address on the back. "Of course, this home isn't listed, but it gives you an idea of my tastes."

He pocketed the picture without taking his eyes off Libby.

"What's a gal like you going to do when it comes time to shovel the walk in the middle of January?" He propped his chin on his hand and let his gaze slither over her face and bodice. "Then again, I could always provide my walk-shoveling services."

Libby tensed. She was about to make her escape when Sybil breezed in with her characteristic clamor, backcombed hair penny copper today.

"She's not an easy customer, this one," Clive said to Sybil. The two snickered as though Libby weren't there. "We were just discussing the pros and cons of condominium living."

"There are no cons to the lock-it-and-leave-it lifestyle." Sybil smacked her gum and plunked onto the padded bench. She picked up the napkin dispenser and checked out her reflection. "Come on, girlfriend, get over this fixation with buying a house. You need your freedom."

"You mean *you* need me to have freedom to travel with you to Tibet, or Timbuktu, or wherever it is you'll think of next." Libby's banter sounded less amiable to her own ears than she intended.

"Catfight!" Clive hooted. "Bring it on, ladies."

Humiliation burned Libby's face at the attention from other customers trying to read or enjoy a quiet lunch. She reached for the realtor's binder and paged through a few listings.

Clive seized his opportunity. "Look, how's about I line up a couple of places for us to view together this week sometime?"

How could he make a realty appointment sound like a date?

"I'm not sure yet what I want exactly." Libby was hedging. "Maybe I'm not ready for this step." She closed the binder and nudged it back towards Clive. Of course she'd thought long and hard about the house of her dreams, but it would be no simple task to find and purchase a property. And she hadn't given enough serious consideration to the cost, either. A mortgage was probably still out of her reach in spite of her scrimping. Before going any further down this road towards home ownership—maybe a pipedream after all—she'd better take a look at the mortgage application sitting on her kitchen table.

But the way Sybil went on remonstrating about the superiority of condo life reminded her how tenacious her friend could be once she took to an idea. The intensity became too much.

Libby stood abruptly. "Please excuse me." The restroom would provide relief in more ways than one, and she made a beeline for it.

Sybil shook her head at the retreating figure of Libby. The woman walked like a dancer. Her dark ponytail was sleek as a girl's, and it swung back and forth in an arc as wide as her shoulders.

Sybil turned to Clive. "Honest, Libby would be perfect for that condo. Keep working on her."

"Oh, I intend to, since you won't let me work on you." Clive's smirk was naughty.

"Ever the player, aren't you?" Truth be told, she could go for him herself if he weren't Iggy's cousin. Her boyfriend didn't know the thin ice he skated on when it came to anything like security in their love life. To top it off, Clive didn't even smoke. Libby would be a fool not to snap him up.

"So what's the ice queen's problem?" Clive asked.

Sybil checked that the restroom door had closed behind Libby before answering. "Just a bit skittish. Though stunning, isn't she? Constantly turning heads wherever we go."

"Ah, she's your competition, then." Clive snickered.

"Hardly." Sybil didn't bother hiding her scorn. Libby once confessed that, in her thirties, she'd gone out with a few guys— but they all ended up leaving her feeling dirty, disappointed. How unnatural was that? "I'd like to see her happy," Sybil added, meaning it.

"I'd like to *make* her happy."

"Well, she doesn't date anymore. That's what she told me, anyway."

"Really?" Clive cracked his knuckles. "We'll see about that."

Libby patted her hands dry in front of the restroom mirror. Should she reapply lipstick? It might give a false signal to Clive, lead him to think she welcomed his attentions. Sure, every woman appreciates being appreciated. But he wasn't a quality man, from what she could see. She needed him for his professional services alone.

Libby zipped open her cosmetic bag anyway. The peach gloss was moisturizing, justifiable on that basis alone. And maybe, while she was at it, she'd take a minute to fix her hair.

Clive rose from his seat, picking up his empty cup for a refill, and Sybil put in her order with him before he had time to offer: "I'll take a green-tea frappuccino and one of those seedy honey bars." Buying her snack was the least Clive could do to thank her for bringing Libby into his orbit.

Sybil valued Libby. Really, she did. She'd sensed a kindred-spirit connection the day Libby came through the door of Amulets for an antihistamine and left with an aquamarine crystal to clear the throat chakra, even if she did return it for refund a week later. The close proximity of their two stores fostered the women's friendship, and they'd fallen into the habit of sharing most workday breaks. Sybil bought the odd greeting card from Hearsay, and Libby countered with the occasional purchase of vitamins.

But Libby forked out her money meagerly when Sybil recommended this product or that treatment. It was as if Libby couldn't bring herself to believe in essential oils activating the limbic system, or in Reiki replenishing the vital life source, or—for that matter—in angel readings introducing people to their spirit guides. Sure, naturopathic and spiritist medicine was Sybil's bread and butter, but she was only thinking of her friend's wellness.

She still had some talking to do to convert Libby. There were signs of progress. Today Libby wore the scarf Sybil had given her along with instructions on linen's healing properties. The goldenrod shade looked fab with the amber flecks in her black-brown irises although, come to think of it, iridology might suggest liver and gallbladder congestion. Maybe Sybil should recommend a cleanse and detox, especially with the onset of hormonal changes.

Clive stood with hands in pockets facing the barista. He turned, caught Sybil's eye, and winked. Her belly fluttered; he was such a flirty Aries.

On the other hand, Libby was a typical Scorpio—resilient and wise and perhaps even an old soul reincarnated time and again. In fact, Sybil often wondered if she'd known Libby in a past life. Sybil's regression therapist had identified two of her former personalities so far; she'd been a Mongolian herdsman and an eighth-century poetess. That could explain their best-friend bond. For whatever reason, being near Libby centered her.

But Libby definitely needed educating. Sybil twirled a strand of hair around her pointer finger. Libby had no idea she was harming herself with her ongoing melancholy about her grandmother's crossing over. Ye gods, it'd happened almost six months ago. Death was a passage; death as a final end of life wasn't a thought anyone should entertain. It gave power to negative energy. After acting so long as conscientious caregiver—and Sybil didn't see that as a particularly noble endeavor—Libby should be kicking her heels up now, free at last from the chains of responsibility to her sick, old grandmother. But she flat-out refused Sybil's invitation after the funeral to the retreat near the sacred Mayan ruins of Chichén Itzá.

So Sybil had gone to Mexico alone, forgoing the beach this time and instead heading inland for the Day of the Dead celebrations. The festival was a great way to deal with the often painful process of the soul's transmigration. One afternoon she took in the Guanajuato Mummy Museum—now that would be cathartic for Libby to see. The collection of disinterred corpses deceased through cholera, with leathery hides stretched over knobby bones and desiccated faces screaming in silence, had left Sybil feeling consecrated, as if she'd been in the company of loitering spirits—although, in all honesty, for a moment she'd almost wished for the rosary of her childhood. She topped off the tour with an outstanding visit to Parícutin. The holy volcano, within the time span of only weeks, had arisen from a farmer's field like a blemish on the skin, as though Earth was purging her system of impurities.

Then, icing on the cake, Sybil had hooked up with Tomás, a bodyguard from Mexico City, and continued with her journey tradition of finding no-strings-attached male company along the way. What Iggy didn't know wouldn't hurt him. And didn't she and Iggy have an unspoken understanding about the openness of their arrangement? Mexico was months ago and she was itching to get away again soon. Her business line of credit could handle the strain.

Clive returned to the table at the same time as Libby and blurted without warning, "What're you doing tomorrow evening?" Sybil cringed at the pick-up line.

Libby retained her cool. "I'll be taking inventory at the card shop Tuesday. Then I'm off to sign up for a cooking class downtown. It's the last day of registration." She turned to Sybil. "I don't think I mentioned the seminar to you."

She hadn't. Sybil wouldn't have gone along anyway. She wasn't interested in learning to cook, of all things. That's what restaurants were for.

"How's about Wednesday, then?" Clive asked Libby. "I'm sure we can arrange a couple of suitable houses for viewing that evening, then catch a drink later?"

"Nope, she's occupied," Sybil said. Libby wasn't the only one who kept secrets. "I've organized her Wednesday."

"You have?" Libby asked.

"I've got a new line of Arabian beauty products coming in, and I've booked the rep for a private consultation for the two of us." As if Libby needed instruction in skin care. Whatever she used, her creamy tan complexion looked much younger than her fiftyish years. But the pampering session would be another step in teaching her friend to chill—to enjoy her new liberty and the way of living Sybil could show her.

Clive glanced at his wristwatch. "Got to run, ladies. Listen," he said to Libby, "I'll give you a call when I've got a couple of places put together."

Libby stood to leave, too. She was never late for work after lunch break, although why she put up with her boss's ridiculous demands was beyond Sybil.

Well, she'd just keep doing her best to drag Libby out of her morbid headspace. That girl definitely needed to mellow out.

✒

Libby detected a subtle aroma of cilantro emanating from the snooty reservations clerk standing at the entrance of the Minneapolis restaurant inside the Belle Boutique Hotel when she stopped by the next evening to register for the class. Either the woman had been sampling in the kitchen or she'd kissed the cook. Libby pressed her lips together as she pictured the second scenario. It wouldn't do to laugh.

The maître d' flared her nostrils. "We don't accept personal checks."

"I don't own a credit card, but I can go get cash."

"There's a late fee, as well. Most of our clients don't wait this long to register, especially because we're bringing in such a renowned chef as Virgil Oxenbury, all the way from England. You're fortunate someone dropped out."

Libby prickled beneath the woman's chastisement. "I suppose my money is as good as anyone's."

The hostess cocked an eyebrow, and Libby couldn't help but compare the woman's chic black dress to her own togs—a simple pencil skirt and blazer. What sort of hostess would wear off-the-shoulder formal attire on a Tuesday, anyway? But just then a table of diners dressed to the nines raised flutes of champagne in a group toast. This was some swanky establishment.

Libby originally assumed the cooking classes would be held at the vocational arts college center, another casual extension program like the scrapbooking lessons her boss's soon-to-be ex was crazy over. And so, arriving at the street address given in the paper, she'd been taken aback that the kitchen of the hotel, known for its elegant catering of small weddings and fine events, would be hosting the culinary sessions. How had she missed that detail when reading the *Tribune's* advertisement?

In Libby's estimation, and despite the popularization of Gordon Ramsay, Britain was more famous for its fish and chips than the soups advertised in the newspaper ad. By the sounds of it, this was a cooking class for epicureans, not the likes of her, just a working girl wanting to brew up a pot of homage to her dead grandmother. But she wouldn't back out now—as Gram often said, in for a penny, in for a pound—so she followed the direction of the hostess's finger to the ATM in the hotel lobby.

Libby counted the stack of twenty-dollar bills the machine spat out, most of which she left at the reservation desk. It was ridiculous to spend so much on a workshop when the purpose of making soup in the first place was frugality. Squandering wasn't her style, but hopefully the seminar would be worth it for the chance of somehow reclaiming Gram.

Libby left the hotel to catch her bus home, slipping her registration receipt into her wallet. She could justify the cost by proving herself a keen participant, throwing herself into the class. She wouldn't have to fake enthusiasm, at any rate. Maybe tomorrow she'd pop in at Re-Leaf Used Reads, in the same block as Hearsay and Amulets, to find one of Oxenbury's older books. She always wondered what kind of person would get rid of a cookbook with food-spattered pages and bindings showing the wear and tear by a loving homemaker over her steaming stove. But one could never have too many soup recipes. She was an armchair traveler when it came to cookbooks—or, more precisely, a soup kettle traveler—cooking her way through cultures by experimenting with the fare of Peru and Portugal, Egypt and Ethiopia, Italy and Indonesia. Who, besides that spendthrift Sybil, needed to take expensive vacations to get exotic experiences?

THE RED JOURNAL

Red Journal entry, dated November 23, 1898:

My Beloved, My Very Heart,

At sundry times and in diverse manners over the past months I have attempted correspondence with you. Now I must confess that, in all likelihood, you will never set eyes upon this script if the message brought me in these last days by the cart driver is indeed true. Along with news of the epidemic, he carried back to me your few possessions and, unopened, my most recent letters to you and the child. I have little recourse but to grieve the word from your own People of your probable death, and yet I can scarce believe it. I will not believe it.

Oh, My Heart, today if you could hear my voice I would exhort you not to fall away but to hold fast the confidence of our someday meeting again and of your return to this house I have prepared for you. But you have wandered far from home, and so this journal is obliged to stand as the prevailing testament of my love for you.

In full assurance of hope I remain, as ever, Yours Truly.

CHAPTER SIX

Two-and-a-half weeks ago

If Paige hadn't been awakened at six on Wednesday by magpies squawking from the branches of the quaking aspen outside the bedroom window, Danny's diesel four by four would have done the trick. It made an awful racket as he fired it up and left their North Dakota farmyard.

Paige nestled back under the duvet momentarily. She should've made sure her husband ate a decent breakfast, at least. Might as well get up and going herself. She swung her feet out onto on the cold linoleum. Today she'd get those books back to the university library in Grand Forks—a perfect excuse to visit her parents.

A few hours later, Paige slouched over a plate of warm gingersnaps at her mother's kitchen table.

"Where's Dad?"

"He's off to pick up supplies for the lawn sprinkler system," her mom said.

"Retirement seems to suit him well." Paige helped herself to another cookie and dipped it into her milk. Since her brother had taken over the construction company, Mom and Dad had lots of free time.

"How've you been feeling, dear?" Her mom removed a baking sheet from the oven. Paige wanted to complain about late nights with her books and sore eyes from staring at the computer screen, but Mom continued, "Have you decided on a name yet?"

Good question. The cross-disciplinary nature of Paige's studies made coming up with a thesis title challenging. "I was thinking maybe *Victorian Architecture as Domestic Expression of Typology in the Home Life of Moses David Melchizedek Laird.*"

Her mom stood stock-still, eyes wide, lips parted. Then she placed her oven mitts on the counter, sat down, and covered her daughter's hand with her own. "I meant the name of the baby." Mom's brows pulled together. "Goodness, it's as though you're possessed these days—as though you have a living relationship with this dead Laird."

"Oh, Mom, I know." Tears stung behind Paige's lids. "Danny's saying the same. I wish I had my thesis over and done with already."

"I wish you could leave it for a few months. How close are you to finishing?"

"I'm waiting for material from a museum up near Winnipeg to complete my inquiry so I can get my last draft off to my advisor. There's something weird I can't figure out about MDM's family."

"His background?" Mom refilled Libby's glass of milk and then her own coffee mug. "I remember you telling me his parents came over from Scotland through Minnesota on their way up north to Canada. Before the Civil War, wasn't it?"

"Your memory never fails you."

"I occasionally check the museum website to keep up with your professional life."

"Goodness, don't judge my research by that horrid site." Paige's job didn't extend to technical maintenance.

Mom picked up a cookie. "So what is it about the Laird history you can't figure out?"

"I'm unclear about the family line after MDM left his parents' home to establish Kirkton in the late 1800s. I know he spent a year at school in Saint Paul, living with friends of his parents there, and then pushed back up northward to Dakota Territory. But apparently he never married." Paige couldn't figure that one out. MDM, town founder and local magnate, was obviously a catch. "He was an only son, and the story circulated that he died alone and childless himself. Except for some innuendo regarding his widowed housekeeper."

That subject consumed a whole chapter of her thesis; the Farris-Yeast scandal held enough water to keep the courts arguing its merit with the housekeeper's descendants to this day.

A related research aspect had arisen as well, but Paige gave no credence to it, convinced that MDM had sincere concern for the aboriginal population. But rumor had it he was a "squaw man"—these days an offensive term but one deriving from the Algonquian word for "woman"—who took liberties with already-mated Native American girls because of the shortage of European females in the Red River Settlement. No, that didn't fit in with his character as Paige knew it. Part of her determination to finish her studies involved clearing MDM's name from the taint of immorality still remaining.

"I have to get at the truth about it, Mom. A principle is at stake, and I can't drop the ball now. Not when I'm on the verge of discovering my answer."

"You've always held yourself to high standards. I'm sure you'll finish well." Mom squeezed Paige's hand.

"Thanks. Your support means a lot to me."

Mom smiled. "That's what family is for."

And what a family Paige had—not only the unit she formed with Danny and now Baby, but their parents, grandparents, and great-grandparents who'd gone on before. Her heritage traced generations back to the time their Scandinavian forebears immigrated and was one she intended to project forward to successive homes full of the same bonding love.

Family was her bottom-line motivation for her research, too. Paige hugged her mom goodbye and made her way back out to her vehicle, but she couldn't dismiss her study subject as she drove away. What kin did MDM have left to disclose his bloodline? In spite of the dead-end trail of his life, she wanted to record his legacy—not limited to an empty museum of a house and the shell of a frontier town but a real story that kept on being told. And with thesis submission cut-off and pregnancy due dates both imminent, the clock was ticking.

Bells tinkled and Libby looked up from the stock list on her clipboard. Serving customers at Hearsay Card and Gift Boutique held priority over taking inventory. She removed the pen from between her teeth and rearranged her face as she greeted the girl before showing her to the Mother's Day section. Libby's boss was likely glowering through the two-way mirror of his office in the back of the store. Even regulars were subject to his distrust, and students from the nearby campus were his prime suspects. Terence, a disgruntled and unwilling proprietor, was better off leaving the sales and the client relations to Libby.

In the ongoing melodrama of his divorce, Terence had taken up grudging supervision of Hearsay last year, stopping in to micromanage whenever his regular job as an investment broker allowed it. Gone was the laissez-faire attitude of Alana, Libby's original boss and Terence's wife. Libby had been as blindsided as he by Alana's desertion of the shop and the family when she ran off with a university language professor. Hearsay was Alana's venture, funded by her husband's more stable income. She'd joked about being a kept woman and ignored his dire prediction that the establishment would never survive in the high-rent zone of specialty boutiques. Nevertheless it seemed to flourish, despite Alana's laxity, before she up and left.

Now Terence's whining about recouping his losses while he sweated over the books raised Libby's doubts about the shop's solvency. But even after his wife's departure, the store was as popular as ever and retained its artsy reputation for high-quality merchandise, much of it locally produced by independent crafters—bean-to-bar chocolates and blown-glass jewelry and hand-tied boar-bristle shaving brushes.

Libby checked that the student was still looking for the perfect card. Hearsay's overall stock was a delightful mishmash, but Libby valued the greeting cards most. Every morning during her first patrol, she allowed herself time to choose at random from the stacks a thought for the day, based on a word leaping out at her, perhaps, or the way the ink sat on the paper's surface. And every morning its truism charmed her. Today she'd plucked an embossed vellum card from its cradle and read its message—*Home is where the heart is*—to be bolstered again as though Gram was cheering her on from the great beyond.

"Excuse me." The student interrupted Libby's reverie, clutching two cards for purchase. Libby almost asked her if she had two mothers—maybe she did—but thought better of it as they walked to the till. After the girl left the shop, Terence thumped on the glass from the other side of the office mirror, and she heard his muffled bark, like a muzzled dog's, telling her to take the office phone.

Libby nearly tripped on her way to open his door. Her boss hated fielding calls, especially if they were personal.

"It's not a supplier," he snarled, so that she took the handset back out to the shop floor.

"Hey, cupcake." The voice was slightly familiar . . .

"Clive." Libby tapped her foot. "Why are you calling my place of work?"

"I tried to get you on your cell, but you weren't answering. And it seems so cold to just leave a message for a beautiful woman like you."

She waited a beat before answering, keeping her voice neutral in case Terence was eavesdropping. "What can I do for you?"

"That all depends on what you're offering." His voice was oily, suggestive. Libby didn't grace his insinuation with any response and so, after another moment's silence, he swallowed audibly and began again. "Well, actually, I've set up appointments to view a few houses on Friday evening, if you're available."

"I'll have to check my calendar." Libby had nothing going on, and she wanted to keep it that way.

"I've got hot listings for you," he said. "They're right up your alley and a great price. I think we'll be able to make a quick transaction."

Already? Libby had wanted a house of her own for so long; it couldn't be this easy. She pulled on her right ear lobe. "I don't know. I haven't even finished filling out the loan application yet."

"No problem. This is a perfect time to arrange a mortgage. Rates are low, realty prices are great, and a gal like you will have the banker eating out of your hand."

Libby set her jaw, about to protest, but then Terence skulked out of his office.

"Look, I have to go." Libby cupped the receiver and turned away from her boss's frown. "I'll see what I can do."

"I'll pick you up on Friday, then," Clive said at the moment she disconnected. Terence grabbed the phone out of her hand and stumped back towards his lair. But he stopped midstride and turned back to her.

"By the way, get rid of the piece of human garbage that's been hanging around here lately."

"I don't know what you're referring to."

"That scum." Terence sneered. "You must have seen the woman with the shopping cart who's taken to sleeping on the corner this past while. It's hard enough to keep this place afloat as it is without rabble of her sort scaring away customers." He shut the door behind him.

The description didn't ring a bell with Libby. The vagrant population always swelled in the neighborhood in spring, and right now she was more worried about how in the world she'd make the necessary financial arrangements to avoid homelessness herself. She could hit Terence up for a raise, but squeezing blood from a banker would be easier than getting money out of her stone of a boss. She sighed. No time would be the right time for a raise; all she could do was ask.

And so, towards closing, Libby tucked her hair behind her left ear and straightened her collar before venturing into the presence of her boss. Terence was still engrossed at his desk.

"I've been thinking that we might start a social media page for Hearsay," she began. "It could bring in a whole new crowd."

Terence growled at her. "Whose genius idea is that?"

Why not hers? "I could do the work myself. I know someone who can supply a few ideas." Sybil, after all, advertised hot deals online regularly. Surely Libby's marketing attempts would add value to her boss's perception of her work contribution.

Terence dropped his pen on the desk top and sat back to glare at her. "What's this going to cost me?"

"Nothing." Had she stammered? "Of course, I'm willing to do this as part of my job."

"Your job? That's clearly outlined. Just follow routine." His voice was dismissive and he picked his pen back up.

Libby took a deep breath. "Since that's come up, don't you think it's time for a performance review?"

Terence spurted a short, bitter laugh. "If you're asking for a raise, forget it. No way can I manage to up your salary, Libby. I could hire a university kid part time for less than I pay you. At least they have some education." Libby's face burned. "I don't even know how I'm going to keep this shop afloat as it is."

She bit down on her lower lip, composing herself. "I'm not asking for a lot. It's just that I'm thinking of moving out of my apartment to a safer—"

"Yeah, yeah. Well, I can't take responsibility for you and your rent when I can barely make payments on my own four-thousand-square-foot blue elephant of a house your friend, the errant mother Alana, insisted on buying at the top of the market and then abandoned, along with her kids."

He was so unfair. For one thing, Libby had never fraternized with his wife. Besides, especially in light of the measly pay, his callous reaction to her own situation flabbergasted her. True, he had a huge burden to bear. And those poor children of his. Libby's chest tightened in visualizing their agony when they woke up one day to find their mom gone. But Libby in her own distress, eager to make a real home for herself in a real residential neighborhood, was only asking for her due.

"My loyalty is to you and the shop—"

"Prove it, then." He shot to his feet and jutted his chin into her face. "If you value your employment, do your job and let me get this place stabilized enough so some other poor sucker will take it off my hands."

He wrenched open the office door, marched down the aisle, and set the chimes in the front of the shop jangling as he stormed out.

Libby considered her situation as she cashed out. With Terence dashing all hopes for a raise, the chances of affording her own house grew slimmer.

She glanced out across the pavement. Sybil had already turned off the lights of her shop, shuttered the windows of Amulets Alternative Apothecary, and put up the "closed" sign.

Sybil was a secondary problem. She avoided her huge Tansey family of siblings and cousins and their spouses and offspring, so she didn't comprehend Libby's sorrow over losing her only kin or her craving the security of hearth and home. Sybil was a whirling dervish of activity, and her radical extroversion demanded constant stimulation. Why, last week she'd wakened Libby after midnight to natter on about her dad's intrusive late-night phone call, never noting the absurdity—like father, like daughter. When Libby said she'd give her right arm for a face-to-face conversation with a loving father, Sybil changed the subject. So Libby didn't bother mentioning her frequent if silent discussions with an invisible, unreachable parent.

Friendship with Sybil had its upside, for sure. But Sybil didn't understand Libby's dismay over her dysfunctional background. Libby would do almost anything for the family connection Sybil outright rejected.

Libby slung her canvas bag over her shoulder and locked up Hearsay behind her. For such a livewire, and despite all her talk about spirit manifestations, Sybil sure seemed nervous about anything to do with real-life death. She made excuses about missing Gram's funeral and never asked directly how Libby was dealing with Gram's passing away. Sybil did sit with her through one crying jag, saying, "There, there" and patting a knee, and somehow that'd helped Libby. Her friend must have suffered over the loss of her own mom to breast cancer. Her compulsive insistence that Libby try this therapy or that potion seemed to be a grasping after life, a defiance against what was unavoidable for each human. After all, there was no antidote for death. Sybil's remedies were a temporary cure, in the end. Life, Gram used to say, is but a breath.

Libby crossed the street. The door to Amulets swung open when she put her hand on the knob, and oriental strains from a lute swooned out around her. She wasn't too keen on this beauty consultation Sybil had arranged, but perhaps her friend needed it as much as she insisted Libby did. Maybe it would relax them both.

Entering Amulets stirred Libby's senses, as always. Sometimes the background music blended birdsong with Beethoven, and other times yogic mantras fused with the vibrato of a sitar. Vanilla-scented candles might flicker in alabaster bowls or island torches light the way to a display of lava clay from Hawaii.

This evening the whole interior was a labyrinth of hanging silk draperies colored paprika and olive and wine. Sybil stepped out from behind a tapestry wearing baggy chiffon pantaloons and a bikini top, a belly dancer's coin-fringed girdle jingling with every step. Libby stifled a laugh. Sybil bowed deeply, holding out a tray bearing two steaming glasses and a silver-domed saucer.

"Welcome to Little Istanbul. May I offer you refreshments?"

"Are you a genie?" Libby lifted the glass vial, hot on her fingertips, and sipped the apple-flavored tea. Delish.

"No, I'm the Prince of Persia's favored concubine." With a flourish Sybil removed the silver lid, exposing two powder-dusted cubes. Libby picked one up and took a tentative bite, its sugar dissolving on the tongue to give way to nutty chewiness. Sybil licked her lips. "It's pistachio Turkish Delight. I bought it at an import shop here in the city, but it doesn't come close to the real stuff sold in the Grand Bazaar."

"I thought you didn't eat sugar."

Sybil had been reaching for the second piece but now withdrew her hand. "Of course not. I bought it for you." She ushered Libby back to Amulet's lounge area where she held her homeopathic and other consultations, the couches piled high with cushions for tonight's occasion. A melodious chanting began, eerie wails floating from the store's speaker in a foreign language.

"That's the famous Blue Mosque's call to prayer," Sybil said.

"I see it all now. Next you'll be asking me to travel to Turkey with you."

"Darn, you saw right through my ploy." Sybil grinned and flopped onto the cushions. "No, as enthralling as the city is, I've done Istanbul already. Unless it might interest you? The *hammam* by itself is worth the trip over."

Libby raised her hand to ward off the suggestion. "No, thanks." She'd heard Sybil's account of her visit to the bathhouse but couldn't see herself ever lying nude on a marble dais in a roomful of strange women, being lathered and pummeled and loufa scrubbed and doused by a half-naked, hefty Anatolian matron who didn't speak English.

Sybil exhaled with a soft moan. "You don't know what you're missing—the colors, the sounds, the tastes of Istanbul. I'd go back in a heartbeat if I could convince you to come along." She squinted at Libby through the steam rising off her tea.

"No chance." Lazing here with Sybil in the mock spa atmosphere was enough. "What happened to Tibet?"

"Tibet's still on too, girlfriend. I've never believed in the policy of moderation and, anyway, if I give you a choice of destinations, maybe something will appeal. Wherever we go, the flight will be free for you. I've got points."

"Your offer is generous."

"But . . . ?"

"No buts," Libby said. "You're generous. And if I ever traveled anywhere with anyone, it would be you."

"So you might change your mind, then? Good."

Libby was about to object when a gust of wind blowing through the shop's door set the tapestries stirring. A woman's voice called out, "Is Sybil Tansey here?"

"Ah, the beautician has arrived." Sybil yelled, "Turn the lock, Katie, and come on back, will you? You can set your tables up here."

The flurry of activity gave Libby a moment of respite. Imagine Sybil's offer to pay for her flights! It was a temptation. Her friend's open-handed approach to spending made Libby look miserly. What would be the harm in accepting the unasked-for gift? She sighed. Even if Sybil declared there were no strings attached, Libby herself attached strings to such extravagance, and she didn't want to be indebted. She'd soon have other obligations of her own to deal with, if all went well.

First things first, as Gram used to say. Before Libby spent money that wasn't even hers, she had to re-evaluate her personal finances. But sitting down with bank officials at this point? Libby's eye twitched. On the other hand, she'd met with that decent Mr. Jordan after the funeral, and he'd helped her close Gram's account and offered his services without pushing. Maybe she could give him a call to feel him out about her options.

"Hop up here and settle in." Katie patted the massage table. Sybil was already on the other one, her face swathed in a steaming, white towel.

During the ensuing treatment, Libby gave herself over to melon facial cleanser and tangerine sugar buffer and hydrating papaya mask, to a hand massage with citrus firming oils, and a foot treatment of coconut exfoliator. She smelled like a fruit salad, but she lost herself in the pure luxury, laying aside her stress if only for a while.

With raspberry-infused compresses on Sybil's eyelids, she couldn't very well look at Libby, but purrs of pleasure came from the other folding table. Taking her to Istanbul in the flesh would be better than a makeshift facial in the back of her Minneapolis shop. Still, she shouldn't dump all her proposed changes on Libby at once. Verbal descriptions of her foreign adventures could never do them justice, anyway. A girl had to go there for herself. The best part about her trip to Turkey had been its incredible sensuousness—the perfect fantasy material for zoning out during moments like this. And so Sybil set her imagination free to relive it all over again.

Istanbul had fired up her senses, all right. She'd prowled its maze of narrow, snaking streets dating back to the time of Byzantium, crossroads of East and West, expecting to meet Aladdin around every corner.

Mosques of age-polished stone hunkered close together, with cascading domes heaped like scoops of melting ice cream and pencil-point minarets outlined against the blue of the Marmar Sea. Their soaring interiors were decorated with ceramic tiles in colors so brilliant they made a mockery of the rainbow. In the marketplace, fragrant spices overflowed their bins. Egg-sized rubies spilled from chests in the treasury museum of the royal palace, home of the sultans. Carpets of intricate pattern hung in open shop windows, and ornate scarves draped the heads of the few women to be found in the streets—a veil, Sybil had learned, meant to separate their humanity from Allah's deity.

She snorted just thinking about it now. Those poor women didn't discern their own godhood within. Of course, it didn't really matter what they believed, did it? Just that they believed in something.

The sounds of Istanbul played through Sybil's mind as she lay beneath Katie's hands. The melodious, haunting call to prayer echoed in a minor key five times a day through the skies of the city—as it played now on her shop speakers, part of her Eurasian medley collection—drawing men to the mosques like ants parading through the winding alleyways. Russian cargo ships boomed as they lined up for entry on the Bosphorus Strait, and vendors roasting chestnuts shouted out in the square.

While Katie massaged in apricot moisturizer, Sybil remembered the warm crush of bodies on the tram, the textures of supple lambskin and silky pashmina in street-side stalls. Enticing aromas wafted from open-air stands, and daily she feasted on feta in herbed oil, figs, stuffed grape leaves. She took her fill of desserts made with sweet cheese caked in coconut, baked in honey, and topped with walnuts—no one she knew around to witness her sugar ingestion.

The whole exquisite city captivated her, and no single experience separated itself from the web of sight, sound, smell, touch, and taste. But the pinnacle of her sightseeing might have been the subterranean vaults of the sixth-century Basilica Cistern.

Dim lighting undulated off the wall-to-wall pool, flickering up eerily onto the squat pillars supporting the ceiling. Cross-hatching walkways nearly even with the surface played an optical trick so that she and the other tourists were dark shadows walking on water. The life-giving liquid had flowed from above onto the rooftops and roadways and gutters, making its way into the basement of the city to be consumed by thirsty mouths fifteen centuries ago and recycled through emptying bladders back to the ocean, purified by uptake into the clouds, raining down to the cistern again. That same water surrounded her there beneath Istanbul's streets. It moisturized her skin and entered her lungs. The very molecules she absorbed might well have been resident in the bodies of great historical characters such as Constantine in the fourth century or, a millennium later, Mehmed the Conqueror—peace be upon him. She might even have breathed those heroes in.

Katie smoothed a firming cream of coffee grounds and cinnamon onto Sybil's décolletage, recalling to her the caresses of Bahar, a waiter who appreciated her tip and offered his company at the end of his shift. Bahar meant "spring of life" in Persian, he told her, and he was a fountain of delight to her that night.

Yes, all in all the culture immersed Sybil in blessings as lavish as any Ali Baba might have discovered in his fabled caves of treasure, as lascivious as the Arabic text of *The Perfumed Garden* that Bahar had given her as a souvenir.

If only she could transport Libby to these sacred places, she could diminish her friend's sorrow at her grandmother's passing over and maybe even her fixation on buying a house. In the first place, if the old woman had really been as good as Libby always insisted—a trait Sybil hadn't picked up on the one time she met her—then why did Libby mourn her so much? After all, what goes around comes around in the great circle of life and rebirth. Libby would bump into her grandmother again, perhaps in a different body but still recognizable. Sybil herself had met many such people ascending through the soul's evolution towards completion.

And about Libby's quandary between buying a house or leasing a condo near Sybil, it was self-evident that short-term rental gave a woman maximum choice without imprisoning her in a lifetime of mortgage payments. Maybe a sublet would come up in her complex and place her friend within proximity to her own, more positive, influence. One way or another, she must give Libby a subject other than morbid physical death and stodgy loan payments to think about, as she herself used thoughts of men like Bahar and the divine springs of life to keep her mindful.

Katie's voice eased into Sybil's ruminations. "We'll finish your treatments off with an invigorating spritz of lemon water." Beside Sybil, Libby gasped, and a second later she received the same shock of mist.

"Funny, I was just thinking about water." Sybil sat up and adjusted her towel. "The *hammam*, the sea, the fountains of the deep."

"I was dozing," Libby said, "dreaming about eating fruit."

Sybil ignored the quip, full as she was of lecture. "Water is so nurturing, the primary antidote to disease, you know. *Dis-ease*," she clarified for Libby's edification. "On every trip I've taken, water plays a pivotal role."

"Like, for swimming or as a drink mix?" Libby's eyes twinkled.

"I'm serious. The water bathing me in a *hammam* in Istanbul might be the same ice I skated on in Amsterdam's canals. Water returns to its source with a memory of its own as part of the balance of the universe, a physical indication of metaphysical reality, of harmonic convergence."

Katie nodded along to her sermon, but Libby, cheeks rosy from the treatment, blinked sleepily at them both. Sybil had better dumb it down. "Come on, Libby, haven't you ever thought about the planet's system of evaporation, condensation, and precipitation as Mother Earth's waterworks?"

"*I* have," Katie said. "The dew is her sweat, the rain her tears of sorrow."

"Yes, and snow is her menses, the cyclical shedding of productivity." Sybil waited for Libby's response.

Libby picked at her towel. "I've thought about how a huge gulp of water quenches my thirst after a long walk, and about how much water I use when I'm making turkey soup."

Katie met Sybil's glance with empathy in her eyes as she handed her a glass of water afloat with cucumber slices and mint leaves. At least Katie understood what she was getting at. Sybil wasn't giving up the teachable moment so easily, and she pressed her point.

"Water has been hallowed since the dawn of humankind." She held her tumbler up to the light of the candles, watching the flame waver and warp through its lens. "Think about how Cleopatra floated on a barge down the Nile into the arms of Mark Anthony, or what bathing in the Ganges means to India's Hindus. Water makes me feel so clean from the inside out. It's the most sacred of Gaia's elements."

"Last week you told me fire was most sacred," Libby said. "But I'm all for bathing rather than burning, and this treatment was heavenly." Libby gave Sybil her cool, serene smile. But the friendly lines at the corners of her eyes deepened, so she knew Libby was still teasing her. Even with no makeup at all, Libby was beautiful with her contoured jawline, long neck, straight nose. And hair she never colored—imagine that.

CHAPTER SEVEN

Today

Libby waits in the thin sunshine as the tour group convenes on the mansion's outdoor terrace high above the ground, the teens jostling for a view. The two aging sisters finally appear, red faced and puffing from their ascent up the circular iron staircase, and the guide pitches into her commentary. Libby, though fidgety with unnamed dread, is immediately engaged.

"The Laird Mansion was built around the turn of the century. This rooftop walk is typical of late Victorian architecture, where the master of the residence might take his tea of a summer's afternoon while surveying his domain."

A strand of hair escapes the girl's starched cap and she sweeps it away from her sky-blue eyes. She'd introduced herself as Paige when Libby and the other tourists gathered by the gate in the picket fence outside the yard. Libby knows who the guide is, having exchanged e-mails with her and seen her photo on the museum website. But Paige doesn't recognize her, of course. The girl had lumbered ahead of them up the stairs, heavily pregnant and dressed in period costume as a parlor maid in a black frock with creamy lace at throat and wrists.

Libby, too, had been pregnant once, though never heavily. Now without warning, as she takes in Paige's fertile silhouette, Libby recalls the butterfly fluttering of those first fetal movements in her own womb, the growing intensity of a promise not kept.

Paige continues her animated spiel. "Moses David Melchizedek Laird—known in these parts as MDM—was a true philanthropist, the builder and founder of Kirkton here in Pembina County around the time North Dakota achieved statehood. Modern-day Kirkton resembles many depopulated prairie hamlets, with houses set around a country store, post office, and gas station all struggling to survive these days." Libby had insisted on paying for Sybil's fill-up this morning at those pumps, just out of sight from where they're standing. Paige goes on. "Below us—there, along Salem Drive—you can see the old schoolhouse, chapel, and remains of residences built as part of the Laird Estate."

"Blah, blah, blah. History is so dry." Sybil's whisper is loud, and Libby wants to shush her. "But doesn't that ridiculous bump of a belly make you want to giggle?"

It doesn't. Libby honors pregnancy. Still, a burst of nervous mirth bubbles up inside her before she can stifle it, as though some good humor is finally pushing its way into her grief.

"Shh," she reprimands both Sybil and herself. The Australian couple frowns in their direction. What kind of example are they for the students? She shouldn't have agreed in the first place to taking this road trip. She's still reeling from Gram's death and it's unfair of Sybil to drag her out of state and then insist on making her snicker like this. But it's her vivacious impulsiveness that's made Sybil so fun from the start of their friendship. She's an emotion carnivore, sucking every sensation—the very marrow—out of the bones of life.

Besides, now that she's here, Libby can't deny her growing fascination with the ring, the mansion, and her conviction that they hold answers to questions she hasn't known how to ask. So Libby strains to catch Paige's words before the wind blows them out over the grasses to become just another bit of history in themselves.

"MDM was born at the Red River Settlement in Manitoba, Canada, in 1865 to Scottish missionaries. He grew up in the era of steamboats, smallpox, and the Indian Wars. Raised in the rectory, he was sent out by his father as a young man to Minnesota to study humanities at university in Saint Paul. At heart he was a pioneer who wanted to live out his dreams in a practical rather than academic fashion."

"See, Mr. Nelson?" one boy says to his teacher. "You don't have to go to university to be successful."

Mr. Nelson turns to Paige. "Let's not discourage the students here. There's nothing wrong with academics."

"Absolutely not." Paige smiles and admonishes the kids: "Stay in school."

Sybil bats her lashes at the teacher, and his eyebrow creases upwards.

Paige raises her finger into the air. "But MDM was not first of all a scholar. He lived in a time that valued rugged individualism, and he believed in getting his hands dirty rather than just moralizing about the plight of the starving Plains people, whose livelihood was disappearing along with the great herds of bison that no longer roamed the Dakotas. His revolutionary plan demanded he actually dwell among the indigenous population, so he left university and came to Pembina County to launch an agricultural enterprise here in partnership with his father, who remained with his congregation at the colony in Canada."

"Agricultural enterprise?" The question comes from a student with wind-chapped skin, sporting a huge rodeo belt buckle.

He looks as though he might be a farmer's son himself. "Grain or beef?" His adolescent voice cracks and his face reddens further.

"Good question." Paige nods briskly. "MDM grew several crops over the duration of his long life including wheat, and of course he raised livestock—chickens, sheep, cattle. But principally MDM was an innovator who adapted to the current market needs with his eye always on the wellbeing of his neighbors. For example," Paige points to the right and traces boxes in the air, "he subdivided that parcel of his richest land into those many garden plots in a sort of collective, to feed the families settling down in his little kingdom here. He even put together a study program for the children of resident and migrant workers."

One of the elderly siblings peers at the tour guide over the rim of her glasses. "Sounds to me like one of those institutional schools. You know, where the poor Native American children were dragged away from their parents and starved and beaten and"—here the dainty lady nods in the direction of the students—"well, worse."

Libby knows why she disapproves. After all, news of the government-sanctioned boarding schools and the abuse inflicted in the name of organized religion has been in the news again recently.

Paige, too, furrows her brow and hesitates before answering. "Similarities existed in that MDM's classroom education was supplemented by manual labor, for adults and the older children, in agronomy, construction, blacksmithing, and homemaking."

"Cool," the shortest of the boys in the school group says. "Just the skills we'd need in a zombie apocalypse." The girls titter, and so does Paige before composing herself. Libby, hungry for more information, ignores the interruption and awaits Paige's next words.

"MDM distanced himself from the earlier movement's desire to suppress family culture, however. Instead, his purpose was to keep families together in community by hiring those still resisting policies that would confine them to reservations. So, in Kirkton, kids remained with their parents or older relatives in the sanctity of their 'homes,' some families partially maintaining their nomadic patterns and living here only portions of the year, others moving permanently into houses built here by their benefactor."

Paige motions towards the crumbling hamlet spread below them. Libby spots a mangy dog padding through a lot full of weeds.

"MDM's educational ideology was radical for its time," Paige tells them. "He came alongside the people he served. He became one of them. It's said MDM learned the languages so that his employees needn't learn English. He was fluent in Ojibwa, Dakota, and Cree, and spoke a smattering of many other tongues."

"I have a translation app for that." The teacher pulls his phone out of his back pocket. The kids quiz Mr. Nelson about how to say "Hello" in one dialect and "You moron" in another.

Come to think of it, Gram used to mutter strange syllables that Libby's long forgotten how to pronounce, with meanings like "It thunders" and "Eat your soup." Gram is never far from her mind these days but, even so, Libby feels vulnerable, defenseless somehow. In spite of the chill in the air, her skin flushes and beads of sweat break out on her upper lip.

What could be waiting for them inside the mansion that is

inspiring such disquiet in her that she fears her legs won't carry her inside when their tour guide decrees that it is time?

CHAPTER EIGHT

Two-and-a-half weeks ago

Libby fit her key into the apartment lock on Thursday evening. She was drained because Terence had been holed up in his office in a foul mood all day, making her run to the back room every time he had another gripe. Before she turned her door handle, Zinnia was at her side with a juicy morsel of gossip.

"You hear about them bigwigs busting down this place?" The old lady twisted the hem of her apron.

"What are you talking about, Zinnia?"

"Rosie on second told me Maria in three-nineteen found a crumpled letter on the floor by the mailboxes when she got home from the chiropractor. Something about the landlord's license not being renewed and us all getting kicked out and the whole building being smashed."

"Where is this letter?"

"What's Rosie going to do, with her gimpy leg and all? They say we got to get out of here before—"

"Who says?" Libby let her purse drop to the floor and placed both hands on Zinnia's shoulders. "Who says you need to move?"

"You, too. We all got to leave, if the landlord won't fix this. And you know him."

Libby nodded. That scoundrel seldom showed his face around the block except to threaten some poor senior for overdue rent.

Zinnia's big head swayed back and forth, her jowls jiggling. "Everybody was talking about it, and Roger in seven-twelve got chest pains this afternoon. Poor Roger. Maybe I got to look into the Haven after all."

"Well, I haven't heard anything about this, and I won't believe it without proper notification." Libby hugged Zinnia. "Now, don't you worry. I'll call and ask about it, but I'm sure it's nothing."

In her apartment Libby changed into her sweatpants. Was there anything to the rumor? Given the landlord's resistance to keeping up maintenance, the city might finally have decided to level the building. But surely the authorities would alert the occupants formally.

The light blinking on her phone caught her eye and she picked up the receiver to retrieve the message.

"Ms. Walker, I'm calling on behalf of Mr. Jordan at Cedars Credit Union. I'm following up on the bank mortgage application you dropped off this morning. We have a file opened for you, and Mr. Jordan would like to book a meeting with you, preferably for Monday as he'll be away from the office for several weeks after that. Please call me back tomorrow morning by eight to confirm."

Libby set the receiver back on its cradle. Boy, that was fast. She hadn't anticipated a face-to-face meeting with the banker yet, especially having just been turned down for a raise. That realtor, Clive, had commented about the necessity of getting loan preapproval, and she sure didn't want to deal with some random bank official. Her chances might be better with Mr. Jordan. At least they'd met amicably already. But did she have enough disposable income to qualify for a mortgage? Did she even have enough cash for a down payment? She needed to convince the banker that her job was secure and that she was a good risk.

If Zinnia's news held any truth, Libby could be homeless in a flash, hanging around the bus stop, begging passersby for change, sleeping under a bridge—

"Stop it," she said aloud, as Gram would have done were she here. "Don't borrow trouble." No one was chasing her out of her home. No one was threatening to displace her. She had to think this through methodically, coolly.

Libby sat down at the kitchen table and tapped the fingers of her right hand on its clean, worn surface—thumb, pointer, middle, ring, baby, then baby, ring, middle, pointer, thumb—one to ten, over and over.

She didn't want to engage with the banker so soon to formalize her mortgage request, when it could be easily turned down. Thumb, pointer, middle, ring, baby. Drat that Terence for his stinginess. Baby, ring, middle, pointer, thumb. But waiting longer to meet with Mr. Jordan might lessen her chances, and the bank was her only recourse.

She smacked her hand on the tabletop and stood up. She'd call the bank tomorrow morning and hope her job prospects were firmed up enough with Terence before she had to physically sit down with Mr. Jordan.

Libby took the soup kettle out of the cupboard. There was nothing like a hearty brew to calm her nerves. She'd had barely a moment to enjoy yesterday's facial before the stress returned to stamp wrinkles back in. Libby placed the pot in the sink and added enough water to cover the smoked ham hocks. When it came to a boil, she turned the temperature down and added a muslin bag she'd stuffed to bulging with black peppercorns, dill weed, and bay leaves. Chopping onions let her cry without the emotion. She allowed her thoughts to wander.

Sybil had made several odd comments regarding water

yesterday, silliness about rain being the tears of Mother Earth. It was her way of making sense of life, Libby supposed, which she herself was in the process of doing, if using a totally different vocabulary. But it got her to thinking about how necessary water was for cooking and cleaning and slaking thirst. Sybil had talked about it in a detached way, dispassionately, as though water was more of a philosophical idea than a materially useful substance. Had Sybil never cried in mourning or remorse? She suspected Sybil didn't even sweat at the gym; she'd once told Libby she drank herbal sage tea to avoid perspiration.

And then, without warning, Libby recalled the waters of her miscarriage as though it were yesterday and not thirty years ago—the gush and flood of mucous and blood, the delivery of that tiny, half-formed body with translucent eyelids and blue-veined skin. And she buckled for a moment with the unexpected pang of it, over the kitchen counter where chopping her onions made her eyes run with tears that, now, soaked down into her heart. She dabbed at her face with a tea towel while tidying the mess, but the tears kept seeping out. She put on a load of laundry while the meat cooked; she washed the bathroom floor and cleaned the toilet and then the shower. But still she couldn't scrub out the stain of that long-ago memory.

When the ham flaked off the bones, Libby skimmed the fat from the broth and added new potatoes, green beans, and baby carrots. While the soup simmered in the kitchen, she put her feet up in her living room amongst her half-packed boxes, weeping still. By the time she scooped a bowl and garnished it with a dollop of sour cream and a few sprigs of young dill, she'd cried herself dry and once again tucked the thought of her baby—and Gram—away.

Sybil was dancing, plastered up against the guy in front of her and moving to the bump and grind of the one behind. The floor of the club was crowded, despite its being midweek. Thursday was hip-hop night at Sonix, the perfect time and place to build her energy and renew her inner and outer selves. Why should she be limited to partying on the weekends anyway? The Thursday crowd was younger, but she fit in. Iggy hated hip-hop and never went out with her on weeknights anyway. Just as well, because Sybil preferred coming alone and cherished the anonymity, craved the surging of the mass undulating to the rhythm as though one body.

Blaring music throbbed, colored lights blazed, and no one's eyes registered recognition. The atmosphere was conducive to clearing Sybil's thoughts and centering herself, alone in the throng and touching without giving anything away.

Libby could benefit from an evening out like this. It would take her mind off her obsession with death. Sybil recognized Libby's moods by now and knew when she was thinking about the old woman, the grandmother. She got a look in her eyes—a faraway look that wasn't only sadness but a sort of yearning.

Sybil shook the picture from her mind and shimmied harder. The guy behind her nudged closer and the one in front leered back at her. She was working it! Sonix on half-price Thursday was better than the gym any day.

But the thought of Libby's eyes wouldn't leave her.

"We're all dying, you know," Libby had said one day at the café when they were both taking a work break. "It's not just Gram."

"That's a depressing view."

"Got to be realistic. No one lives forever." Libby's voice had held a catch.

Sybil had snapped a comeback. "You don't need to focus on physical decay to know that part's inevitable." Then she'd changed the subject to travel again.

Now she clenched her teeth thinking about that convo. Her bodily mortality was not her favorite topic to contemplate. Her one recent scare, the lump that went away on its own without the doctor, had been enough warning for her to add dandelion root to her daily regime and double up on her mistletoe tea. And happy energy helped, of course—thinking positive thoughts, being kind to herself, and meditating, at times even falling into soul travel through out-of-body trances. That harmonizing energy was what she always found on her trips to sacred places, and it could be the answer for Libby as well. Never mind Libby's insistence on the certainty of death. Of course they all had to pass over eventually in order for rebirth to occur, for the fullness of love to blossom. But she, Sybil, intended to keep herself alive in this world as long as possible by sheer self-determination. And love, too, of course. Lots of love.

It all had to do with the attitude anyway. Her weak-willed mother's problem hadn't been a rogue genetic aberration but rather a caving in to the belief that genetics ruled her fate. Sybil wasn't about to allow that to happen to her. Despite the tireless harassment of her aunts and sisters to get tested, Sybil rejected intrusive "scientific" methods and cures that were often carcinogenic in themselves.

"*Om namah shivaya*," she chanted as she gyrated to the frenetic beat of the music. She forgot what the words meant exactly, but her mantra often took her to the edge of pure consciousness, of empty bliss. It wasn't effective tonight, so she switched to her favorite English inspirational axiom that blended so nicely with the pulse of the dance—"My body is my temple, my body is my temple"—until she purged herself of any contaminating thoughts of death, remaining in the now, in this moment as though it was her last.

She left Sonix with the guy who'd been dancing behind her. He really knew how to move.

Paige hit "send" a little too aggressively. She prized her occupation in the archives of the Laird Mansion in Kirkton, but not late on a Thursday night when she and Baby should be at home on the farm with Danny, and not when she'd been waiting so long for the curator up in Canada to deliver the promised files. Maybe this message would get his attention. The museum there had located a small stash of letters from the days of the Red River Settlement that held promise for her studies. It being the eleventh hour, she needed to tie up the remainder of her investigation so she could send her thesis draft off to her advisory committee readers.

Paige slumped in the office chair and stared out the attic casement at the late April moon. It would look better through her own bedroom window. She swiveled around to appraise the stacks of research piled on her desk and on the shelving, all alone with her papers and the ghosts of the Laird family.

"There is no such thing as ghosts," she said aloud, in case Baby could read her thoughts after all.

Not that there'd ever been a hint of spiritualistic activity in the mansion; in fact, the opposite was true. Tourists always asked if the place was haunted, deflated by her answer that peace reigned in this house even now, half a century after Moses David Melchizedek Laird had ceased walking the halls at more than a hundred years of age. Those settlers were a hardy lot, and this one, at least, left no poltergeist behind to rap on walls or make lights flicker.

But something otherworldly inhabited the Laird Mansion—an inexplicable sense of presence, of a being greater than the self. Paige felt it every time she came to work. The anticipation of it started as soon as she stepped into the yard through the gateway, the path pointing her straight—were she to walk through walls—to the epicenter of the house. Entering the mansion, musty with the smell of history, was like opening the cover of a book, each room another chapter in the rereading of a favorite bedtime story. Entering the mansion she felt an invisible guardian placing a worn quilt around her shoulders. The moment at the end of a tour when she walked across the threshold into MDM's den, the unseen host welcomed her back as if to a once-forsaken room where she rightfully belonged.

So Paige couldn't blame tourists for expecting tales from the dead. Even if they didn't sense the subtle hospitality, the history of the museum demanded a conclusion, a closure. Some said MDM had built this home with hopes of filling it with a family to carry on his name. But the registry of weddings, births, and deaths—vital records supposedly safeguarded in the Pembina County Courthouse—was incomplete when it came to this era, in large part due to a fire that had wiped out many files. No will was ever found. No legal Laird beneficiaries remained, although Kirkton gossip propagated by certain family members of MDM's housekeeper had insisted for years that they deserved recompense from the estate.

"All they would have inherited was debt," she told Baby. Musing aloud helped to clarify her puzzlement.

MDM's legacy was a philanthropic one, for at age eighty he'd set up a charitable foundation remaining today as a force in education and municipal health care—if more of a psychological encouragement than a monetary actuality. The money was long gone. Much of the land had been sold off as MDM's vigor declined and the said housekeeper held sway. After MDM's death as a centenarian, when the town's population decreased so that it all but closed its doors, the state stepped in to keep the historic site afloat. Now the Kirkton Preservation Society operated under a board of directors with the help of, largely, volunteers. Paige's part-time position as docent and archivist put her in charge of the collectables and a cataloging system, such as it was, with the responsibility of data entry and so on added to her tours.

"But I need more than cold statistics, Baby. Of course, I've gotten a glimpse of MDM's private life. I think you'd like him." She tickled Baby's skin through her skin. MDM's few handwritten notes, his neat ledgers, and his single mourning announcement from his father in Canada only whetted her appetite for a sharper, more immediate picture of the son. Sure, a fair bit of information existed online about the town and its history, but each tidbit needed to be cross-checked and verified against existing documentation, and often proved faulty. The graveyard, kept neat by the few remaining residents with long-deceased relatives, yielded little information; the Laird name appeared on only one headstone. All in all, the dearth of personal documentation astounded

Paige and couldn't be explained away by a random courthouse fire. The personal record of MDM's presence was almost negligible except perhaps in his artistic creation of the residence—that is, the evidence of the estate itself.

Indeed, the mansion and holdings were a clear display of the painstaking work of MDM's hands, his labor of love. Paige saw his thumbprint in the resulting product, the premeditation of it showing up in the masonry sketches of the fences and foundations and fireplaces as well as in the more recently discovered blueprints of the house itself, all authorized with his signature and much of it accomplished by his own hand. A news story in the *Kirkton Crier* published in 1897, titled "Laird Sets Cornerstone of Grandest House in County," recorded that MDM drew all the lines of the plans himself, and that he oversaw the choice of each rock marking out the boundaries of his ownership, and that he manually set each fieldstone of every fireplace. MDM's personality especially proclaimed itself in the inscriptions he'd carved into the sandstone mantelpieces or etched into wood—cryptic phrases that, room by room, threaded the home together.

"And then, of course," she said to her child, enclosed within, "the final surprise in the den at the end of the circuit always delights the tourists. *You* will love it, too."

So she could *sense* the man in his handiwork but, really, that wasn't proof supporting the research claim in her graduate thesis that the architecture was an expression of MDM's private home life. As far as hard documentation about MDM's personal life, his official biography, it seemed as if the evidence had been tampered with, letters and photos and diaries possibly destroyed.

"What am I missing, Baby?" She tapped fingernail on front

tooth, pondering.

Her cell phone on the desk clattered to life and she fumbled to answer it. Danny sounded beat. "I'm in from the fields. Long day."

"Did you find the potato salad and fried chicken in the fridge?" She could use a bit of that herself about now.

"I stopped in for a bite with Mom and Dad on the way back," Danny said.

"A hot meal? Good." That was one of the perks of the in-laws living so close. She'd never have made the town-to-farm transition without the backing of Danny's mom, in particular. Though her mother-in-law might not understand her academic objectives and would never read her thesis after publication, still, her support in filling the gaps while Paige studied was providential.

"When are you going to be home, Paige? I worry about you driving after dark."

"I'm just revisiting two of MDM's financial registers to verify an element of my thesis index and then I'll be on my way."

"It's showering," he warned. "The roads will be greasy, so be careful, okay?"

She suspected the weariness in his voice was less because of his bodily labor today and more about her academic fixation. The studies were getting on her own nerves, but in just over two weeks—in the middle of May—the museum would open and take up all her energy, leaving no time for writing other than clarification and editorial polishing. Even though she wouldn't see the tourist season out due to the baby, she looked forward to guiding those first tours.

But her submission date was rushing upon her; the manuscript must be in the hands of the UND's profs within the month. Paige swallowed the lump lodging in her throat. She was cutting it close, especially if Baby decided to make an earlier entrance than his imprecise due date of the third week in June.

If only she could get her hands on those personal letters MDM had sent his father after he struck out on his own to found Kirkton. Then she could finish off her current draft by filling in the holes—and what gaping holes they were. MDM's personal past had been shrouded in mystery until Paige took him on as her graduate subject and sorted through the existing but disorganized documents. Questions kept coming up. Every fact Paige learned about MDM's life raised another two uncertainties worthy of investigation. But, as her main advisor at UND kept telling her, at one point every graduate student has to call it quits and save some exploration for the Ph.D.

Libby woke up on the couch to the nasal whine of a balding, late-night TV host hawking kitchen gadgets. In her sleep, she'd slopped the last bit of congealed soup onto Gram's lap blanket. She blotted at it with her napkin. The hand-quilted throw was a gift from the aides at the Haven in appreciation for Gram's selfless service. Libby had made sure to take it to the hospital in the ambulance the day of the heart attack, tucking it in around her grandmother in those last hours of her life. Gram had fingered the soft binding like a baby swaddled in daddy's arms until her shallow respiration slowed and, bit by bit, her life ebbed away.

Libby checked her watch. It was two already and she had to be up by seven, coherent enough to phone Mr. Jordan's assistant on her way to work. She hated discussing money almost as much as she hated spending it. If she'd ever learned to bank electronically, maybe there'd have been a way to arrange for the mortgage without having to submit her finances in person for scrutiny. But homelessness, especially in light of the rumor Zinnia was circulating, was too real a possibility to shirk facing the banker.

Of course, the eviction story might be bogus. That was another phone call she needed to make. She wouldn't dare spend time at the shop, even over her break, to call around for such information, what with Terence's snarky mood these days. She'd keep her personal life hidden away out of sight and lie low. No need to aggravate her boss any further.

Libby stood up and yawned. Maybe she should unstack all the sheets and towels from the linen cupboard. It wouldn't take long to sort through the pile and decide what to pass along to the Haven; they were always short on cleaning rags. Besides, she might find another shoebox full of photos and clippings and overlooked information stowed away on the top shelf.

What was she looking for, anyway? Gram's soup recipe, of course. But there was more to it than that. All along she'd been searching for something bigger than that recipe.

She'd been searching for rest.

The thought stopped her in the middle of folding the quilt. She'd been engrossed in the search and until this moment hadn't really understood what for. The word "rest" didn't even make much sense to her. After all, it wasn't as if her life was a blur of busyness, and she certainly slept well most nights. But ever since Gram died she'd been missing the tranquil optimism Babette brought to life in her daily tasks—her daily utterances—as she puttered about the kitchen or straightened the hall carpet or studied the crossword puzzle through her huge magnifying glass. Gram had been so full of peace, always looking beyond her situation with a confident assurance of a thing unseen, as though the future was a better reality sure to meet her one of these days.

"This world is not our home," she'd say to Libby.

"We're American. Of course it's our home," Libby always replied. And Gram would smile and go on humming. She was so full of a wisdom Libby never seemed to get to the heart of, although this sorting through Gram's possessions was yielding bits and pieces for her—a sort of postmortem.

So, yes, she'd do the linen closet as soon as she could get to it, but at a reasonable hour. Instead she brushed her teeth and climbed into bed with the lap blanket, burying her nose in it and smelling for Gram.

What if she couldn't convince the banker, Mr. Jordan, that she had enough money for a down payment and that her job was secure? What if she didn't qualify for a mortgage? Well, she thought as she drifted off, she could always take Sybil up on her suggestion to throw away her dream of home ownership and give in to life as a renter, with enough cash to follow her friend on her madcap travels.

"Slide right in there, cupcake," Clive said. Libby pulled away from his clammy grasp as he opened the passenger-side door of his vintage Cadillac, a car that impressed her not at all. "The next place is a bit of a drive from here, so we'll have time to get to know each other."

"I assume this is the last viewing? Because it's getting late." Libby snipped off her sentences like the ends of green beans bound for her soup kettle. With someone else she might have mentioned she was hungry, but she didn't want to give Clive the opportunity to suggest supper together. As it stood, this was too much like a trick date—a couple out together on a Friday evening, the guy all solicitous with his hair spiked up in a silly rooster comb. The realtor had picked her up from Hearsay as he'd arranged, but she wasn't in the mood for listening to his lame rationale behind each choice of residence he declared to be "just perfect" for her—three condos so far, all out of her price range and all uninteresting anyway. And now he was likely dragging her up to Sybil's even pricier complex near Arden Hills.

"As I mentioned to you before, Clive, multi-family dwelling is what I'm trying to get away from."

"Got a treat for you next, then." He grinned, his eyes sliding sideways at her. "Yessiree, this little gem of a residence should do it for you, chickadee. Just what the doc ordered." He swung the Caddy into the flow of traffic and launched into a dubious pitch about how she might be able to score a mortgage more easily if he wielded his influence at the bank. Clive knew most of the assessors at Cedars Credit Union, he assured her. Perhaps he'd have a few words with the one handling her file.

"No, thanks." Libby pulled at the seatbelt, turning away from Clive.

"Your loss, dollface."

Libby tuned him out as he rattled on about the next walk-through. She leaned her head back onto the shabby upholstery and closed her eyes. She'd never agree to be part of his scheming. It was going to be difficult enough to convince Mr. Jordan of her validity without risking fraud. This morning on the bus she'd called the bank to make the late Monday appointment with him and—what with the all-day cooking class Saturday and the apartment turned upside down—she'd have to scramble to get her books in order over the weekend. It was all going too fast for her.

But what was her option? She was so *done* with apartment living. The condos she'd seen today, though newer and less suffocating than her tenement flat, only cemented her resolve to find a house—a real home all her own, with a yard and a tree. Libby felt herself slipping into a doze as the car swayed and Clive's voice droned on, but his tone changed before she sank into unconsciousness.

"Okee dokee, here she is." Clive braked and Libby sat up. She blinked at the house on her right, her thoughts sleep tousled. Was this a sick joke? She turned to Clive.

"But this is Seven Canaan Lane."

"Yep." Clive stuck out his chest. "What the little gal wants, the little gal gets."

"But how did you . . . I mean, it's not for sale, is it? I haven't seen a listing."

"I tracked the owners down using the photo you gave me. The address was on the back, remember? They haven't listed it formally yet, but I convinced them to let me walk through it with my 'very interested client.'" He made air quotes. "I told them they could essentially name their price."

A prickly flush washed over Libby and she opened her mouth but no words came out.

Clive laughed. "Don't worry, it's just a come-on line. In the end, they'll deal. Let's go, kitten. We've got a house to view."

Libby almost wanted to hug the man, anticipation for the

moment overriding her skepticism. She followed Clive up the sidewalk to the porch on which she'd first seen the blonde girl playing forty years ago, through the door he unlocked and into the entry. They left their shoes on the mat and stepped onto the original hardwood floorboards polished to a warm glow.

The interior of the house was exactly what Libby had always envisioned, with wide white sills and baseboards standing out against the plastered walls painted in heritage colors—mossy greens and serene blues. The living room was lit with ceiling and wall fixtures that were either original or expensive replicas, and the kitchen had glass-fronted cabinets and open shelving and a farm sink with a backsplash of subway tiles. Upstairs Libby found low-ceilinged bedrooms and a claw-footed tub.

It wasn't the décor per se that enchanted her most but the way the cushions were plumped on the davenport by a loving hand, and how the family portraits were hung in the hallway. It didn't matter that the electrical and plumbing systems were antiquated or that heating costs might spike in the winter because of the obsolete insulation. This house could be hers.

"How much . . ." Libby's voice broke. "How much are they asking?"

Clive mentioned a price and she sagged against the doorframe. "That's out of my range completely, almost double what I estimated in the best-case scenario."

"Not so fast. I might be able to talk the owners down." He led her back outside and opened the car door for her again. "Why don't we discuss our prospects over steak and a nice bottle of red?"

"Thanks, but I'll take the bus home from here." She buttoned her coat up right to the top, bundling her disappointment away.

"Not a chance, cupcake." He gripped her elbow again. "I insist on at least getting you home safely."

She withdrew her arm under pretense of needing a tissue from her purse. "I have an early commitment tomorrow and, look, the bus is coming right now."

As she stepped away from his car, Clive protested, saying he'd set up other viewings on Sunday. But after this past half-hour of immersion into the intimate life of the residents she had so long fantasized about, Libby had no desire to consider other properties at all. Before mounting the bus steps, she turned back towards Clive's car.

"Thanks for arranging the viewing," she called out over the idling of the motor. Though Clive couldn't have known the depths of her dreams about this house or the implausibility of her ever affording it, he deserved credit for opening that door to her. "I'll contact you after I think about it."

Really, what was there to think about? She wanted something she couldn't have, and deprivation wasn't new to her. Yet, in spite of the hard, cold facts of her situation, optimism took hold of her heart.

THE RED JOURNAL

Red Journal entry, dated December 24, 1911:

My Heart,

As is my custom, this Christmas Eve I spent whittling another plaything for the child—a miniature copy of the occasional table I recently purchased for the Blue Room. But would she be too old to enjoy her stocking this year? The halls of the mansion are empty save for the housekeeper and her brood, whom I have forbidden to enter my inner chambers lest they discover and defile the handiwork I have crafted.

How I lament your absence. I have undertaken countless excursions throughout the Great Plains and beyond, seeking traces of you along pathways familiar to your People but ever shifting. Just this past summer I came across another institution offering indigents temporary refuge, the records of which hold the shadowy stories of orphaned girls admitted as infants only to be exiled in shame to some unknown end. The shame is not theirs to bear, and yet they suffer it.

In that I myself have suffered, I am able to comfort the suffering. I so long to comfort you and our daughter in your travails.

In full assurance of hope I remain, as ever, Yours Truly

CHAPTER NINE

Two weeks ago

A dumpy male employee in a stained bib apron was putting trash out in the alley when Libby found her way to the back of the Belle Boutique Hotel on Saturday morning.

"You looking for the cooking class?" The greasy fellow lit a half-smoked cigarette and pointed his chin in the direction of the door. Libby entered the steamy room noisy with the bustle of food preparation, but none of the plentiful restaurant staff acknowledged her.

A robust man wearing an official white hat and pristine white jacket embroidered with the words "Chef Virgil" emerged from the hallway entrance at the far end of the kitchen.

"There's our last participant." He was chirpy with British pomp. "Come along, then. The rest are waiting."

"I didn't know I was late." It wasn't quite eight, and on a Saturday morning, at that.

"You're not, but this is an enthusiastic group." He handed her a hairnet and drew her into a smaller kitchen furnished with four stations, each replete with sink, fridge, chopping block, and stove, and occupied by three or four people already engaged in rinsing vegetables and browning meaty bones.

Libby squeezed between a slender woman dripping diamonds and a Johnny Depp look-a-like with a five-inch wire whisk tattooed on his inner forearm. The group as a whole bantered back and forth about previous sessions held here at the Belle and elsewhere in the Twin Cities—a demo on locally sourced ingredients in the kitchen at Hotel Ivy, last fall's croissant tutorial at La Patisserie, the televised tastings with the late Anthony Bourdain at the Piccolo. Several of Libby's classmates, she learned as she listened, were employed in top-rated establishments themselves. But most were hobbyists, with what sounded like unlimited grocery budgets, who planned vacations around Le Cordon Bleu academies in Paris or Madrid.

Libby was way out of her social league, and a few minutes of the chef's instruction let her know just how *haute* the *cuisine* was. No one there flinched at his terminology, all of them following his staccato instructions throughout the morning about clarifying a consommé with egg whites or binding a thick soup with a liaison of boiled bread pulp. They negotiated the layout of the kitchen as though it was second nature to so easily find stockpot, sieve, and ladle, to say nothing of food mill, mandolin, or mortar and pestle. Transferring smoking fat from one pan to another over the flaring gas elements didn't faze them. By lunchtime, each cook had produced at least one remarkable dish: a shellfish *velouté*, a chicken *pot-au-feu*, a *potage* garnished with diced aromatic spring vegetables like chives and paper-thin slices of shallots and grated daikon radishes. But Libby's own oxtail soup—or *grand hochepot*, as Virgil magnanimously named it as he went sniffing past—seemed to her very humble indeed.

For lunch everyone enjoyed a bowl of the chef's Stilton-leek soup. Libby lifted a spoon to her lips; maybe her own cheese-infused invention for Zinnia last weekend would prove she was a natural. While they ate, the chef served up a lecture regarding his culinary philosophy, referring often to his latest publication. The glossy book titled *Simmer, Scoop, Slurp: A Savory Soup Sampler* was a compilation of favorite recipes he'd gathered on international forays throughout his career. Libby flipped through the copy nearest her while he chatted, appreciating the full-color shots of the multicultural fare: tomato-lentil Moroccan *harira*, Mexican *pozole* with avocados, Vietnamese noodle *pho* in a translucent blue-and-white bowl, cockle soup of clams gathered at low tide along Ireland's shores. This was as close to international travel as she was ever likely to get.

"I believe in using what's at hand." Chef Virgil sounded like Gram. "We see this in the traditional dishes of every country. You there"—he addressed a gregarious brunette who'd been dropping comments all morning in an exotic accent—"what's your gastronomic background?" The woman shrugged. "Come now, I'll bet your mother made *avgolemono*."

She nodded. "You're right. We grew lemon trees in our yard in Greece, so it was the cheapest thing, and Mama cooked it almost every day." She pressed the back of her hand against her mouth, bulging her cheeks out in mock nausea. The room erupted in laughter.

"We take our culture for granted," Virgil said, "but all of us, I'll wager, would pay dearly for Mama's specialty on a wintry Minnesota evening."

Another student lifted a hand. "My brother-in-law brings his sister's *shkedei marak* back home with him whenever he visits Tel Aviv."

"Yes, Israeli soup croutons." Thank goodness for Chef Virgil's translation; Libby couldn't keep up on her own. "We import our heritage into our kitchen as a way of celebrating our own roots. You all know the folktale of Stone Soup, I'm sure, as variations of it occur across ethnicities."

He settled back on his stool and assumed the narrative voice Gram used at bedtime. "Long ago, a penniless wanderer happened upon a town and begged the inhabitants to feed him, but they refused, as they themselves had so little. The rascal convinced them he could produce—as if by magic—a great soup if he had but a pot, water, and a stone. This they could provide, and when the liquid was boiling, one onlooker volunteered a few onions, another found a potato in his pocket, a third added butter from his cow, and so on until the soup was a succulent mixture, a veritable feast."

Libby smiled to herself as she stood to help clear the lunch dishes. How similar his fable was to the real-life story of Redpath and the hobo jungles.

The afternoon's session dealt with choosing herbs and spices for the perfect *bouquet garni* and included a discussion about the best varieties for an indoor garden. At one point, Chef Virgil made a comment that caught Libby off guard.

"Before we disband later today, remember that I'll need ingredient lists from each of you for your specialty at next weekend's function. And don't forget to give your soup a name to appear on the menu."

Libby turned to her tattooed workmate. "What's he talking about?" She hadn't heard about any function.

"The fundraiser next Saturday for the . . ." he picked up a sheet of paper and read, "'Network of Community Collaborators Ending Homelessness.' The Belle does it every spring in conjunction with a visiting chef." He handed her the page. "You didn't get one when you came in?"

Libby stared at the bulletin, the words popping out at her.

The two-session cooking seminar would culminate in a professional project—participation in a dinner to be attended by gourmands from around the state, perhaps even restaurant scouts looking for new talent to hire or new recipes to popularize. Each class registrant was expected to produce a novel soup. Sample-sized bowls in flights of three would be on the tasting menu to be deemed as worthy, or not, of receiving certification. Cash prizes were also on the table.

No wonder the participants in the class were so focused. They were in competition against each other—against Libby herself. Only the young man cooking alongside her had offered her conversation.

"I'm hoping a foodie will blog my soup," he said now, keeping his voice down. "It might score me cred with my boss. I'm up for a promotion to the *sous-chef* position."

Libby pursed her lips. What was the motive of the other workshop attendees—arrogance, prestige, money, or perhaps the sheer pursuit of art? Her own reasons were much simpler, and in this first session she'd already received skill-enhancing information she could use in her humble kitchen. She didn't need the stimulus of a contest to sharpen her interest, and in fact the idea that her soup would be evaluated nettled her. She fiddled with a set of stainless steel measuring spoons until Chef Virgil's final words of lecture broke through and sent her to her coiled pad to scribble down a few notes.

"It's all about the seasoning," he said. "A *purée* requires a light hand when it comes to, say, cilantro or cloves. But quantities of pungent chili and fresh ginger are intrinsically necessary for the integrity of a Brazilian *vatapa*."

In late afternoon Virgil dismissed the group with a summary regarding their assignment. "As you refine your recipes for next week, don't be limited by familial preconceptions, but rather improve on those inherited flavors. Be bold, be innovative." He collected lists from most as they exited the kitchen. "I'll be checking for fresh produce at the market early Saturday morning according to your requirements, and I'll have all the ingredients ready so that we can recreate the soup anew here in the Belle kitchens. I see we already have"—he shuffled through the stack of hand-ins—"a fat- and gluten-free *caldo* from Portugal, a vegan chowder cleverly named 'Don't Meat Me,' a mutton pot using both *halal* and kosher ingredients to observe religious restrictions, and a fruit *coulis* and a *sopa de chocolate* that both look delightful."

Libby's paper was as blank as her mind. She still had no idea as to her specialty, though of course she knew what she'd *like* to cook. Chef Virgil, maybe noting her lack of ease, assured her she had time to e-mail him before Friday morning, when the printer would need the dish titles and final listings of ingredients for the menus.

The telephone clamored at Paige from the wall, breaking her out of her bookish concentration. She strained to rise from the floor, her feet asleep from sitting cross-legged, and answered on the fourth ring to her mother-in-law's jolly voice.

"It's Donna. What are you up to this fine Saturday evening?"

"Same old," she answered. "Research. I'm getting near the end, though."

"And it's a good thing, too." Paige detected not a trace of rancor. "You're so diligent. All of us Paulssons are proud of you, of course. But you should take a break. Can I bring a huckleberry pie over for coffee?"

Saliva gushed in Paige's mouth. "Thanks, but I can't take the time." She was snacking on celery dipped in the peanut butter jar at the moment and would fill up on leftovers while she proofread her current chapter later on.

"I'll send a slice along with Danny when he stops in. If Martin leaves him any, that is." Donna sighed. Danny's dad had been putting on the pounds and his mom worried about diabetes.

"Are you donating pies for the fair again?" The museum's opening event loomed two weeks away and, though Paige as docent was the official overseer of all the institution's events, she'd learned early in her marriage that the community ladies had a long-established routine for who contributed what to such events. Paige had seen Danny's mom in baking mode, when every surface in the kitchen was covered in pastries and breads and cookies. But she was known for her berry pies, which last year had brought in enough to pay for professional steam cleaning of the mansion's carpets.

"I'm afraid not." Donna's voice held real regret. "The food committee insists that it's time for the younger generation to take over the baking. Besides, all the surnames beginning with 'P' are to bring salads."

"Oh, maybe I should bring—"

"Don't you think about it. I'll make enough coleslaw to feed the whole alphabet." She chortled. "Shredding cabbage is a lot easier than rolling dough."

"Well, it's Kirkton's loss, but Danny will be happy to have more pie for himself."

MDM had loved pie, too. Paige once read a newspaper article about his attendance as guest of honor at the lunch following the ground-breaking ceremony for the new town hall, when the founder had good-naturedly eaten a piece of each pie on the insistence of the matrons showcasing their daughters' culinary skills.

"By the way," Paige said into the phone while she had her mother-in-law's attention, "I've been meaning to ask if you've come up with any memories about MDM, as we talked about a few weeks ago. You told me to remind you. I'm attempting to fill in blanks about his private life, and I know your side of the family has been in the area for several generations."

"No." Donna's tone was hesitant. "I've been trying to recall if I ever met him, even as a girl. He was somewhat of a recluse, you know."

"Only in his later years." Paige cringed as soon as she uttered it. Did it come off as academic snobbery? After all, Donna had grown up here. She softened her tone and added, "But of course you'd have been pretty young at the time."

"My mother once described him as an upright gentleman, and I got the impression she'd spoken to him on the street once."

"Could we ask her about it?"

"Um..."

"Oh, sorry. Never mind." Paige was sure putting her foot in her mouth this evening, but she'd forgotten momentarily that Danny's grandmother was in a care facility in Grand Forks, not expected to see the summer out.

She hung up the phone and, before resuming her weekend activity of searching computer databanks and journal papers for factual substantiation, she stared out the window at the trees swaying long limbs at her, beckoning her into the springtime dusk. She ignored their pleas as she'd have had to ignore Danny, were he home, and so it was just as well that he was taken up with seeding. He'd be eating his chicken sandwich about now as he went 'round and 'round in circles. Paige took in the broader sweep of the fields he'd already worked beyond the willows, clods of newly turned, dark brown earth lying in neat rows as though waiting, expectant, for the germination beneath to sprout out a fuzz of bright green.

Her research was a tyrant. She groaned and turned back to her notes on the variation of building styles employed in the Victorian era, when the Industrial Revolution allowed wide distribution of ornamental decoration so that Romanesque and Colonial, Italianate and Gothic revivals blended together. MDM used this architectural composition to express not only his aesthetics but also, symbolically, his personal, communal, and governmental policies. Paige shook her head; she was overthinking this. The information and meaning she could layer into her thesis was endless, but the more bulk she added, the more vigorously she would be grilled at her oral defense.

Why hadn't she chosen a simpler premise confined to straight history rather than the psychological and philosophical and even political mess she'd gotten herself mired in? She might have stuck with MDM's fundamental role in the colonization of Kirkton and how his house set trends in his day. But no, her thirst for knowledge demanded she jump into the deep end. And so she'd plunged, helpless, under MDM's spell—not least his moral outrage for the well-being of Pembina County's original populace, shown through his hospitality to the Native Americans and in the messages hidden within his design and decorating and furnishing choices.

And where had all her diligence gotten her? Why, whole days passed by without Paige spending even fifteen minutes looking into Danny's eyes, never mind preparing herself or the nursery for Baby. But now that she was so far into her studies, there was no turning back.

Paige shuffled through a file of her notes. She sighed when she noticed that the willow tree—breeze having died down—no longer summoned her.

Late Sunday morning sunlight streamed into Sybil's bedroom. She stretched and ran her fingers through her hair, which last night, after Iggy left, she'd bleached yellow and then tipped in a vibrant violet semi-permanent dye. Iggy would be over for an in-house lunch today. Although cooking was not her prime talent, she could bake a mean fish. Yesterday she bought a grouper fresh in from Florida and a large bag of limes—enough for a pitcher of mojitos, too.

The thought of the menu put her in mind of one of her travel escapes from a cold Minneapolis winter. She'd flown to the island of Eleuthra, a skinny squiggle on the map of the Bahamas, and chartered a boat to trace its shoreline. That week the sailor, charming Charles, fed her conch fritters on coral sand beaches, walked her out on rocky ledges above the ocean's crashing waves, and snorkeled with her among sea turtles, one of which he illegally caught and cooked up for her later. She'd made an exception to her self-defined vegan rules, which Charles had no way of knowing about anyway. Turtles and conch and their scaly cousins were, after all, only ugly marine creatures without the precocious personality of fur-bearing species—hardly animals at all.

But the highlight was spelunking in a cave said once to have held pirate booty. Bats swished out in a cloud as Charles and Sybil entered the yawning cavern, stalactites hanging like uvulas from the ceiling. They were alone, though decades of graffiti showed the grotto to be a long-used trysting spot. They descended, Charles's torch piercing the dense darkness and lighting up the mineral columns that surrounded them in a bewitched cloister.

Charles happened to have a bottle of rum in his pack.

For hours that night in the bowels of the island, he riveted her with stories about growing up spear fishing, marrying a girl who made peas and rice as good as his mama's, and passing along to his own five children—three from his official wife, the others his "out family"—the traditions of *obeah*, the folk religion akin to voodoo. His great-aunt had taught him how to cast spells and hear the spirits and use talismans. He gave Sybil a demo of his incantation and, though she suspected this might be part of his tour-guide routine, thrills ran up her spine when his eyes glazed over in a trance.

Now, in the solitude of her Sunday morning meditations and revived by her reminiscence of Charles, she felt the time was right for her personalized version of contemplative, centering prayer. Operating by reason in the supernatural realm was impossible, so she disengaged her mind and prepared to celebrate herself as an incarnation of pneuma, as one fragment of deity in the unity of the All. She decided on Pranayama yogic breathing, except that she was lying down—so much more comfy than sitting on the floor.

"Be still and know that I am," she began chanting slowly, inhaling the life force and exhaling time-bound thought, over and over. "Be still and know . . . Be still . . . Be . . ."

All consciousness of time fled, leaving only the delicious sensations imparted by rendezvous with men like Charles, the double portion of life allotted to her by the Oversoul—whether called Vishnu or Allah or Great Spirit. As she came back to sentience, she took a few moments to give thanks for the gift of self-realization produced by her intentional lifestyle of honesty and authenticity.

Sybil flung back her bedding, ready for the day. Her morning sessions of replaying an amorous memory as a prelude to connecting with the wider universe were not only for personal entertainment in the moment but helped in her communion with others. Iggy was the main beneficiary of her pleasant retrospections, her life-affirming meditations, and her feminine magnanimities. Even if he was oblivious to his own soul wounds, Sybil accepted that her special purpose—for this day, anyway—was to release love to him.

And yet, the thought intruded as she turned on the water for her shower, how could she be sure she wasn't missing something? She caught her reflection without meaning to, before she'd arranged her face, and the dark melancholy there cast a shadow over her heart's invigoration.

CHAPTER TEN

Today

Libby hugs her jacket around her, chilled on the exposed portico high above the museum yard. Sybil is prying at the mansion's cedar shingle siding with her thumbnail, her bangles a-jangle. Libby disregards her fidgeting and directs all her attention onto the tour guide, Paige.

The young woman's eyes are sparkling like a child's at Christmas as she talks to the group. She leans forward a bit, the corners of her lips turned up slightly. The moment an elderly lady or student asks her a question, a dewy rose glow washes her cheeks and her posture loosens as she launches into the answer.

It must be so gratifying to be *heard* by her. But Libby isn't yet ready to speak up herself.

The enthusiasm of the mother-to-be is all about her subject matter, her glance now and then dancing out over the prairie as though to catch sight of a straggling buffalo like a phantom from the past, even as she rubs her swollen torso and shifts her weight from one foot to the other. Libby's become increasingly intrigued with the museum herself over the past week or two, ever since she discovered the out-of-date tourism pamphlet in Gram's bedside table. And then, after what happened Friday night in the apartment parking lot, she couldn't avoid thoughts of the museum and didn't sleep much before Sybil picked her up yesterday morning for this trip.

"MDM was also an entrepreneur." Paige continued her discourse. "Born too late to fully capitalize on the fur trade, he also missed the bonanza of the Black Hills gold rush. But during the population boom that followed the laying of the railroad from Winnipeg south to Saint Paul, he soon made his fortune in shipping grain to flour mills, cattle to packing plants . . ."

"What's with the *feng shui* of the fences?" Sybil's interruption is rude, but Paige turns to listen. Sybil jabs a thumb out towards the fields. "I mean, there seems to be some flow of life force in the layout of the fields, as though the fences form a rune or a symbol."

Paige tips her head to one side, perhaps as bemused by Sybil's madcap manner as Libby had been when they first met. It's partly Sybil's appearance that's so mesmerizing. Today, for example, she's decked out in striped leggings and cowboy boots, her hair a mass of braided, beaded, teal-blue extensions. But that doesn't stop Paige from answering Sybil's question seriously.

"Yes, the fences," Paige says. Libby, too, looks down and out again upon the symmetry of the landscaping as Paige explains. "The outer dry-stone hedge, you can see, is punctuated by a dozen rock pillars and still in decent repair. It encompasses a forty-nine-acre tract. It's only four feet in height, but the century-old wall was meant more as demarcation than protection. It was never intended to keep anyone out but rather to differentiate MDM's wider agricultural holdings and pasturelands beyond from the homestead within.

"Then notice how, at the center of this walled-in parcel of land, the smaller, domestic yard is enclosed by a right-angle ribbon of picket fence equidistant on all sides to the mansion, which in turn is positioned at the center."

Yes, Libby can see it. She follows the square-within-square layout as Paige traces the path she and Sybil had taken this morning.

"Look at how straight the road is out there"—Paige points beyond the property line—"where you turned off the highway onto Salem Drive and passed beneath the fieldstone arch hung with its nineteenth-century gas lantern, still manually lit when the museum is open."

The words of welcome inscribed into that arch had struck Libby at the time. *Laird Estate: Better one day herein than a thousand elsewhere.* It smacked of ownership pride, like Gram's welcome mat in the apartment: *Home Suite Home.* As the father of Seven Canaan Lane, shrugging off his jacket after work, might swing his daughter up in to his arms and she might squeal, "Welcome home, Daddy!" Libby banishes that last picture from her overactive brain but, instinctively, her spirit implores an unseen father of her own.

"As you approached the museum," Paige goes on, "you drove within sight of the livestock corral and the small lake and the vegetable plots inside the stone fence." Libby's first sight of the mansion itself, full on as it appeared in Gram's brochure, had stunned her in its familiarity, with its formidable proportions and heavy shingles, its opulent front door, and its encircling veranda. "Then, passing into the inner court of the yard through the gate—you can see the pattern easily from this height—we walked by the remains of a reception gazebo, a hand-pumped water well, the iron lamppost, and the kitchen garden attached to the north side of the house. It's as though MDM's personal landscaping mimics the larger farm layout."

Libby strains to decipher the correlation between elements of the outer periphery and the domestic yard—the corral to the gazebo, the lake to the well.

The teens are getting restless, and Libby resists hushing them, trying to hear Paige. "Salem Drive is the sole entrance to the museum grounds, and the road lines up with the pedestrian walk leading through the rusty yard gate into the inner courtyard, taking the visitor from the outside world to the front door of the mansion in deliberate, orderly design."

It appears, as Sybil suggests, to be a code of some sort.

"Look for this pattern of enclosure, which is repeated again as a motif in the floor plan of the mansion." Paige clatters free a brass key from the ring in her apron pocket and fits it into the lock of the paint-flaked door beneath the eaves of the rooftop terrace. "Now, please follow me into the house itself. Watch your step over the raised sill."

"Finally we get inside." Sybil sounds bored already.

Libby's stomach tightens with the creak of the hinges, her uneasiness rumbling like a hunger pang as awareness of her situation crowds in on her again. What is she doing here? Despite the abundance of museums and galleries available back in the Twin Cities, she's never fancied herself a history buff—that is, not until learning about the existence of this museum. She chews her lower lip, she fingers the new-to-her ring-hung chain around her neck. What in heaven's name possessed her to travel out of state to the remote Laird Mansion in the first place?

But, in her heart of hearts, she knows. It all began when Gram died before Christmas, and it really started coming into focus last month, in late April.

CHAPTER ELEVEN

Two weeks ago

Monday morning, the first of May, didn't feel like a fresh start. Libby stepped down from the bus a street away from Hearsay, vaguely registering the commotion coming from around the corner. Her mind was full with distractions. First of all, she couldn't settle on what soup to make next weekend, though of course she was leaning in the direction of Gram's mystery recipe, the taste of which still missed the mark of the original. Then, distress over today's upcoming bank appointment merged with her shaky hopes of purchasing the house and her growing unease regarding the story circulating in her apartment block about a big corporation pushing to buy the whole building for the land value. Added to this, Sybil nattered nonstop at her about traveling rather than nesting. She'd recently even sent her a list of links to the world's most sacred places, badgering Libby on the phone until she promised to check them out.

But Libby's lack of concentration today was primarily due to the ongoing emotional upheaval in packing away Gram's life. All day yesterday she'd been occupied in the living room, taking down and sorting through the abundance of postcards and news clippings and greeting cards her grandmother had plastered all over the walls. It took hours because recollection attended each scrap of paper: *To err is human* and *Laughter is the best medicine* and *Charity begins at home.*

Charity—love. What a good motto to finish up with. At that point, Libby had stopped reading the cards and placed the remaining batch into her file for later consideration, suddenly wearied of all Gram's cheer. Just as she'd begun to tackle the linen closet as her last job of the evening, she glimpsed the corner of a faintly familiar pink box way high up in the back. But then a telemarketer demanded her attention, and fatigue made her sit down for a cup of decaf before retiring. Thinking back about it this morning, there was something both familiar and unsettling about the box's pebbled surface. She'd have to dig into that closet soon.

No wonder, then, Libby didn't notice the crowd gathering and the raised voices coming from the direction of Hearsay until she walked into the middle of it. The sirens weren't wailing, for one thing—sirens always set childhood panic rattling her bones—but the flashing lights almost blinded her.

Terence stood in the open doorway yipping at a stocky policeman as he poked his finger repeatedly towards the cracked plate glass and the illegible graffiti sprayed on the brick exterior.

"Who knows what that old crow would have done next?"

"Calm down, sir," the officer said. "We'll get this sorted. You allege the suspect has been loitering near your premises lately?"

"'Suspect'?" Terence's top lip lifted in a sneer, showing off one eyetooth. "I caught her red handed, defacing my shop and slamming her cart into the window. And yeah, the hag was hanging around here last week, too. I almost tripped over her when I left Friday."

Terence's howl overrode the scuffle between a second officer and a bag lady. Libby looked more closely. Wasn't that the same homeless woman with the crocheted cap who'd peered in at her through the café window? This must be the "scum" Terence talked about the day Libby asked for a raise. She hurried towards the shop door through the alcoholic fumes emanating from the woman, who craned her head towards Libby while the policeman restrained her.

Suddenly the thrashing bundle of rags went still, and then she stabbed a long, gnarled finger straight at Libby and shrieked, "I seen you! I know you!" Squinching through straggly gray hair, she shot resentment at Libby through rheumy eyes until the officer folded her into the patrol car, arms and legs again flailing.

Libby's skin crawled. Terence turned glaring eyes on her.

"I have no idea who she is." Libby clamped her arms over her chest. "That is, I think she might be the same person I saw at the café last week, but—"

"Then you recognize the accused?" The first officer had his notepad out again, pen at the ready.

"Absolutely not." Everyone on the scene was watching her. "I mean, maybe she's been following me, come to think of it. Somebody's been following me." Why was she blundering on? She composed herself, counted to ten silently. "I saw this woman pass the coffee shop and look in at me a week or so ago. I believe it was the same woman. Her cap . . ."

The policeman nodded at Libby's weak explanation and slid his pen and pad into his pocket. "It's okay, ma'am. We'll follow up on this when we've questioned her, once she's sober."

A new chorus of the woman's howling swelled out of the car as he opened the driver's door, abating again when they drove off.

"Well, go on then," Terence growled, as if Libby had anything to do with the vandalism. "Clean up this mess and call someone to patch the window." He stomped off, grumbling that she'd better solve this problem if she expected him to keep her employed—that it was *her* problem, after all.

Libby wobbled back to the storeroom for cleaning supplies but had to sit on the closed toilet seat lid for a minute to gather herself. That outlandish woman had scattered her into a billion pieces. Terence's veiled threat wasn't lost on her, either. Her income was at stake and she needed the job security, what with her mortgage application pending. How would she answer if Mr. Jordan demanded verification of her employment status during the bank meeting later today? What if he called Terence to confirm her situation while her boss was so irate? Why would that ridiculous old woman bring such misfortune down on her?

Libby relived the scene again—the bag lady's ugliness, her violent spasming as if in seizure, her piercing glare and blaming eyes.

How dare that rotting stranger arouse such shame in her?

Libby's repulsion took her aback. Years of helping at the Haven with Gram and then her ongoing volunteerism there had ingrained in her a sense of mercy towards seniors, even those in the throes of senility. But now, though she tried to dismiss her repugnance of the homeless woman, all she saw was a drunk—and a mean one, at that. Her screeching accusation insinuated they had a sort of connection, and it clawed at Libby like the old lady's dirty talons had scraped on the metal doorframe of the patrol car: "I seen you! I know you!"

Libby vaulted to her feet, grabbed the bucket and brush, and ran from the accusatory words, wishing she could flush them away behind her. She had *never* seen that woman before last month. Or else she had seen her over and over again in every demented woman at the Haven and on the streets of the city since she was a girl.

No, she didn't need to think about it. She needed to do her job and suck up to Terence and forget the ugly affair of this morning. This wasn't her problem. The cops had taken the woman into custody and thrown her into lock-up. It was *their* issue and had nothing to do with her. The incident was finished.

Somehow she'd get through this day and slip away early to meet the banker.

Paige drove towards the museum on Monday afternoon, following another long morning at home of editing and rewriting her thesis manuscript. She slowed to a stop as she approached a slim figure strolling on the right-hand shoulder of Salem Drive. The cute teen with a turned-up nose stopped walking and stuck her head into the open passenger window, smiling through her freckles. She was almost certainly part of the Farris-Yeast clan; they occupied more than half of the remaining habitable houses in Kirkton.

"Can I give you a lift to the mansion?"

"Thanks." The girl hopped into the front seat.

"You must be one of the new museum volunteers this season?"

The girl nodded. "I'm off classes early for my first day of training."

"My name's Paige."

"Oh, everyone knows who you are. I came with the junior class for a tour in the fall, before the museum shut down for the winter." Paige couldn't recall her face. "I'm Jamie Farris." Jamie snapped her seatbelt buckle with a sharp click. "But not one of *those* Farrises."

Paige kept her expression neutral. "Pleased to meet you. You'll enjoy working at the mansion." She hoped so, anyway. Local animosity abounded, what with the current Farris-Yeast family lawsuit that just went on and on. Jamie must be significantly removed from that branch for the board to accept her application for the student position. The museum offered one of the few opportunities for area kids to get formal, though unpaid, vocational experience. "If you need any historical information, Jamie, I'm the one to ask. At least for a little while longer." She patted her belly.

"When are you due?"

"Third week in June."

Jamie's eyes popped. "Wow, you're big. Oops, I mean . . ."

Paige laughed. "I really am, and I have another seven weeks, if I go full term." She'd already gained twenty-five pounds. "The doctor assures me it's not twins."

"My sister Rika's pregnant. I'm going to be an auntie any day now." Jamie arranged her book bag by her feet. "Hey, maybe you want to come to the baby shower tonight?"

Paige thanked her but deferred with some misgiving; she should get to know the locals better. She was so immersed in the historical records that she tended to forget the current-day living going on around her, preferring the faded text of out-of-print books to the full-color present. She glanced at Jamie.

"You like babies?"

"Sure," Jamie said. "Everyone likes babies."

Paige nodded. That was true, and MDM must have liked them as well. Children definitely played a role in the mansion's history. Maybe she could get confirmation of a few facts if she asked the right questions; even shirttail relatives had memories, if only of ancestral gossip.

She'd ease into it. "They used to have grand parties in the mansion, with lots of community kids in attendance." According to Paige's initial interviews, the Laird house once knew the pitter-patter of little feet—if not of MDM's own offspring then at least of those belonging to the housekeepers. The presence of children in the historic home was the origin of the lawsuit, which alleged the Laird estate remained morally obligated to continue financial support of the Farris-Yeast kinfolk.

Jamie sat forward, straining against her seatbelt. "I saw photos of that—a bunch of them around a huge tree at Christmas. The kids of some of the, uh, housekeepers or something." The girl sat back, suddenly silent. Was she blushing?

Paige mentally reviewed the history of the litigious family Jamie disavowed. The housekeepers were at the base of the story, long before the Laird Mansion was built.

It had all begun with a local girl, Henrietta Adams—ten years younger than MDM and not even Jamie's age in 1889 when she eloped with Robert Farris, a cross-border whiskey runner, in rebellion against the matchmaking efforts of her parents. Paige bit her lower lip—it was not the sort of detail she'd be comfortable sharing with Jamie. The esteemed Mr. and Mrs. Adams, who admired the ambition of the young industrialist MDM, had been pushing their daughter in his direction and were devastated by Henrietta's wanton actions with another man. They disinherited her, and both parents died shortly thereafter. Widowed in 1905 at age thirty with several children, Henrietta Farris fell into destitution. That's when MDM took her on as housekeeper out of pity over her unfortunate turn of events. He opened his home to her children and even saw to their education as though they were his own.

Then Henrietta Farris died, leaving her grown sons to fend for themselves—as well as one married daughter, also named Henrietta. This suggested to Paige a possibly fruitful line of inquiry.

"The two housekeepers were related, weren't they?" She didn't need to ask, but bold-faced honesty might be too direct, might spook the reticent Farris. "I noticed their graves side by side in the estate cemetery."

Jamie laughed. "How could you miss that? One Henrietta would be bad enough. What an ugly name."

"Not such an uncommon name for that era," Paige said, "and the tradition was to keep one's first name alive by recycling it down the generations." In fact, her research showed that girls far back on the family tree of the two Henriettas were known by variations such as Hettie and Etta and, as Jamie's own sister was named, Rika—damning evidence had Jamie known about it.

The wind buffeted Paige's car and she gripped the wheel more securely. By all accounts, the younger Henrietta lived up to the meaning of her hand-me-down name, "powerful ruler of the house." After wedding William Yeast and being widowed herself in 1925, when his neck snapped upon being thrown from his horse, she moved back into the mansion of her youth with her own batch of children and took over her mother's stewardship of MDM.

Consequent to this business arrangement, offshoots of the Farris-Yeast progeny seemed to feel entitled to the Laird birthright, if Paige rightly read between the lines. Some of the family promoted the story that the second Henrietta had once been engaged to marry their patron, MDM. They went so far as to claim that Laird blood ran in their own veins through one or the other of the Henriettas, elder or younger.

This was the source of local legend about MDM's connections, perhaps even intimacies, with the Farris-Yeast women—and was likely the remembered detail that had caused Jamie's blush. It was preposterous that MDM might have sired children with Henrietta Farris or that he cavorted with her daughter, Henrietta Yeast. Yet the Farris-Yeast family had brought forward a will listing as benefactors several members of the household, purportedly signed by MDM but subsequently proven to be forged. Neither Paige nor the courts had found any supporting evidence for the complainants' allegations.

Paige did, however, believe the stories of the housekeepers ruling the Laird domain with a tyrannical hand. Perhaps Jamie would have a perspective on it.

"Have you ever heard any stories about the housekeepers?"

Jamie scratched her eyebrow. "Well, my grandma once told me that everyone in this town knew the housekeepers bossed the whole family around—even the old man."

Yes, common knowledge held that the Henriettas lorded it over the staff during seasons of plenty and then, as the estate's riches waned, bullied the aging MDM himself until he died, when Henrietta Yeast was still in her sixties. This second housekeeper outlived him—and was certainly still around in the days of Jamie's grandmother. Both Henriettas seem to have passed along greedy bitterness over perceived injustices to the very children who benefited from Laird's generosity. Paige assessed the girl sitting beside her. She hardly looked the bossy type, yet several of her extended-family members—remnants of the Henriettas—continued to petition the court for what was "rightfully theirs."

"You know," Paige said, reverting to her earlier subject, "children other than the Farris-Yeasts would have run along the halls of the mansion. In MDM Laird's day, the displaced Native families who lived on and worked his land—along with their own garden plots he provided for them—were welcomed every Sunday to a feast laid out in the great hall."

"Right. The picture I saw showed older and younger kids wearing strange clothes. Like, I mean, lacy frills on some of the girls and others in fringed leather outfits."

Yes, children of varying age and race would not have been unknown in the Laird mansion.

Paige lapsed back into silence as she drove the last few minutes. The courts had fended off each new attack by the Farris-Yeast aggressors but were handicapped without a clear enough paper trail to once and for all disprove their claims. Talk of sabotage circulated—speculation that the housekeepers had destroyed what could be used to finally put the case to bed.

And then there was that other longstanding rumor.

One eyewitness alive in the pioneer era was said to have told a grandson, who told a cousin, who told a nephew, that MDM Laird had indeed been officially married. That a decade into his Dakota residency he'd taken a bride not of the social standing expected for a man of MDM's professional reputation. That it had been a matter of passion resulting in a short-lived union. But again, Paige ran into a dearth of official documentation—and this wasn't a subject she cared to broach with young Jamie, whose grandmother's witness would be completely unreliable anyway.

Paige pulled the car into the lot of the Laird Mansion Museum, gravel crunching beneath its tires. She and Jamie opened their doors simultaneously, and a prairie gust swept through the interior to send her record files flying.

"Yikes!" Jamie leapt from the car to help Paige chase down her notes blown against the fence.

Paige panted until she caught her breath. "That's spring for you."

"Yeah. It's pretty cold for the first of May."

"May Day," Paige said.

"Right. My grandma tells stories about May Day celebrations in Canada when she was a girl."

"It was once suggested to the Kirkton Preservation Society," Paige said, "that this date might be a good excuse to advance the museum's opening day by two weeks, erect a maypole in the yard, and have local girls dance around it in costume."

"What a great idea." Jamie's net of freckles moved with her smile.

Paige laughed. "That's what I thought at first, but they didn't agree." And neither did she, once she learned more about what both May Day and MDM stood for. "The chairman told me that, in spite of MDM's European connection, pagan May Day celebrations were never held here, out of respect for his puritanical sensibilities. Besides, they couldn't very well risk rescheduling the museum kick-off in case the area farmers hadn't completed seeding."

"I see I have a lot to learn." Jamie handed her a pile of papers. "My job is mostly in the gift shop. I've already memorized the instruction manual on how to operate the old-time cash register.

But I don't know much about the overall history." She tugged open the gate and started up the walkway.

"It takes time." Paige closed the gate behind them.

Today she wouldn't follow her usual habit of climbing the back steps to her third-floor office through the servants' entrance. She'd been the one to put the neglected exterior staircase into regular use shortly after being hired, when she'd instituted the new tour itinerary starting with the outdoor balustraded terrace at the peak of the mansion rather than at the grand front door. The backdoor approach allowed visitors to appreciate the layout of the mansion without being overwhelmed by its full glory right off the bat, and they never complained about having to climb such a genuine antique as the Art Deco, wrought-iron, circular set of stairs.

But today she'd conserve her energy. What had kept her slim before marriage and pregnancy was wearing her out these days, although the facility's opening in two weeks would mandate regular ascension of those steps, like it or not.

"Wow, what's with all the activity?" Jamie asked. They stood at the head of the path that ran from the gate straight through the mansion's front door, which was wide open to the sunshine this afternoon. "Looks like a celebration."

"The first day in May is earmarked by the KPS for spring cleaning."

The yard buzzed with activity: gardeners digging in flowerbeds, a handyman patching siding shingles, and hands wiping the upstairs windows from the inside. Paige and Jamie passed by the footings for the gazebo, which had fallen into significant disrepair when it no longer served as the receiving lobby for

MDM's purchases. The gazebo was a freestanding atrium that had acted almost as an altar for the offering of skins and pelts brought for trade by trappers—by Blackfeet and Ojibwa, Métis and Cree, Arikara, Hidatsa, and Mandan. A few steps on, Paige let her fingers slide over the cool brass handle on the well pump that still provided water to the pool at its base, once used as an outdoor washing station for bloodied hands or muddied feet. On a stepladder, a girl polished winter off the globes of the lamppost, perpetually lit during tourist season. The herb garden at the side of the house had been tilled and seeded.

"Okay," Jamie said, "I know on the fall tour you mentioned a pattern being repeated over and over on the property. But I didn't quite get it."

That wasn't surprising. Paige's research depended on MDM's highly developed symbolism. She wasn't sure she could swear to its validity herself.

"Think from the outside inward," she began. "We have MDM's wider grazing lands, within which the stone fence encloses the homestead, within which another square delineates the yard's picket fence, within which the square of the mansion sits. MDM's orderly layout of the inner yard's gazebo, well, kitchen garden, and lampstand reproduced the elements of the outer ring of his larger estate."

Jamie nodded. "I remember that part. The yard light represents the gas lantern hanging on the entry gate, I think you said. The well stands for Beulah Lake, where my friends and I always swim. But . . ." Jamie stopped, her forehead wrinkling.

Paige picked up the narrative.

"The potager beside the kitchen door imitates the large

vegetable plots set between the yard fence and the stone hedge's northern edge. Both the gazebo here and the corrals out there had to do with animals."

Of course, Paige had read all of this herself for her graduate studies, antecedent researchers having already made the link between inner yard and outer homestead. One expert even developed the idea that the primary source of the imitation was the natural world of native grassland irrigated by the Red River, overrun by wild prairie animals, and illumined by the sun, moon, and stars—flora, water, fauna, and light represented three times over.

However, in one eureka moment Paige had singlehandedly discovered the next level of repetition—the design of the house itself. This was the genius kernel of her thesis, but she'd stumbled on it out of pure luck so she almost hesitated to take credit. When examining an aerial photograph dated 1927 of MDM's estate, she'd inadvertently placed alongside it a sketch of the house's floor plan. That's when she first observed the enclosing schemata within the house itself—the outer walls of the home forming a perimeter of hallways and salons, a secondary ring within that incorporating the high-ceilinged foyer and staircase, and MDM's most private room, the den, at the hub. The replication of pattern corroborated for her the purposeful planning of the house blueprint by MDM.

Paige had detailed her contention in the thesis through claim, evidence, warrant, and qualification. But she never tired of walking through the concentric maze of the mansion in real life although, throughout winter, shuttered parts of the museum had been inaccessible even to her. So now, with cleaning staff removing dust covers and polishing silver and oiling hinges, its mirrored mysteries beckoned Paige.

"Jamie, I don't know if you recall from your class visit in the fall what I said about the house layout?" Paige might as well make use of her audience to practice for the upcoming premier tour of the new season, and teach the girl at the same time.

"I couldn't hear much. I was near the back of the group." Jamie hung her head at the excuse; more likely she wasn't thinking at the time that she might be taking on a job at the museum. In fact, Paige hadn't fleshed out her research fully last fall and didn't speak then with her current confidence.

"Well, come on." Paige gestured towards the entry. "Let me remind us both."

The front door of the Laird Mansion, facing east, opened inward onto the foyer or great hall, at the left edge of which a smaller replica of the outside lamp stood sentinel. The walnut reception desk beside this indoor lamp, as Paige explained to Jamie, once welcomed trappers and hunters in a continuation of the business begun in the gazebo outside. It still held receipt books for traded goods showing payment by MDM to signatories with names such as Abooksigun—meaning "wildcat," Paige told Jamie—or Hokoma meaning "guide," or a simple X in the case of illiteracy. Beyond the floor lamp and desk, a free-standing bronze basin reminiscent of the outside pond was empty but would soon be filled with floating water lilies, which Jamie seemed to remember from last fall. Against the right wall, a sideboard held a silver tray and pot, where scones and tea had once waited to refresh—just as the outer gardens and fields provided nourishment.

Jamie's eyes glittered. "How cool. Did you really tell us all this last year?"

"Probably not in such detail." Every month Paige's own understanding had gained clarity, and the whole system of analogy was too complicated to explicate to large groups. Right now Jamie's time had almost run out, too. Her first shift started in a few minutes, so Paige summarized.

With their backs to the eastern door, Paige pointed out how the south and north wings opened out on either side, connected through the western corridor—with music parlor, library, dining room, pantry, and kitchen arranged in a semi-circle. The room flow led back to the great hall, and to the den, of course, the innermost chamber, the core of the house.

"The orderliness of it can't have been a fluke," Paige said, more to herself than to Jamie as she considered the multiple tiers of her proposed typology. Straight ahead from the entrance, a wide oak staircase, its surfaces rubbed with seven coats of hot beeswax to a lasting luster, rose from the floor of the great hall towards the ceiling two stories above. The lounge chairs and billiards table of the upper hall were visible from here, but bedrooms clustered around the balcony behind the second-floor wall. Paige didn't lead Jamie onto the carpeted steps but let her go on down the hallway to the back porch, converted into the museum gift shop, to begin her shift.

When she had gone, Paige made a beeline on the main floor past the grand staircase towards the den, almost hidden behind the staircase like a secret.

At the center of the floor plan, and the final room on the tour towards which Paige now hurried, the den proved once again her conceptualized schemata of correlation. As usual, she couldn't wait to see it. The outer part of MDM's personal office incorporated a cherry-wood secretary inset with a Star of David design, a porcelain washbasin with pitcher, a kerosene lamp, and a fruit bowl. One more furnishing in the den clinched beyond all doubt her argument about MDM's architectural reproduction in the square-within-square structure—den within house, house within yard, yard within forty-nine-acre farmstead, walled farmstead within the greater estate. The treasure lay at the heart of the mansion, concealed in the den for shock value behind a heavy linen curtain acting as a room divider. That apex of the tour waited now for Paige's attention.

She grasped the brass doorknob of the den, a wild sort of joy rising in her at the anticipation of flinging it open.

But the door was locked and the cleaning staff were all occupied elsewhere at the moment. Paige blew out her breath like a deflating balloon. She stood arms akimbo and addressed her belly.

"Well, Baby, you and I really ought to get at that office computer anyway. Next time I won't forget my master keys. We'll just have to wait to re-enter the sanctum."

Paige approached the elevator, a remarkable contraption in MDM's remarkable turn-of-the-century house, and scraped open the cage door of the lift. It was still working even though no longer in use for tourists because of insurance concerns. Squeaks and moans accompanied her upward journey to her office. "Don't worry, we'll get there safely," she said aloud in case Baby was frightened. Had the fax machine, against all odds, received the promised copies of MDM's letters to Father Laird? Why couldn't the Canadian curator scan and e-mail them to her? Maybe that museum was as technologically archaic as this one. The Red River Settlement would, of course, need to retain the original letters.

Paige pushed away the jolt of envy at the thought, wishing she could procure them for her own archives. No, not *her* archives. Her job here would soon be completed. Soon she'd have the thesis done with no need to be occupied in these archives any longer. Besides, she'd have other priorities. She looked down at her bulge and heaved a sigh. Baby must never guess about her impatience over the timing of his conception.

Manipulating the lever and dragging back the iron gate of the lift, Paige stepped into the quiet of the attic. She picked her way around an oak barrel, several pieces of rattan furniture, and a bale of twine to her desk, where she turned on the lamp. "They're here, Baby—what do you know?" The faxed letters had indeed arrived. She retrieved the stack of sheets from the tray but, before she could peruse them, her cell whistled an alarm from her bag on the chair. What appointment had she forgotten? Paige fumbled for the phone and caught sight of the calendar notification; her obstetrician in town expected her in ninety minutes! She grabbed the sheaf of papers and headed at a run for the stairs. She couldn't wait for the elevator if she wanted to make it all the way to Grand Forks in time.

CHAPTER TWELVE

Two weeks ago

Libby wiped the moisture from her forehead as she stood on the street in front of the bank. She wasn't prepared in any way to plead her case for a mortgage before Mr. Jordan, who at this moment must be looking at his watch. Maybe she'd been too quick on the draw by letting Clive pressure her into making the application when she wasn't even sure she had an adequate down payment.

But every time she thought of Seven Canaan Lane, her breath caught in her chest. How Gram would have loved it. Libby couldn't sleep last night just thinking about the way the screen door spring had stretched with a kitty-cat meow when Clive opened it—was that only on Friday?—and how her own soul purred when she crossed the doorsill. Then, when she finally dozed off last night, she had another of her recurring dreams about being a child in a strange house. She couldn't call them nightmares, really, though the expanding plotline now included scenes of blood and of witchcraft—a miscarriage? that homeless crone?—and of her freezing in a stinky sleeping bag under a bridge on the shore of the muddy Mississippi.

And if poor sleep wasn't enough, Libby was still jittery over the ugly scene at Hearsay this morning. What if the cops made good on their threat to phone her, looking for more information about that delusional woman? She couldn't shake the impression that the bag lady could mess up her living plans, which were tenuous at best anyway.

With so much insecurity all around, how could she face

Mr. Jordan with confidence?

Libby sucked in air. She checked her bag again to make sure her file was still intact: list of assets and debts, bank statements, insurance policy, her pay stubs, tax returns for the past three years. And of course she also carried a record of her inheritance from Gram, such as it was—money Gram had squirreled away in an unmentioned account over decades of scrimping and saving, of making soup from leftovers with the future of her granddaughter in mind. Gram had always thought first about her. Libby recalled their turning-point conversation, when she was eight and still officially resided in the trailer park. That evening she'd taken the public bus all by herself to Gram's apartment when her mother again hadn't shown up at home for supper.

"Child, how did you get this bruise?" Gram had touched her cheek.

"Um . . ." Mom had told her what to say, but she hated lying to Gram.

"Now, don't you tell me you tripped again." Gram squatted down to look into her eyes. "Is it the man Elsa has been seeing lately?"

"I dunno which one you're talking about, Gram. Uncle Tommy or Uncle Sid—"

"Don't call those men 'Uncle,' Libby."

What was she supposed to call them? Not "Dad," that was for sure. No one else in third grade had three or four dads at the same time.

"Uncle Tommy—I mean, Tommy—is real nice to me." Even if the others weren't. But Tommy was always kissing her mom. Gross. "Sometimes he babysits, and he gives me candy if I let him take pictures of me."

Gram had looked away, quiet for a minute. Then she set a bowl of chowder in front of Libby, thick and steaming on that cold winter night, and left the room. She talked on her bedroom phone and her tone went from soft to severe. "That's enough foolishness, Elsa Walker." Libby heard phrases like "needs a stable home" and "climbing into a bottle" and something about lying down with dogs and getting fleas. And when Gram came back out to make Libby a yummy dessert of cinnamon-dusted frybread, she told her granddaughter she'd be sleeping at Gram's apartment now, that she wouldn't be going back to the mobile home except to get her clothes, and never again without Gram.

A few days later she went with Gram to the trailer she no longer called home, and she fetched her favorite toy—the only treasure from Gram that survived her mother's cruelty, easy to hide away under her mattress when Elsa was in a rage and breaking dishes in the kitchen. She and Gram had found the miniature tea set at a garage sale, tiny cups and saucers made of green glass thin as fingernails.

Soon her mother left the trailer in the Twin Cities for the sunny state of California. Gram broke that news to her with a shake of her head, saying, "Two wrongs don't make a right." Gram's rare tears weren't for herself, Libby had been sure even at age eight. The sadness in her eyes seemed to well up from deep inside, where feelings usually hid. Gram didn't cry often, so Libby knew this was an important date—the day she began taking a regular lunch to school, and the night she could finally sleep without worrying about the disturbing noises coming from the next room. And she didn't ever miss Tommy's candy, either.

But she missed her mother.

Now, standing on the street in front of the bank, Libby swallowed hard. Where had that last thought come from? She glanced again through the glass doors, past the wall of automated tellers, into the threatening interior.

At the time of her separation from Elsa, Libby fell easily into the rhythm of living with Gram, bonding of course, leaning on her for every childish need. Had she grieved back then? She remembered thinking, for a long while, that it was her fault her mother had run away, that it was because Libby had skipped along the schoolyard at recess and sung with her friends: *Step on a crack and you'll break your mother's back* . . . Had she gone through the stages then that she was experiencing now over Gram's death—the shock, denial, anger, bargaining? She wasn't sure. Maybe her loss of Gram was reviving sorrow she surely must have felt back then, a little girl abandoned by her mother and never knowing a father.

The ten-word rhythm ran through her just then like a knife: *Once upon a time in a land far, far away* . . .

Libby opened the bank door and entered at the moment Mr. Jordan himself stepped towards her, navy tie a perfect match for his suit.

"I'm sorry I'm a bit late." Libby checked her wrist though she knew the exact time.

"Not at all, Mrs. . . . . " he checked his file, "Ms. Walker. That's the same name as your grandmother, if I recall correctly."

"Oh, please, call me Libby." Neither the "Mrs." nor "Ms." bothered her. She didn't care that she hadn't married, but she never encouraged the use of her surname. She loved sharing Gram's genetics but hated their joint illegitimacy.

Mr. Jordan smiled and held the door open for her. "Come on into my office and we'll get this mortgage process underway for you."

🖋

"*Namaste.*" Sybil bobbed her head in a bow, her palms together. Her last customer of the day—whose name she couldn't recall at the moment—was a regular, one of her more liberated clients. She was always popping into Amulets for a product or process to take her to the higher dimensions of the spirit realm.

"Have you got any books about João de Deus?" The woman placed a pack of price-reduced tarot cards on the counter, her charm bracelet jingling with an eclectic assortment including a Pisces fish, a silver St. Anthony medal, and a cinnabar bead.

"Ah, yes, the healing medium from Brazil." Sybil led her over to the bookshelf section. "I'm thinking of adding one of his colored-lamp quartz beds to the back of the shop. Only approved practitioners can purchase them, you know, and that would mean a trip down there myself."

South America had been back on Sybil's agenda for a while. Although she'd traveled to Argentina and Chile once, and had even driven amongst the stone monoliths on Easter Island, she'd missed Machu Picchu and the Inca trail in Peru. And at that time she hadn't yet heard of the isolated Brazilian village where thousands from all over the world convened to watch the astonishing physical surgeries performed by the Portuguese-speaking, full-trance medium who incorporated various light beings. Channeling their power, João the miracle-worker could heal the lame and give sight to the blind. Sybil pulled out a couple of his books for her client. Of course, João was currently under investigation for sexual misconduct, but the client needn't be told about that. Come to think of it, maybe the timing was right for Sybil to get a better deal on that quartz bed.

"I'm so blocked lately, you know?" The woman frowned. "Can you recommend a treatment?"

Of course Sybil could recommend a treatment.

"I've noticed you haven't been manifesting wellness lately." Sybil let warmth flood her voice. "At Amulets, we care about the individual journey that takes you to supreme happiness." The woman looked up from the book in her hands, her eyes pleading. Sybil led her down another aisle, hawking this box and that bottle to the client, oldest stock first: organic apple cider vinegar, Epsom salts for a liver flush, tiny vials of real saffron for appetite suppression.

"You've had my ionic foot bath detoxification recently," Sybil said, "and cupping and ear-candling, so you should be okay there. You're using the Goji powder you bought last time, right?" She was musing aloud more than questioning. "Maybe quantum laser treatments to neutralize and clear cell memory?"

"Okay, I'll take an appointment for next week."

But Sybil had a little more in mind. "I think perhaps you're ready for a few specific modalities I've been studying." Sybil hadn't achieved Ascended Masterhood yet, but she'd been doing lots of research on the 'Net. "I'd like to try to read your akashic record."

"My what?"

"Akasha is the unseen substance from which all life is formed. It's the field of energy created in the astral plane through all our thoughts, feelings, and desires, from the time our discarnate souls leave their point of origin to their return to divinity."

Sybil had never attempted this procedure before, but it couldn't be that hard. She and her client only needed to align themselves to the vibrations of the mindstream. She was naturally—some said supernaturally—intuitive, and what could prepare her better as a teacher than simple openness to all the universe had to give her? "Let's make room for that consultation along with the laser treatment."

Sybil locked up after her client left the shop, glancing over at Hearsay. Any one of her techniques would prove greatly beneficial to Libby's wellbeing, if she'd take Sybil's advice half as seriously as her customers did. But a girl could only lead her friend so far, and the fastest way to help Libby attain any elevation in her level of consciousness would be through external stimulus. Clothes shopping today would be a good place to start.

"Sorry about that." Libby fumbled for her phone at the bottom of her bag. "I forgot to silence my cell." The text from Sybil demanded she appear at Marshall's for a bargain-hunting spree in forty-five minutes.

"No problem. I think we're about done here anyway." Mr. Jordan shuffled papers together. "You should hear back from us in a few weeks. I'm confident it'll be good news." He stood to shake her hand then opened the office door.

Libby was anything but confident as she headed for her appointment with Sybil. She didn't have the cash to spend on frivolities, but she envied Sybil's carefree glee. When she walked into Marshall's, Sybil met her wearing a fuchsia sari, Birkenstocks, and a cloche hat. She carried an armload of clothes.

Yes, Libby was about to be sucked into the vortex of Sybil's vivacity.

"Found the perfect LBD for you," Sybil announced. She waved one of the dressed hangers like a pirate flag so that several other shoppers stopped to stare. "And look at this fantastic lipstick named"—she turned over the tube in her hand—"'Gore.' Let's try it on you." Sybil dumped the mass of clothing onto a tabletop makeup display, ripped off the protective tape, and screwed up the hideous lipstick. Libby ducked.

"Not for me, Sybil." She laughed and then almost burst into tears, a mess of emotions. "What a day I've had."

"Tell Mama Sybil all about it." She pushed Libby towards the change rooms and came right on in with her. "But first I want to see this black silk velvet on you. Here, let me help you get your sweater off. " She tugged it over Libby's head before the lock was fastened on the door, and all talk of bank loan and bag lady was subsumed in the flurry of undressing and redressing. Sybil tossed one outfit after another at her, stuffing discarded garments into the corner on the floor or piling them unfolded onto the stool, zipping Libby up before she had a skirt over the hips and vetoing those pants as too saggy, that blouse as too dowdy.

"Show off your body, girlfriend." Sybil unbuttoned the top to expose Libby's cleavage and shook her head. "You need a new bra."

"The bra I have is fine." Next Sybil would be dragging her into a specialty lingerie shop, forcing her to try on underwear in front of her. "I'm not about to spend a hundred bucks on a bit of sheer lace."

"At least give this bathing suit a chance. You'll need it for the beach."

"I'm not going to a beach." The girl was relentless in bantering her about travel.

"You are no fun." Sybil crossed arms over chest. "I could help you look so good if you'd stop resisting my advice."

"Okay, then," Libby said, casting her gaze around for common ground, "which do you like better, this purple T-shirt or the green jeans?"

Sybil grinned in victory. "The T-shirt. That's the *orchid* T-shirt, not purple. You need to update your vocabulary, too." She kicked her way through the discarded pile of clothes, yanked the change room door open, and pushed Libby in the direction of the checkout. "No, leave those things for the staff to hang up. It's their job. Come on. I need a chai latte, pronto."

Over steaming cups, Libby filled Sybil in on her meeting with the banker. Yes, it went well, and no, she didn't notice if he was cute or married.

"What was all the commotion in the street this morning?" Sybil asked.

"I was getting to that," Libby began. "This old lady turned up—"

"Right. I saw a bag of bones hanging around with her shopping cart this morning when I opened up Amulets." Sybil's eyes narrowed. "So what happened?"

Libby outlined the situation, but her story came across as lame. She couldn't quite explain the threat she'd felt, not only about her boss's foul mood but about the cops' flashing lights and their promise to call her. And especially about the look in the eye of the crazy woman.

Her inability to properly communicate her frustration didn't matter. Sybil's short attention span took her off on another tangent, and in this instance Libby didn't mind a bit. She wanted to forget the whole morning scenario, anyway.

"Have you ever even stepped out of state?" Sybil asked.

"Of course I have." She wasn't totally naïve. "You're not the only one who's traveled, you know."

"Where have you gone, then?"

"Flew to Vegas for a couple of days when Alana was still around." Libby's old boss had insisted on taking her to a trade show back before Terence got wind of her lavish spending.

"Ooh, isn't it fantastic? Did you see 'Absinthe' at Caesars Palace? Or maybe that was before your time."

"We were busy browsing the booths and collecting brochures. But tell me about 'Absinthe.'" Libby leaned forward on her elbows, feigning interest. The ensuing description of the raunchy performance told with Sybil's typical vim served Libby's intended purpose of rerouting the discussion. In fact, she'd left the state of Minnesota only one other time, and so long ago it didn't bear repeating. Or remembering. Avoiding those memories was getting more difficult each day.

Libby's tactical ploy backfired once Sybil got back onto the subject of trips.

"So, did you look through the travel links I sent you?"

"That was just this morning, Sybil. How would I have found time?" Especially on the sort of day this one had turned out to be.

"You don't have to get snippy about it." Sybil tipped up her cup for the last drops. She wiped the corners of her mouth with thumb and index finger. "It's almost as if you're scared to leave home."

Was she? Libby jiggled her right leg five times, left leg five times. Did she even have a home to leave?

Sybil went on about how Libby should listen to the sages of the past and more recent poets, too. She talked about the wind, the salt wind, the sea wind beating a cloud through the skies. "Like Yeats, 'I would wander always like the wind,'" Sybil said, ever the drama queen. That poem, probably learned back in high school, must be her life's motto.

But Libby herself was tired of wandering—of wandering and wondering where she belonged. Her whole life, especially now with Gram gone, seemed restless and rootless. She'd always been a loner, and now she was lonely in earnest. She was a cloud chased by wind if ever there was one, and she couldn't imagine Sybil actually liking the feeling.

Paige snuggled under the afghan on her sofa, home from the obstetrical checkup in town after too many hours on the road. Of course, she'd stopped in to see her mom and drop off a bouquet of flowers and a card. This was the third time she'd miss celebrating Mother's Day in person, what with the museum tours beginning, but her parents would be up to Kirkton's Saturday festival, at least.

Now, with supper dishes stacked into the dishwasher and Danny back in the field finishing up seeding the northwest quarter, Paige settled down to her research—just she and Baby. She'd had not a moment to read and assess the faxed letters received this morning from her historical counterpart at the Canadian museum. She sipped peppermint tea and delved into the extant words of Moses David Melchizedek Laird, written to his father at the Red River Settlement after MDM had left Manitoba for the American university.

She'd failed so far in finding the human element behind the figurehead of her research subject as founder, pioneer, and builder. So Paige pinned her last hopes on these letters to give her something juicy to nail down her dissertation's main argument. After all, if it was true that MDM articulated his view of domestic life through the design of his estate—as she purported and, for the most part, had supported—surely he must have left behind evidence of his personal passions. Not that her thesis strictly demanded private and subjective evidence of MDM's inner life, but Paige craved details to convince herself of MDM's upstanding character.

"He *has* to have been good," she said to Baby.

She sifted through the eleven pages, six letters in all, handwritten in a fine and flowing script and dated over an eight-year span. The curator had prefaced the letters with a note of explanation that Uriah Laird, having returned to his homeland of Scotland at the turn of the century, likely took with him the remaining correspondence from his son and merely overlooked this small packet.

"If only I'd been able to spend more time during my grad studies exploring the backdrop to MDM's early life—especially his relationship with his father." She murmured it so that Baby would know how important fatherhood and sonship really was.

Laird the elder had for five decades served the spiritual needs of the settlers in the northern colony at the junction of the Red and Assiniboine rivers. In-depth treatment of this aspect was beyond the scope of her research, but a cursory survey told her old

Laird had a reputation for standing against political, social, and economic iniquities as he spoke against moral decrepitude from the pulpit and through his pen. She'd read his scathing denunciation aimed at both whites and Native Americans. In his estimation, the diabolic greed of the whiskey trade and the self-mutilating paganism of the Sun Dance were both based more on human nature than on race.

Not only did she know about his public *condemnation* but also his words of *commendation* for MDM. She'd read the Reverend Uriah Laird's *Daily Nor'Wester* editorial remarking on his upcoming return to Scotland, in which he praised his son as "the express image" of the father because of MDM's continuation of the family work and values south of the border in Pembina County. Father Laird was evidently proud of MDM, the entrepreneur who put their joint strategy into action on the ground.

Paige shifted, her body stiff, and reached for her cup of tea. "Baby, you are going to make Daddy and me proud, I just know it." She stroked the back of the child's head through the barrier of her abdomen. Would their son ever gain the distinction of her thesis subject? Would he make history?

In Uriah's published writings, he fervently opposed the dissolution of community life through the breakdown of the family unit. His thundering sermons and axiomatic tracts might actually have made a difference to the cultural fiber of mid-nineteenth-century colonial life, if Paige's brief analysis of the Red River Settlement's social structure held water. At any rate, the father's thinking seemed to have formulated the views of the son. As was natural in family life.

"Will *you* end up farming like your daddy?" Baby kicked her just then and she grinned, imagining cowboy boots like Danny's on their little one.

Paige leafed through notes substantiating that Uriah and MDM together developed a proposal independent of any other religious or governmental organization of their time, although in some respects—at least on paper—the father-son plan resembled earlier missions of mercy to the aboriginal people. However, that humane system was followed by the secular Carlisle Indian Industrial School model, founded in Pennsylvania in 1879 by Richard Henry Pratt, whose militaristic and racist approach to the Native American was to "kill the Indian in him and save the man."

How different Pratt's idea was from the Laird way!

By the time MDM settled Kirkton and began his program a decade later, Pratt's officially sanctioned method was widely disbursed throughout America. A few day schools were located on reservations but, for many Great Plains tribes, children were ripped away from parents and home for the sake of "education" and placed in boarding schools far away from parental influence. It turned Paige's stomach to think of Baby being abandoned like that. She was well read on current sociological criticism of those historic schools as "central to inculcation of the civilized ethic" in subjugating the indigenous populace.

In direct contrast, the Laird prototype allowed maximum freedom for families to stay together at a time when the stresses of societal upheaval arising from European colonization clashed with nomadic ways and tore families apart. Father Laird's ideological blueprint provided for the needs of the First Nations in Canada, and MDM put it into practical effect with the establishment of his American estate.

As for MDM continuing a family life, he seemed destined to remain a bachelor. None of the young ladies at the Red River Settlement, with their kid gloves and corseted waists, turned his head before he left for his session at university. And none of the wishful parents in Pembina or neighboring counties succeeded in securing the attentions of Kirkton's leader for their daughters, either. Maybe he was looking for something altogether different, not only in livelihood but also in matrimony.

"He was so selfless," Paige said aloud. She couldn't get over MDM's character—something she could hope to encourage in her own child. Obviously MDM's upbringing had formed the basis of his self-giving work among the Native Americans of Pembina County as he applied his father's intellectual ideas and philosophical ideals to real-life practice. He put his hands to the till and delivered many Plains people from starvation to more secure and meaningful occupation in his fields and in their gardens, his barns and the bison compound he established for them. He taught them horticulture, carpentry, and animal husbandry. And he learned from them to hunt, craft leather, and speak in several Algonquian and Siouan languages. Paige chuckled to herself; she'd have to homeschool if she expected Baby to learn anything like MDM's syllabus. History recorded that MDM even intervened in governmental-Indian land treaties, but always on behalf of the Native American people.

That is, MDM performed in action what his father had preached in the words Paige had read through old-fashioned sermons published in the literature. He put the flesh of love onto the skeleton of knowledge by entering into the very life of the tribal nations, bearing the reproach of others, unashamed to call them his brothers. In his hospitality he might well, as he once said, have been "entertaining angels unawares."

Paige raised her swollen feet up onto the coffee table and leaned back into the couch. Before reading MDM's letters to Father Laird, she flipped to the last page of the printout and studied the blurry photocopy the curator had sent along for her interest, marked 1890—an image taken in the fall before the Wounded Knee Massacre. She was familiar with the daguerreotype because the original formed part of the Laird Mansion Museum collection. In it the husky MDM stood dressed in full costume beside a Lakota warrior, several teepees pitched behind them. Though the picture was in black and white, she imagined the rainbow palette of the decorative buckskin shirts, the sleekness of the warrior's braids tied with quillwork strips, and the outrageous red flame of MDM's beard. She knew firsthand the beauty of the beaded moccasins, as MDM wore them in many photos. In fact, this very pair hung today in the mansion's foyer closet.

Paige turned her attention back to the text. The letters weren't an exhaustive or cohesive record by any means, but surely they would give her a glimpse into the man's psyche.

CHAPTER THIRTEEN

Today

Mildew pokes musty fingers into Libby's nostrils as she enters the third floor of the mansion museum from the outside terrace, the attic smelling like a vintage suitcase. Diffused light filters into the hallway through the few mullioned windows to illuminate a crate of oily rope, a splintered sled with metal runners, a rocking horse painted like a zebra with a bristly tail. Libby follows along with the tour group as Paige explains the functional nature of this space.

A cozy office with a potbelly stove and a grouping of oak cabinets fitted with brass hardware, once used for the landholder's record keeping, is now devoted to file storage housing museum archival documentation. A taxidermy room showcases moose antlers and a fluid-preserved bat specimen, and the laundry features an ingenious system of drying racks. In the sewing area, a sturdy wool tweed is laid out on a long table for the cutting alongside scissors, and a measuring tape is wound around a wooden spindle. Much of the attic is given over to maids' quarters—a dormitory with six cots as neat as though made up this morning, and a simple bathroom with, Paige boasts, running water even for the staff. The male gardener, stable hand, and valet "lived out." A large section at the center of the attic is blocked off from traffic with walls and, facing the office, the rusty cage doors of an elevator of dubious safety.

Libby registers each fact with studied appreciation in spite of Sybil's apparent detachment, but she quickens her step as the group wends its way towards the next level below them. The gloomy painted stairwell is narrow and low ceilinged, so that Libby has to bend her neck to avoid bumping her forehead. It's all fine and well to look behind the scenes at the workings of the Victorian household staff, but what she really wants to see are the personal rooms of the family once occupying this home. The steps creak beneath her feet as she descends behind Sybil. She trails her hand over the waves of the lath-and-plaster walls.

"This is more like it," Sybil says when they're ushered into the second story. Her right dimple winks at Libby.

"It's plush." Libby keeps her voice to an undertone. The hallways are papered in crimson damask, with metal fixtures casting soft light onto carpeted floors and coffered ceilings. Quarter-sawn oak trims the doors, and a built-in fire hose curls into itself behind a heavy glass panel.

"Reminds me of the Saint Paul Hotel." Sybil tips up her nose as though she regularly spends the night at that luxurious downtown landmark. Maybe she does, for all Libby knows.

"You're from the Twin Cities?" the Australian woman asks. "We're flying out from there tonight."

"Imagine that." Sybil's eyes are hooded. "Small world." The woman nods amicably. She doesn't recognize the demeaning tilt of Sybil's head or the wry putdown in her voice. Libby winces. Sybil elevates her own glamorous excursions far above the mundane experiences of mere tourists.

The group gathers around Paige and the Italian onyx water fountain at this far end of the hall, matching the one downstairs. All at once parched, Libby wants to sip and maybe dribble on her top. What impulse is this?

Paige explains the floor's layout. Living quarters, sitting areas, and work spaces are arranged around the perimeter of the house, which has in total twenty-six rooms on all three levels. Libby trails behind as the group sets out in a clockwise direction through halls hung with maps, an ivory fan, framed bits of embroidery. An intricate needlework sampler in silk threads of heirloom colors bears the motif of a flying heart and the quaint words *Let brotherly love continue*. Libby's step falters in front of it. Where has she read this before?

The group peers through doorways into a bathroom, a storage cupboard stocked with hunting gear, and various chambers with four-poster beds and tatted lace dresser scarves and ebony hairbrushes with bone inlay. Painted-and-papered bedrooms—the rose room, the violet room, the sage room—feature bay seats and leaded glass and oriental carpets. Libby pulls at her necklace, toys with the gold ring at its end—the ring that Gram wore. Is there a forget-me-not-blue room, too?

"This games room," Paige says as she leads the way, "separates the guest wing from the master suite beyond, which we'll view later. The recreational atmosphere here is set by the nine-foot billiards table with decorative, turned legs, imported by MDM from France."

Some of the boys whistle, and several admire its mint-condition green felt, but the atrocity reminds Libby of a casket.

The rest of the room, though, is decorated in a style that would have delighted Gram, with quilts draped across overstuffed chairs, a braided rag rug, and—lining the lower walls—dark wood wainscoting topped with a plate ledge cluttered with figurines and photographs and postcards.

"Oh, don't touch the cues. They're fragile." Paige removes

one from the boys who are manhandling it. She redirects their attention to the collection of stuffed animal heads on all four walls. "But you can feel the shaggy mane of the bison here. Buffalo robes used to be in great demand."

Libby abstains, but the students and Sybil take turns burrowing their hands into the fur and petting the shiny snout as though the beast might purr for them.

Sybil sniffs her hands. "Smells wild."

Paige gives her head a shake. "Strictly speaking, Pharaoh wasn't wild. As the dominant bull, for many years he serviced the herd MDM established for the preservation of the species after the last great bison hunt of the 1880s. MDM's work in this area signaled good will to the starving families he adopted as his own people."

Sybil snaps her head around, beaded extensions bouncing. "Eww. They *ate* him?"

Paige laughs. "Likely not. His old flesh would have been pretty gamey. But yes, bison meat was a staple on this estate, as it had been the main menu item for the people of the Great Plains. Now, if there are no other questions, let's move on."

Libby's not sure she wants to move on. A dim memory of violence flits through her mind, unrelated to all talk of bison and pool cues. Where did it come from? Maybe Sybil's right—maybe she's a reincarnation of a Victorian lady or Plains warrior brave who visited once, who toured the home of the illustrious MDM Laird. She laughs a single silent syllable at the silly notion. However, there must be a reason she can't put her finger on the source of her sudden alarm.

CHAPTER FOURTEEN

Two weeks ago

Paige nestled under the couch throw, crocheted by her mom for evenings like this, and turned to the packet of faxed letters originally drafted by MDM. Would she find what she was looking for? The opening words of the first handwritten letter, dated 1882, gave her a peek into his personal life.

> *Father, I am moved in sorrow over Mother's passing and wish to come home from university to bring you comfort in your mourning. However, I shall heed your caution about the weather; the situation here is little better and it is likely I would not arrive before you were well taken up once again in your work.*

Right, this letter was probably in answer to the black-edged announcement Laird had sent his son. It was currently displayed behind glass on the music parlor wall, above the joyous fireplace inscription: *In the midst of the assembly will I sing praise to thee!* But in this letter Paige could sense MDM's sorrow, though he didn't dwell long on it.

> *Speaking of work, Father, I have had a change of situation myself. Keeping in mind your seminal purpose, I shall not continue my studies in Saint Paul after this first year is complete. My disposition is ill suited for lectures, and I have heard of great opportunity elsewhere, what with the railway expansion and resulting population boom. The Minnesota forests are being felled* . . .

Paige skimmed over a description of how, soon after his writing, pine logs cut and stacked onto the frozen river would be floating northward down the Red River and taken by train to sawmills in Grand Forks. This offered several immediate prospects for MDM's livelihood if he could find his way into employment with the Northern Pacific Railway, with an eye towards homesteading himself. This first letter ended with a forward-looking paragraph:

> *A fellow student from Dakota Territory has extended me the privilege of partaking in a buffalo hunt, and I simply cannot pass up the chance to undergo such an expedition myself—one of the last of its kind, I am certain, though promised to be much smaller than the wondrous events having taken place in years past. It is told that the extinction of the beasts, the primary sustenance of the Plains People, has caused them much desolation, and I have intense desire to inquire into how I might be of service to these impoverished souls. I will write again with details of the hunt.*

Sure enough, the second letter, dated later that spring and composed mid-excursion, gave an eyewitness account of the slaughter. Tens of millions of bison that once roamed the Great Plains were, by the time MDM penned this letter, almost obliterated under the urgent demand for fresh meat to feed railroad workers, and for hides and tongues that were sold across North America. But what impressed Paige was not the sorry litany of facts regarding this late-in-the-day buffalo hunt carried out by men wielding guns for sport but rather MDM's air of concern for the human stragglers he encountered along the way:

> *Father, these People, once so hardy and beautiful, are now miserable creatures—destitute, afflicted, and tormented, this last remnant still resisting placement on the governmental reservations. You taught me to love righteousness and hate wickedness; the wandering homeless wretchedness of the starving Indians is wickedness if*

anything is. Yet the government's Peace Policy has afforded them no peace, hostilities everywhere seethe, and I fear true assimilation and reconciliation are but an illusion.

MDM's compassion surged through Paige, too.

On our campaign, clusters of hungry drifters with their women and children follow along behind the jubilant hunters and skinners, perhaps hoping to glean from the killings. I am particularly moved by one boy and his younger sister, left orphaned by epidemic, who scavenge among the crowd. The girl, whose cough is alarming, cannot be more than ten or eleven years of age. I am told the children sold off their only asset, a horse, to a scoundrel who gave them little recompense and left them eating gophers.

Paige sipped her tea to calm her gag reflex.

The sunlight reveals this People's pallid and pocked complexion. The moonlight, as they huddle beneath tattered blankets, glints off the whites of their piteous eyes. Would that I might offer succor and deliver them from their suffering, their fear of death, their bondage. Would that I might make intercession for them, mediate a better covenant for them, and give rest to their restless souls.

How had Father Laird responded to reading of such grace extended to the same ethnic group that had killed MDM's own mother? Paige tipped her head back onto the couch cushion and turned her face upward, eyes closed, her hand massaging Baby. Yes, this was the stuff she'd been seeking, full of emotional intimacy. Nothing she wanted to repeat aloud—not with Baby listening in. She went back at her reading. In a following paragraph,

MDM spoke of the hallucination-inducing tortures used in ecstatic ceremonial rituals meant to make and maintain kinship between earth and heaven, between the seen and unseen realms.

> *It is said that over and over they pierce their flesh to appease the wrath of their gods, purging their consciences as if it were possible that their blood should take away their transgressions.*

Paige groaned. Some of these rituals were still, in this day and age, honored and practiced among Native American groups.

She sped through the next three letters written over the following seven years. They showed development in the business plans of the father and son regarding their venture, but nothing further of a personal nature. In 1887, MDM wrote of his early financial successes in Dakota Territory, gained through his occupation with the railroad and subsequent investments, and of his staking a claim and erecting a small house on the banks of the Red amidst the shacks being hammered together by varied tradesmen.

In 1888, he told of procuring land grants and setting up an agricultural enterprise with an eye to those unwilling to give up their communal interdependence for life on reservations or state-run allotments. They could come and go as they desired, MDM promised them, and commit only to seasons of sowing and reaping to feed their children. But the men considered farming women's work:

> *Father, so often they say to me, "It is easier to hunt than to dig."*

They would come again, they told MDM, when they had hides to sell at the top price he was willing to pay them. So he cleared his land without them, and as he tilled they passed by the fields in roving bands, disbelieving that his intent was not to force but to welcome them as self-supporting guests.

By 1889, Paige read, MDM's cross-cultural friendships in the recently established state of North Dakota began attracting the attention of agents from the Office of Indian Affairs. The government approached MDM to become an Indian agent himself and promote their integration into mainstream American culture. He refused in order to carry on his own mission of mercy in his own way. As he and Father had discussed, MDM wrote, he wanted to give the People freedom rather than constriction, communication in their mother tongues rather than enforced English, childhood learning within the family unit under parental supervision rather than exile to faraway classrooms and, above all, relationship rather than regulation. MDM would expect no payment in return from them, as he and Father Laird had worked out—nothing but joint participation in the blessing.

Paige sighed. Much of this was familiar, basic information. She patted her rounded belly. "I know the historical facts of MDM's struggle to establish Kirkton and the nearby farm. But I don't want just the facts. I want the emotion behind them."

To her relief, the first words of the last letter, dated 1890 like the portrait of MDM in tribal costume, again exuded emotion:

> *Father, I have such touching news. As you know, although my fortune ever increases and our interracial endeavor grows slowly, still I experience a deep chasm separating me from true intimacy with those who visit our farm. They seem skittish, lacking faith that I am*

> *truly harmless and disinterested in defiling them. If only I could put into their minds and write on their very hearts the law of love you have taught me in speaking forth the truth. Instead, a great movement has arisen among the People; the so-called Ghost Dance unites them under its self-proclaimed prophet who predicts the imminent elimination of evil from the earth. Their enthusiasm frightens the governing authorities.*

What was this "touching news"? Paige's eyes flew over the text.

> *In all this uproar, the Cree orphans Hokoma and his younger sister Nuttah, whom I met on the hunt in 1882, have found their way to our property and are zealous to till a plot all their own and take in a harvest.*

Ah, those must be the kids in that one photo in the library . . .

> *I have helped them build a shelter on the outer yard, and I believe our actions have aroused interest among others of the People.*

MDM continued to discuss, in sloped handwriting, practical aspects about his objective to build the grand house he and his father always envisioned—in fact, the very museum Paige would find herself in today, more than a century later. She turned to the final paragraph of this last letter and came upon an unexpected hint that sent electricity coursing through her body:

> *I am heir to your fortune, Father, not simply of mammon, slight as that is, but of name. And although I have not yet provided you with grandchildren, I am sure to remedy this eventually, although I am very busy, as you know, with enlarging our land and business holdings.*

What was this? Paige had read nothing elsewhere indicating MDM had aspirations towards fatherhood himself. This was just the sort of tone she'd been digging around for since she took up her studies.

> *But in reminiscing over my childhood, I yet hear echoes of your late evening conversations with Mother by the fire, in which you spurned the barbaric habit common in the early years of the Settlement among the French fur traders who took multiple Indian women already mated. I recall to you my boyhood friend Armand, whose father the canoeman knew the paddle and the song, and who is said to have sired a goodly portion of the Colony. I think as well of our fellow Scotsman, old McDuff, who, lonely in the wild new land, took a wife (albeit legally) from the Métis inhabitants to produce even more mixed-blood offspring—to the general disapproval of the pious folk of Kildonan.*

Paige wrinkled her nose. Was Laird a bigot? Of course, language was different in that era, nothing like the politically correct jargon used today, but still... She read on.

> *You explained even then that your position neither prohibited nor consecrated the mixing of races, and that your concerns were only as regards the holiness of matrimony.*

Yes, that sounded much more rational to Paige. But she read the next words, the last paragraph of that last letter, with increasing incredulity:

> *Any uncertainty I might have harboured about your intentions for me were totally resolved upon your last missive, Father. Your approval of my request for freedom in seeking a mate of my own choosing and your*

trust in my judgment has anointed me with the oil of gladness.

"No!" Paige flung back the afghan and leapt up, nearly weeping at this final, insufficient word, and Baby leapt inside her as well. In all her combing of the material, she'd found nothing, other than the housekeeper rumor, indicating MDM had an inclination towards romance. To be left hanging like this infuriated her. She stomped her foot, and then she did it again rather than screaming as she wanted to do. The letters had hinted at, but *not* given her, the breakthrough she anticipated between MDM's professional and private lives. In the end, Paige was left with nothing of value to add to her thesis about her research subject.

Never mind her "thesis" and "research subject"—this had become *personal*. Like a lover jilted, she'd riled herself up into a crabby mood by the time Danny came in from the fields, dusty and tired.

Ten days ago

Libby's feet were killing her. The weight of the grocery sacks plus six flights of stairs, after a long day at Terence's beck and call, sent all her misery to her big toes. The sooner she could kick off her pumps, the better. She pushed into her apartment, past open boxes in the hallway packed up during every spare moment over the past few days, and into the kitchen. Cleaning and organizing had consumed her and kept at bay Sybil's accusation that she was afraid to leave home for the pleasures of a trip. Gram's presence crowded the flat with bits and pieces of her life—and not the right bits and pieces, either. Surely Libby would come to the end of it soon.

She was putting her parsley in the crisper when her phone rang.

"You've got to see this," Sybil said into the receiver as she navigated through her favorite metaphysical tourism website. Libby wouldn't be able to resist her latest find.

She pushed a fresh stick of gum into her mouth, and ripe watermelon exploded on her tongue. She hadn't eaten supper yet. She'd texted Iggy earlier, asking him to pop by with curry from the hole-in-the-wall near his place. But tonight, he said, his wife insisted they celebrate their kid's birthday, and he couldn't get away without arousing her suspicion. Sybil blew a sticky bubble. Oh well, that was the downside to dating a married man. Missing a few meals here and there was a cheap price to pay for the insurance his family provided in stopping him from getting too possessive of her. As it was, to her chagrin Iggy had been mentioning the idea of divorce again lately.

A panorama of the Himalayas zoomed out at Sybil from her high-resolution monitor. She cradled her phone between ear and shoulder as she clicked onto the site of a luxury hotel in Lhasa, Tibet.

"Not too shabby," she said into the receiver. "Check out the link to the resort I just sent you."

"I told you I'm not online." Libby clipped her words.

"Bad day at work? Is Groucho Terence giving you grief again?"

"I can't talk. I've got groceries all over the counter and so much to do."

"You don't have five minutes for your friend?" *Only* friend, Sybil might have added but didn't because Libby moaned, sounding properly resigned. Sybil clicked her mouse again. "Ooh, the photo of the Potala Palace is spectacular. It says this is where the Dalai Lama used to spend winters."

Tenzin Gyatso was one of Sybil's heroes, of course. She'd read half a dozen books by His Holiness in the last couple of months, ever since inspired by the idea of Tibet as her next possible destination. She wasn't a politically minded person and for the most part didn't keep up with events taking place on the world stage. So she'd been horrified to learn that more than a million people had lost their lives in the Communist occupation of Tibet, resulting in a massive exodus. The outcast population looked to its supreme spiritual leader for return to their homeland. The current Dalai Lama, fourteenth in the cyclical reincarnation of Buddha himself, had fled his country in 1959 and now, from his temporary home in northern India, promoted world peace, religious unity, and ethical living.

"I haven't got time to talk, Sybil."

"But here's a fantastic shot of the scenery. Don't tell me you haven't always longed to get a real-life view of Mount Everest."

"Not really, especially with all the earthquakes happening there. What I'd like to get a view of right now is a particular recipe . . ." Libby's voice trailed off and in the background a drawer grated shut.

"You would get terrific soup recipes if we went to Tibet together." Maybe the way to Libby's sense of adventure was through her stomach. Sybil did a quick Google search. "Have you ever eaten, uh," she guessed at the pronunciation, "*thukpa bhathuk*? Where else are you ever going to get the chance to eat noodle soup made with yak meat?"

Libby blurted out a short laugh. "Honestly, Sybil, you don't let go of an idea once it lodges itself in your pretty little head, do you? And you, of all people, are showing your desperation if you're offering me animal flesh."

Sybil turned to the mirror mounted beside her desk and smiled at her reflection. She actually *was* quite pretty today, as last night she'd thrown a ruby rinse onto her bleached hair and strategically placed a few strands of tie-in tinsel that glittered like a Yule tree.

Should she disclose her change in agenda for tomorrow evening, to warn Libby? No, she'd keep mum on it right now. Libby needed a man but wasn't admitting it yet, whereas Sybil had found an ingenious way to incorporate men with travel. Possibly travel would loosen Libby up to romance as well.

She turned back to her computer. "I'm sending you a couple more links. Promise you'll check them out."

"Okay, already. I'll see if I have time later on. But I need to put on a test pot of soup. I told you Chef Virgil is expecting my list of ingredients before midnight for his menu printing and shopping." Her voice held the edge Sybil used to hear from classmates before a big exam. At least Libby had promised to look over their traveling options.

Sybil disconnected the phone and took a virtual tour inside Lhasa's Jokhang Temple with its heavy wooden timbers, gilt statues, and maze of chapels and corridors. The colors flared out at her from the walls and halls. Reds and corals symbolized both the divinity of the life force and destruction by fire.

Saffron robes declared humble renunciation and the transcendent state of empty nothingness. The structure was surmounted by a gilded dharma wheel on its roof, a visual for Buddha's way to enlightenment.

The photo reminded Sybil that her favorite earrings were a set of enameled dharma wheels, and that every time she wore them her customers engaged her in discussion about the Eightfold Path and the Four Noble Truths. Maybe she should set up a rack in Amulets dedicated to Buddhist jewelry. She might as well capitalize on a trend.

Not that she'd ever seriously studied Buddhism. The outline of its development she'd read online was dizzying in its complexity. But she'd learned enough about Asian beliefs in general to order appropriate stock into her shop representing a wide range of Far Eastern denominations: sand mandala kits from Bhutan, lotus pins from Hong Kong, miniature Zen gardens from Japan. Tibetan Buddhism's religious customs were particularly energetic, with ecstatic and animistic rituals performed by possessed oracles to placate local spirits and demonic powers. The introductory book of Tantric practices she ordered for the shop had to be kept under the counter wrapped in brown paper—too racy for most.

Yes, Tibet was definitely the next sacred space on Sybil's list of must-sees. Although she liked to vary her destinations, delving into oriental mysticism during her visit to Japan had whetted her appetite for more of the East.

She pushed away from the keyboard, closed her eyes, stretched out her padded recliner, and for a few delicious moments relived her Japanese vacation. What a whirlwind trip, with almost more time spent on planes, trains, subways, and cable cars than in formal sightseeing. But the brevity was worth it for her glimpses of the national contrasts. Tokyo's urban dynamism of the Ginza was juxtaposed against the snow-tipped tranquility of Mount Fuji rising far in the distance. The intense rush of bodies bursting out of the Harajuku station gave way to the sublime serenity of the Meiji Shrine. The stench of the fish market was washed away in the waters of the local bathhouse.

Aboard the Bullet Train, Sybil had whizzed by rice and tea fields interspersed among villages along the way to Kyoto. There she watched a flower-arranging demo, tried on a multi-layered silk kimono, and ate with chopsticks from a lacquered tray—tofu and miso and pickled veggies. The next day she took a local line, her seatmate an aged woman in wooden sandals cooling herself with a bamboo fan, to the holy settlement of Koya set amidst eight mountain peaks. The music of bells and cymbals led Sybil along a walking path through monastery grounds wreathed in thick mists. Pruned pine trees genuflected over koi ponds. In a red pagoda, a thousand-year-old scroll showed cherry trees in full blossom.

On Sybil's last evening back in Tokyo, she'd headed to a karaoke lounge featuring all-you-can-drink sake and ended up on the tatami mat of a traditional inn with Nobu. All in all, the vacation had been otherworldly, reconnecting her physical body with the spiritual source of pure awareness.

But enough reminiscing. Sybil sat forward again to check out availability of flights to Tibet, but her stomach grumbled out its emptiness. She should eat.

Libby had just hung up from Sybil's call when the landline rang again. Hopefully it wasn't the cops. Officer Garcia from the "crime scene" Monday had left his name and number on her voicemail yesterday, asking her to please contact him. She'd no intention of doing that. Anyway, arranging Gram's possessions and juggling her own obsessions was taking up all her spare time.

"Hello?"

"Yeah, cupcake, Clive here." He waited as though expecting an enthusiastic response. Why was he calling her? Libby had told him after the viewing Friday that she would phone him, not the other way around. "So, Sybil tells me you're a gal in need of distraction. I know this great bar downtown. How's about I pick you up for a pick-me-up?"

"Thanks, but I don't think so, Clive."

"Okay, then." He changed his tenor. "Have you given any thought to the tidy property we looked at last week? The owners are primed and ready to move it. I've been schmoozing them and have them all tenderized for your offer."

"Of course not," she fibbed. *Of course* she'd been thinking about Seven Canaan Lane, but she could hardly admit it to herself, much less to Clive. "I haven't heard back from the bank about my mortgage yet . . ."

"No problemo. We can write up the contract with a proviso."

"I'm not comfortable with that." Libby wasn't comfortable with anything at the moment—not Sybil's constant bantering about travel, not Clive's pressure, not the stress about the bag lady. She checked Gram's sunburst clock above the kitchen table then thrummed her fingers on the recipe box she'd searched through three times already today—*one, two, three, four, five* . . . "Look,

I don't have time to deal with this tonight. I'm kind of under a deadline." She needed to identify and finalize the soup seminar ingredients for Chef Virgil. If only the financial components of her life were so easy to sort out.

After hanging up, Libby waffled over her last practice batch of soup. Maybe she should use unsalted butter this time. But Gram wouldn't have used that, come to think of it. No, she'd stick with bacon grease. At the organic grocers today Libby had picked out a mild onion instead of the leeks provided in class, and bought a parsnip in addition to the suggested carrots, trying to keep the flavors as close as possible to Babette's likely choices. The butcher helped her decide on cheaper cuts of beef that Gram could have afforded—a blade pot roast, some ribs, and the chuck end of the shoulder or "clod," as Chef Virgil called it. Libby's instructor had suggested, as well, adding chicken bones and giblets browned in the oven for extra flavor, and they were roasting right now. Gram always said that old chickens make the best soup.

Marrow bones, broken and wrapped in pieces of muslin, were known to improve a good stock, and Gram would have had access to both, though she'd never have bothered with the fabric. Or would she? Libby recalled her tying up spices in a piece of worn cotton ripped from an old dress and bleached clean of color. But Gram tended to toss the stripped carcass of a roasted chicken or the leftovers from a turkey directly into the pot, not willing to waste any bit of meat—always sweetest nearest the bone.

Libby would take no chances with this last test soup, and so she unwrapped and rinsed the muslin for the aesthetics of a clear stock, or "bone broth" as trendy young homemakers were calling it all over the Internet. Buying the ingredients had put a dent in her budget, but the soup wouldn't be wasted even if the recipe didn't go over with the clientele at Belle Boutique Hotel. She'd take whatever concoction resulted to the Haven this weekend for the old folks there. It was about time for a visit anyway.

As she cooked up her trial batch, Libby paid close attention to every detail so she would attain maximum "sapidity," the word Chef Virgil used for flavor. She placed the meat into cold water, brought it to a boil, skimmed off the scum—which she now knew was called "albumen," like with eggs—then added coarse salt and the veggies. She took it all down to a simmer and then checked the clock. This broth wouldn't be ready until pushing midnight. She might as well make one more pass through the file she'd collected of Gram's papers—her recycled cards from the shop, magazine clippings, bits of correspondence, and anything that might hold a clue to the formula for her signature soup.

That's when she found the pamphlet.

It was a thin, tri-fold sheet stained with a coffee ring, easily overlooked in her searches for the recipe. It fluttered out of the file folder onto the kitchen floor as Libby sat down on the vinyl chair. She reached for it and turned it over to the front, printed in black ink with the title "Laird Mansion Museum, Kirkton, ND" appearing above a simple line sketch of an old house.

Libby's skin prickled from her chest up to her scalp.

She knew that house. Somewhere—in her dreams, maybe—she'd seen it, the straight path leading past a well pump and up to a porch with a swinging bench. She remembered the swing and how she'd wanted to sit in it.

Her apartment table disappeared and she was back on the porch.

"Get over here and stay right beside me!" Her mother's voice in her memory is accusatory, harsh, not the manner of a mommy protecting her little girl. A screen door slams at the back of the house—or is that the sound of the door on Seven Canaan Lane?—and the dusky shadows on the porch are long and deep. She shivers, but her mother doesn't draw her close. The pink train case, borrowed from Gram, is heavy to carry, but she grips its plastic handle with both fists. Mommy warned her not to drop it. Another lady stands in front of the door, with an apron tied around her thick waist and a face more wrinkled than Gram's, but with sad lines rather than Gram's happy ones. Libby wants Gram. Why did Mommy make her leave the city and drive all the way out here, where there are no trees but only the big, big sky and long, flat fields? The lady talks and Mommy talks, but five-year-old Libby can't understand the words, just the sour anger oozing out of their mouths.

Hammering at her door broke Libby out of the unbidden recollection.

CHAPTER FIFTEEN

Ten days ago

Sybil pounded on Libby's apartment door until the one across the hall opened. A weary face with double chins peeked out. "You wanting Libby?"

"Isn't she here? I just talked to her on the phone."

"She's got to be home, what with all them grocery bags she hauled in tonight." The woman pulled a hanky from her housecoat sleeve and wiped her nose. She stepped into the hallway. "You are making enough racket to raise the dead. And at this hour."

Libby finally opened her door. "It's okay, Zinnia. You remember Sybil, my friend?"

The neighbor shuffled back into her apartment, muttering, "Funny kind of friend hardly shows her face around here then about breaks the door down trying to get in."

"Don't mind her," Libby told Sybil. "She's my protector. What are you doing here?"

"Hungry," she said in half-truth. "I knew you'd have food." Sybil pushed into the shabby entrance and breathed a noseful before coughing it out. "Yuck—meat."

"I'll make you a cucumber-and-cream-cheese sandwich. It's a rare celebration to have you visit me at home."

"What a dive." Sybil picked her way over piles of newspaper and cartons. She didn't remember it being quite so slummy.

"It's not always such a mess. I'm packing up Gram's stuff."

But Sybil saw beyond the upended drawers and bags of clothing to the cracks in the walls and the condition of the carpet.

"This place should be condemned."

"There's been talk, but I don't think it's serious."

"What on earth kept you from hearing me knocking, anyway?" Sybil asked. "You didn't have music on."

"Just . . . I don't know. Daydreaming, I guess."

Sybil took a closer look. Libby's eyes were rimmed in red. Had she been crying? "You've got to take a break, girlfriend."

"I'll drink decaf while you eat your sandwich."

"I don't mean a coffee break." Sybil stopped herself from saying more. Libby's need for a real vacation was becoming critical. Maybe she'd change Libby's mind tonight, though she'd have to approach the subject of travel gingerly.

"I brought you a treat." Sybil withdrew the plastic bag from her jacket pocket. Libby's eyebrow arched. Sybil laughed. "It's not drugs, you idiot. It's Goji powder."

"If you think you're going to pep me up by forcing one of your magic potions down my gullet, I'm afraid it won't do the trick this time." Libby took a cucumber from the fridge.

Sybil huffed. "What are you saying? Goji berries are an antioxidant super-food often prescribed as a blood tonic."

"Nothing wrong with my blood."

Sybil almost called her on that statement. Libby carried toxic shame around with her—unspoken but, she'd bet, related to her family line and her complexion. Sybil had once asked about the ethnic roots of her surname, but all Libby had responded was that her forebears had a habit of walking out, and that the Walker name had followed them from at least the time of her great-grandmother although she wouldn't know about family before that.

"Anyway, I didn't bring the Goji for strictly medicinal reasons." Sybil opened the bag.

Libby placed a whole-grain sandwich in front of Sybil then sat down herself. "What's it for, a face mask?"

"No, bimbo, it's for your soup. You've been complaining that it lacks something, and so I grabbed a packet from my own supply for you." Also, it was dated and needed to be moved off her shelves. She licked her pointer and stirred it around in the powder before popping it in her mouth and smacking her lips. "It's got a tomato-like tang to it, a *je ne sais quoi* to add mystery to your brew." Sybil was no cook, but Goji powder might help. It couldn't hurt the meaty mess on Libby's stove. Besides, this was a way to introduce her friend to more of the great product she stocked at Amulets.

Libby cocked her head. "Do people use this in soups?"

"Yeah, I have a client who adds it to her shitake cream of mushroom." Libby took a pinch from the bag and put it on her tongue. "Also, Goji boosts the immune system."

"I'm not sure it would be a good idea to try it out for my weekend workshop entry. I can't take chances on the upper-crust diners coming to the Belle for the charity event Saturday." Libby tapped her foot. "Besides, you say those berries are from Asia. My recipe is linked to my heritage. I'm calling it 'Babette's Bowl,' and Gram sure wouldn't have even heard of Goji berries, let alone used them. Sorrel, maybe, or lambsquarters. But not exotic powder from a specialty health store."

"I thought your chef wanted you to play around with spices this week." Sybil bit into her sandwich.

"I don't know . . ."

"Well, I'm not taking it back home with me, so keep it. You'll change your mind." Sybil jammed the plastic bag into Libby's purse and then took another bite. "This sandwich is delish."

"One of Gram's standbys. It's nothing fancy but, as she used to say, 'Hunger is the best sauce.' I often took it to school in my lunch kit." Sybil noticed Libby relax when she mentioned her grandmother.

Libby was constantly referring to the old woman as if that biddy's "wisdom" applied in any way today. Her friend was stuck in a long-gone era, where platitudes were the answer to any problem. Why, Libby had once preached at her for caring so much about her looks, using that tired phrase about beauty being only skin deep and telling her she was going to get burned if she kept playing with fire by dating so many men. And yet look at her today. Sybil was more desirable than ever and definitely not burning.

But thinking about Gram seemed to calm Libby, so maybe now was the moment for Sybil to mention her other reason for coming over so late on a midweek night.

"I brought my laptop here to show you something special." Sybil reached for her bag near the door and opened the lid as Libby began protesting.

"Not more trip propaganda."

"You've got to see this wonderful hotel in Lhasa . . . Hey, aren't you wireless?" Sybil couldn't connect to the 'Net, though her computer detected a weak signal coming from an apartment nearby. But it was locked. "Boot up your dinosaur of a desktop, won't you?"

"Sybil, I'm not going to Tibet with you."

"Sure you are."

"No. I. Am. Not." Libby drew her words out, as if speaking to a dimwit.

Sybil laughed at the silly show of childishness. "Don't be a party pooper." She nudged her friend's calf with her booted foot.

"How can I hammer this in?" Libby clenched her teeth.

Maybe Sybil's approach wasn't the best way to bring up the subject, but she was too far into it now to back away. "I wanted to show you my surprise through the online photos, but you're forcing me to spell it out for you." She paused for effect. "You and I are booked for a first-class trip to Tibet in June."

Libby's mouth fell open.

"Yep." Sybil slapped the tabletop for emphasis. "I was browsing and happened onto a great deal for two. I had almost enough travel points to cover the entire package, so I entered my credit card number and—*ta-da!*—nonrefundable tickets. They're so cheap that it isn't costing much more than the flights I've already promised to give you." Her cheeks almost hurt with her smile. "The balance you can pay me back over time. Say a hundred bucks a month."

Libby didn't gasp or bounce around in delight. Her reaction was much less gratifying—the plate clattering back onto the table, the eyes sparking with irritation or maybe self-respect. She drew herself up to full height.

"No, I'm sorry, Sybil. It's generous of you, and I'm sure you mean well, but I can't up and leave at the last moment like this."

"Of course you can." What nonsense the woman believed. She had weeks left to pack for the trip. "This is a once-in-a-lifetime deal, I tell you. I should know. I've never seen a vacation sale like this before."

"But I haven't got a passport, for one thing. And Terence won't give me time off. And I've never even owned luggage." Libby mumbled something about a small, pink suitcase, but Sybil couldn't quite make it out.

"Excuses, Libby. This will be an adventure *par excellence*. Think of the food, the mountains, the temples." To say nothing of the guys Sybil would pick up for them along the way.

Libby wagged her finger under Sybil's nose. "You're not listening to me. There's the house I'm looking at buying, and I can't jeopardize the sale or the financing. A hundred dollars subtracted from your monthly income might not be much, but it's way out of the question for me."

"We'll figure it out."

Libby tossed her long, straight hair like a show pony, one or two pewter strands subtle amongst the dark. She fixed her amber-flecked eyes on Sybil, pausing as though about to make a dire announcement.

"To be completely honest, Sybil, if I ever took a trip anywhere, it sure wouldn't be to Tibet. I don't *want* to go. And if you keep bringing it up, I'm going to start avoiding you."

The set of her jaw said it all.

Sybil had never heard Libby take this tone before. Maybe it wasn't the smartest idea after all to have locked in the trip reservations without convincing Libby beforehand. If in fact this was her final word, Sybil had no idea what she'd do with the tickets.

No, she couldn't let the conversation conclude on this note. Speechless for the moment, she put her elbows on the table, her chin in her hands, and she squinted at Libby.

Despite the petulance in her own voice, Libby didn't let her eyelids flicker under Sybil's glare. Her friend should know better than to push her like this, when the tornado of life was twisting and crashing around her. Sybil's incessant battering only added to the pandemonium of death and stress and restlessness Libby was fighting. Even the wild disorder of her apartment mirrored the shambles of her life right now.

Out of the corner of her eye, Libby spotted the brochure she'd dropped earlier on the tabletop—the worn, folded paper with the drawing of the North Dakota museum. She steeled herself against breaking visual contact with Sybil. She didn't want to draw attention to the pamphlet, didn't want Sybil digging around in this last, sacrosanct haven of her privacy—the ground of her uncharted fears.

The brochure was within Libby's reach. She sat down and edged Sybil's sandwich plate in its direction to cover it, itching to snatch the paper away before Sybil spotted it lying there. But the girl was too quick for her.

"What's this?" Sybil swept up the pamphlet in an instant. She silently read the front, opened it and perused the information inside, and then with exaggerated deliberation placed it back onto the table. She thumped it with her finger and then pointed at Libby. "You're planning a trip, and without me."

Libby crossed her arms over her chest, rubbing little circles on one elbow to her internal rhythm: *Once upon a time in a land far, far away . . . Step on a crack and you'll break your mother's back . . .* It did look bad. After Libby's peevishness about Tibet, Sybil would leap to false conclusions.

"No, you're wrong." Libby let her arms drop to her sides and forced softness into her voice. "I mean, the pamphlet was in Gram's stuff. It must have been sitting around here for a long time."

"Was she wanting to go to North Dakota? Did she ask you to take her?"

"Of course not. She was too old to travel." Why *would* Gram have had this in her papers? "She was a packrat about cards and clippings, Sybil. This must have been another random bit of reading she came across." Mustn't it? But why then did the sketch on the front disturb Libby so much?

Her doubt only fueled Sybil's enthusiasm. "I'll bet she wanted to see this museum." She stood halfway and stretched across the table to bring her face close to Libby's. "Let's go in her honor."

"No, I—"

"It's hardly a day's drive away, Libby."

"But it's—"

"I'll pay for gas and motel."

"Work is—"

"We'll go on a weekend. The pamphlet says the museum opens annually in mid-May."

"I've got—"

"*You owe me!*" Sybil plunked herself back into the chair and fixed Libby with eyes of granite. "You owe me, Libby Walker. I pile you up with destination magazines, I take you shopping for a great travel wardrobe, I tell you all about my trips just so you can live them vicariously. And then I generously spend all my airline points and more on a vacation *for you* that you refuse to take. What ingratitude."

Aghast at the onslaught, Libby had no ready comeback on her tongue. Of course, she took no ownership for Sybil's outrageous decision in the first place to reserve the nonrefundable travel package. And her own refusal to go to Tibet was only logical. Sybil's declaration of her indebtedness held no validity. Her sheer presumption, her egotistical self-focus, her opportunistic reproof left Libby speechless. But this wasn't the first time lately she'd been called ungrateful.

Sybil rose and replaced her laptop in her bag. "Think about what I'm giving up to be your friend before you reject my compromise of a simple, two-day road trip."

She slammed the door behind her.

Libby touched the hot spoon to her lips, blowing on it before tipping a bit of the broth into her mouth. Tears stung her eyes, not on account of the scalding soup but because Sybil's acrimony lingered in the apartment. And when Libby blew away the ire and bitterness of Sybil's manipulative demand—intended, of course, to induce shame—still she was left with the fact that a road trip wasn't too much for Sybil to ask of her, especially in light of her friend's overarching generosity. However, this admission brought Libby no relief. She didn't want to go to North Dakota any more than she wanted to go to Tibet, but for altogether different reasons.

As for Libby's soup, the flavor was good but not outstanding, a wholesome blend of tastes without a distinguishing note of zest—a lot like the watery stew of her life.

She threw the spoon into the sink, all at once giving up on her experiment. It'd have to do as her prototype for the weekend.

It might not feed the five thousand, as Gram would put it, but this pot wouldn't be wasted because several seniors at the Haven would welcome anything made in Babette's kitchen.

The hour was late and she might as well send off the list of necessary ingredients to Chef Virgil and call it a night. But after completing that chore, and tidying the kitchen, and having a steamy shower, Libby still wasn't sleepy. She retrieved the Laird Mansion leaflet and sat down again at her computer, typing in the URL to take her to the museum website.

She had a bad feeling about this.

Libby read all of the site's information, examined the substandard images of blurry Victorian costumes and kitschy giftshop ware, and further searched for history on this Laird guy. None of it brought her any closer to understanding why her chest constricted when she thought of Gram holding a secret regarding the mansion from her beloved granddaughter. This pamphlet was meaningful to Gram or she wouldn't have kept it. Every scrap and slip in her belongings indicated a memory saved against dementia.

What was Gram's connection to the museum, and did Libby really want to know? It would mean she had a connection, as well.

Libby clicked the "contact us" button. She drafted a one-line e-mail asking for the exact date and time of the Laird Mansion Museum opening, information not obvious anywhere on the website. She didn't mention her name—that would be too much of a commitment, as though she were seriously intending to travel to North Dakota. Before she could delete the whole thing, she hit "send." What harm could there be in asking such a simple, anonymous question?

CHAPTER SIXTEEN

Today

The tour is getting tedious. Sybil drops back from the group and watches the brats clear out of the billiards room in front of her. Kids can be such a pain. She should know, having in her thirtieth year birthed one herself at home in a tub of tepid water with the aid of an acupuncturist. She hasn't thought about that for a while.

She'd breastfed the boy for a few days then surrendered him up to the originally reluctant father, who after all insisted on sole custody. Not that Sybil had any intention of challenging the claim. Was her "sacrifice" a type of appeasement for—or maybe condemnation against—her own dad's rebuff?

Having rejected the initial pleas of the sperm donor, Sybil had gone through with the pregnancy and first stage of lactation only because every woman should have the experience at least once. It is her right and her pleasure to encounter the sensuous event denied to the masculine gender. But that was as far as her desire for matriarchal power took her. Two earlier pregnancies and one later had been terminated in the accustomed manner.

As the students scrabble about in the hallway, Sybil does her math: the boy she birthed would be about eight or nine now. She'd bumped into father, son, and barren wife last summer. When the woman averted her gaze, Sybil made the "call me" hand motion at the still-yummy husband. Of course, she barely glanced at the child.

Well, she has nothing to apologize for, even in comparison to the fusty Victorian morals represented on this historical tour. The American settlers were too narrow in their intolerant philosophies.

Sybil approved rather of the aboriginal morality of old. She might not be able to duplicate the sexual liberty enjoyed by the Native Americans before the European invasion leveled them with sickness and avarice and white-man religion. But she can always buy the international version with another flight, another encounter with foreign cultures, to further expand her horizons.

Sybil is last to leave the billiards room; she wants another go at old Pharaoh. She digs her nose right into the mass of buffalo hair, puffy around the old bull's neck. The musk takes her back to her South African expedition, when she'd slept in a thatch-roofed lodge on a game reserve and been forced to step on the hides of wildebeest and zebra. The cooks grilled kudu and warthog and springbok, to her disgust. She thought she'd signed up for a photographic safari and assumed she wouldn't be subject to the spoils of a hunt. Even today the idea of slaughtering the beautiful beings and snuffing out their divinity just to feast on their flesh or walk on their skins almost makes her bawl.

Her real destination on that trip had been Cape Town's Table Mountain, and she saved it for the last day of the vacation. The cable-car ride to the top was prohibited due to high winds. Having worn sandals inappropriate for heavy hiking, she stuck to open pathways on an easy route to a flat plateau. There she sat in the lee of the sacred summit, known for its primal spirituality pulsing with light in a convergence of nurturing, sustaining energy. Many people reported healings at Table Mountain. Hadn't she herself been cured there of the herpetic rash that, since high school, sporadically blistered up on the most inconvenient body parts at the most inopportune times? And on the mount that day she met Senzo—of Zulu extraction—who occupied her evening quite nicely and fed her cornmeal porridge for breakfast.

Considering all her expertise, Sybil should write an autobiography detailing her geo-psychic-amorous exploits. She might call it *Sybil's Sensual Search for Sacred Spaces*. It has a nice ring to it and would be an easy sell in Amulets. Her customers grab any material she recommends straight off the shelves, and a self-help guide like this would be so useful to them.

And of course she'll need to gather more data. Meaning more trips and more lovers. A shiver quivers up her backbone. In all her research, she hasn't yet found "the one"—that perfect swain who checks off all the boxes for more than a night or two at a time. But that's the fun of the chase, isn't it? Total satiety of the soul—that sense of really catching her breath as in a deep yawn—might be just around the next corner.

She exits the billiards room, still thinking about travel. Maybe she can take Libby with her to South Africa someday, since Tibet doesn't appeal. Sybil catches up to the lagging sisters in the hallway, who are admiring the needlepoint handiwork on a chair cushion.

*

Libby enters the master bedroom ahead of Paige, who pitches into her discourse.

"This apartment with *en suite* bathroom—a unique feature for the era—was inhabited by Moses David Melchizedek Laird himself. It boasts a Russian sleigh bed with a silk-lined, linen coverlet." Paige smooths a wrinkle from its surface. "You'll note that the closer we move towards MDM's presence, the richer and more personal his possessions."

Yes, Libby has indeed noted that. Her scalp is tingling and

her sense of the dead owner's presence is growing.

Paige continues. "The focal point in this bedroom is the fieldstone fireplace with a saying carved by MDM's had into the sandstone lintel. This fireplace is one of ten needed to heat thirteen thousand square feet. Watch for other unique mottos engraved throughout the mansion." She straightens the mantel clock sitting on the stone shelf then points to the inscription below it.

Before Paige can read it, Sybil spouts out, "*The bed undefiled.* Ye gods, what does *that* mean?"

Libby would expect Sybil to display more literary insight, in light of her formal education. But likely Sybil's confusion arises out of a moral rather than an intellectual vacuum. Immediately Libby rebukes herself. Who is she to judge Sybil's morality when she's had her own iniquity to deal with?

In an aside, restrained, she explains to Sybil, "It's about the sanctity of marriage. Gram used to quote it to me when I was a girl." It made sense to her only after her own failed attempts to find love—shacking up with her high-school boyfriend and then dating guys she had no real interest in. And has she found what she's looking for yet?

"What did you say?" Paige asks. Libby shakes her head without repeating herself, and smiles to make sure the girl doesn't take it as a snub. Her explanation doesn't concern a stranger. It's meant only to fill a gap in Sybil's knowledge.

Sybil, however, in her striped leggings and clacking teal hair beads, is already sticking her nose through another door, this one into the master bedroom closet. Libby moves closer. A message is stenciled this time above a teeny leaded window, across from shelving stacked with period clothing: *As a vesture shalt thou fold them up.* Are the words instructions on how to care for clothing?

The inscriptions captivate Libby. She'll have to keep a keen lookout for them. As the group moves back into the hallway, she finds one or two sayings embellishing other surfaces as well. On a stone slab above the door to a fourth bathroom, she reads *Our hearts are sprinkled, our bodies washed,* MDM's sentiment sounding like Gram's notion of cleanliness being next to godliness. On a plaque beside the second-story speaking tube, part of the mansion's elaborate intercom system, MDM fairly shouts *See that ye refuse not him that speaketh.* Libby's reminded of her mutinous adolescence when Gram would admonish, "Children, obey your parents," and when she'd yell back at Gram that she had no parents. Gram would pull her close and hold her fast and weep a moment with her.

Libby moves along with the group, duly noting the points of interest indicated by Paige—a bird's-eye maple dressing table, a silk calligraphy scroll MDM acquired on one of his many travels before dying at the ripe old age of 102. But she finds herself balling her fists, digging them into the pockets of her jeans to stop the trembling that has only increased in the past half hour since entering the museum. She registers the appreciative remarks of the elderly sisters, the shuffling of the teens, and Sybil's flirtatious comments aimed at the teacher. But she's more aware of the inner tension building inside her gut, and suddenly—as she steps around the final unexplored corner of this floor and finds herself overlooking the great hall on the main floor below—in a flash she knows positively that she's been here before.

CHAPTER SEVENTEEN

Nine days ago

MDM's faxed letters lay scattered in front of Paige. She rubbed her eyes, her lids burning, and refocused on the text of the missive in her hand. She'd almost memorized the lot of them, word for word, over the past four days. It was after midnight and Danny was fast asleep upstairs. They'd barely made eye contact while she read over supper. She'd promised him quality time this coming weekend, but her research was a jealous lover and she doubted she could deliver. Maybe she should crawl in beside him now, waken him with kisses, and warm her chilly feet.

The *bing* of a received e-mail stopped her from shutting down her computer—probably automated junk delivery. Who on this continent would write so early in the morning? But the "from" line piqued her interest: *gramsgirl1@outlook.com*. The e-mail read:

> *Can you tell me the date your museum opens this spring? I couldn't find it online.*

Paige popped off a quick answer:

> *Noon on Sunday, May 14th. Sorry about the poor website. It needs attention.*

Paige returned to thoughts of her strict timeline. In a week and a half she'd begin her final season as museum tour guide. More to the point, the weeks to Baby's birth were counting down just as quickly as the hours left until thesis submission. Another e-mail from "Gramsgirl" appeared almost immediately:

> *Thanks for the info. I'm sort of thinking of coming up from Minneapolis to check out the museum.*

Paige typed back:

> *History buffs love us. Ever been here before?*

Gramsgirl wrote:

> *I'm not really a history buff.*

Not much of an answer to her question. Paige wrote:

> *The Laird Mansion Museum might change that for you. Fascinating place. Hope you can make it.*

It was always nice to open someone's mind and emotions to the story of the past, but this casual e-mailer was a doubtful bet. Most visitors to the museum were either school kids on a field trip from Grand Forks or else genuinely interested internationals looking for the local flavor of the American frontier.

After a short but deep sleep, Paige arose to eat breakfast with Danny and see him out the door. She checked her e-mail again before showering and found another note from Gramsgirl:

> *Can you tell me if the museum has one of those swinging porch benches, with a dark brown, buttoned leather cushion?*

What an odd question. Paige knew of no bench swing although, come to think of it, there might be screw holes in the porch ceiling. She didn't answer with a message of her own yet; she'd see if she had time to check the archives for a telltale photo later today.

Bag of popcorn in hand, Sybil slid into the theater row after Iggy while the previews blared from the big screen. She winked at Clive, triumphant over their success in positioning Libby between them—a bit of a trick, given her friend's bad attitude.

"This was supposed to be girls only. Why did you invite him?" Libby hissed in her ear.

"Shh, you'll hurt his feelings." To avoid smiling, Sybil took a long draw from the straw sticking out of her diet cola, to which she'd surreptitiously added the contents of a tiny bottle of bourbon she happened to have in her purse. She didn't want to give away her glee at one-upping Libby after her friend's impulsive refusal last night to agree to Tibet, a subject that was definitely not yet closed. Libby pretended she didn't care for Clive—or for any men—but Sybil knew what was best for her. That's why she arranged for the guys to meet them tonight. Clive let her know crashing the party would be his pleasure and that the Odeon was the perfect venue—that is, dark enough in case one of his wife's friends showed up.

From the time she was a girl, Sybil liked to double date, even later when "date" came to have a much more complex meaning than sitting in a movie theater holding hands. Group experiences were always good, in her book, though she might never convince Libby to enjoy the riskier liaisons available these days. No matter. It was sufficiently amusing to watch her fend off Clive's paws tonight.

The movie volume ramped up as the climax approached. The lead male vampire bit down on the leading lady at the same moment Clive, teeth bared for comedic effect, went for Libby's neck. Libby squawked. Then she excused herself for the restroom. She stayed there until Sybil collected her at the end of the show.

"Where's your sense of humor?" Sybil dried her hands and checked out her hair in the mirror. How could her roots be showing already? "Poor Clive sat through the rest of the show pining for you."

"It's time for me to go home."

"He told me he thinks you're cute." Sybil was all about the thrill of the chase, especially if she could urge things along. Pushing Libby and Clive together should result in real fireworks. And Libby was showing a bit of remorse over refusing her gift of travel, at least enough to make her cave when Sybil insisted she borrow her new tank top for the evening—not that Libby twigged to its being almost sheer. Next she'd get Libby to agree to the out-of-state road trip. She'd bide her time. Libby would give in eventually.

"This is not middle-school intrigue, Sybil. You need to respect my boundaries."

"Sure, sure." Sybil knew what Libby really wanted—what every woman wants—despite her prim exterior and talk of boundaries. Guys liked a challenge and Clive was no exception. But Libby could ruin this if she wasn't managed correctly. "You'd better be nicer to Clive or you're going to lose your chance on that house he's talked the owners into selling you."

Libby's swallow was audible. Sybil smirked into her reflection. "Come on, let's go have a beer."

"I told you, I'd like to go home. You know I don't drink."

Right, Sybil had forgotten Libby's twelve-step pledge, taken long ago because of an imagined addiction. She said, "They have non-alcoholic drinks at the club I have in mind, and the dancing will be heating up about now."

But there was no budging Libby and, in the end, Sybil let her catch the bus while she enjoyed the company of her two men. Iggy hung out at the Sonix bar ogling the hostess's cleavage, but that didn't faze Sybil because Clive really knew how to shake it on the dance floor.

Libby turned her face away from the boozy breath of a fellow passenger and shifted her feet to avoid the crush of partyers flooding onto the bus. Good thing she had a library book along to stick her nose into. She'd be transferring at the next stop to the Metro Blue Line anyway, although there was no guarantee the train commuters would smell or behave any better. Spending time on public transit in downtown Minneapolis was not her best pick for a Friday night activity, but it was preferable to enduring another moment with Clive, who'd clamored to drive her home when Sybil refused to deliver her back to her apartment after the movie.

She sighed. There she was, being ungrateful again. The realtor held a key for her, quite literally. Was she staring a gift horse in the mouth? Clive could snag Seven Canaan Lane for her if the bank approved her mortgage. The annoyance on his face tonight let her know he was unimpressed about her skipping out on the dancing segment of the trick date. Good grief, didn't he have any sense of professional comportment? What realtor would risk losing a sale for the chance of a kiss in a darkened theater?

Clive was attractive enough, with his silvering temples and saucy smile. And his carefree way of standing with hands on hips while gazing into a woman's eyes might be called charming by some. But he was a decade younger, closer to Sybil's age, though that in itself could be considered a compliment to Libby. And the way he pulled out her chair for her and even pouted when she brushed him off—well, it wasn't unflattering.

Libby tugged on her ear. She hadn't been pursued like this in a long while. There was a reason for that. She pinched her earlobe to bring herself back to reality. She just didn't trust men. It's not that men hadn't been looking at her, but she wasn't looking back at them. And she saw no reason to put her trust in Clive.

Eight days ago

Libby scribbled notes along with the rest of Chef Virgil's acolytes during his morning lecture on this second Saturday of the two-part soup seminar. The others treated his words with reverence, craning forward into his voice, and now and then asking him to repeat a poetic phrase. But Libby, though thoroughly enjoying what she was learning, wouldn't again spend so much money on another seminar.

"Soup is a relationship," the chef said, punctuating his grandiose words with a broad sweep of his hand.

"Soup is a relationship," the guy beside Libby repeated as he wrote it down.

"What do you mean, a relationship?" she asked Virgil.

"All the separate ingredients must unite in a homogenous communion, a perfect whole greater than the sum of its parts," the chef explained. "Choice of ingredients is of utmost importance. For example, I'd never add watermelon chunks to a split-pea soup, but I often top off my stewed fruit compote with a crunchy tangle of pea shoots. "

Libby needed clarification. "So you mean you want the soup to be balanced?"

"Oh no. We talk about wine being balanced when no dominant note stands out. But in soup, we want the special 'zip' that gives the dish its quirky individuality without overwhelming its basic temperament."

Yes, that was the problem with Babette's Bowl. Libby's version lacked the zip she hadn't tasted since her youth.

Virgil went on. "This is why I say soup is a relationship—like a family. Every family is a blend of the personalities within, yet one quality often predominates and defines it. Perhaps an extroverted mother imbues the home with her flamboyancy, or the introverted father sets the mood with his quiet steadiness." Libby wouldn't know about that sort of home, but how she longed to.

Virgil sounded more like a psychologist than a chef. "Then again, maybe a daughter is a musical protégé who, through her calling and career development, steers the parent-sibling unit in a particular direction. It's the same with soup. Do you see what I mean?"

Several in the group nodded. Libby couldn't quite grasp his illustration and, perhaps seeing her perplexity, Chef Virgil inclined his head towards her.

"A good soup must retain its integrity. It must be pure and true. Complex, yes, but not complicated. A soup's essential character is an infusion of characteristics giving it its 'consubstantiality,' as it were, with one flavor dominating and the others not in 'balance' as such but in agreement with the base note, complementing and nuancing the flavors without subjugating itself."

Libby, unsure how to spell some of his words, gave up taking notes and attended to his meaning. The ideas he raised were new to her. Who'd have thought there was a philosophy of soup?

Chef Virgil picked up his ladle and waved it at them in passionate appeal. "A good soup has a singularity of nature made up of a multiplicity of elements. It should beguile the mouth, and will calm or excite depending on its purpose—like your lemon soup." He pointed at the brunette who'd grown up in the Greek lemon grove.

That woman nodded vigorously. "But I'm sure Mama never intended to excite me any more than I was already excited." The class members laughed.

"Of course, we must not try to force emotions when crafting." Virgil put his spoon down and placed both palms flat on the countertop. "We don't 'go for a feeling' when cooking soup, but rather trust that our soup will elicit feeling."

Maybe Libby's problem was her desperation for the feeling Gram used to give her, the missing spice in her life.

"We begin with a sound base," Chef Virgil said, "perhaps a brown stock or maybe a *fond blanc* made with a *mirepoix* of carrots, celery, and onions. Even this core substance of the soup will show variety depending on its source. Chinese celery, for example, tastes very different than Mediterranean celeriac. This, in my view, gives soup its own *appellation,* as wine can be identified by the soil in which the grape vines grew."

Libby closed her notebook. The loss of her soup recipe paralleled her loss of Gram. No matter how she tried to recall the original taste, her current soup—like her life—was a boring slurry of sameness rather than the dynamic interrelationship Chef Virgil described. She herself had none of this *appellation*. Even her name, Walker, denied her a sense of origin, of place, of home.

The lecture ended and the kitchen erupted in a flurry of activity. For the rest of the morning and well into the afternoon, the group members bustled and bumped and milled about the kitchen as they filled the room with gorgeous aromas, spooning up samples of each other's inventions and making suggestions towards improvement or, perhaps, sabotage. Late in the afternoon, Chef Virgil once again took center stage, clapping three times.

"Class, attention. The diners will be arriving shortly and we must be ready."

Libby lifted her spatula from the stainless pot and placed it on the spoon rest. The success or failure of the soups being presented at the function tonight would affect the teacher's reputation as well as determine the career fate of several of Libby's fellow students, with their dreams of gastronomic notoriety. She didn't have such skin in the game, but the strain in the kitchen was almost palpable.

Virgil asked, "Any final questions as we complete our masterpieces?"

One student inquired about finishing a peanut-yam gumbo with *kefir* rather than yogurt, and another wanted the chef's opinion on garnishing with popcorn. When Libby's tattooed workstation mate asked about his salmon bisque, Chef Virgil advised him to trust his artistic impulses and add in more lavender.

"Not everyone should feel so unrestricted," Chef Virgil

cautioned. "It takes a certain sensibility of palate to avoid too heavy a hand in seasoning. We're aiming for the perfect marriage of flavors—a combination of sweet, salty, sour, and even bitter—enhanced by qualities of color, temperature, and the *nappé*." Libby mentally reviewed her glossary. Right, he was talking about texture and consistency. She'd had no idea when she registered for the class that she'd be learning so much French.

Virgil approached her and took up a spoon to sample her broth. She shrank back. The soup wasn't ready for assessment, much as she needed an analysis to figure out what was wrong.

"Yes, it's lacking . . . " he said. She expected it, but Chef Virgil's critique stung. "Tell me again the background of this formula."

"My grandmother—who learned it from her mother, who might have gotten it from further back—made it for special occasions. Well, not *this* soup, exactly. I never got the full recipe from her before she died, and I just don't know what I'm missing."

"But where did it originate? Is it from Europe?"

"I don't know." Gram never mentioned any overseas relatives and surely hadn't ever gone there herself.

The chef smacked and then murmured more to himself than Libby, "Perhaps a tablespoon or two of lemon juice to acidulate it?" He leaned over the pot again and inhaled deeply. "You might try anchovy filets or dark beer, both used on occasion to give a beef base like yours some punch. Though, if you're wanting to retain compliance with your genealogy, I'm not sure what to suggest."

No, Gram wouldn't have had access to anchovies, and beer wasn't allowed in her home. Over the next half hour, Libby poked around the stock of fresh herbs and other ingredients piled onto a counter for the group's ease of accessibility. She rolled a sprig of mint between her palms to release the bouquet and sampled from a bottle of liquid smoke. Nothing seemed quite right. She'd never discover the "enigmatic taste of ethnicity" Chef Virgil expected of each creation. She found she cared about his approval after all.

Then he was counting down the minutes left before their soups must be plated. Libby, in reckless desperation, remembered Sybil's powdered Goji berries. She grabbed her purse. She turned the flame up for a quick blast of flavor-infusing heat and dumped the contents of the plastic bag into Babette's Bowl, praying silent forgiveness for her culinary blasphemy. Asian Goji berries were less likely than mint or smoke to have flavored Gram's original soup, but they were no worse than the chef's suggestions of beer or anchovies. They might at least add that *je ne sais quoi* Sybil described. A quick lick of her spoon gave her taste buds a pleasant zing. And then in a fluster, as waiters stood by, she and the other seminar participants filled and tidied the white miniature bowls, arranged them on trays, and handed them over to be whisked out into the dining area.

Two hours later, Libby and her fellow soup aficionados traipsed out of the kitchen into the formal dining room of the Belle Boutique Hotel, wearing their splattered aprons like pageant banners, to receive general recognition as participants in the fundraiser. Individual acclaim went to the top three winners of the contest.

She didn't place, of course. But before the night was out she'd received a business card from one of the judges, Quentin Hardy, who asked her to please call his office at her convenience. She pocketed the card imprinted with the logo of a leaf and the words *Folkways Nutrition Group*, but she couldn't wait to get home and relax, maybe sleep in on the remaining day of her weekend. Libby left the restaurant with the other seminar participants, Chef Virgil telling them they would receive their certificates of completion in the mail. And, he reminded them, they could order his famous cookbook, *Simmer, Scoop, Slurp*, online.

Sybil spent Saturday afternoon at the hairdresser preparing for her evening with Iggy. At the luscious touch of head massage and scent of citrus argan oil shampoo, Sybil closed her eyes and took herself away to the wondrous country of France, where she'd once luxuriated in a world-class treatment in a famous salon along the Champs-Élysées.

Ah, Paris! The city was a consumer's Nirvana, and she'd left her mark in one or two stores. Thus fortified, she pushed forward in her calculated search for the sacred in Paris.

There'd been too many museums so she skipped them all. And she walked right by one cathedral after another. Instead of following the run-of-the-mill tourist circuit featuring the Eiffel Tower or a cruise on the Seine, she identified three portals to take her through to the numinous aspect of the City of Lights: nature, music, and the mausoleum or—easier to remember—trees, tunes, and tombs.

Sybil had begun by strolling through a couple of the pocket-sized parks that sprouted up behind iron gates and on street corners. In the famous Tuileries *jardin*, she joined in on a demonstration of heaving and hollering university students covered in chocolate meant to symbolize dirty oil, and then she sat on a bench beneath a flowering cherry tree in the square facing the flying buttresses of Notre Dame. Paying homage to green Paris took most of the day. Along the way, buskers had her tapping toes to an accordion, swaying to the singing strings of a street-side violin, and stopping for a full-blown orchestra in the underground tunnels of the Métro. That evening a jazz band in a smoky bar on Île Saint-Louis topped off her musical foray.

Yes, nature and music had spoken to her soul in Paris. She'd chosen those themes well. But the pinnacle of experiential bliss in her hunt for the holy came the next day with the third element in her city self-tour itinerary: the afterlife.

As the hairdresser today worked dye into her scalp, Sybil revisited the Père Lachaise Cemetery in her mind. There she'd spent an invigorating afternoon contemplating the purpose of this life as the opportunity for individuals to learn the lessons of love that would transport them to their next plane of consciousness. She tarried by monuments celebrating the writers Balzac and Proust and Oscar Wilde, the composer Chopin, and the rocker Jim Morrison. She strolled among the headstones and sepulchres forming a city of shrines, the lanes and family vaults dating back centuries. The graveyard was cheery with flowers sprouting among stone effigies of prone corpses and lively skeletons immortalized in marble.

And a very lively *monsieur* to help her find her way.

"*Salut*," he'd said as he approached her standing still in the crowd exiting the grounds. "Are you lost?"

"Not anymore." She tried out her French: "*Je m'appelle Sybil.*"

"*Et moi, Luc.* Pleased to meet you." His accent was adorable and his smile smouldered. Sybil pushed aside his extended hand and bent forward to administer the famous French cheek-kiss greeting. In polite society this was reserved for more intimate relationships, but she fully intended to have one of those with this gorgeous specimen.

Luc grinned with boyish charm. "Why are you hanging around a graveyard?"

"I might ask the same." She swept her bangs aside and, extending the movement, traced her lips, Luc's eyes following her finger. Already the chemistry between them pulsed. "For me, it's the atmosphere here."

"Then I insist you join me in a visit to the Catacombs." Moments later on the crowded train, they stood within each other's breath, until Luc warned, "Next stop."

The hairdresser interrupted Sybil's memories to rinse. Then, as she snipped away and gabbled about her kids, Sybil slipped away again to dream about the hallowed halls of the underworld. Luc drew her towards the threshold of the Catacombs to descend into the pit—an ossuary of quarries honeycombed beneath the city. Carved into the rock above the entrance was a phrase beginning *Arrête!* and Luc hissed to her its meaning in English: *Halt! This is the Empire of the Dead.*

They plunged downwards into the deep gloom, trailing along rough corridors hewn out of limestone oozing with moisture. They burst into first one chamber and then another, met by the dancing shadows of stacked-up bones and skulls bleached by the centuries, the mouldering decay of decomposition having had its way long ago. It was positively macabre. They followed the pathways, flickering lamps in the abyss dimly lighting plaques upon which were written epitaphs of verse and prose in a French beyond Sybil's grasp, and in Latin, and in another language she couldn't identify—maybe Italian?

Soon she had Luc translating them to her in his exotic whisper: *It is among these tombs that time and death come to cross their scythes* and *Believe that each day is your last.* Every ominous declaration brought another palpitation, delectable because of Luc's very flesh-and-blood presence: *It is by demonic malice that death has entered the world.* At every vocalization, Luc pressed closer to her. *Pale death knocks indiscriminately at the doors of the cottages of paupers and the palaces of kings.*

Of course, Sybil couldn't agree with the sentiments, believing as she did that "death" is only a doorway to the next life and the ones following. That each individual's soul determines its own rebirths according to spiritual needs. That love is the ultimate lesson to learn in every cycle of incarnation. The archaic words served to remind her that death is only an illusion.

In salon after salon, the bones of the deceased were piled high, one atop the other and close as wooden matches in a box. Femur and tibia aligned with humerus and fibula—terms rushing back to Sybil from high school—the domes of crania wedged in between like sulphurous tips about to ignite.

If you have ever seen a man die, always consider that the same fate awaits you.

But Sybil felt the presence of tarrying spirits winking at her through empty eye sockets. She peered back through them into eternity.

Where is death? Always future or past. Hardly is she present before she is already gone.

At every opportunity the pair would duck into an alcove or slide behind a pillar of bones to read yet another maxim. And at every interpretation Sybil would curl herself closer to Luc's body and try to disbelieve what she'd long ago decided to be false.

At death, we leave everything.

They spent much longer than the mile-long subterranean maze demanded, sneaking off from the authorized trail to squeeze into yet another passageway, interlocking fingers with damp palms tight, Luc's lips grazing Sybil's neck, sensuality coupling with trepidation to birth gooseflesh all over her body.

The sting of death is sin . . . Precious in His sight is the death of the saints.

And each cavern with another pile of skeletal remains brought more poetry calling out to her as she prompted Luc to read the inscriptions, horrified at them yet drawn to them.

Come, people of the world, come into these silent mansions. Then will your soul be struck by the quiet voice that rises from within: "It is here that the greatest of masters, the Tomb, holds his school of truth."

When at last they emerged from the womb of the earth onto the streets of Paris, the sun was hiding herself behind a massive thundercloud so that the early dusk came upon them like a storm as they made their way through the cobbled streets to the

Frenchman's apartment.

On that trip to Paris, Sybil found fear to be a powerful aphrodisiac.

Souvenir is French for "recollection," and Sybil left France with the souvenir of Luc. Yes, she recalled him quite regularly, even as she strove to forget the out-dated cenotaph readings that imprinted her psyche and repelled her with their magnetism. She tried to keep the paramour separate from the proverbs, but she never quite succeeded.

Sybil left the hair shop a new woman, almost not recognizing herself. She'd taken time for eyelash extensions, too, and determined to wear her sequined number and her highest heels for Iggy. After all, she'd sort of ignored him after the movie with Clive. Iggy liked her to dress up, and she did enjoy titillating him now and again—not a difficult task when his wife was such a home-bound drudge who thought a good time meant spritzing on cologne before going to choir practice. Not a difficult task at all when Sybil had spent the afternoon with her travel memories.

CHAPTER EIGHTEEN

Seven days ago

Strong arms encircled Paige from behind.

"Hey, sweetie," Danny said, "want to take a Sunday afternoon nap with me?"

"You startled me." She'd been slouching over her research, and the wind outside—and her concentration—must have muffled his approach. She twisted around to face him, her belly more in the way this week than last. "I only wish I could nap." Her voice sounded whiny even to her ears. "I have so much left to do today if I want to keep on schedule. Will sandwiches be enough for supper?"

"Don't sweat it. I'll barbeque." He pulled her to a standing position and gave her a long kiss. "I'm missing you, Paige."

"I'll be back in full swing once this thesis is submitted."

"Really?" Danny dropped his arms. "I'm afraid your perfectionism won't allow you down time in the few weeks between submission date and the baby's due date. You sure do a thorough job of whatever project's got your attention." He moved away to look out the window.

"I've been too focused on the research, I know." Paige's apology rang hollow to her own ears. "I suspect my paper is acceptable as I have it now, but my contribution to the literature could be so much greater if only I had more time."

"Time is not in our hands."

Paige nodded. He was right, especially when it came to gestation—in either the academy or the uterus. He went on, "You want to do a thorough job, but it's looking like overkill to me. Some things are more important than educational accomplishment."

She joined him at the window and looked straight into his face. "That's easy for you to say. You finished your degree in agriculture and have found your identity in farming. It satisfies you."

"I do this for you. For *us*." His shoulders drooped.

"I didn't mean offense, Danny." His sacrifice was for the sake of the family—not only for her and Baby but for his own parents, who were too tired to carry on the farming much longer. "And I don't mean I'm not satisfied with life, because I am. I'm just not sure where I belong right now, in the classroom or the nursery. I want to finish one thing before I start the next."

"Who says you can't do both?" Danny took her hand, brushed his lips against her knuckles. "Anyway, accomplishments aren't what give us value."

"I know," she said. Did she?

"And your standard of excellence is going to carry you through all sorts of life events. Be patient with yourself." He kissed the tip of her nose. He was a good man, and he knew how to lift her mood even when her hormones raged.

"I don't want to quit in the middle, that's for sure. I don't care if I don't work at the mansion after this tour season. I'm even looking forward to having Baby as my main responsibility." In fact, Paige had been feeling increasingly less threatened about this perceived loss of identity so common among the young professionals she knew who were resisting the commitment of marriage and all it entailed. Perhaps the hormonal surges were softening her towards impending motherhood. Whatever the cause, she was beginning to sense the personality of this child growing within. But scholarly pride had its place as well, and so she added, "However, the record needs to be set straight about MDM. If only he'd been clearer in those letters so I could use them as verification of his integrity. The world needs to know the truth about him."

"Such passion," Danny teased. "Seriously, I love your commitment to knowledge. And, you know, you'll always be the resident expert in this community, whether you work out of the museum or go on with studies to eventually teach in the city as 'Dr. Paulsson.' Either way, you're going to be a terrific mother." He patted her abdomen and then knelt down to put his ear against its taut surface just as Baby kicked. Danny laughed.

"He's been giving my ribs a real beating today." Hunching over her keyboard or reaching for printed documents scattered around her on the floor crowded the little guy, and now she stretched her arms high to give them both room. Danny drew her up onto the couch for a quick cuddle before he went to the basement freezer to fetch steaks to thaw.

Paige's situation was less like a crossroads now. Danny always put things in perspective for her and re-established the emotional tone of the household when her disposition set things topsy-turvy. Lately he even did that for Baby; last night when she awoke, her back aching with all the child's tossing and turning, Danny's deep voice hummed endearments that calmed Baby as though he was already under the influence of his daddy's commanding presence. Danny would make a wonderful father.

Paige's mind turned to her research in comparing her husband to the less tangible "other man" in her life. MDM would have made a wonderful father, as well, she was sure. She clicked her laptop awake and inspected the wallpaper she'd installed over the weekend—a rare color photo of MDM she'd found in the ever-surprising archives, taken by a Brownie camera in the fifties. He'd have been at least eighty-five years of age.

MDM perched on his wing chair like a king on his throne, like a royal who, after having made a proclamation to his nation, sits down with the authority of one whose unalterable word has been spoken. His eyes were the variegated golden-brown of the beads on the amber teething necklace Paige had gotten as a baby gift from a fellow graduate student at the university. In the photograph, MDM stared into the camera, the heavy folds of his lids giving an impression of great wisdom and even sadness—except for the glimmer of a smile peeking out amidst his mass of facial hair. His brows and beard and moustache still held a tinge of gold, a vestige of the glorious red that would completely disappear before his death.

Perhaps MDM's air of nobility had earned him the title "Pioneer Prince of Pembina County," according to a governmental tract recruiting back-country frontiersmen for North Dakota. It described him as a mercantile leader who became rich and made others rich along the way, a captain who led others in his procession against injustice, an empathetic servant who gave up his own traditions to leave a new heritage for his fellow man. The famed vigor of his youth was still apparent to Paige in this photo on her screen. He had about him a bearing of sovereignty.

Paige pulled herself away from her reveries to dig back into her thesis for the next few hours. Before she called it a day, she checked her e-mail. Her academic advisor had written to ask about their next meeting. Consulting her calendar, she set a date with him and then, before arising to toss a salad for supper, she revisited the last question received from the anonymous

THE RED JOURNAL

Gramsgirl. She tapped out a couple of lines:

> *Sorry for the delay in my reply. I checked the records and found there was, indeed, once a porch swing that hung near the front door, but it was removed in the late 1960s.*

Paige learned yesterday that the old rattan porch swing had been stored in the mansion attic ever since, eventually pressed again into service—perhaps by the Farris-Yeast teenagers living there?—as a casual couch on the floor in a cluttered corner, unrecognizable as a swing and partially hidden now with a horsehair blanket thrown over it. Paige would never have realized its original purpose if not for the e-mailer's question.

She bit her thumbnail. How had Gramsgirl known about the porch swing in the first place, and why would it matter to her? Straight-out asking might spook the writer, and so Paige took her time in drafting the rest of the e-mail, keeping it a light invitation. Her job and delight was to promote the public's historical knowledge of Kirkton and of the Laird Mansion Museum, in particular—enough of a reason to answer with care. But beyond that, the evasive Gramsgirl caught her interest, although she wasn't sure why, and she didn't want to lose the connection.

Paige reread the original question. She'd found no "dark brown, buttoned leather cushion" described by Gramsgirl, only a shredded, canvas-covered pad fitting the dimensions of the white wicker bench.

But something niggled at Paige. She looked again at the uploaded photo on her computer screen of MDM in his den, with the edges of his chair barely showing up against a backdrop of dark paneling. She pictured the chestnut leather, button-back, scroll-armed chair still squatting in its full glory at the heart of the mansion, where MDM spent his later years alone in contemplation as he rested from his lifetime of work. It was a grand piece, imposing in size within the small room that held only one other piece of furniture: the matching footstool.

A tremor hit Paige at the thought of the secret inside that footstool positioned before that throne in that inner sanctuary. The den with its majestic two-part furnishing was the grand finale on her mansion tour, the hub of the whole house, and, she suspected, the key to her remaining uncertainties about the life of Moses David Melchizedek Laird.

She scrutinized the photo. Then she gasped.

The covering of the mammoth, buttoned, chestnut brown leather chair and its matching ottoman corresponded exactly with the description given by Gramsgirl of the porch swing cushion! She must have gotten the two mixed up. Could she have seen the inner den and confused the seating there with the outside swing?

Questions leapt into Paige's mind, but she wouldn't risk scaring off the Minneapolis e-mailer, so she sent her answer as written. Hopefully it would stimulate further communication.

Libby's feet were sore from standing in the kitchen and serving line at the Haven. It was the first Sunday evening in a long while she'd come back to lend a hand. The staff wore relieved smiles when she walked in, and many of the residents had a word of welcome. But the population had changed even in the past three months. She heard the same stories over and over from the old gals—very few men lived at the Haven—who were still able to line up for their buffet choices, about how one friend finally succumbed to the Alzheimer's and how another was found in her room taken by a stroke.

Now the last of the diners, in wheelchairs or hooked to oxygen tanks, were fed and watered, some of them asking for a bowl of the test soup she'd made before the weekend and lugged over to the Haven in Gram's eight-quart kettle. They still expected her to bring a taste of homemade comfort from her apartment fridge, as she and Gram had done for so long. One of these days the staff would tell her health regulations prohibited her from bringing in food from outside the facility, but for the moment they turned a blind eye. Maybe they sensed Libby's need to give as much as the residents' need to receive.

Libby leaned against the wall by the door and let her vision skip, like a stone over water, across the silvery heads as the old folks chatted quietly, one or two still agile enough to crochet, several being fed the last of their vanilla pudding by aides with aprons. How many more inmates were confined to their rooms?

She couldn't avoid comparing the depressing panorama in this bare-bones dining room to the swanky ambience of the Belle Hotel's restaurant full of high-end clients taking part in yesterday's benefit for the hungry. How ironic that none of the Haven's residents, let alone the city's street people, ate the sort of fare conjured up by the workshop magicians—the exquisite *avgolemono* or lavender-scented salmon bisque—even though the Belle's stated purpose was raising funds to feed the poor. Chef Virgil's high-minded philosophy of soup translated into nourished bellies only by way of tax-deductible donations from the soup-sipping wealthy.

Was Libby's own approach any more moral? Her attempt in making Babette's Bowl for the purpose of quelling her hunger pangs for Gram did, in fact, result in a sort of consumable product—her soup was being eaten by Gram's friends at the moment, after all. But Libby's involvement in the sophisticated seminar for the purpose of finding the rustic recipe from her youth was almost a paradox. She spent money on high-end culinary training to learn how to save money on her forgotten, homey recipe so that money could be spent on subsistence programs to feed those with neither home nor money. Gram grew up on that soup, and then made it for Libby, and then some form of it had entered the mouths of the gourmands in the Belle, opening their pockets to stock the breadlines for the poorest of the city's poor. Wasn't that process convoluted?

The recipe Gram cooked up for Libby, lost now in time, had almost certainly gone through various stages of evolution and devolution since its inception. If Libby hadn't discovered its ingredients after all her own rigorous experimentation and the tutelage of a world-renowned chef, how could she ever recreate the real thing?

"Nice to see you again." At the words, Libby brought her attention back to her surroundings and the sprightly senior in a floral dress standing before her. "I don't think I told you last time how sorry I am for your loss."

"Thank you," Libby said.

"Your grandmother always encouraged me with just the right words. She'd say to me, 'Keep your chin up' or 'Tomorrow is another day.' It boosted me."

"And how's your arthritis, Mrs. Lundberg?"

"Oh, no worse than can be expected."

"You're looking well." Libby gave her a hug.

"Your soup sure reminded me of Babette." The lady's eyes misted over. "She's gone on to her rest now."

Libby slumped back towards her flat, longing again for the hopefulness Gram always expressed after their joint visits to the Haven. She saw the silver lining to every cloud. What little Gram had, she gave away, serving up soup and sympathy to her fellow elders out of the abundance of her heart.

But Libby was not giving out of a plentiful inner resource. She was only trying to expunge her repugnance for the less fortunate—the aged in wheelchairs awaiting death or the homeless in torn sleeping bags—and maybe work off her week-old guilt over rejecting the plight of that stinky bag lady who just wouldn't leave her conscience, or her memory, alone.

Red Journal entry, dated April 4, 1916:

My Heart,

Today marks twenty-five years since I took you as my bride, when we entered the covenant of marriage as partakers of such a blessed calling; for matrimony delivered us both—you from the state of orphanhood as much as me to the state of belonging.

Having tasted of this heavenly gift and labored in love alongside me on behalf of your outcast People, you now forfeit their joy. Would that you could see their exultation as they attain this same deliverance from alienation unto communion one with the other, and with the government insofar as I am able to make intercession for them. Dislodged and banished, the People now find their home in the refuge of our estate at Kirkton; spurned and forsaken, they now prosper in one accord as true family.

Yet you wander, and for almost two decades have I yearned for your homecoming. My Heart, I am persuaded of better things for you who, through faith and patience, might obtain the promises you have inherited.

In full assurance of hope I remain, as ever, Yours Truly

CHAPTER NINETEEN

Six days ago

Monday started off sweetly enough for Libby. She didn't even read on the bus ride, taken up instead with watching a giggly little girl playing peek-a-boo with her grandfather, his white wisps mixing in with her yellow curls every time he drew her close for a hug. Libby talked to him herself, silently, as though the old fellow were her own: Hold my hand, Daddy; Kiss my cheek. But the morning deteriorated when she got to work.

She opened Hearsay before Terence arrived in his usual sulk and then faced his wrath over her clearance pricing of the homemade jams Alana had ordered before she left him, as though Libby was personally responsible for his misery in both marriage and business.

Next she wasted her fifteen-minute break over at Amulets subjected to Sybil's account of the vision she'd had during her Qigong meditation session the previous night—something about a Sufi mystic spouting Kabbalistic teachings to a statue of Vishnu. The girl's wanton blending of belief systems got to be a bit much at times. Libby was used to Sybil's wacky thought patterns, but this vision was over the top.

"What do you mean, it involved me?" she asked.

"I received a warning. A prophetic message." Sybil stood at her till, counting a stack of twenty-dollar bills. "I was told you need to search out your emancipation with fear and trembling."

Libby scoffed. "That's ridiculous." Emancipation from what?

"You're pretty judgmental." Sybil's lip curled. "How can you deny my personal experiences when you're so closed to trying anything new yourself?"

"And how can you say you've got the answer to my life?"

They'd had this discussion before. Sybil would next chastise her for lack of mindfulness or advise her to chew fresh *ashwagandha* root to nourish her spirit. Her proselytizing urges knew no bounds; she'd once dragged Libby to a meeting where a kundalini practitioner caused hideous spasms in his followers as their awakening serpents uncoiled. It was plain creepy.

Today Sybil dismissed Libby's objections by tipping her nose into the air and saying, "You need to let your inner voice guide you, and to watch for road signs pointing the way to your destiny. Which means you really do need to go on a trip with me to find a sacred space of your own."

No wonder that, given her boss's mood and her friend's harping, this morning Libby's stomach was tied in knots even before she spotted the patrol car driving up to Hearsay. At least the lights weren't flashing this time. Libby dropped her cleaning cloth and scampered to the shop door to intercept the officer and forestall any scene that might attract her boss's attention. But when she saw the second officer open the vehicle's back door, and the passenger swing out scrawny legs to emerge from its interior, she froze with her hand on the knob.

"What's going on?" Terence's yelp broke her spell and she whirled around to face him, shifting her body to block his view of the curbside gathering.

"I don't know. I'm sure it's nothing." But that third person stepping out of the police car almost sent her over the edge.

"Get out of my way." Terence had barely grated his words past his teeth before the shop's entry bells clanged into service and the silhouette of the policeman from last week filled the breadth of the frame.

"Ms. Walker, would you step outside, please?" He raised his hand against her boss. "No, sir, this doesn't concern you." The scowl Terence shot Libby before returning to his desk in the back indicated he'd be sure to make it his concern later, when he got her alone.

The old woman, elbow gripped by the second officer, stood beside the front fender. Her head was bowed and her gray hair tied back, no longer an untamed mop tentacling out from beneath a grubby cap. Libby faced the shop so as to turn her back to the street—to the woman.

"You didn't return our calls." Officer Garcia frowned.

"Right. Sorry, my weekend was pretty full."

"We have a situation needing your attention." Her attention? Libby heard the woman's movement behind her.

"I thought this was all taken care of." Libby's hands locked into fists. "My boss isn't pressing charges." Terence had declared that the recompense wouldn't be worth his bother, so the situation concerning the vandalism had nothing more to do with her. The police had removed the woman from the scene and incarcerated her for disorderly conduct. That should be the end of the story, as far as Libby was concerned. So what was their official business with her now?

The officer's facial features softened. "Our interest is of a more personal nature. Please join me by the vehicle." Libby made herself turn around, commanded her legs to step.

"That's her." The old woman muttered her words towards the sidewalk. Then she lifted her chin, and dread fused Libby's spine.

She couldn't have taken her eyes off the crone if she'd wanted to.

Officer Garcia said, "Our investigation has traced the subject's recent move from California, where she's got quite a history with the LAPD for public intoxication and, further back, for solicitation." The woman shrugged off the restraining hand of the second officer and limped forward until her nose was six inches from Libby's.

"That's her, all right. The first time I seen her, I knew it." The breath was free of alcohol now, and the voice deep and raspy but not angry. Instead it held an emotion Libby couldn't identify—didn't want to identify. Her belly churned in visceral denial and she swallowed back sour stomach juices.

Garcia took his hand out of his pocket and opened his palm. "We have papers for you to sign down at the station regarding the perpetrator's care arrangements."

"What does her care have to do with me?" Libby wanted to vomit. She knew the answer to her question. "You threw her in the drunk tank and she's sober now. Just put her back on the street."

Silence settled onto the group for a moment, and Libby didn't know where to look. Then Officer Garcia, in a conciliatory tone, said, "Ms. Walker, this woman is physically weak and in need of medical attention. As she maintains you are her next of kin, we naturally thought you—"

"Next of kin?" Libby's forehead broke out in sweat.

"And she had this *Tribune* clipping, dated four years ago, on her person, as well—a photo of you with her own mother." He held it out.

Libby didn't grace it with so much as a look. She gritted her teeth. "You must be mistaken. I don't know this woman."

But she did. Libby did.

And then Elsa spoke her daughter's name. She uttered it in a quavering voice this time, through those wrinkled lips with the bit of saliva clinging to the corner.

"Libby." The old sot blinked her bleary eyes. "Libby, it's me. It's your mom."

The words, spoken so brokenly, echoed like thunder in Libby's shrinking soul. Her hands flew up of their own accord to cover her ears against the memory of her mother screeching at Gram in a long-ago fit of rage, demanding nonexistent money, shrieking for what was rightfully hers, bitterly wailing, "Where's your heart?" so that tears leaked down Gram's cheeks and Libby cowered against the overblown emotions hurled like wayward projectiles against the curtain of callus she'd layered up to protect herself.

She stood like that, hands over ears and gaping at Elsa, until the officer prodded her arm. "We need a signature to have her released under your supervision with custodial obligations." Garcia adjusted his cap. "If you'd like to make arrangements to—"

"You don't understand." Libby turned towards him, coughing back the acidic phlegm in her throat. "I reject any responsibility. I have no obligation to this woman, and I don't believe you can legally force her on me."

Libby swiveled on her heel and stomped back through Hearsay's door, swinging it shut behind her so that the whole shop filled with a ringing racket. She jerked the offending chimes off their moorings and threw them onto the floor, Terence looking on with fury twisting his face.

Across the pavement from Hearsay Card and Gift Boutique, Sybil took in the goings-on through the window of Amulets. She grabbed a packet of sugar-free gum from the counter display—a new product imported from the Caribbean, made from the sapodilla tree and flavored with organic cinnamon—and unwrapped it as she watched the spectacle unfolding outside.

So Libby was in trouble with the cops. Maybe karma was catching up with her for consistently resisting good advice. Take their visit this morning; the way she ignored the clear direction of Sybil's dream proved her foolishness. Sybil didn't have such visions often, so the spirit world must be raring to get hold of Libby. A dream, after all, is the hidden door to the sanctum of the soul, as Carl Jung put it—or was that Brigham Young? Whoever the author, he understood metaphysical revelation through the subconscious.

Across the street, Libby tossed her hands up and spun away from the old woman, and then she crossed her arms over her chest. What was their connection? But Sybil knew Libby didn't like connections. Take her ridiculous action on Friday night, bailing out on the date when she could have scored big time. Clive was getting cold feet even though Sybil coached him not to give up. He might still sell Libby on the condo unit in her complex. And if it would be through romance, well, so much the better for frigid old Libby. She could do worse than hooking up with a guy like Iggy's cousin. But Clive couldn't be blamed for his doubt. From what Sybil could tell, Libby wasn't giving him much hope of either a realty sale or a good-time romp. The longer Libby resisted Clive, the more Sybil adored his cute persistence.

Voyeurism pushed Sybil out into the street to join the hubbub just as Libby stormed back into the card shop. What mischief was this? Sybil approached one of the policemen.

"Officer, can I be of any help?"

She was dying to know what the kerfuffle was all about. The old lady bowed her neck until the other cop guided her into the car's back seat. The main officer stared in the direction of Libby's retreat and then closed and pocketed his notepad, still without acknowledging Sybil's presence. She had no way of interpreting the incident that had just played out. The direct approach was needed.

"My name's Sybil Tansey. I own the shop over there. Do you need a witness for anything?"

"Thanks," the officer said, "but this isn't a public matter."

"Libby Walker is a good friend of mine." Sybil glanced into the darkened car glass but couldn't see the face of the passenger. She turned back to the short but muscular cop, definitely her type. Most men were. "I'm sure there must be information I could give you about the situation."

The officer paused at that, maybe thinking of asking her if she knew the old broad or maybe thinking of asking her out for dinner. She stepped closer, and he answered all stiff and businesslike, "No, but we do appreciate your concern."

"You know where to find me if you change your mind and need to ask anything. Anything at all." The guy pretended not to hear her—he really was quite adorable—and she blew a kiss at him while his colleague in the front seat, door opened, outright laughed. It was such fun to tease.

But, nosiness unabated, Sybil entered Hearsay and walked

right into the middle of a storm. Libby stood with both arms thrust out and palms fending off Terence, who was straining forward with a mottled face, his neck sinewy.

"This is the final straw," Terence shouted, pounding a fist into his thigh. "You're dragging my business into the gutter. The cops are harassing me because of a drunk you tell me is claiming to be your mother. What do I care about your personal life?"

Sybil cranked her head around to look at Libby. What was this about a mother?

Terence continued his tirade. "I can't balance the books that miserable Alana left me, no thanks to you." His spittle sprayed. In a culminating crescendo, he bellowed at Libby, "You are fired. Get out of my sight!"

He marched towards the back of the card shop, the striking of his boot heels on the floor causing the glass shelves to rattle. He disappeared into his office, and Libby's purse came flying down the aisle from the back, knocking cards off their perch. Sybil picked it up because Libby, with pasty face and fixed stare, wasn't moving.

Before he slammed his office door, Terence again howled, "Out!"

Libby stood immobile on the street corner beside Hearsay, clutching her purse to her chest, a wave of internal heat flushing her whole body. She couldn't make out Sybil's words coming at her in a low purr. She stumbled as Sybil steered her into the café, where a sip of espresso burned her tongue and brought her back to her senses.

"I'm finished." Libby teared up.

"The miserable cur, to dump you like that."

"He warned me. I should have listened." But Libby couldn't have done anything to stop the termination. She'd been working on borrowed time ever since Alana left Terence. She pushed her fist into her stomach to stop the jabbing pain in her gut, but the panic kept building. She slopped her coffee over the rim.

Sybil cupped Libby's hand with her own and it helped to stop the shaking.

"That man should be shot," Sybil said. "He's a misogynist pig. Let's launch a suit against him."

"It's no use." Libby dropped her chin. Losing her job wasn't the worst of it; she'd pick up work elsewhere. But what horrible timing. How would she meet the mortgage conditions now? And as for her *mother* . . . Libby shuddered.

For the next half hour Libby wept out her concerns, and it was good to have Sybil's ear if not her interjected and relentless advice. Libby worried aloud about missing out on the mortgage and ending up homeless, and Sybil offered to lend her money towards renting the condo in her complex. No, Libby declined, she was anxious to find a real home and settle down. Sybil insisted that her offer of a ticket to Tibet was still on, that Libby could join her in beating the mundane realities of life—beat death itself— by seeking the sacred through travel. When Libby tried again, admitting out loud that she felt lonely and unloved and silently blaming the lack of a father, Sybil made cooing sounds and mentioned something about Clive being able to fix that.

In the end, Libby couldn't force herself to face the question of Elsa's return from the dead, let alone discuss it. And when she didn't bring it up, Sybil did.

"Is that old bag lady really your mother?"

Libby shook her head back and forth, her chin brushing the top button of her blouse. "I can't believe it." She didn't *want* to believe it. This was not her idea of how to redeem a sense of family.

"Well, she looked a lot better without the shopping cart and with her hair tamed, if I do say so myself." Sybil smoothed her own bangs—today a tiny fringe held back with a barrette. "Maybe she's changed."

"You have no clue what I went through as a child," Libby said, astonishing herself. She'd never brought this up before.

"Do tell." Sybil leaned forward.

Libby fiddled with her spoon. "You come from a real family, with parents and siblings and cousins." She didn't mean to sound jealous, but she'd put her foot in it now and might as well confess. "I never even had a real mother, Sybil. She was one sick drunk from the beginning. Never mind the boyfriends; she abandoned me completely. If it hadn't been for Gram, I'd have ended up in foster care, which would have been better than what Elsa could give me, anyway. Gram and I thought she was long dead."

"No wonder you dumped her, then."

"Well, I wouldn't use the word 'dump' . . ." Yet wasn't that what Libby had just done?

"She's a huge liability," Sybil said.

Libby nodded reluctantly. She took in a lungful of air and exhaled slowly. "I should forget about the whole thing with her. Elsa's made her own bed and she should lie in it." Had Gram said that? No, never about Elsa.

"As for coming from a huge family, lucky me." Sybil rolled

her eyes. "But if it's family you're needing, I've always thought about you as a kind of mother."

"Me?"

"Nothing to do with the age difference, of course. You could as easily be my sister or, for that matter, my great-granddaughter born again from a past life. You and I are true kindred spirits."

Sybil prattled on ridiculously, and the sound of it pacified Libby for the moment. Getting stuff off her chest hadn't helped after all, and her complaining only left her feeling soiled. Of course, she'd never given Sybil details about her early life and the events landing her in a child psychologist's office. Acute stress, dissociative amnesia, and sleep problems had plagued her off and on for years after Gram took her in. She'd learned how to numb those emotional responses long ago and now wished she could retain the sense of distance from her past. In the end, airing her concerns didn't take care of her very real problems. Sybil's show of support, directive as it was, left her unsure about how loyal a friend Sybil really was.

Before catching the bus, for the first time riding it homeward in the morning rather than at evening rush hour, Libby bought a newspaper, and not this time for the realty section. She had to find a job, and quickly. She'd give her résumé immediate attention when she got back to her computer, and meanwhile she might as well spend her commute time constructively.

CHAPTER TWENTY

Today

Paige, bellied up against the railing, overlooks the great hall on the main floor below. She's enjoying her first full tour of the season, though her legs ache already from the burden she carries. The group is larger than most that will show up throughout the summer, with school now still in session, but it's still tidy enough that everyone will hear her explanations and she can assess each reaction. She loves when they ask questions.

The group mills towards her from the area of the bedchambers. The older two ladies are keeping up the pace despite puffing. In an accent pleasant to the ear, the Australian couple converses about the quality of American craftsmanship. The teacher has been clicking away on his cell phone—likely saving material for a classroom quiz—despite the distraction of the woman with teal-blue extensions and the crazy outfit, whose more reserved companion seems engrossed in every detail of the tour. Are the students catching on to her own fascination with the story of MDM?

History is such a living organism. It keeps on thriving and growing, whether a person is ready for it or not. She pats her tummy.

Paige enjoys her role as guide—as, in a way, mouthpiece for MDM himself. But bringing knowledge to life for others demands first learning the subject matter inside out, in this case the details of the luminary's life. As a researcher, Paige is a listener first; she's been listening for the voice of the old gent through the documentation he's left behind in all sorts of records and writings and registers, and through his estate's architecture and art and atmosphere. And then she passes it on to interested parties.

But lately her commitment to piecing together the historical elements of MDM's life has been replacing the reality of her own living. Danny says her head is so up in the clouds of research that sometimes she can't see where to plant her feet on the ground. He's got a point. MDM certainly wouldn't have approved of learning at the expense of living; he saw education not as self-fulfillment but as a means to the end of improving the wellbeing of those in his care.

Three teen girls, wearing matching emerald eye shadow probably applied in the bus after leaving home, sidle up to Paige. The one in the front asks, "Was the guy who lived here married?"

"Well, we've never found proof that MDM had a wife."

"Why would he make the place so pretty, then?"

"Yeah," the second one chimes in. "My mom would kill for a house like this."

Paige answers, "There's lots of evidence of women residing here—the housekeepers and their female children, for starters. But it's part of the mystery surrounding Kirkton's history."

"She rhymed." The third girl giggles. "Mystery—history." They titter and move away. Paige is not so easily satisfied.

Maybe, before leaving the master bedroom, she should have brought up MDM's marital status, a frequent tourist question she hasn't answered herself yet. Of course, unanswered questions are what fuel research, and she's normally glad for them. But having just submitted her thesis manuscript for approval, she can't afford to push much further into this uncharted area or she'll risk jeopardizing her whole project. If only she could fill in the blanks of MDM's interpersonal life.

But she's been so careful all along not to introduce problems into her research that she has no way of countering—issues of, say, economic interaction between rival fur-trading companies, or the role of the Scottish colonists in the Red River Settlement up north. Or political realities of the government's assimilation policies forcing Native Americans onto reservations and away from the "vagaries of the hunt," as one historian had put it. No, Paige has followed her advisory committee's direction to keep her focus narrow and save content for future doctoral studies. Shifting the lens of her research at this late date would be unfeasible.

But the question of MDM's marital status is pivotal to her work. Why have a "master bedroom" if there is no bride to share the bower, no heir proceeding forth from it? Where is MDM's family line? Of course, Paige knows the answer or, at least, the official answer: MDM is the end of the Reverend Uriah Laird's line. Anecdotal sources imply the existence of illegitimate children from Native American women—the fact that some colonists bedded the locals was well established in the literature—but Paige has found no formal evidence of this in the life of MDM.

Yet she's sure she hasn't discovered all elements in this line of inquiry. The beauty of the mansion, the care taken in its design and execution, the choice of furnishings such as the Russian sleigh bed all speak of subjective, even romantic, intent. What greater reason can a man have for building such a home than enduring love for a woman and the prospect of posterity? The validity of a legal marriage would be of fundamental concern if MDM had left behind any children. Indeed, it's of fundamental concern to the courts right now, what with the ongoing Farris-Yeast lawsuit.

Paige's musing is interrupted by a soft moan beside her. The quiet woman—Libby?—approaches the banister and leans over with a dancer's posture, her necklace swinging free like a plumb line. She's riveted on the view below. Paige studies her regal profile and aquiline nose. Throughout the tour, she's carried herself with dignity, in dramatic contrast to her companion, craning to hear Paige over the noisy kids and examining every detail upon entering a new area. Her few comments, murmured to her friend, intimate she knows more than she's letting on. She must have read up on the museum, but it's not just her evident background knowledge that catches Paige's attention. Something about her vocabulary, the way she uses a particular word—what is it, now?—tweaks a memory, but Paige can't quite place it.

Yes, there's more than meets the eye about Libby.

Sybil's had almost as much history as she can take. With the inspiration of her travel title, *Sybil's Sensual Search for Sacred Spaces*, still fresh in her mind, she pushes through the bottleneck of kids. Her book's a marvelous idea to float past Libby, an excuse to get her back on track about coming along to Tibet. Now where has she gone?

Sybil enters the hallway to find her friend staring out beyond a balcony over a huge, open area below.

"Don't jump," Sybil quips. But Libby doesn't respond. Sybil taps her shoulder. As in a trance, in slow motion, Libby twists her head around but doesn't seem to see her even now.

The light in her eyes! Sybil stumbles backward under that beatific expression of faraway yearning, forgetting what she was going to ask. Would Libby hear her anyway? Something supernatural is obviously happening here. Sybil's felt it herself many times, although not at the moment. Not in this old house, which isn't even haunted according to the tour guide.

What is it, then, that possesses Libby?

Maybe the museum is situated on a ley line Sybil hasn't heard of. After all, North Dakota resonates with the vibrant spirituality left behind by early tribes, whose ceremonial grounds surround them here. The founder of Kirkton might have intuitively chosen this geographic site because it aligned with a power apex, perhaps the gravitational anomaly of the Montana Vortex just to the west. Sybil had been intrigued by its inexplicable force when she visited.

She breaks a piece of diet-friendly pomegranate chewing gum out of its blister pack and then situates herself in a corner to watch Libby and to reminisce about her last visit to the Wild West.

Sybil had made a proper pilgrimage of it by visiting the site of a buffalo jump, where for two millennia herds of the beasts were stampeded over cliffs onto waiting spears below. Thirteen feet of compacted bison bones at the base of the canyon attested to the provision of the spirit world for the people of that culture. Talk about history. Then Sybil cleansed herself in a sweat lodge. From a chieftain's daughter—not some white-skinned tour guide dolled up as a parlor maid—she learned the story of how the Great Spirit turned a hump of dirt into the first buffalo. And she heard about the buffalo stone, a medicine object that sang out from among the sagebrush a song that called the bison to the slaughter. She partook in a smudging ceremony, the sacred smoke of braided sweetgrass—the hair of Mother Earth—fanning out over her in a purifying and healing ritual that took her into a meditative state of self-consciousness.

After Montana, Sybil had flown down to Arizona to experience a vortex on yet another ley line in the mesh crisscrossing America. The vibrant colors of Sedona's Cathedral Rock and the healing waters of Oak Creek formed the perfect coupling of geology and metaphysics for the true seeker walking in the ways of the aboriginal people. Up close and personal, Sybil studied the desert through the three themes of flora, fauna, and faith. First, the flora of mesquite and yucca, prickly pear and hedgehog cactus tied her to the physical realities of the sacred space. Then, the fauna of Gila monster and coyote, tarantula and rattlesnake communed with the shared life force in her.

Finally, her faith soared when she'd had her soul mapped by a descendent of a powerful Hopi shaman who had direct access to the Great Spirit, and who was also a passionate lover. Later she bathed her feet in waters from a well sacred to the Yavapai Nation and sat mesmerized before the Singua cliff dwellings. To top the trip off, she followed a path to the divine feminine while treading a seven-circuit rock labyrinth that reminded her of the hedge maze in the gardens at Versailles—all of that ageless wisdom converging for a moment in the center of her own being, the synergy of the ages released to enrich her own vitality.

Arizona had reinforced Sybil's perception of the interconnectedness of life, perhaps symbolized best of all by the Medicine Wheel. Its cross represented balance and its circle denoted the flowing energies of the universe—the thread of consciousness linking a vortex in one American state to a labyrinth in another, a mystical meditation in a medieval garden in France to the dharma wheel atop a temple in Tibet.

She nods to herself. Yes, the made-in-America Medicine Wheel presents a perfect example of the oneness of life—body, mind, and spirit.

So the stilted and old-fashioned phrases littering this mansion baffle Sybil. And Libby's regressive explanations make no sense, either—her commentary concerning "sanctity of marriage" and "bed undefiled." How limiting such "truths" are.

And yet, Sybil's heart whispers, how consoling . . .

She opens her eyes to mute that unwelcome voice. Libby is still possessed by an unnamed entity, her eyes alight with an awareness Sybil, for all her resistance, covets.

Well, she isn't about to interrupt the animus exerting itself on Libby. Let her steep in it, whatever its source. Maybe this is the breakthrough to her encountering the sacred in more remote corners of the earth.

CHAPTER TWENTY-ONE

Five days ago

"Thanks for submitting your application in person," the office receptionist said to Libby, "but we use a commercial janitorial service."

"I was in the area and thought I'd take the chance." Libby placed the paper on the counter and returned the thinning file folder to her bag. She'd walked all morning, south along Hiawatha Avenue and east into Longfellow towards the river, dropping off her résumé wherever she found a possible employer.

"I'll pass it along to the management anyway."

Libby thanked her and stepped back out onto the Minneapolis sidewalk. Tomorrow she'd blitz Dinkytown, but of course her first choice for a job had been the neighborhood surrounding Seven Canaan Lane. It wasn't a busy shopping scene, but restaurants and banks and theaters all needed entry-level staff. Even a cleaning job would tide her over for the time being.

Now, so close in proximity to the residence and unable to resist, Libby turned left. After all, she hadn't seen the house since the weekend before last, when Clive took her for a walk-through.

The Arts and Crafts bungalow appeared unoccupied this Tuesday afternoon. The latticed windows glinted a sunny smile, their lacy curtains a delicate backdrop and the only feminine characteristic about the house. With its broad proportions, its stucco and sandstone walls, its lowering roof with heavy shingles, the house looked anchored, like a boat sitting low in the water. No, on second thought, not a boat. A boat goes somewhere. Seven Canaan Lane had its roots sunk deep into the earth.

She'd never own that house now. Libby's chest ached, but she had to be realistic. Without a reference from her boss at Hearsay, she'd have a hard time getting a job in retail sales, and her loan was sure to be denied. Maybe she could find work at the Haven—they knew her there—but the wage would be a pittance. If only she had a college degree to add to her credentials. "Self-education through wide reading" didn't fill in a blank on job applications.

When it came down to it, this was Elsa's fault. All of it. If only her mother hadn't deserted her in the first place—if she'd listened to Babette's good sense and admitted she was powerless over alcohol in a life that had become unmanageable and been ready to get her own hands into a pail of sudsy water like Gram did—Libby would not be forced to repeat the cycle of poverty she'd inherited. If only Elsa Walker had thought about someone else for once in her miserable life, if she'd been there for Libby when she was growing up and choosing the wrong boy and miscarrying a baby and burying a grandmother, a case might be made for Libby reaching out to her now. Her initial guilt over rejecting Elsa dissolved under the recollection of her maltreatment.

Libby knew her own hypocrisy. She saw the disparity between her compassion for, say, Zinnia or any of the old folks at the Haven and her revulsion against her own mother. But it wasn't a matter of logic. This was an issue of the heart, and she didn't have any room in her heart to forgive without even the semblance of an offered apology. Even then, Elsa could never make up for the abuse she'd inflicted.

Libby pivoted away from the house and headed in the direction of Minnehaha Falls. She needed brisk movement to jostle away the rock in the bottom of her belly, and she almost broke into a jog. Why hadn't she packed along her running shoes? Bare feet would do. She yanked off her heels, careless about the sidewalk chill or even possible glass. By the time she hit the cottonwood and hackberry trees waving their new embryonic flags of green, she was puffed out and much more mellow—at least for the moment. The pavilion restaurant served a great seafood chowder. Though the cost of dining out wasn't in her budget, she condoned it by promising herself she'd drop off another application there. Waiting tables couldn't be that difficult.

Libby arrived home in the early evening to find many of the block's residents on the steps outside, a humming swarm of bees. Zinnia, stooped and shuffling towards her, pulled the hanky out of her cardigan sleeve.

"They gone and done it to us, Libby." She dabbed at her glistening forehead. "I told you they would. They drove up here in their fancy van and stuck that paper on the front door just about the time Rosie was fetching her groceries up them stairs."

"What are you talking about?" Libby placed her hand on Zinnia's fleshy arm. "Who had a fancy van?"

"Rosie got right on up to my apartment and dragged me out here. Well, she let me dress first. Wouldn't want to be indecent for them boys." Zinnia cracked a toothy grin. The five or six gang members who lived on the top floor were subdued for once, sucking hard on their smokes and ignored by the other tenement dwellers clustering around the door. "When I clapped my eyes on that poster there saying the building is unsafe, I just knew we were in for it."

"Unsafe? That's ludicrous." Sure, the landlord turned a deaf ear on tenant pleas to replace shattered windows, and the intermittent odor of sewage lingered near the parking lot in the back. But most likely a developer looking for a building site was behind the rumor.

She climbed the steps and the crowd parted for her, falling silent except for the sobbing of one old gal. Libby froze when she saw the official City of Minneapolis Placard of Condemnation in bold black print ordering all occupants to vacate the premises within ten days or risk discontinuation of their utilities. The tenants picked up their carping. One dialed a mobile phone and begged her daughter to come get her, another kicked at the wall with his paint-splattered work boots.

"I guess it's the Haven for me after all." Zinnia tugged her sweater close around her buxom chest. "Rosie and me will make out fine at the old folks' home, Libby. But you're young. What'll you do?"

What would she do, indeed?

Back in her apartment, Libby loosened her knot of hair, locked the door behind her, and rested her forehead against its blistered paint. Zinnia's gossip had been right all along. Libby should have called someone to find out about it, as she'd meant to do, instead of sticking her head in the sand and not getting around to it. One of the block residents had tried to reassure the others downstairs that compensation must be coming their way—a month's rent, maybe. That was all fine and good, but how far would a few hundred dollars take her?

Facing homelessness was Libby's nightmare come true. Sybil once said about her health, "Don't think you're off the hook because you avoided tobacco. Your mom and her boyfriends puffing away in your presence poisoned you with second-hand smoke—forced it into your lungs." Had she been imputed with homelessness, too?

Libby sprang back at three sharp raps on the other side of the door.

"You in there, cupcake?"

She unhooked the chain and turned the knob. "Clive." Her timbre must have told more than she intended because he slid right on in, his arm snaking around her waist before she could withdraw.

"Sybil suggested you might need a shoulder to cry on after getting fired yesterday. I've been calling since this morning."

"I turned my cell ringer off while I was out job searching." Why was Libby explaining? And why was Sybil talking about her private life with him? She moved to escape his hug, but his arm tightened around her middle, the other hand now stroking her back.

"That rat of a boss deserves to be slapped with a lawsuit for wrongful dismissal—discrimination, maybe. You want me to look into it?"

Libby shook her head, long hair tickling. She wouldn't pull out that card. Terence would contest any accusation she might levy against him, and he'd likely win.

"Poor gal." Clive's voice was soft. "And on top of it all, I see by the notification on the block's front door that the city's shutting down this hole on you."

Libby wedged her arm into Clive's muscled chest to get distance between them. "I'll be fine." Would she?

"I know this might be a bad time to put more pressure on you, but we need to strike while the iron's hot." Clive placed his briefcase on the stack of boxes next to the couch, extracting a sheaf of papers stapled at the corner. He sat down and patted the seat cushion next to him, as though he were the hospitable host. "The owners of the property we're looking at are entertaining offers, and an initial bid was placed this morning."

"Offers?" Libby sat down beside him without meaning to. "On Seven Canaan Lane?" She'd thought this was a private sale with Clive approaching the owners on her behalf alone. Had he been soliciting potential buyers, upping the ante by peddling her house to other parties? *Her* house . . .

"This is your big opportunity." Clive's knees bounced. "How's about you look over this conditional purchase agreement? Hey, don't shake your head so quickly."

"I've told you, I can't come up with even the down payment on this place. And, what with having no employment, the bank's not going to approve any loan."

Clive blinked once, twice. "You called the bank about your being fired?"

"Not yet." But she'd thought about stopping in to see Mr. Jordan today.

Clive whistled between his teeth. He twiddled with the heavy silver bracelet on his wrist and then slid his eyes sideways at her between slatted lids. "What they don't know won't hurt them."

"What do you mean?"

"You don't need to mention your current unemployment. It's temporary."

"The bank will find out on its own." She gnawed at her knuckle. "I mean, Terence will tell them."

"Maybe they've called your references already and gotten the all-clear."

"Yes, but even if they okay the house loan, how could I make monthly payments without a job?"

Clive gave a half-hearted shrug. "You worry too much. Let the future take care of itself."

"You're joking, right?" Living one day at a time was quite different than refusing to make commonsense plans.

"Look, dollface, the mortgage process is underway. The paperwork is in the hands of the decision makers by now. You say you applied over a week ago?" She nodded. "So don't sweat it. They'll have the money to you lickety-split is my bet. Meanwhile, you'll get a new job and they won't be any the wiser. All they want is their interest."

She bit on her inner cheek. It sounded shady to her. "I've got to get out of this apartment right away, and I have nowhere to go." A video played across her mind's screen of her huddling in a sleeping bag beneath a bridge. Sybil might let her couch-surf at her place. But even if she welcomed company, her condo was a couple of miles from the transit, and Libby hated to be dependent for a ride.

Clive shifted sideways on the couch until they bumped elbows. She could smell the mint in his mouth—not unpleasant. But she wasn't expecting his next words.

"So why not move in with me for the time being?"

Libby vaulted to her feet, clasping a toss cushion to her chest.

"Whoa, no offense meant." Clive stood up himself and touched her arm. "Just a friendly offer, kitten. I've got a second bedroom, big kitchen. Pay me rent, if it makes you feel better."

"You hardly know me." What she really meant was that she hardly knew him.

"I'd like to get to know you better." He examined his fingernails, his facial expression neutral. What sort of arrangement was he suggesting?

"I, uh, I don't know what to say."

"No need to say anything right now," Clive said. "But the space is yours for the asking. It's a standing offer." He passed the papers to her. "For the time being, take a gander over this contract for the house. I've already filled in the price we discussed the other day—subject to the bank approval, of course. And if this other interested party doesn't manage to undercut us with their price, we can tie the sale up pretty fast. Give me a call after you sleep on it."

Libby locked the door behind Clive. She had a lot to think about. Maybe she should give up on the idea of owning her home and settle into renting—if she got a job fast enough. Maybe she should take Clive up on his offer of temporary shelter. It seemed innocuous, the way he formally shook her hand before he left instead of snatching a quick kiss as he'd done at the movie theater. Clive's mixed messages could indicate he was picking up on her restraint and backing away in order to let her get used to his advances, yet his optimism about the house purchase and his bristling over her job loss both gave her the strange sense of being taken care of. Whatever his reasoning, Clive's attentions—brotherly or otherwise—and his offer of shelter did give her a last-ditch fallback, at least in the short term. She had an out if she really needed it.

Libby rubbed her eyes to clear the fog. What was she thinking? She'd be foolish to misread his motivation. She changed into her sweats, studying herself in the bedroom mirror. Not that she was taken with her own looks, but she could see why he had come on to her in the first place, if appearance was the draw. The question, though, was more about what *she* felt towards *him*. And for all her resisting his hug on entering the apartment tonight, she couldn't deny the comfort of his arm around her waist and his hand patting her back.

Libby gathered her hair up into a ponytail and pushed back her sleeves. Whatever emotions needed dealing with, her first concrete step would be to finish culling Gram's things by filling the garbage bags with rejected items and the boxes with clothes for donation. Sorting out Gram's possessions had turned into packing up for her own move. Her gaze swept across the kitchen, into the living room, and down the hallway. She had only the two bedrooms and a couple of closets left to sort. One way or another, she'd be leaving this hellhole.

Libby had just finished cleaning out the bathroom cupboard when Zinnia popped over for a bedtime cup of celery soup and a chat. Good timing; she needed a break. They commiserated about their housing troubles, and Libby offered to help her friend with her imminent move to the Haven, or at least get boxes for her.

"Just like Babette, always going out of your way." Old Zinnia's eyes got shiny. "I'm going to miss you like I'm missing your Gram. Like she used to miss your mama after you moved in here. Though, heaven help me, Elsa was one miserable person."

Libby reared her head. "You knew Elsa?"

" 'Course I did. Babette would go on and on about that wild girl before you were born." Zinnia's nostrils flared, but then she turned a soft smile on Libby. "You brought joy to your granny. She told me, 'Everything comes to him who waits.' How old were you when you moved in here?"

"Eight, but I never remember a time I didn't know you." Libby stroked Zinnia's arm.

"From the beginning, long before you come to stay, we talked about your mama, Babette and me. I was her—what do they call it?—her confidante. Every morning she put the coffeepot on and we had us a session. She'd tell me how Elsa was always drinking and carrying on. Getting in trouble with the police. Taking you places a child oughtn't be going. Then she disappeared altogether. My, Elsa gave Babette worries."

"She's back again."

"Elsa's come home?" Zinnia's words tumbled out. "I thought she was long dead. Babette always insisted she was alive, even if she never wrote, never called. A mother knows this sort of thing, she'd say."

"No, not dead." Libby only wished that were the case. "Close to it, though. Apparently she's been crawling the streets of L.A. this whole time and now she's come back to torment me."

"You mean you met her? She came here to the apartment?"

"No, to my workplace. In fact, she got me fired from the card shop." Libby flexed her jaw, grinding her back teeth together.

Zinnia insisted on hearing the details of the job loss, her eyes welling up over Terence's foulness and the bad spot this put Libby in. Her empathy made Libby sorry she'd shared any of it.

"Well, I got to let you do your packing." Zinnia licked her soup spoon clean and lumbered to her feet. "When you seeing Elsa again?"

"I won't be," Libby stated flatly. "She's a ward of the state, as far as I know. They'll have to deal with her now."

Zinnia clucked but didn't offer her view on the situation. Instead, she placed her bowl and utensils into the sink and said, almost to herself as though she was replaying it in her mind, "One time she came around with you, they had a terrible row. Elsa was boiling mad and ripping up them letters, whipping them up into the air like she was making a snowstorm. Begging for money as if Babette had any more to give. Demanding she pawn her jewelry."

But Gram didn't wear jewelry.

Libby had only the faintest recollection of this tantrum, and she didn't care to recall the particulars of Zinnia's story. It didn't matter to Gram now and, as far as Libby was concerned, the subject of Elsa Walker was closed. What with Terence firing her, the resulting financial crunch—why had she wasted money on that soup seminar?—Clive's proposed living arrangements, and Sybil's high-pressure manipulations, Libby had enough of a mess to sort out without muddying her situation even further with thoughts of that bag lady.

Libby booted up her computer before she headed for bed Tuesday night. She found her inbox full and opened first the most recent e-mail, which was from Clive:

> *Just a quick line to put it in writing, cupcake. I know you want to buy that house and I can help make it happen. All the faster if you move in with me.*

Was that a bribe?

Next she read a lengthy message from Sybil, who didn't often have the attention span for more than a quick text. In this tirade, she complained about Libby's cold treatment of Clive after all she'd done to get them together, and she advised Libby to give the man a break. She signed off with her customary bossiness:

> *Embrace the present, ignore the past, and let the future unfold as it will. Just move in with him already.*

Had Clive and Sybil been talking about her again after he left tonight? Libby squinted at the screen and then trashed both messages.

She yawned and checked the time on the corner of the computer screen. Maybe she should answer the remainder of her mail tomorrow. Then she spotted a message from Paige at the museum. Libby opened it to read that a porch swing had indeed hung outside the door of the mansion. As if by reflex, Libby shot back a quick query:

> *And is there any record of a very young girl who came to visit the museum in 1967?*

She'd barely clicked "send" before a flush flamed across her cheeks. What a stupid question to ask. She didn't want to get into a real dialogue with this Paige, certainly didn't want to bring up memories she was trying not to remember. But her message was in cyberspace and irretrievable.

After dumping several spam e-mails in a row, Libby started when she came upon a message from the Belle Boutique Hotel, its subject line all in caps: ATTENTION WORKSHOP PARTICIPANTS. The restaurant manager hadn't bothered to use blind carbon copy, so she could see the names of all the recipients, including Chef Virgil's. One of the diners at Belle's benefit event three nights ago, the message read, had suffered a serious allergic reaction. The facility's four-star kitchen kept rigid control over all regular menu items, and so the soup seminar cooks were asked to immediately resubmit their ingredient lists.

Libby clapped her hand over her mouth. The Goji berries! She'd added that bag of powder on impulse, without having itemized it ahead of time for the menu printout. Doubtless the administrators of the Belle were trying to cover their backsides and divert any legal blame. Could Goji be the culprit?

A quick 'Net search confirmed to Libby that, indeed, some people had a strong sensitivity to the berry, developing swollen gums and a fiery rash. With shaking hands, she composed a response and deep apology to the restaurant, admitting her oversight, and copied it to Chef Virgil. Would she be held liable?

Libby's head pounded and she crawled into bed without washing her face. She was such a failure. Furious at herself for adding the pulverized berries to her soup, she was almost as mad at Sybil for forcing the Goji powder on her in the first place, though in the end using it had been her own desperate decision. At the same time, she likely deserved Sybil's criticism about her treatment of Clive. Did she have any chance of getting a decent-paying job in time to qualify for the loan, or would she end up out on the streets or, worse, in Clive's bed?

But Libby suspected these troubles were only distractions. Her personal moral failure ran much deeper than soup and sleeping arrangements, and Zinnia's earlier disclosure about being acquainted with Elsa only stirred up the emotional waters more. Wasn't Libby just as culpable as her loser of a mother? She was no better than the rejecting mother she'd rejected.

Libby fell into a troubled sleep to dream about pawnshops

and screaming drunks, porch swings and pink train cases and paper snowstorms.

*

The antique regulator clock on the farmhouse wall ticked its way towards midnight, and every blink of Paige's lids sandpapered her corneas. Three days remained until her submission deadline of Friday, May 12. She'd spent the last ten hours editing one of the final chapters regarding the decoration of the Laird home. MDM had been a trader at heart, and his international travels resulted in a fine souvenir collection, photos of each piece included in her thesis appendix. His home was adorned with such exotic paraphernalia as a drum from Zanzibar, a painted hand fan from Spain, a Maori stone ax from New Zealand.

Baby was kicking up a fuss in her abdomen, so Paige stretched back on the couch and mused about one particular excursion MDM had taken in his mid-twenties, a decade before the turn of the century. MDM had cruised to the Orient on business with a private stop along the way: Taiwan, then called Formosa, a territory of China. There he visited his shirttail relative—a Scottish anthropologist, educator, and missionary affectionately called by the locals the "Black-Bearded Barbarian." MDM brought back an elaborately embroidered, three-inch-long silk slipper resembling a doll's shoe, now encased in a black shadow-box frame and residing on a shelf in the museum's library.

"It would likely fit your restless foot," Paige said aloud to Baby.

A note she'd found in MDM's papers told how it had been worn by a grown woman, victim of the hideous tradition of foot-binding that produced excruciating pain and horrible infection, immobilizing females and subjugating them beneath cultural and conjugal tyranny. The tiny shoe was a symbol of emancipation promoted by the distant relative, who to this day retained a lasting reputation in that country.

Paige sat forward and chewed on her pencil eraser. Perhaps the relative's complete immersion into the culture of the indigenous people—including marrying across racial lines in taking a Formosan wife—was what so impressed MDM that he redoubled his own efforts to identify with the Great Plains populace of North America.

The historical record showed that MDM admired his father's earlier dedication to the dignity of the Canadian First Nations up at the Red River Settlement. He mirrored this attitude when he made a name for Kirkton as an American haven against the dehumanizing zeal of colonialism here in the U.S. Not that MDM agreed with the barbaric savagery tribes wreaked against each another—the wars and horse thieving and murder. But in his writings MDM expressed disapproval over the white man's practices of forbidding children to speak in their mother tongue, or cutting off their braids, or, especially, breaking apart the family unit, all of which did nothing to promote the real, humanizing love he espoused.

Paige straightened up her nest of papers spread over the coffee table so she wouldn't come down in the morning to a mess. But she was wired up. If she climbed into bed now, she'd only wake Danny with her insomnia. Maybe a warm bath would soothe her and Baby both.

Before running the tub, she checked her e-mail one more time. Two days had passed since her last, mincing communication with Gramsgirl; maybe there'd be a response tonight. Her hope was met by a brief and utterly frustrating one-line message asking about visitors to the museum back in summer of 1967. How was she to deal with such obtuse questions? She chose her words carefully; this skittish e-mailer might yet offer value to her. Then halfway through her answer she realized the significance of the date.

MDM Laird had died in the summer of 1967.

Gramsgirl knew something! Somehow this anonymous tease held answers. Wild impatience threatened to take over as Paige typed back in a frenzied staccato, using bold and caps:

> *The Laird Mansion Museum was not instituted until the mid-1980s. We do have a stash of earlier estate guest books kept in the archives and, while I can't speak for the next docent, I would be delighted to open them for you if you'd come see me before I leave my post here in a few weeks.* ***It's of urgent personal interest to me to speak with you AS SOON AS POSSIBLE.***

If this didn't scare off Gramsgirl, nothing would. But what choice did Paige have? She groaned. Even a bubble bath wasn't likely to work its tranquilizing magic tonight.

CHAPTER TWENTY-TWO

Today

Libby gapes over the banister at the main floor of the mansion. The hand-rubbed oak rail and the sweeping, curved, carpeted stairway bring to her wide-awake mind the setting of her night terrors, never before faced in the daylight.

Yes, she's stood at this very spot before, long ago as a girl, back when the nightmares started. A massive weight descends on her now—of horror or glory—so that she sags forward and the air goes out of her lungs. She's rooted to the spot and hardly hears the tour leader's explanations.

"In this great hall MDM received visitors entering through the front door," Paige says as the international travelers, the elderly pair of sisters, and the mingling batch of kids trail down the steps. "As the only entrance to the mansion, the great hall sets the tone of grandeur we see throughout the home. Note the walnut reception desk, and check for signatures in the guestbook. The floor lamp is original, as is the silver tea service on the sideboard. As with many of the furnishings in the mansion, they were at one time sold off, to be purchased back and restored by the Kirkton Preservation Society when the museum was instituted."

Libby observes motionless from above, unable to move, paralyzed by the cognizance—the sudden *knowing*—though she can't fit her certainty into words yet. Gram might have said she was "feeling it in her bones." The guide steers the group towards the south wing, past the colossal, water-filled, polished bronze basin in the center of the hall. Some of the teens are tall enough to peer over its edge at the water lilies floating on the still surface, but others strike goofy poses that reflect in the convex surface of the bowl.

Once, on a summer evening long ago, Libby had stood tippy-toes there, too, giggling at the distorted image of herself clutching a pink train case.

"Libby, snap out of it." Sybil has come back up the stairwell.

In a daze, Libby follows her down to the expansive lobby floor. She would go on to where she's being drawn by an invisible force—*wants* to go on to that other, windowless room to see if there's any blood left. Instead Sybil pushes her towards the crowd.

Libby stumbles on the doorsill into the music parlor. Her purpose for being here drastically changed the moment she overlooked the great hall from the second-floor balcony. Yes, she registers the guide's words and the visitors' appreciative comments about the hand-painted linen wall coverings, the Battenberg tablecloth from Belgium, and the rosewood harmonium that was moved back in this morning from temporary use elsewhere on the property. But her surging yearning to cross another threshold threatens to engulf any interest in the remainder of the circuit. She steels herself against running, fast and hard, to that room.

That room. Where is it, again?

Libby inhales deeply, willing her stomach to still and stepping on Paige's heels as they enter the library. Paige points out the breakfront cabinet showcasing leatherback books and the curios MDM brought back from his extensive travels throughout the Dakotas and far beyond—a Cheyenne peace pipe, a silk slipper from Formosa, a Tasmanian spear. Paige shows maps tracing MDM's travels from early in his life—his 1882 emigration from Manitoba to Minnesota, the bison hunt in Dakota Territory. In addition to several overseas excursions and beginning in late 1898, the year the mansion was completed, MDM took many short-distance trips. He traveled western North America right through the Great Depression, when he was already in his seventies. Throughout Paige's explication, Libby clasps her hands to steady them, squeezes them to release the tension building inside.

When she's calmed herself, she gravitates towards the library's maps, bound into a large album ignored by the others as they drift off to explore the rest of the room's offerings. She pages through them, yellowing paper ensconced in plastic to protect the fragile edges. Several maps are inked over in long, squiggly lines, thick and thin as the nib followed its path.

"Did MDM take these domestic trips for business or pleasure?" Libby voices it aloud to the guide's back. It's the first time she's addressed Paige directly.

Paige turns her head, her eyes widen, and she swallows before answering. "The locals say he was searching for a lost love, that he was on a quest."

"Was he?" Libby strains to catch some inflection, some validation. She's trembling.

"I've never figured that out. Maybe." Paige's eyebrows bunch. She looks as though she has more to say but is interrupted by one of the seniors asking to be shown to the restroom.

Quest. It's such a mythic concept.

On the other hand, the word "journey," a favorite of Sybil's, is one Libby hears a lot. "It's the journey that matters," Sybil will say to condone another brash decision or to badger Libby to jump in alongside. "Life is all about the journey." But it's not. Lately Libby's been so tired of the journey, the momentum of that unending spiral set by the mistakes of her mother and grandmother and great-grandmother—by her *own* mistakes—disallowing her to finally arrive at wherever it is she's going.

Libby spots Sybil cornering the teacher, pressing her chest up against his arm. Sybil's journeying—geographically, sensually, emotionally—comes from her itchy feet, her compulsive insatiability for experience. To her, it's all about living in the moment and embracing the process. But as far as Libby can tell, Sybil's journeying dissipates fairly quickly into footloose wandering.

It's not only Sybil who's restless. Sure, Libby might have no desire to travel around the world poking her nose into other cultures for the sheer fun of it. But is she any further along than Sybil in identifying and attaining her goals? She fends off Sybil's constant demands for a travel partner but at the same time longs for her own unclaimed, unidentified purpose—her internal place of abode. She's a half-century old and is unemployed, virtually homeless, a rotten daughter, and insecure enough to consider shacking up with a man she's not even interested in. She's physically worn out with the packing of the last month, and she hasn't even gained the reward of finding Gram's soup recipe. To top it all off, she's losing the memory of Gram herself.

So, no, the journey of her own life hasn't been anything to boast about. Running away is completely different than running towards.

A boy jostles her arm, mutters an apology. It breaks Libby out of her rumination for a moment, but the books in the cabinet before her prove her very point. She's read enough old literature to know that a quest is at the heart of every great story, in which a hero—King Arthur or Jason the Argonaut—undertakes his journey specifically in order to attain his prize. The journey is only the means. In contrast, a quest is something the traveler in this life is almost irresistibly *summoned* to, the pursuing of a goal that must be grasped in order for success to be claimed.

Gram had been on a quest, too, though not for a Holy Grail or Golden Fleece. Libby herself, her safety and wholeness, had always been part of Gram's prize. Not all of it, she's sure—not with the way Gram died, leaving so many questions unanswered, as though she saw the goal from afar without reaching it herself. As though she pointed the way but was unable to draw a concise map for getting there. Libby lets her gaze flicker back down to the maps. She touches the ring through the fabric of her blouse—the ring that once encircled Babette's finger.

Was Gram pointing her towards the Laird Mansion Museum?

Even if MDM hadn't been on a quest for a lost love, as Paige seems to think, his life as represented in this house hints about a purpose almost within Libby's grasp. The carving on the mantelpiece across the room reads *They which are called receive the promise of inheritance.* Libby is being called to a quest but doesn't know by whom or to what. It has to do with the rediscovery of the ring, the letter, and the memories of a five-year-old girl being restored moment by moment.

Something more is waiting for Libby, if only she can articulate what *her* quest really is.

CHAPTER TWENTY-THREE

Four days ago

Sybil held the phone to her ear as she surveyed Hearsay's store front from inside her own shop on Wednesday afternoon, about the time she and Libby would usually take a coffee break together. The two days since Terence had fired Libby had passed slowly.

"I'm here for you, Libby. Call me." Sybil drew out her words in a show of the empathy her friend likely needed about now, but she smacked the phone back down onto the counter. What was up with Libby's isolation since being fired? How did she know Sybil wouldn't give her a job stocking shelves if she didn't ask? Sybil wouldn't have; who needs friends complicating business? But that was beside the point. Clive was the one to inform her about the apartment block being condemned, and Libby hadn't even called her about it yet. Sybil huffed.

Well, if she wanted space, Sybil would give her space. How long could she keep it up? After all, Libby needed her more than she needed Libby.

Amulets had been quiet lately, business slow. It should pick up soon, what with the psychic fair coming to the city next week. Riding on its tails, Sybil's shop would feature several specialty sessions. She'd retained three speakers to give informational classes in the diverse fields of numerology, astral projection, and body talk. Such tutorials always boosted her product sales. She might then offer, as a future service to her clientele, consultation with a travel agent to promote sacred destinations. Of course, she'd taken so many spirit journeys already that she herself could easily lecture for hours.

Sybil picked up her feather duster and ran it over the shelves, hands busy while she contemplated possible topics for her own imaginary workshop presentation, and the outfits she'd wear to illustrate her theme. For one, she'd deliver a discourse on the Recoleta Cemetery in Buenos Aires—a cityscape of mausoleums and vaults and grand sculptures within fifteen walled-in acres. There she'd paid tribute at the graveside of Eva Perón but, mostly, just basked in the presence of so many resident if invisible entities. For that lecture she'd wear gauchos and a felted wool hat or, maybe better, her tango-worthy, ruffle-hemmed scarlet dress and strappy stilettos.

But she wouldn't mention the Argentinian barbeque. Tempted by the delectable aromas wafting from an open-fronted restaurant, she'd fallen from her vegan state and succumbed to a fat-dripping feast of marbled T-bone. No one here needed to know about her weaknesses there. On her return to Minneapolis she did make confession to her sympathetic but non-English-speaking greengrocer, who nodded and grinned and bobbed as he packed up her purchases, good as any priest. And she'd detoxed for weeks, cleansing her system of the epicurean poison with a salt-water colonic, and abstaining from dairy and alcohol. Thus she'd cleared her conscience and purified body and mind.

Still, every now and then—usually when she was chewing on a soy burger—she thought she could hear the sizzle of raw beef hitting hot grill, to say nothing of the sizzle she felt at the memory of dancing in the seedy Argentinian *milonga* with Esteban. He'd shown her why tango was famously defined as "a vertical expression of a horizontal desire." She could proudly share that tidbit with her future class of dreamy-eyed, middle-aged matrons mooning over the trips they'd never take.

Sybil stuck the feather duster under the front counter and put her imaginings back into place, as well. Whether or not she managed to get a series of talks together for later in the fall, she could at least publish *Sybil's Sensual Search for Sacred Spaces* by then and have copies on hand to sign. And she'd display them right here, next to the till.

She glanced out the window again to see a bedraggled Terence locking up Hearsay across the street. Sybil didn't feel one bit sorry for him, after what he'd done to Libby.

Sybil next unpacked and shelved a shipment of elixir, letting thoughts turn to Libby's obvious inner turmoil. Fear hamstrung her friend. What was so awful about being without a roof over her head for a while? That was the whole adventure Sybil incorporated when she took off with a suitcase and a passport, never knowing for sure where she might lay her head at night. Sybil clucked her tongue. Libby was her own biggest problem and had a lot to learn.

Sure, Libby had been having a streak of bad luck lately. But bad luck could strike almost anyone who wasn't attentive—like Sybil's own mother, who'd let the cancer get her. If her mom had fought back harder, if she'd lived her life in an ethos of happy energy instead of inviting the cancer to begin with, she'd be alive today.

If only Mom had fought, had not given in, had not *invited* that freaking disease . . .

Sybil couldn't stop the abrupt flood of emotion, like sewage spewing from a backed-up toilet. Why had she been orphaned by her mother's negligence, her father's spiteful remarriage? It was

Mom's fault for challenging kismet by ignoring the cosmic and spiritual laws of the universe. After all, everyone has the seeds of cancer growing within, waiting to overtake the body's immune system. Hadn't her mother loved her enough to fight the negative confession that created the negative reality?

Hadn't her mother loved her enough to fight?

Hadn't her mother loved her?

All at once dizzy, Sybil crouched down on her haunches in the aisle, glass bottles in both hands. Was she having a breakthrough? Was the fervor in her dying mother's eyes, which Sybil had always taken for love, actually hatred?

Love didn't hurt, and so Mom—in her renouncing of life—must not have loved.

Rather than give in to despair, Sybil was washed with such gratitude that she'd found answers her mother never knew—empowerment to take what was rightfully hers, to live fearlessly, to find and show love her own way. Only Sybil could redeem herself, and only through the gnosis she'd gained in the years since Mom's passing. This knowledge, this *knowingness*, bolstered her even in the moment.

Maybe, if she called a séance with her monthly support group, she could still show Mom what real love looked like. You get back at hate by loving, after all.

Libby's fate came into this, too. Sybil suspected she herself had capacity to take on only one acolyte at a time, and Libby was soaking up all her mojo. Maybe Sybil had been asking too much of herself. Switching genders might be the key, allowing her to concentrate all her loving instruction towards men. Men were so much more expressive—physically, at least.

She'd have to think more about that.

Meanwhile, she heard the universe telling her the time had come to take another trip. Tibet was still on the radar, of course. She couldn't just throw away the tickets even if Libby felt justified in wasting that kind of money.

Sybil shoved the last of the Immortality Potion into place on the shelf, chipping the bottle's glass. She wasn't taking Libby's refusal at face value, for Libby's good as well as for her own sense of self-control. After all, since Libby lost her job, she had no argument about missing work. She only needed to have the ice broken, maybe go on that road trip up to North Dakota to get the juices flowing. She'd find a way to force her hand yet, if Libby would respond to the voicemail message and call back. For good measure, Sybil picked up her phone again and tapped out a text to her: *Call me.*

But she received no response over the following days.

Two days ago

Libby ran her soapy hands under the kitchen tap, washing off the newsprint ink that stained her cuticles and worked itself into every line of her knuckles. She hadn't known she owned so many breakables, but this was the first time in her life she'd ever packed for a move.

Yesterday, when she ran out to deliver another couple of résumés after the apartment's power went off again, she noted with dismay the formerly pristine sheet she handed to the owner of Phil 'Er Up was smeared with inky fingerprints—not a great specimen of cleanliness when applying for a position as line cook. The mom-and-pop diner was a modest establishment. It had attracted the attention of a restaurant reviewer and captured a one-line mention in the *Tribune* last month. At least it wasn't a big chain with a fixed menu she had no way to influence.

"Experience?" Phil had wiped his hands on his apron.

"I've dealt with the public for much of my adult life, mostly in sales." Maybe he'd skip over the part of her application showing lack of references from Hearsay.

"Cooking experience?" Apparently Phil didn't speak in full sentences.

"Uh, well, none in a restaurant, per se, but I'm handy with soups."

"Sorry, no openings." Phil turned away, crumpling the sheet of paper into a ball and aiming at the garbage can.

"I should mention that I just completed a seminar over at the Belle—" She hadn't finished her pathetic pitch before Phil whipped around.

"Virgil Oxenbury's seminar?"

"Yes," she said. Was he that famous?

"Got *Simmer, Scoop, Slurp* right here." Phil indicated the cookbook. "You certified?"

"My certificate is coming in the mail." She hoped so, anyway, and wasn't about to comment on any possible legal action by the allergic diner. "I love to design soups. I've been cooking since I was quite young and have a real repertoire of recipes I could share with you."

"Such as?" Phil removed his bib apron, waved towards a table, and poured two cups of coffee. She assumed she should sit.

"I make a terrific beet borscht with garden dill—"

"No Ukrainian."

"Well, I have a great Thai chicken coconut soup with lemongrass and chili seasoning—"

"No Asian."

Libby sipped her scalding coffee. This wasn't an ethnically diverse restaurant. What attracted Phil to Chef Virgil if not his global palate? She'd describe her fantastic concoction of butternut squash and mango soup fragrant with fresh ginger and turmeric, but his ban on Oriental flavors put the kibosh on that idea. Then the placemat menu caught her attention. Ah, he was playing to the Midwestern taste for down-home farm cooking. She could do that.

"My corn chowder would knock your socks off, Phil."

He perked up. "Go on."

"I sauté locally sourced, double-smoked bacon with onion and celery. Then I add scraped red Idaho potatoes and, of course, the sweetest corn. I don't overdo seasoning, preferring the clean flavors of the pork and dirt-grown market veggies." Here Phil graced Libby with a discreet nod. "I thicken it with rich farm cream, finish it with dry white wine, and top it with a sprinkling of chives, crumbled bacon, and a grating of aged American cheddar."

"Hmm." Phil accepted the fresh résumé and circled her contact info.

Libby forced her lips into a firm line to resist the grin straining at the corners. It would be just her luck to get another grumpy boss. And yet Phil's terseness was altogether unlike Terence's canine rage, his shut-down attitude towards her suggestions. Phil might even be interested in Babette's Bowl.

As soon as she thought it, Libby pushed the idea from her

mind. No use dwelling on the impossible. She'd lost any chance to find the recipe that truly brought Gram back to her, but she could honorably cook the other soups, the nonessential soups, that she'd learned at Gram's knee and afterward. She still had that much of Gram, anyway—that, and the cache of common-sense sayings ingrained in her psyche, though they never quite met her need for answers to the big questions in life.

Now, standing at the sink and scrubbing off today's newspaper ink from chapped and dried-out hands, Libby couldn't believe the work week was almost over—the first one without income in many years. In the busyness of packing and job searching, she hadn't missed Terence and his beastly attitude one little bit. But, wow, she was tired. She could use some mindless downtime in front of the computer, but likely she was offline for good. News of the building's condemnation must have filtered through the system because the utilities had been undependable ever since that notice got stuck to the door of the block.

Libby patted her hands on a tea towel and looked over the apartment, full of boxes and only needing a day or two of deep cleaning to remove the last traces of more than four decades of life with Gram.

Oh, and that last linen closet hadn't yet been cleared out.

When the squall hit, Paige dashed into Kirkton's tiny general store to shake off the raindrops. Coffee row was alive and well; several area farmers lounged on mismatched chairs around a table, their legs stretched out in front of them with the heels of their riding boots propped on the oiled hardwood floor. They fell quiet at her entry, staring as though they'd never seen a pregnant woman before. Paige couldn't blame them. Her immersion in her studies precluded town activities like curling and baseball in which most area women engaged, so society hadn't seen much of her since the wedding. She was an import, an outsider, the high-falutin' city girl over at the museum with no time to rub shoulders with locals. She must try to change that perception. Paige smiled at them, but they shifted towards one another, began chewing the fat with each other again.

Paige turned to the graying brunette at the till.

"Hi, Yvonne." She was glad to recall the name of the store-and-café owner. She picked a granola bar from the candy selection by the counter, not wanting to admit she'd ducked in to avoid the weather. "I'll just take this for now."

"Paige," Yvonne said in greeting. "Everything ready for tomorrow?"

"It's all coming together, thanks." Paige refused the paper bag and pocketed the bar. She'd taken a break from her editing to check on museum festival preparations but needed to get home again and polish off her thesis, due for submission before midnight tonight.

"You look like you're ready to pop." Yvonne's eyes assessed her belly. "How are you going to manage all those stairs if you're guiding tour groups this season?"

"Oh, it's good for me to get the exercise." Paige smiled, but she noticed the men were listening in again. "Besides, I won't be at the mansion for the full summer. I'll get the program going and then turn it over to my replacement. Are you coming out tomorrow? We're serving a variety of cookies from the museum's historical recipe book."

"I know that. After all, I donated the ingredients for Molly's baking spree yesterday."

"Oh, um, of course," Paige stuttered, reminded of the connections. Molly, Yvonne's daughter-in-law, was formerly a Farris and the aunt of Jamie, the girl who worked in the museum's gift shop. Paige would never catch on to rural community life if she didn't become more observant, but it seemed everyone was related around here. At that thought and on a whim, Paige blurted out to Yvonne and the half-dozen eavesdropping farmers, "By the way, did you ever meet MDM Laird personally?"

Yvonne gasped and seven pairs of eyes focused on Paige. What could be so stunning about her question? After all, MDM had died less than fifty years ago, and a couple of these old fellows would have been out of their teens by then.

Finally Yvonne broke the stilted silence. "Why do you ask?"

"It's for my research. I'm looking for a couple of anecdotes about him, personal stories so I can get more of a feel for his private life." She shouldn't have brought it up, what with the ongoing litigation. For all she knew, every one of them might be connected to the court proceedings with an eye on remuneration. But Paige had put her foot in it now; she might as well carry on. "For example, there's ongoing blather about his once having married."

Yvonne averted her eyes and busied herself by straightening up the counter.

One farmer spoke up. "No way. My grandfather did business with Laird. He was a fair man, in Grandpa's view, but a bachelor if there ever was one." He stressed the word "bachelor" with a sneer on his face, and the other men snickered. Ah, yes. Paige recognized the indirect reference to the unsubstantiated allegations about

MDM's immorality.

"Might I interview your grandfather?" Paige couldn't keep the intensity out of her voice.

"He's long dead."

"Besides," another farmer spoke up, "you should keep your nose out of it, what with the lawsuit."

"I only—"

"It really is none of your business," the first man said, and his cronies nodded in agreement. "This is a family matter."

"Family? But there *are* no Lairds left." Paige, of course, knew they were referring to the Farris-Yeast relatives, who grafted MDM into their family tree without any proof. It was absurd and academically reprehensible to her, but that was the nature of countryside tittle-tattle. The men didn't respond but tugged their caps low on their foreheads, one or two digging their truck keys out of their pockets.

"Good luck with the opening tomorrow. I'll make it if I can." Yvonne's voice held a hint of apology despite her 'fraidy-cat shirking at Paige's question.

Leaving the store, Paige didn't regret her spontaneous, last-ditch attempt to glean information, even though she'd sounded like a reporter. But if she kept up her inquiry, she'd alienate these people for good and she couldn't afford that, if only for the sake of Danny and Baby. Small-town minds are unforgiving, despite the locals' neighborliness in welcoming newcomers with pies and casseroles. Real friendship was harder to forge. Paige was glad she had a growing bond with her neighboring in-laws.

Sybil was driving home in rush-hour traffic on Friday when her car phone rang, showing Libby's number. She thought about not answering but relented after three rings. "It's about time you called. I've been wondering if you died and were rotting in your apartment." Her words were not as harsh as her mood. Let Libby hear the scorn. She'd earned it.

"Sorry to worry you. Have you heard my block's been condemned?"

"Yes." Sybil gritted her teeth. "Clive happened to tell me."

"I misplaced the cord for my cell in all my packing and only just found it to power up this afternoon. And the land line's been cutting out, so my computer's down right now, too." Libby's excuses didn't placate Sybil, but the edge of hysteria in her friend's voice sounded real.

"You couldn't have stopped in at Amulets?"

"I've been run off my feet. I'm exhausted, Sybil."

"Well, you should have asked for help." Sybil flipped on her turn signal and cut off a green Honda in the right-hand lane. She spoke crisply so that her voice carried well through the Bluetooth connection. "Anyway, everyone's trying to get hold of you."

Libby paused a beat or two. "Who's trying to contact me?"

"Clive for one. He's stopped in a couple of times and you haven't been there. Or else you're ignoring the doorbell."

"I did leave the apartment between boxfuls, but only to drop off job applications. He could have jotted a note."

"Then your old boss called my shop," Sybil said. Why he hadn't just walked across the street, Sybil didn't know. Not that she'd give that scum the time of day.

"Terence? What did he want?"

"Don't know and didn't ask. The guy's a psycho."

"It's about the mortgage, for sure." Libby's voice rang with panic. "The banker's gotten hold of him."

"Don't get your knickers twisted." Sybil couldn't stay mad at Libby for long, and she'd bet her friend hadn't eaten much today. "Look, why don't I swing by and pick you up for supper?"

"No, thanks. I have a pot of soup on, and I can't take the time to go out anyway. I'm almost packed, but I'm not even sure yet where I'm moving."

"Yeah, well, Clive mentioned he's got that problem covered." Libby should thank her stars over the break the realtor was offering her. He sure had it bad for Libby, lucky girl. He was a catch.

"He told you about asking me to move in with him?" Libby said it like it was a moral failing on Clive's part. And maybe on her own as well.

"He's obviously lusting after you."

"It would be strictly a roommate situation." The chill in Libby's voice almost frostbit Sybil's ear. "And I haven't decided about his offer yet."

"I wouldn't throw that fish out so quickly." Sybil pulled into the lot of her condo complex. "Oh, and one other thing. The cops came around here today asking for you."

The phone went dead quiet this time.

"Libby? You still there?"

Libby stammered, "What did they want?"

"As if they'd tell me. The short, well-built guy—" she checked the name, "um, Garcia—gave me his personal number to pass along to you." She recited it to Libby but tucked the card back into her wallet in case she had an excuse to call him herself one of these days.

They disconnected, but Sybil would phone her again soon, maybe even drop by tonight. After she met Clive for a drink, that is, ostensibly to fill him in on Libby.

✒

Gram's kettle, one of the last items to be boxed up, sat on the stovetop and simmered with the final brew this apartment would know. Libby was making refrigerator soup. All leftovers went into the pot, including a chunk of salami, everything in the vegetable crisper, leftover gravy, a half-eaten rice-and-tomato casserole from the freezer, and even some currant jelly. It wasn't only that Libby didn't want to waste good food but that, like Gram said, old habits die hard. Since the seminar was over and she'd given up on her search for Gram's long-lost recipe, making soup was once again simply a creative release.

She thought talking to Sybil would calm her, now that she'd had a few days all to herself with the apartment drapes closed against the sunlight and yawning cartons swallowing Gram's possessions. But this call had only stressed her out more. A flush crept across her chest and up to her face. She fanned herself with a notepad.

What could the police want with her this time? Surely they wouldn't be the ones to deal with her faux pas in Chef Virgil's workshop. Maybe they were contacting apartment dwellers about the eviction. More likely it had to do with Elsa. The authorities would hound her until she convinced them she wouldn't take any responsibility for her mother, who had denied all responsibility for *her* so long ago. Deep down Libby knew that refusing to deal with the familial situation was not the end of her problem.

Libby might as well get it over with. She dialed the number

Sybil had given her and, as the phone rang on the other end, began pacing from kitchen table to living room couch and back again, counting her steps: *One, two, three, four, five . . . Step on a crack and . . .*

"Officer Garcia? This is Libby Walker. You were trying to get hold of me?"

"Yes, Ms. Walker. Thank you for returning the call. I wanted to inform you about Elsa Walker." *Six, seven, eight, nine, ten . . . you'll break your mother's back . . .*

"I told you I don't want anything to do with her." Libby wasn't obliged to explain this or obligated in any way to keep tabs on the woman. *Once upon a time in a land far, far away . . .*

"Be that as it may, for your own safety I'm alerting you that your mother was admitted into the state mental hospital a week ago but has now gone missing."

Libby stopped midstride.

"My own safety?"

"The psychiatrist believes she presents some danger and that she might well contact you." Garcia paused. "Please let us know if she does."

CHAPTER TWENTY-FOUR

Two days ago

Libby tied thick knots in the tops of two garbage bags holding the dregs of Gram's cards and clippings, the debris of broken pencils and plant pots and pancake flippers, and the detritus of knee-high nylons with holes in the toes. She'd compressed Gram's wearable clothing into two boxes that Zinnia's movers would deliver to the Haven. Libby opened the apartment door and dragged the bags behind her into the dim hallway. Only the linen closet was left to deal with, but she needed air. Officer Garcia's news about Elsa made her legs wobble.

Libby depressed the elevator down button and sagged against the wall, waiting. The situation might not be too bad. So what if a random doctor thought Elsa was dangerous and might come after her? Sure, the woman was a sloppy drunk, but she didn't have a gun or anything. Libby could probably fend her off even if she wielded a knife, so the risk of Elsa injuring her was not great.

But Libby's fear of Elsa had never centered on physical pain.

There, she'd admitted it. She was afraid of Elsa N. Walker. Her stomach roiled as she replayed her mother's shrill shrieking of Monday afternoon. It melded with a barrage from a distant past—"I seen you! . . . Get over here and stay right beside me! . . . These stupid letters are useless!"—and with Libby's disgust as she pictured herself morphing into that homeless hag of a mother via the café window reflection.

Her apprehension over Elsa was irrational, but she dreaded all that her mother represented.

The dumpster was almost full, but Libby managed to tip her

bags up over the edge. Car tires squealed a block or two away in the general buzz of city traffic, and a siren wailed. Libby pulled her sweater collar up around her neck against the chill of night darkness, for the lot light was still burned out and shadows shifted in the breeze. She shivered. Someone walking on her grave?

"Libby."

The voice croaked from out of nowhere. Libby lurched, jittery as a Siamese cat. She looked for its source and then backed up, backed away from the trash bin and towards the tenement wall, almost tripping on the sidewalk curb but not stopping until her shoulder blades met the siding.

"Who's there?" Her whisper quavered. But she knew who was there before the pale phantom, Elsa, emerged stooped and drab from behind the massive metal bin.

Libby frantically grasped after the knob on the back door, her wrists bent up behind her. Locked! Where was her key? She avoided meeting Elsa's creepy glare. She dug into her empty pocket and then eyed the distance to the corner of the building. Could she make the front entrance without Elsa tripping her? Could she scream loud enough to be heard?

"Baby, it's your momma," Elsa rasped. She extended her shaking hand.

Libby's belly clenched and she commanded, "Get away from me!" She was facing a crazy person, a madwoman, a character in a horror flick. All her nightmares flapped around her, a cloud of vultures descending upon her with beady, red eyes blazing and flesh-tearing bills gawping open.

Elsa drew closer, snagging at Libby's sweater with those bent and gnarled fingers, a demon from the pit of Hades murmuring endearments that chilled her to the marrow.

"My sweet girl. My darling little girl." Sheer terror strangled Libby's bowels, and she choked back bile.

"The cops are looking for you." Libby was desperate. "Go away."

But the voice scraped on. "I should have came back here for you long ago. I seen you working at that store and I wanted to touch you again."

When Elsa raised her claw towards her daughter's face, Libby reacted from her gut. She thrust both arms straight out and knocked the witch off the sidewalk towards the pavement just as a car, blasting music, careened around the corner.

✦

Tremors shook Libby's whole body, wrapped in Sybil's cashmere throw in the passenger seat of the Prius parked outside the apartment block. She couldn't stop her teeth from chattering.

"Drink this." Sybil offered a steaming take-out cup. The ambulance sirens had wailed out of Libby's range of hearing, and the rowdy boys from the top floor had been dealt with as well, charged with reckless driving by the officers chasing close behind them and hauled away in the patrol car. But Libby was the one feeling imprisoned. Bewildered, she faced Sybil.

"How did you get here? I didn't call you . . ."

"You're in shock, Libby. I was cruising by to check on you and your packing for the move. I was worried about you. You didn't sound so good when I talked to you on the phone earlier."

Libby tried to sip, but she spilled the drink onto the expensive shawl.

"I'm sorry, I'm sorry," she heard herself say, and she blotted at the liquid soaking into the weave.

"It's okay. Leave it alone. I'll get it dry cleaned."

"Some stains don't come out." Libby wasn't thinking about milky tea on a cashmere wrap. "The blood . . ." She plucked at her own t-shirt, the drying spots crunchy.

She couldn't help but picture the sequence of events that had taken only moments to play out. Elsa tripped—no, Libby had *pushed* her—and before the frail woman could regain complete balance on teetering feet, the car was barreling straight towards her. Its headlights lit up her skinny body, its tires locked, and it screeched to a stop.

But not in time.

Elsa flew backwards several feet and slammed into the dumpster, eyes wide in her wrinkled face and staring right at Libby, who ran forward to catch her as she collapsed. Blood spurted from Elsa's head, and Libby was hyperventilating before the cops took over.

"The paramedics got here in time. They stabilized her before they left." Sybil groaned theatrically. "Ye gods, Libby, it was an accident."

But Sybil wouldn't comprehend the remorse that was settling into Libby's heart.

And Elsa's physical welfare wasn't her only concern, anyway. The incident—the blood—brought into crystal clarity the nightmarish moment Libby had been avoiding for almost fifty years, when she was a tiny, blood-splattered girl hiding herself in the heavy folds of a purplish-blue curtain, shrinking out of sight until long after the corpse had been removed. And the consternation roused by that mental snapshot now kept her silent.

She wouldn't—she couldn't—explain this to Sybil. The picture was too vivid and too brief, with no context whatsoever. Libby fought to put the fragmentary memory back where it had come from, in the depths of her denial.

Finally, outward composure regained, Libby said to Sybil in an unsteady voice, "Maybe we should go to the hospital and check up on Elsa?"

"Nope. You signed the medical forms. They know where to find you if they need to."

Libby sagged against the inside of the car door. "That's true." But it wasn't, was it? Her conscience whispered "Guilty!" over her shameful aggression against her mother. She didn't voice it, hadn't admitted aloud her blame to Sybil who, like the policemen, seemed to assume Elsa had stumbled into the path of the oncoming car. Libby didn't disabuse them of the notion. It would do her soul good to tell Sybil the truth about having pushed Elsa—a trouble shared is a trouble halved, as Gram would have said. And Libby's action was self-defense, in a way. Before she could open her mouth, Sybil made a suggestion.

"Let's take a drive. I don't want to leave you alone yet, and you need to calm down."

Libby nodded. But apparently what Sybil really had in mind, as she steered her car aimlessly down one residential avenue and up another, was a pep talk. No—more like a psychoanalytical lecture about Libby's resistance to the advances of Clive, who would be perfect for her at a time like this, what with his take-charge attitude and his well-developed buttocks. Sybil prattled on about Libby's vulnerability and frigidity and emotional dysfunction. The harangue only heightened her soul's aching over the real problems in her life—the bloody image of her little-girl self, her lying by omission to the police, her imminent homelessness. Sybil didn't pause long enough to notice that the sweat beading on Libby's upper lip had less to do with hot tea than with humiliation over her own culpability.

"Clive could be such a support to you," Sybil gushed. "I'm not talking financially, though he's rolling in cash, from what I can see. You deserve to be happy, Libby, and that means surrounding yourself with positive energy. Clive would be a great distraction, now that your grandmother finally isn't taking up all your precious time."

A muscle in Libby's cheek twitched. "Gram was *never* a bother." How could she repay Gram for the years committed to her upbringing, to rescuing her from the attentions of the visiting "uncles," to keeping her out of the child welfare system Elsa's lack of parenting would have eventually consigned her to? Babette took Libby in as a young girl abandoned and then again the second time when miscarriage brought about a new sort of abandonment. Libby couldn't earn such grace—it was all because of Gram's sacrificial nature. Libby loved Gram for what she gave, but Gram loved Libby when there was nothing in it for her.

"And here I am, turning my back on Elsa." Gram's own flesh and blood. No longer just abandoned, Libby was abandoning—not just a victim but a transgressor herself. She was swamped, her life a mess of unpalatable soup that had been boiling hard for too long, surely no longer salvageable.

And all Sybil could do was go on and on about Libby's lack of love life.

Libby slapped her hand down hard on her thigh, the sting

waking up her senses. "Enough already! I'll figure it out about Clive."

Sybil's jaw muscles corded. "I'm only trying to help you." Her profile was severe and chiseled in the glow of the Prius's dashboard light. But Libby wasn't sorry she'd made Sybil stop the nonsensical and constant bombardment.

She'd once introduced Sybil to Gram, bringing her new friend home for supper. It had not gone well, what with Sybil's silly talk about the sacred bond between animal, plant, and mineral, and about the life force residing in rocks and trees. Gram in gentle reproof said that only living hearts were able to house spirit. Sybil, usually so sure of herself, had left in an offended snit smacking to Libby of self-doubt. And Libby never brought the two together again, having no desire to submit Gram to Sybil's dogma.

For her part, Gram warned Libby against Sybil's dabbling in the "dark arts," as she put it: "I once worshiped rock, tree, and weasel, too, before I learned they only hinted at better things to come. As they say, there is none so blind as the one who will not see."

After a few minutes of driving, Sybil parked again in the pool of light at the front entrance to Libby's block. She turned off the ignition and placed her hand on Libby's arm before she could open the passenger door.

"You never take my advice, Libby. Look how happy *I* am. Considering my vast dating experience, don't you think I'm qualified to give you input?"

Libby couldn't stop her eyebrows from popping up.

"What?" Sybil fixed her with a stare.

"Lack of chastity isn't a great qualification for counseling."

"It's not like I'm promiscuous. I'm monogamous—one guy at a time." Sybil laughed.

"Okay." Libby didn't want a fight. She and Sybil had discussed this once, with Libby labeled judgmental even when she tried to mend fences.

"Never mind." Sybil snorted. "I know men. And believe me, I know better than you do what's best for you. And what you need"—she pressed the point—"is someone who will wine and dine you, someone to sweep you off your feet. You have no idea how useful guys can be."

Useful? Manipulation wasn't Libby's style. Gram had taught her by word and example to say what you mean and mean what you say, without scheming.

"What you need right now," Sybil said with finality, "is a boyfriend."

"A boyfriend?" Libby choked on her tea. Sybil's lack of insight into her situation was profound. "I don't want a boyfriend. I don't need a man, Sybil. I need a *father*."

And as Libby put it into words, she realized at once how true it was, and something deeper yet broke inside her orphaned heart.

"Fine." Sybil squared up her shoulders. "I can't sell Clive to you. I get it. And I agree that you're in a tight spot." She cleared her throat. "But distance would give you a whole new perspective. Let's make that happen for you." She riveted Libby with her gaze. "I insist on taking you away from all this madness, if just for a day or two."

"I can't. The apartment, my job search, the house offer—"

"I said I insist. It's what friends do." Sybil flung her right arm around Libby and drew her close, above the armrest. "We'll drive on up to that museum in North Dakota. No arguing." She tightened her grip, almost pinching. Libby didn't have any strength left to withstand Sybil's persistence, and she dropped her chin towards her chest and then slowly nodded.

"All right. I surrender."

Sybil hurtled into high gear at that, instructing her with terse phrases to pack a bag and be ready for pickup by ten o'clock in the morning. Sybil pushed her out of the car and sped off before Libby could renege, if she'd wanted to.

⁂

Ten minutes before midnight on Friday, in the living room of their farmstead with Danny asleep upstairs, Paige submitted her thesis by e-mail to her advisory committee at the university. Had she not been pregnant, a celebratory glass of champagne would have been in order. But instead of jubilation, Paige admitted a sense of defeat. She'd tried her best to ferret out that clinching bit of personal information about her subject, but MDM Laird's secret—if indeed one remained—had eluded her, and full admission of this fact was all that was left to her.

In a way it was a relief. She'd done her best and now, with only the formal defense left and any requested changes to be made before official printing and binding of her thesis, she could concentrate on her upcoming delivery. Paige looked down at her massive belly full of movement and life. She suspected the physical ordeal of birth would be even more laborious than the academic effort she'd expended.

Before joining her snoring husband for the remainder of the night, Paige checked her e-mail one last time, but Gramsgirl hadn't answered. Maybe, Paige admitted, she'd been too enthusiastic—well, even vehement—with her last message, using words like "urgent" and "imperative" in demanding the woman contact her. She grumbled loudly enough that Danny, all the way upstairs, stirred in bed, setting the joints of the old farmhouse groaning. It was too late to make changes to her research now anyway, with thesis sent, but her curiosity still demanded answers that she'd likely never receive.

Paige pushed herself to her feet, stiff in the hips from her latest sojourn on the drafty wooden floor. She wanted to be fresh for the museum's opening ceremonies, and she could still get six hours in before Danny woke her for a goodbye kiss. The museum's big kick-off would feature a speech by a functionary from the state arts council, and evening fireworks, and, of course, tables of treats like Molly's baked goods. Paige wouldn't be giving a full tour until Sunday, but the Saturday festivities commencing at noon were a community tradition, with most farmers done their seeding and children fidgety for the beginning of summer still a month away.

Paige was impatient for new beginnings, as well.

✦

Bone weary, her vision bleary through salt-crusty eyes, Libby reached up into the top shelf of the linen closet and felt for Gram's pink train case, finally recognized. She moved aside the cushions blocking the dusty overnight bag, carried it into her room, and set it on the floor. She rifled around in her dresser drawers for pajamas and a change of underwear. That, along with toothbrush and makeup pouch, was about all the case would hold, and all she would need anyway, for a single night away.

She sat down on the edge of her bed and balanced the pink case on her knees, stroking its bubbled, fake-leather surface. Gram used to let her pack it for sleepovers with her girlhood classmates and always hid a surprise in it when Libby wasn't looking: a new ponytail elastic, a bag of candy to share, a glittery card with a sentimental message inside. What would she find in it today? Libby hugged a smile to herself. The last time she used it as a teenybopper, her oh-so-necessary bottle of hairspray leaked all over the satin lining and dried into a brittle mess. The next Christmas, Gram bought her a new backpack printed with the cast of Happy Days, and she had no further need of the train case. Had she even seen it from that day to this?

Libby lifted the vintage case from her knees to heft its weight, much lighter in her adult hand than it had been the first time she carried it when she was five. On a bright summer day, she and her mother had stopped in at Gram's, who begged Elsa to let her babysit. But Mom insisted Libby come along with her somewhere as proof—of what, Libby didn't understand. Gram with a fierce scowl shook her head, and Libby hoped Gram wasn't angry with her. Funny what fragments of the past come to mind half a century later. At any rate, Gram let Libby take the cute pink case to hold her nightie, and then she put in a box of crayons and a coloring book for the excursion. That had cheered Libby up. On the trip, the radio of the borrowed car blared country-western music and her mom sang along at the top of her voice, windows open to the fresh air.

Libby had no memory of the ride home.

Now she clicked open the rusty metal clasp and lifted the lid to a treasury of childhood mementos. She rummaged through elementary report cards and school photos, a homemade valentine, an orange potholder she'd crocheted under Gram's supervision—the sort of trove a proud mother might keep to capture the growing up of her beloved child. When had Gram last added anything to the stash, or had she long forgotten the pink box concealed high above reach in the back of the top shelf in a linen closet?

Libby shoveled the contents into a haphazard pile on her nightstand, her nails scraping against the scab of hairspray on the bottom. Before she refilled the case with necessities for the road trip, she noticed a slight bulge inside the gathered pocket of the lid's lining. She slipped her hand past the elasticized edge and extracted a once-sealed envelope and, falling from it, a chain attached to a delicate gold ring—a child's ring, maybe. Under the light of her bedside lamp, she examined the tiny, worn band, its surface rough as though scored.

Had she seen this ring before?

She turned the envelope over. Addressed to her, a simple *Libby* was written in Gram's hand, not so spidery as in her later years but firm and sure. She further loosened the crackled glue of the envelope and pulled out two sheets of paper with Gram's close penmanship filling all four sides. *Libby, my dear*, it began, and her breath hitched.

> *I suppose every family has a skeleton in the closet. I've been meaning to write this out for you and there's no time like the present. You have a right to an explanation about your mother and my mother, the story of the ring.*

Libby paused her reading and checked in vain for a date on the top corner of the first page. When had Gram composed it? She fanned herself with the envelope, faster and faster the further she read.

She'd never heard any mention of this from Gram in all the time they lived together in the apartment. Libby had asked, that was certain. Time and again she'd asked Gram questions about the family or, rather, the lack of family. Gram evaded the subject, simply hugging her when she was in elementary school and outright dismissing the questions when Libby was in junior high by saying she had all the family she needed right here, and that it would all come right in the wash. Maybe, by the time her grandmother believed Libby was old enough to understand, Babette had lost the knowledge of her heritage as Libby herself had lost the details of that night of blood—the source of her recurring nocturnal terrors.

Like an exhalation from Gram's dead-cold lips, the epistle's story unfolded for her.

The ring was a Walker heirloom, Gram wrote, the only article of material value other than the soup kettle handed down to Babette from her mother, Elizabeth—Libby's great-grandmother. According to what the workers at the Minnesota orphanage told Elizabeth, she'd been wearing the band the day she was dumped on their doorstep at the turn of the century—a traumatized little girl whose English was all muddled up with Cree, broken cries of "Mama" mixed in with "Nisis"—meaning "Uncle," as Gram explained. The swarthy but freckled, auburn-haired youngster with baby teeth still intact arrived at the orphanage dehydrated from dysentery. She clung to a rag wrapped around three tattered, illegible letters. Word had it that her mother's brother, Nisis

Hokoma, had brought her to the institution and died there himself the next day. How he and Elizabeth came to be wandering the Midwest Gram had no clue. And she offered no explanation as to whether the orphanage tried following up on the girl's letters. But the engraving inside the tiny ring gave a date, presumably of Elizabeth's birth, and hinted at wealth—if indeed the ring hadn't been stolen in the first place, Gram wrote.

Libby loosened her grip on Gram's letter in order to scrutinize the inner surface of the oddly familiar ring, which she could swear Gram had never shown to her. Libby made out faint scratches but nothing identifiable. Perhaps if she used a magnifying glass? It would be packed at the bottom of a box, and she couldn't think which one it might be, fatigued as she was at two-thirty on a Saturday morning. She resumed reading.

Elizabeth was given the last name of Walker by the orphanage authorities. She'd walked into their lives, they said, and they sought to root her there. But Elizabeth left the institution in disgrace a mere three years after the onset of puberty. Gram used elusive language here, as though distressed:

Your great-grandmother had been offended by a man in a position of power. I was the result.

Settled in Minneapolis, Elizabeth gave birth to Babette in 1910 and worked at whatever came to hand to feed the pair of them, but Elizabeth died before her hair turned gray.

Babette had worn the ring until outgrowing it, she wrote, first on her pointer and then on her middle digit and so on until it no longer fit even her pinkie. Then she carried it in her brassiere by day and clutched it beneath her pillow every night, until she saved enough to buy the gold chain at JB Hudson. The family memento rested close to her heart until the birth of Elsa, sired by the scoundrel Redpath, who was the descendant of a Siouan tribeswoman and a Scots fur trader.

Libby let the sheets of paper lie on her leg as she pondered the news of her lineage. Who knew what other ethnicities might flow in her veins, given—besides Gram's indiscretion—the rape of her great-grandmother and then Elsa's outright harlotry? No family line remained for Libby to trace, and these latest tidbits only complicated her genealogy. She read on. By the time Elsa was old enough to care for the ring, her behavioral problems stopped Gram from handing it over. Elsa's tantrums gave way to a troubled adolescence and then to alcohol abuse and reckless living:

> *I knew she'd sell the only inheritance I had to pass along to you, my dear granddaughter. So I hid the ring away from her greedy eyes the night she brought you back from the trip up north. She carried on about the letters not being any use at all, tearing them up in front of you like that and throwing the pieces into the air to scatter around our feet. Do you remember, Libby? Oh, but you were so tiny then.*

Was that the night Zinnia had been talking about, with the paper snowstorm and Elsa stinking of booze?

> *I didn't even know Elsa had found those letters. I forgot I had them, stuck away for years in a file in a kitchen drawer. Out of sight, out of mind, I guess. But it seems she took them along on the trip. I managed to sneak a ripped bit from the floor before she burned the whole mess of them. I don't know what was so important about them that she had the idea they'd get her money.*

> *I think she tried to use them as a bribe.*

Whom would she be bribing?

> *Anyway, there's no use crying over spilled milk. This ring and these words are all I have to leave you, my dear. May they bring you peace.*

Libby slumped on the bed, anything but peaceful. She turned the pages over in her hands, looking for more of her grandmother, scanning the words again. She looped the chain around her neck, the cool gold of the ring nestling between her breasts. Where was the paper scrap Gram had referred to? Libby ran her finger along the inside of the envelope inscribed with her name. Yes, there it was. She withdrew the torn corner of a second envelope, dirty with age or her mother's rage and imprinted with a smudged postal stamp in faded, once-red ink: *Kirkton, ND.*

And at that moment Libby knew she'd indeed once seen a larger version of this ring—a bold, wide band of worked gold hanging upon an old man's withered knuckle.

At the mental picture, she leapt up from her bed, sending the case bouncing and skittering across the floor. Her knees buckling beneath her, she fell back onto the bed with sweating palms and hammering chest. The room spun and she saw, without the usual veil of half-sleep, that ancient man bending forward in his chair, reaching for her with open arms, asserting those ten words she yet couldn't recall, his eyes at that moment still focused and a joyful smile parting his snowy, blood-flecked beard. The wide-awake nightmare rolled on. Libby saw again her mother and the woman in the apron bursting into the room and pushing her aside. She'd shriveled into the curtain then, while her mother spewed profanities over the dying man, and the aproned lady flapped her hands and finally found the telephone to call for help.

Now, in renewed terror over that long-ago night, Libby gulped air to regain control of her runaway memories. Finally, she flipped off the light switch and pushed herself beneath the covers, bunching the pillow over her ears to silence the monsters howling beneath her bed.

CHAPTER TWENTY-FIVE

Today

In the library of the Laird Mansion Museum, Libby closes the album and turns to survey the walls, a frame-to-frame checkerboard of photographs and paintings and sketches—some colorized but most in the sepia and tan of recycled brown paper lunch bags softened with use. The room is an overwhelming collage of history. Where should she start?

"The museum's compilation of artwork illustrating the daily life of the Great Plains people has grown far past MDM's initial collection," Paige says.

The sisters, moving like conjoined twins, have bustled over to the best light by the window and are peering at a landscape painting through their matching spectacles. The Australians snap pictures of the pictures, and the school kids scuffle and poke at one another, almost upsetting a table of old bone arrowheads. Paige deflects their attention to an illustration of pioneers building sod-and-plank houses in the beginnings of old-town Kirkton. Libby overhears a couple of girls comment about the shirtless young men portrayed, and several of the real-life boys stick their chests out in competition.

Paige commands their attention again. "I recommend that as you browse this gallery you attend to the dates, notations, and titles to facilitate a sense of flow to the history. Remember that MDM was born in Canada in 1865, attended school in Saint Paul in 1882 before immigrating to Dakota Territory and founding Kirkton, and completed building the mansion in 1898, which he inhabited until 1967."

"Wow, the dude was really *old* when he croaked." The pimple-faced boy is counting the decades out on his fingers. "Like, over a hundred. Is that him?" He jerks his thumb at a head-and-shoulders sculpture of a straight-nosed man with thick side-whiskers and full facial hair including bushy brows.

From this angle looking up at it, Libby is five again.

"Yes," Paige says, "the cast bronze bust was commissioned for MDM's eightieth birthday, twenty-two years before he died. Over the duration of his lifetime, he participated in the repopulation of the Great Plains bison herd, saw the railway established, and met in person Theodore Roosevelt, who owned a cattle ranch in the Badlands before becoming president."

Paige goes on to detail how MDM suffered through the 1918 Spanish flu epidemic that killed thousands of his fellow homesteaders and beloved Native American companions. "He was around when both Jesse James and John F. Kennedy were shot. He was seventeen when Hitler was born, lived through two world wars, took passage on both stagecoach and airplane, and lost an acquaintance on the disastrous maiden voyage of the Titanic."

"Was it Leonardo DiCaprio?"

Paige smiles at the student's quip while the teacher, having extricated himself from Sybil's snare, stares the silly boy down. Libby feels heat creeping up into her cheeks on Sybil's behalf. The students are sure to carry stories back to their parents about Mr. Nelson's inappropriate involvement with the strange woman on their field trip.

"My point is that MDM's life spanned several eras. The same man who made this history"—she throws her arm in an arc to indicate the full scope of the art on the walls—"lived until some of your own parents were born."

"Until *I* was born," Libby mumbles to herself. Paige must have heard her, the way her mouth opens. Libby pivots abruptly to avoid any questions. She's not ready for Paige's questions. Not yet.

She treads to the west wall, feigning interest in three large pieces. She studies a canvas showing wind-driven braves wrapped in blowing, striped-edged blankets and standing in front of their camp, perched on the banks of a muddy creek that waters the horses. Another scene picturing an oxcart laden with a Métis family, circa 1883, hangs beside a noble chieftain wearing a magnificent feather headdress that cascades down to his heels like a bridal train.

Libby tunes out Paige's genial voice. She homes in on another grouping displayed on the wall across the room, above the chaise lounge upholstered in worn green damask. The photo on the left is labeled "Entertaining Angels Unawares: First Guests Hokoma and Nuttah 1890." Here a duo adorned in beads and fringes—the girl maybe still in her teens—stands at attention, but their eyes slant towards each other as though they're smothering mirth, like young people of any nationality. Are they related? Beside this piece, another identifying itself as "Sod Turning 1897" shows a younger MDM with tamer whiskers, dressed in top hat and tails as if for a great celebration, posing with one hand on a spade and the other on the shoulder of a young woman dressed in a high-necked blouse with hair drawn back into a chignon.

Libby moves in closer. Is this the same girl as in the photo on the left, only a few years older? She looks at the 1890 image again, swiveling her head to compare posture and smile and lovely, high cheekbones. The moccasins of the younger girl ultimately give away the identity of the older, for the toes in the more recent picture peeking out under long silk skirts bear the identical floral pattern.

CHAPTER TWENTY-SIX

Yesterday

The delicious aroma of coffee woke Paige on Saturday morning, the first time in weeks she'd out-slept Danny. He stood beside their bed holding her favorite mug, a big smile plastered on his face.

"You are so cute with your messy hair and baby bump."

Was it really already ten? "Hey, why aren't you out finishing up the seeding?"

"Last night's shower dampened things, and I'm waiting for the wind to do its magic," Danny said.

"It rained? I slept like a log after I finally came to bed." Paige rubbed her eyes. "Oof, Baby is kicking my bladder this morning." She picked up the cell phone from her dresser and dashed across the hallway—no connecting bathroom for them in this old farmhouse. Her exasperated moan brought Danny running.

"What's the matter?" he asked. "Are you okay?"

"Sorry. Didn't mean to alarm you." He was so protective of her lately. She washed her hands and squeezed toothpaste onto her brush. "I'm just annoyed that I still haven't had an answer from the anonymous e-mailer I told you about." Not that it mattered anymore, with her thesis finished and sent.

"The stalker?"

"Danny, don't be silly. It's a woman, I'm sure of it." What guy would use an e-mail address containing "Gramsgirl"?

"How can you tell nowadays?" Danny nuzzled her neck as she rinsed and spat. "Can't say as I blame him. You are irresistible."

She laughed and gently pushed him away. "Go on out to *your* boyfriend, John Deere. He's waiting for you. Oh, did you pack a lunch?"

"I should get the last quarter seeded by noon, so I thought I'd stop over at the museum to grab a carnival snack before parking the machinery." Danny handed her a towel. "Then later I'll come back into town for the barbeque and potluck. It'll be great to see our parents all together."

"Oh no, I forgot I planned to make a salad."

Danny stopped on his way out the bathroom door. "Didn't Mom tell you she was going to fix a salad? No one expects you to bring food, Paige. Not with all the work you've been up to. Which reminds me, did you get your paper sent off before midnight?"

"I did." She gave him the thumbs-up and his eyes shone at her. She warmed at his pride.

Paige dug her costume out of the closet and tore away the drycleaner's plastic protecting it since last fall. She buttoned up the frock, glad for the extra-large waistband that, last season, had dwarfed her. The starched white cap was cute as ever, and the mirror showed her looking every bit the parlor maid, especially once her apron was tied over the massive bulge that was Baby.

She wouldn't have much time today to visit with the folks, what with her responsibility for managing the day's events. Not that either her mother-in-law Donna or Mom would expect attention, and Martin loved shooting the breeze with Myles-to-go, as he called Paige's dad. Besides, there was plenty to occupy them. The museum's official annual opening always saw the whole community turn out, with tables of local crafts: crocheted dishcloths and handmade wooden toys, metal signs and wind chimes, a rack of dried herbs gathered wild from grassland and thicket, and bergamot-scented soaps made with beef tallow. For the first time a beer garden would be set up for the adults, in Paige's opinion not strictly in keeping with MDM's abstemious nature and his advocacy for Prohibition. Even a maypole would be more fitting. Then again, a maypole wouldn't produce the income of a beer garden to pay for the museum's operation.

Libby pitched forward, her seatbelt tightening against her chest as the Prius slammed to a stop in front of Seven Canaan Lane.

"I hope this satisfies you." Sybil spat the words out.

But Libby was under no obligation to apologize. "It's a fair deal. Swinging by the house before we get onto the interstate for North Dakota doesn't cost you anything."

"Except time."

"Saturday morning traffic didn't hold us up at all, Sybil, and we have the full day to get there. You're the one who always says travel is an adventure."

"Plodding through middle-class Minneapolis is no adventure."

"Be a sport." Libby nudged Sybil. "I know you're philosophically against me buying my own home, but what's the chance I'll be able to afford it anyway? I just want to look at it one more time."

"Yep, without that loan you've got nothing." Sybil flared her nostrils. "So why your fixation on this overpriced house"—she stabbed a rigid finger towards Seven Canaan Lane—"when you could move in with Clive for free?"

Libby tipped her head and held her tongue for a moment. "I thought you were through with pushing him onto me. We were going on this road trip for distance from questions of that sort."

Sybil was a bulldog when she got a bone between her teeth. Libby didn't want to think about Clive right now. Increasingly when the subject of homelessness arose, her stomach cramped and twisted. All she'd wanted, when she asked Sybil to include this house in their road trip itinerary, was to sit for a moment with her nose pressed up against the window of her limitations and poverty, like a kid outside a candy store. In reality, not only her dreams of purchasing this house but even her desire for Sybil to show empathy were turning out to be wishful thinking.

"I need my morning chai," Sybil said. "Get out."

"Pardon?" Libby had assumed they'd merely slow down as they passed by Seven Canaan Lane. What if the occupants were watching from behind the kitchen curtains, wondering about the unfamiliar car?

"I'm going back to the drive-through on Lake Street. I'll bring a coffee. You need an attitude adjustment."

Her words were interrupted when the screen door of the Arts and Crafts house slapped closed. Someone must have stepped out, but Libby resisted turning sideways to check. She lowered her voice. "Let's go now."

Instead Sybil punched Libby's seatbelt button, reached over her to open the car door, and pushed Libby out. She scrambled to find her footing. The car peeled off, leaving Libby on the sidewalk exposed to the frank inspection of the stocky blonde woman standing on the porch of Seven Canaan Lane, her fists planted on middle-aged hips.

In an attempt at nonchalance, Libby faced the street again and made another quarter-turn as though intending to walk purposefully towards some destination or other. But there was no store nearby, no obvious reason for her to have been dropped off in this residential area. She must look pathetic.

"It's you. Minnehaha."

The street being otherwise empty, Libby couldn't ignore the words directed at her, and so she steeled herself to face the speaker.

"Excuse me?"

"I've been watching you for years." The woman hustled down the stairs. "Since I was a girl. We must be roughly the same age?"

Libby was mute. She recognized a faded version of the blonde girl from four decades ago who chased her puppy, the same bride who celebrated her wedding with a lawn party, the young mom who moved back home to Seven Canaan Lane with her family when her elderly parents needed help. But Libby assumed she herself had been invisible all this time—when she ogled the house from her seat on the public bus, when she dreamed about a daddy hugging his fair-haired girl, when she made this street her walking route because she wanted a house like that, a family like that. The woman stepped closer, a smile on her face brightening her eyes.

"My name's Gloria. And you can't really be named Minnehaha."

Libby stifled a nervous laugh. "Why on earth would you have thought so?"

"Well, you were always very mysterious to me, since the first day I noticed you—your waist-length hair, exotic eyes I couldn't read, and the way you crept along as though you were tracking a deer in the forest. Just my childish imagination. But this was about the time, in school, when we were studying Longfellow's 'Song of Hiawatha.' You must remember it." Here Gloria placed her palm on her breast and raised her face upwards as though on stage for a variety show recitation. She drew in one long breath and chanted:

> *With him dwelt his dark-eyed daughter,*
> *Wayward as the Minnehaha,*
> *With her moods of shade and sunshine,*
> *Eyes that smiled and frowned alternate,*
> *Feet as rapid as the river,*
> *Tresses flowing like the water,*
> *And as musical a laughter:*
> *And he named her from the river,*
> *From the water-fall he named her,*
> *Minnehaha, Laughing Water.*

She gasped for air and then beamed at Libby without apparent self-consciousness. "I actually memorized that stanza in your honor, and it still comes back to me every time I see you walking by the house."

"*You* made up stories about *me*?" Libby clamped her hand around her throat. She felt exposed, the watched and no longer only the watcher.

"Yeah, and about your grandmother. She did housecleaning for my friend's family down the street. They loved her."

"I tagged along sometimes." Was Libby really conversing with the owner of Seven Canaan Lane?

"Right. You became a legend in our fifth-grade classroom, even though you didn't attend our school. So I made up a story for all of them about how you and I were friends." Gloria ducked her head, her cheeks suddenly pink. "They fought to come for sleepovers at my house for the chance to glimpse Minnehaha at midnight, 'peeping from behind the curtain, from behind the waving curtain, gleaming, glancing through the branches, as one hears the Laughing Water' . . . Well, you get the picture. I was besotted with the fantasy as a preteen."

Libby understood. It was the counterpart to her own obsession. She stared over Gloria's head at the home of her make-believe family.

"Well, my real name is Libby Walker." She stuck her hand out and clasped the other's. Would Gloria recognize her as a potential buyer?

"Nice to meet you. Come in for a coffee?"

"You were on your way out," Libby said. "Anyway, my friend will be back momentarily." She checked up the street, but there was no sign of Sybil's car.

"My shopping can wait. It's not every day Minnehaha visits in the flesh. Come on, we'll sit in the front room, and you can dash out when you see your friend returning."

"Well, I suppose you're used to strangers tromping through your house these days." Although, come to think of it, Libby she hadn't seen a "For Sale" sign posted on the lawn of Seven Canaan Lane. "And, actually, I'd like to see the bronze chandelier again, hanging over the couch."

Gloria, halfway up the steps, stopped dead. "How would you know about the chandelier?" She turned, her mouth a grim line. "You haven't been . . . *peeping*, have you?"

"Oh, good heavens, no. I'm the person Clive Clifton, the realtor, brought by to view your house." Had two weeks passed already?

Gloria's forehead relaxed. "Oh, so you're the 'interested private party' he's representing. That makes sense. He came knocking on our door, flashing his fake Rolex and fast-talking about someone hot to buy this place."

Libby groaned. "I am so sorry he pestered you. I swear I didn't sic him on you. I had no idea you were considering selling in the first place." Her apology was real. Clive was embarrassing.

"We weren't until he came by. But it got my husband and me thinking that it's about time to downsize, what with the boys on their own now." Gloria ushered Libby into the living room and onto the davenport. "Give me a second. I think my breakfast coffee is still hot." She disappeared into the kitchen to re-emerge almost immediately with two china mugs.

"Surely your children wouldn't approve of your selling the family home." Libby toyed with the ring at the end of the chain. She shouldn't even continue on this line of thought, this fancy that—if she believed enough—she could achieve what she conceived. Seven Canaan Lane was out of her reach, and all the faith in the world wouldn't change that fact.

"The boys are joint owners of a car dealership in Palm Springs, with growing kids of their own and wives who adore the sun. It's more likely we'll end up there than ever see them move back up north." She offered Libby cream and sugar, but both women drank their coffee black. "A distant cousin of my husband has been hounding us to sell to him, but I suspect he just wants to reno this place and flip it."

"Oh, no. It's perfect the way it is."

Gloria nodded, her hooded eyes watching Libby over the rim of her mug. "Besides, we wouldn't want just anyone to move in here."

Libby jittered her foot on the floor, her knee jiggling. "But you have the house listed."

"Not formally. I mean, we haven't signed a realty agreement yet, and we're not sure this Clive is the right character to negotiate our interests."

"Right." Libby blew out her breath, her shoulders collapsing. She shouldn't have assumed she still had a chance at it, and not only because her mortgage application was likely to be turned down. "I understand the other potential buyer has already put in an offer anyway."

Gloria blinked. "What other buyer? We gave that realtor leave to show the house only once."

"But I thought—" Just then, the Prius wheeled by, Sybil craning her neck. "Oh, I'd better run." Libby put down the half-empty mug and rose to leave.

"Listen, give me your phone number. I want to talk to my husband first, but maybe we can swing a private sale."

Libby's stomach flip-flopped. She felt around in her purse for pen and paper, finding a small card. "Okay, but I'm pretty sure the finances won't work out." Not now, with eviction and no job and everything else going on in her life. She skimmed the printed information on the business card in her hand, not recognizing it. But Gloria was already scribbling on her napkin and so Libby tucked the card into her shirt pocket and recited her cell number as Sybil leaned on her horn. She blasted away until Libby emerged from the house at run, with a wave towards Gloria behind her.

✒

"You were *in the house?*" The accusation ringing in Sybil's voice struck Libby as impertinent.

"Thanks for the coffee." Libby plucked the go-cup from the car's holder. She didn't respond to Sybil's sneer but, keeping her own voice light and cheerful, she firmly changed the subject. She had no taste for a quarrel. "So what's our ETA?"

"Under five hours to Grand Forks, if we don't waste too much time eating lunch at a greasy spoon along the way." Sybil's lips stretched flat and white in a mock gag.

"Fargo must have a vegan-friendly restaurant. Let's enjoy the road trip." Libby's remonstrance was aimed as much at herself as at Sybil.

"You're finally getting into the spirit of things." Sybil's voice was still sour.

"I'm not likely to take vacation again anytime soon."

If a change was as good as a rest, as Gram always insisted, she might as well make the most of it, use the trip as distraction from the stress churning inside her gut. Where would they stay the night? Even a budget motel, with someone else making her bed in the morning, would be an indulgence for Libby. She looked at the map but could see nothing close to Kirkton that would likely be good enough for Sybil. The drive to the museum from Minneapolis would take them through Fargo-Moorhead to Grand Forks and then on up almost to the Canadian border.

Sybil spun off down Canaan Lane, and Libby sank back into the leather seat, even tilting it for further comfort. The business card in her pocket chafed. She pulled it out and turned it over a couple of times before she recalled where she'd received it.

"What's that?" Sybil eyed the card. She should be giving full attention to merging into the traffic on the I-94.

"A card one of the judges handed me last weekend at the Belle's fundraiser." He'd scrawled his personal number on the back. "I forgot all about it. He told me to contact him."

"Maybe he thought you were cute." Sybil's humor was dribbling back into place. "What's his business, anyway?" Sybil snatched the card from her and read the company name aloud: "Folkways Nutrition Group."

"I suppose I should call him when I get back." Libby scratched the tip of her nose. "He's likely forgotten about me by now, or maybe he's heard about my terrible mistake and won't want to talk to me at all."

"What mistake?"

Libby sighed. "The Great Gourmet Goji Fiasco." Her improv title had a ring to it. She explained, without blaming Sybil, about her rash impulse to toss the powder into her seminar concoction at the last moment. Sybil burst out laughing, apparently finding it hilarious.

"So call the guy," she said.

"I'd rather do a background check on his company first."

"If you had a data plan, you could Google it right now." Sybil shook her head as though Libby were an incorrigible child. "Here, use my tablet."

Sybil sped northwest towards Saint Cloud while Libby read up on the company—a consulting group that delivered quality nutrition services to businesses and restaurants around the country. They counted as clients some of the biggest names in the industry and specialized in ethnic foods customized to meet religious, regulatory, and aesthetic standards.

"It says here they 'develop and test recipes, analyze nutrient content claims, and design menus based on client specification.'" What in the world could Libby contribute to Folkways? There was only one way to find out, so she dialed her phone.

Quentin Hardy himself answered, expressed pleasure at her following up on their contact, insisted she address him by first name, and explained a bit more about his company. Finally he got around to his proposal.

"We're looking at generating a new line directed at indigenous peoples the world over." His crisp articulation caught Sybil's attention, and she hissed at Libby to activate the loudspeaker function. Libby waved her quiet—had Quentin heard?—and pressed the phone closer to her ear. He continued, "My business partner is in Paraguay scouting out ancestral cornbread recipes, and I'll be joining him next in Lima on the hunt for regional dishes of the Peruvian Andes."

"Yes?" Libby's voice was light, polite, though her throat constricted with anticipation.

"I was impressed with your presentation at the charity function held at the Belle."

"My presentation?" Babette's Bowl, at least its current formula, wasn't spectacular by any definition.

"It's your whole demeanor, actually. Your . . . well, your obvious ethnic background, for one thing, if you don't mind my mentioning it. And your lack of pretention so rare among gourmands. Frankly, we need people we can work with, Libby, not some high-strung artist type trying to shock the palate. Your soup was the most accessible dish I tasted all evening."

Libby smiled into her phone. "By 'accessible,' I assume you

mean 'down home.'"

"I suspect you have a few more surprises hiding under your chef's hat," Quentin said.

"But I'm not a trained chef."

"You have the touch."

"I'm not even sure I'll get my certificate from the seminar." She caught her lower lip between her teeth. Maybe she shouldn't have alluded to the possible ramifications of her culinary mistake, but Quentin didn't react. Libby agreed to meet with him, and disconnected.

"Job offer?" Sybil reached to the seat behind her for her bag of sweet potato crisps and offered it to Libby.

"Something like that. I'm not sure." Libby dipped her hand into the bag for a few of the chips.

"He mentioned your ethnic background."

"You heard?"

"Couldn't help it. Loud voice." She grinned over at Libby. "I've often wondered why you didn't claim your Native American status. It's nothing to be ashamed of, you know."

"I'm not ashamed, I'm just uninformed." That fact wasn't as true today as it had been yesterday, before she'd found the letter detailing the little Gram knew. "I'm as Heinz 57 as most Americans."

"Want to go to one of the powwows around the Twin Cities this summer, watch their hoop dancing?" Sybil asked.

"Why?"

"To belong." Sybil crunched a chip loudly. "Cultural identity and all that crap."

Libby had never been too concerned about identifying with

any particular cultural group—not even in school, when her academic counselor pushed her to try out for a race-based college scholarship. It had confused her at the time. Wasn't America a melting pot of nationalities? During high school, she was as friendly with the Malaysian girl in Bio as with the new immigrant Israeli sisters in Algebra. Belonging, Gram held, wasn't about skin color or bloodline but about heart attitude.

Not that her heart had always kept her out of trouble. Not that even Gram's words were enough to convince her, as a teen, to find her heart's content outside of her boyfriend's bed. No, life's lessons hadn't come easily to Libby.

But experience had taught her exactly what she needed to know, even—when she thought about it—guidance in how to answer Clive's offer of "shelter." Hadn't she made her mind up long ago that official marriage was the only avenue she'd ever walk towards interdependence with a man again? Her worth didn't rest on her race, whatever *that* really was, any more than it rested on her gender or her family.

Her family . . . A picture streaked unbidden across her mind, of her mother unconscious on the filthy pavement in front of the dumpster. She shivered.

"Someone walk over your grave?" Sybil turned down the car fan.

"No, I was thinking about Elsa and the horrible scene last night. You know"—Libby paused—"it wasn't a sheer accident, Elsa getting hit by those maniac boys."

"What do you mean?"

"I sort of, uh, pushed her away from me at the wrong moment." Slight understatement, and the confession didn't relieve her. "She was calling me her sweet darling and clawing at me." Libby shuddered again.

"Disgusting. What a piece of human garbage."

That was a little harsh. Libby frowned. "Still, I think maybe I owe her."

"Right. Owe her what?"

"I should check on her when we get back, make sure she's alive." Gram wouldn't have lost hope in Elsa. She'd have spent the night at her daughter's side in the hospital, holding her hand, speaking soft words.

"She was hardly a mother to you."

"Maybe she was as good a mother as she knew how to be." Libby didn't believe her own words. Elsa had had Gram as an example and was left no excuse for her abusive selfishness, her profound lack of parenting skills.

"Then why didn't she have other kids?"

"I explained that to you." Libby's face heated up. "It wasn't for lack of willing men. I was the only one of her 'accidents' to see the light of day."

"So she used abortion as birth control? She was ahead of her time."

Libby withheld comment. The old sorrow of her miscarriage surged, memories of the tiny body with closed eyes bulging as if about to pop open and glare blame at her. She ran her fingers over her left wrist, feeling for the razor-thin scar, the remaining evidence of the cataclysmic event. It still stunned her to think her mother could so easily flush away life, more than once, when Libby had held onto her singular pregnancy with such futile desperation.

Sybil rolled her eyes. "Don't look so tragic. Abortion, from a philosophical perspective, is a merciful procedure. Elsa saved your potential siblings the horror of the life you lived and gave them the chance for another go-around."

"There's nothing merciful about getting rid of a baby." Libby didn't want to discuss this with Sybil, who'd once told her fetuses denied life at one stage were reborn into another body somewhere else along the continuum of infinity's endless progression. But believing something didn't make it true. Trusting reincarnation couldn't return Libby's child to her any more than it could take away the sting of Gram's death.

Sybil glowered. "Your hostility's showing."

Libby was indeed once more filled with hostility over her losses, anger rushing in like the breaking of waters. She hitched up her left shoulder and burrowed into the passenger seat. She counted to the rhythm of the tires—*one, two, three, four, five*—and slipped back half a year, to the day Gram's wizened fingers stroked the quilt binding and her breathing labored and her voice grew softer than ever.

"You'll do fine when I'm gone," Gram had said. "It's always darkest before the dawn." Maybe she'd been thinking, too, about how Libby went to pieces after the miscarriage.

"Why does it always end with death?" Libby had asked.

"Death, like living, is a matter of faith."

"But faith in what, Gram?"

"Ah, now that's the issue, isn't it?" Tendrils of white hair clung to her face. Libby strained to hear, went to her knees to get close to Gram's mouth. "Faith in everything means faith in nothing. Belief itself doesn't get a girl anywhere. It's *what* she believes in that saves her."

"I believe in *you*, Gram."

"But I'm leaving."

"I don't know which way to turn." Libby clutched—too tightly, perhaps—to papery skin that would in any event have no time to bruise. "Should . . . should I just follow my heart?"

"Your heart will be where your treasure lies." Gram's panting was slow and shallow. "Follow your treasure."

"You're my treasure, Gram." Did she have to die now, this minute? "And I can't follow you. I'm trying to find the way . . ."

"You can't take every path," Gram inhaled, "or you'll end up walking in circles," Gram exhaled, "and never find your way home."

"But where is home, Gram?"

Her voice had been so faint. "It's where our fathers rest. Not in the ground, you know." And Gram nodded her head, then, and went home, leaving Libby to her silent supplications: Father, where is the way? Where is home?

The car's music jolted Libby out of her doze and back to the countryside speeding by. She took a swig of bottled water to moisten her mouth—had she been snoring?—and reached for Sybil's tablet again. She logged into her e-mail account, which she hadn't accessed for almost a week thanks to the shambles in her apartment. At the top of her inbox, she found a welcomed message from the Belle Boutique Hotel. The diner who'd reacted to an ingredient in one of the soups had assured the hotel that Goji could not, in fact, be the culprit, as that supplement was a regular part of her diet. Libby almost cheered. Then she spotted a response to the last message she'd sent to Paige at the museum. She opened it, her eyes skipping here and there over the text, the bold and caps of the final sentence yelling at her:

> ... Museum was not instituted until the mid-1980s ... can't speak for the next docent ... come see me ... **It's of urgent personal interest to me to speak with you AS SOON AS POSSIBLE.**

Libby sucked in her breath, clicked the "log out" button, and threw the tablet into the back seat. She closed her eyes once again in what Sybil hopefully viewed as a sign of boredom.

But Libby wasn't bored. The intensity of the e-mail message made her belly spasm. Her lack of sleep last night joined forces with her natural repugnance against the stress of the unknown—against what she didn't really want to know, if she was being honest with herself. She forced herself to sleep again, awakening next when Sybil stopped at a gas station and ordered the attendant to "fill 'er up."

"Phil 'Er Up," Libby heard herself repeat, groggy. "That's the name of the restaurant I applied to."

"Oh, Sleeping Beauty awakes." Sybil slipped her credit card out of her wallet and pushed it at the gas jockey. "You want a candy bar?"

"Ugh, no." Libby disliked junk food as much as Sybil said she did, but somehow her friend hadn't ever noticed, even after all the pots of nutritious, homemade soup Libby had shared with her. Why, just last month, before her world turned upside down, Libby had brought over to Amulets a tub of lemon and lentil chowder with cumin, which her friend ate with appreciation but—come to think of it—without asking for seconds. Sybil's chosen career in the field of alternative health and nutrition made her talk like a clean-eating snob, as though everyone else craved foods forbidden to her. Why press a candy bar on Libby? Maybe, after all, Sybil actually craved junk food herself.

"Pop? Fries?"

"Sybil Tansey, just because I don't buy into your vegan, gluten-free, low-sodium, no-sugar, fat-free diet doesn't mean I eat garbage."

"No offense meant." Sybil opened the door and swung out of the driver's seat. "Be back in a minute."

While Sybil visited the ladies' room, Libby placed a quick call, taking a chance she'd reach a voicemail box rather than the live person. No such luck.

"Hey cupcake, to what do I owe the pleasure?"

"Clive." She straightened up. "I only have a second. Just wanted to let you know—"

He cut her off. "Glad you phoned. I'm just out shopping for new sheets and wondered if you prefer white or tan."

"I definitely won't be moving in with you, Clive." Her voice wavered, but now was no time to start doubting again.

"Kitten—"

"And it's Libby."

"Oh come on. Don't be like that, dollface."

But Sybil was coming out of the gas station now. Libby hung up on Clive.

"So you say you applied at a restaurant?" Sybil jammed the car's stick into drive and pulled back onto the highway. "Planning on taking two jobs, then?"

"Maybe. I've got to support myself."

"Did you know that Terence posted a 'Help Wanted' sign in the window of the card shop?"

"I have no interest in ever working for him again." Libby crossed her legs and linked her hands together over her knee.

"Good last resort, though, if you get hungry enough. You could go back begging for mercy. I'm sure by now he's realized how much you did for that store and is wishing he hadn't been so hasty."

"Last resort for Terence, maybe. I'd rather starve." Would she rather have no chance at all for the mortgage? That was a more pressing question. Phil was likely to call back and offer her the job, and surely the pay would be better than the pittance at Hearsay. But wishful thinking wasn't reality, and Gram's voice whispered to her something about beggars riding horses.

THE RED JOURNAL

Red Journal entry, dated September 13, 1955:

My Heart,

See how feebly I hold my pen. My words, as my days on this earth, are nearly over, my mediation complete, my prophecy fulfilled. I sit now and rest, having attained my ninth decade and finished my work once and for all. Yet still I welcome those who draw near in faith, boldly passing through the veil into my inner sanctum—those who have done their business with me and know me, from the least to the greatest, those who come seeking to take possession of their inheritance of peace with me.

Kirkton, I hear from my cloistered office within these walls, decays and waxes old, though its foundations will never vanish. The People—not all, but those established in their families—live by the law of love written on their hearts, generation to generation. Their failings and sorrows are remembered no more, my own youthful travails for them proven effective.

My Heart, I trust you have passed along this same love to Elizabeth. How I long to see her once more.

But soon, surely, I must leave my body and this paradisal home to enter into heaven itself, for where a testament is, there must also of necessity be the death of the testator. I have run with patience the race set before me. This life, like the blueprint to our earthly home and, indeed, to the project I have so meticulously constructed for our daughter, is but a copy and a shadow of the good things to come. We have in store a better and enduring substance.

Yet I long to bestow on the girl the bequest you and I intended for her. The ungodly heritage of Henrietta's crafty and brutish offspring does not escape my purview; even in my dotage I have learned of the poison as relates to the Laird name being passed along to the whole community. They have despised you in your absence and made a myth of you, My Heart.

But we do not fear what man might do, for we receive a priestly kingdom that cannot be moved, and we have an altar whereof they have no right to eat. And so,

In full assurance of hope I remain, as ever, Yours Truly

CHAPTER TWENTY-SEVEN

Yesterday

Sybil's stomach was growling when she and Libby stopped at Grand Forks for a quick salad. Their conversation had flattened along with the topography as they headed northward, and neither of them was saying much anymore. Sybil was ready to quit driving. She'd never spent this much time at once with Libby, who kept dozing off. She had to do something to amuse herself. It was time to tell a story.

"Did I ever describe the gastronomy of Spain to you?"

Libby perked up. Even Iggy listened to Sybil's travelogues although, of course, she left off the juicier bits when recounting her escapades to either of them.

"Did you come across *crema de calabazo*—pumpkin soup?" Libby asked. "It's quite famous—"

"I didn't waste calories on soup. I virtually lived on tapas in Barcelona." Sybil could taste them again. "Bites of sweet pepper and anchovy. Sun-dried tomatoes skewered with olives. And cava pouring freely, of course. My favorite bar was around the corner from the entrance to the ruins at the city's foundation." Sybil flicked the wrapping off a piece of sour cherry gum and popped it into her mouth, saliva gushing as she slurped around her words. "I walked down steps into the basement of the city, clear back to the Roman settlement—excavated remains of a whole civilization, including a winery and a fish-processing plant and a laundry facility. Did you know the Romans collected public urine to use in their fabric-bleaching process?"

"Too much information." Libby's nose wrinkled.

Apparently, like most moderns, Libby believed that urine was a sort of toxic waste. But beyond its early laundry usage, consumption of urine had been shown in both laboratory and clinical testing to be a rich source of nutrients, enzymes, and antibodies protecting against all sorts of diseases. However, Sybil refrained from mentioning this trivia or the fact that she'd tasted her own urine once, at a party of like-minded, countercultural friends. After all, she'd intended this road trip to be a pleasant precursor to future travel.

"You'd have enjoyed strolling with me in the underworld among the shades and wraiths of such a golden age."

"Really?" Libby's smile was lopsided. "I suppose you saw Nero fiddling around."

"Bad joke," Sybil said. "You should have more respect for the hereafter. Barcelona is crawling with past lives. When I left for the airport, the taxi driver pointed out this incredible hillside cemetery overlooking the Mediterranean Sea. Thousands of crypts and mausoleums and tombs were stacked up on each other, tier upon tier like a honeycomb in a hive. Like a sprawling apartment complex."

"That sounds awful."

"No, it was inspiring." Sybil had wanted to ask the driver to stop, but her Spanish wasn't up to the challenge and she had a plane to catch. "It would be a great place for a séance. Can't you imagine the vital forces in that energy field?" Libby shook her head. Sybil really should escort Libby to a séance one day. "I'm going back to Europe on a funerary-art-themed tour eventually—take in Edinburgh and Dublin. Karl Marx is buried in London, you know, and Vienna has Beethoven and other composers."

"You're rather obsessed with death, my friend." Libby said it without obvious emotion, as though it wasn't an insult.

"You're suggesting I'm obsessed with death when *you* can't shut up about your grandmother?" As soon as her retort was out—and with such nasty inflection—Sybil bit her tongue. But Libby pinned her with those deep eyes and remained silent.

Sybil was hardly focused on death. How could anyone make such a statement when even her chosen career celebrated the fullness of health and wellness? Amulets Alternative Apothecary was dedicated to robust physical life and also to the eradication of this society's linear dualism that saw a chasm between spirit and matter in denying the unity and oneness of the All. Recreationally, too, Sybil always sought out new experiences to wake up her carnal senses as well as her intuitive and preternatural instincts. She bordered on the ritualistic in her endless and frenetic search for uncompromising holism. No, if anything, Sybil was obsessed with *life*.

Yet Libby's comment nagged at her.

Quiet descended again as they rolled through the farmland. Libby, obviously disinclined to chat, kept her eyes closed as she toyed with that ring on the chain around her neck. The terrain passing by Sybil's window reminded her of hairstyle possibilities: corn plots with last year's stalks poking up in bristly Mohawks, pastures bleached white with a green haze of new growth at their roots, and loam-brown fields newly tilled into comb-toothed rows.

In the silence, Sybil had to confess to herself that, yes, her own view of dying was incomplete. She believed the break between this life and the next—that is, "death"—was a misconception regarding the continuum of eternity. She was sure the spark of divinity within every person was unable to be quelled, and that no one really "died" but only entered a different realm to reappear at the proper time and in just the right form.

So, then, why did she refuse to discuss her mom's passing with her sisters? Sybil's palms were making the steering wheel slick. And why could she not call up her mother at will, no matter how many psychics she consulted or mediums she petitioned?

Sybil had seen wonders performed for friends through clairvoyance, cosmic vibration, and telepathy. And she regularly communed with various beings via the Ouija board and table tipping. She once belonged to a scrying group of seven, a divine number, meeting monthly in a room lit only by a single white candle, where they gazed into a mirror to summon up loved ones who'd passed over. On occasion, Sybil even partook of psychography. She'd empty her mind of all thought and, with pen in hand, would wait for a message, tuning herself in to the right frequency and writing down anything that came to her—the great I AM communing directly with her, through her.

But to this day, not one of the presenting spirits had ever identified as Charlotte Tansey.

She'd desperately sought a manifestation in many altered states of consciousness. Nothing was out of bounds to her. Then why did panic overwhelm her when Mom's smile flashed, unbidden, across the screen of her mind in her everyday moments, when she least expected it—at the shop or on a date or visualizing another excursion? What was the alarm that could cripple her soul in the minutes just before she fell asleep, when she caught a whiff of her mom's perfume and knew it had nothing to do with a ghostly visitation but only unmitigated memory—that unmistakable fragrance of rose and orange blossom, cedar and amber Mom dotted onto her wrists and décolletage even in the hospice bed, when the cancer was eating her up from the inside?

Thinking about her now was dangerous. Sybil turned up the volume on her music. She longed acutely to hear from her mother, and yet she hated the thought of hearing from her mother. What might Mom, always so sure of herself—as sure as Libby's Gram had seemed that one time they met—what might Mom say?

For years Sybil had been having great success in speaking affirmation into her own life, creating her own reality. For example, just last week sneezing and coughing set in but, stalwart, she declined to admit she had a cold. Instead, she took authority over that virus by commanding it to disperse, proving the power of the spoken word. It worked like a charm for breast cancer, too. She hadn't succumbed yet to the family curse, had she?

But a different sort of cancer now ate away at Sybil's soul.

She gripped the wheel, nails digging into palms. She'd just have to try harder to break through to her mother and put an end to the uncertainty. The scrap of doubt about the afterlife clinging to her mind like sticky gum was simply lack of faith on her part and had no place in the evolutionary system of transmigration she espoused. And to be sure she wasn't missing anything—just hedging her bets here, covering all the bases—she continued to add to her spiritual smorgasbord any other beliefs that fit in, consistent or not. Truth wasn't a closed book, after all.

Come to think of it, she'd heard about a thaumaturge in the Roswell area, UFO country, whose wonderworking paranormal abilities were making her famous. That might do the trick for

Sybil. She mentally jotted a note to herself to arrange for a consultation on the anniversary of Mom's passing over. Maybe on such an auspicious day Fate would reward her strivings to grace her with Mom's presence. Sybil's official spirit guides—seven in all, from across eons and cultures—never failed to appear when she bade them. And she suspected a poltergeist or two occupied her vicinity as well, if the flickering hall light and the eerie reappearance of the angel number eleven on her clock, her odometer, her restaurant bills meant anything at all.

Her mother had an obligation to appear, if only to confirm all was well on the other side. But when Sybil said so aloud at a family gathering she couldn't avoid, one of her aunts blabbered on about Charlotte finding her peace at the end with the hospice chaplain, praying to her Maker for salvation. What was that all about?

A bird flew at her windshield and she flinched. She shifted in the driver's seat to stretch her lower back. Libby remained in her own little world, if closed eyes and the cryptic smile pulling at her mouth were any indication. Probably dreaming of that house back in Minneapolis. Sybil sniffed. She'd been trying to bring Libby along on the path towards enlightenment or transcendence or awakening—whatever one wanted to call it. But she suspected she was fighting a losing battle. All the holiness housed in the consecrated places of the earth, the sacred destinations so energizing to Sybil, did no good to the one lost in the dark, the one who wouldn't come into the light. Homebody Libby might be a hopeless case after all.

*

Paige sagged against the corndog stand. She'd been on her feet all day.

She shouldn't complain; after all, the community had turned out in droves for the museum festival, and the events had ticked along nicely. The opening address by the arts council representative from Bismark received resounding applause, the kiddie rides resulted in giggles rather than tears, and the craft and food vendors were a great success—particularly the mother-daughter pair selling sizzling-hot Lakota frybread and tart wildberry fruit leather. Paige had enjoyed a sampling of both herself.

During the afternoon she'd made her rounds with a cold juice in hand, greeting the guests like a hostess, welcoming the members of the Kirkton Preservation Society as dignitaries, and introducing the museum staff to the new docent who'd just arrived. Ophelia was a student from the university's history department coming for the summer on Paige's referral. She'd led the girl on a private but truncated tour of the premises, not wanting her pregnancy weariness to blur her enthusiasm about their job. Maybe Ophelia would stay at the museum, wooed—as Paige had been wooed—by the mysteries of the past.

So the community event was going well. It was nice to have this time of farewell before Baby made his appearance, although of course she'd still enjoy acting as head guide into June while Ophelia trained. Paige scanned the busy grounds, the lofty mansion so full of MDM's life. Would the girl be able to fill her shoes?

Paige caught her own hubris and reprimanded herself. Danny had always insisted that no one is irreplaceable, except maybe a mother. Paige left the corndog stand's umbrella shade and resumed her managerial role. Yes, no one else in the world could fill the shoes of a mother, the new shoes she'd be putting on in a few short weeks.

She ambled through the crowd and passed by a table with a few remaining bags of homemade cookies, squares, and brownies, pausing to rub her swollen ankles.

"You look worn out, dear." Yvonne, the grocery lady, stood beside her daughter-in-law while Molly gave change to a customer. "You should sit down." She patted the seat of her wooden stool and then bent her head forward. "I'm glad you stopped by." She spoke in an undertone. "I was thinking about our conversation in the store yesterday, about you asking if MDM had ever married."

All weariness fled, and Paige snapped, "You know something."

The woman jerked her head back, her eyes large as a jackrabbit's before it bounds out of sight into a midnight ditch. Paige held still until Yvonne whispered, "Well, of course I never met the old fellow. He died about the time I was born."

"I see . . ." Paige left the phrase open ended to encourage the woman to continue.

"And my grandparents didn't personally know him, though they respected him. He was well along in years even in their day."

"Of course . . ."

"And in a different social class." Yvonne raised an eyebrow.

Different social class? "But he farmed, like all the other locals." From her research, Paige had found nothing to suggest MDM would initiate social segregation, but others might have been intimidated by his wealth.

"Maybe so." Yvonne's mouth was a thin line. When she spoke again, a smear of orange lipstick smudged her teeth. "Anyway, I don't remember the exact words my grandpa used, but . . ." Yvonne's voice trailed off again and Paige jutted her chin forward.

"I won't quote you." Was Paige's tone trustworthy?

Yvonne's eyes bulged. "Quote me?" She looked around, furtive, but no one other than Molly, engaged in counting cash, was near enough to hear.

"I mean, I'm curious about what your grandfather said to you about MDM, and I won't let anyone know you were the one who told me."

Yvonne blew a breath from puffed cheeks, and she nodded slowly. "Okay. Well, the gist of it was that Grandpa's dad helped break Laird land and get it ready for seeding. This was right around the time Sitting Bull got killed, according to Grandpa."

The warrior's death at the Standing Rock Reservation happened in 1890, which would have made MDM almost thirty when Yvonne's story of her great-grandfather took place.

"Go on, please." Paige forced her voice to remain voice neutral, encouraging, so paranoia wouldn't get the better of Yvonne.

"Well, according to what Grandpa heard, there was definitely a woman involved with MDM. And a wedding."

"Really?" Paige's voice quivered. This anecdotal testimony would hold no water without documentation, so she leaned closer and smiled as though she had all the time in the world for this little *tête-à-tête*.

Yvonne warmed to her subject. "Of course, Grandpa said they were calling MDM a 'squaw man.' You know, that like some of the other settlers he used a Native American woman for his own"—here Yvonne checked right and left—"well, pleasures."

"The history books talk about that practice." Paige hated to admit it.

"Yes, and I think it still gives the men in this community a kick to think they can drag down MDM's reputation. And there's that lawsuit." Yvonne clucked. "You know, there's an old jealousy around here still, though you couldn't tell by the turnout today."

Paige wouldn't get sidetracked into that subject. "Did your grandfather mention the name of the woman?"

"No, I don't think so . . ." Yvonne's gaze strayed over the crowd, maybe seeking another customer to buy out the last of the baking.

"Any children?" Paige's attempt to lock Yvonne into the subject fell flat this time.

"No, he didn't say anything about kids. Anyway, that's all I was going to tell you. Yoo-hoo," Yvonne trilled, hailing a passerby—a woman with four children in tow who likely had little time herself to bake. "I've discounted the last of the huckleberry turnovers."

"Well, thanks," Paige said, though Yvonne was bragging up Molly's culinary efforts to the potential customer and didn't say goodbye.

Paige appreciated the info. But eyewitness accounts held more validity academically than as-told-to testimony, especially removed by three generations. Yvonne's story was nothing Paige could even check up on; she'd examined every shred of existing documentation. Though the woman's report was riveting on a personal level, it had no real benefit for Paige's research. Besides, how could she approach her thesis committee at this stage with a request to contribute an addendum based on such an unverified narrative as Yvonne's? But Paige was intrigued all the same.

Danny and their four parents arrived in time for the barbeque, his mom carrying a huge bowl of coleslaw that Paige avoided because of her heartburn. After a good visit with them, and as the band tuned up their guitars and banjos for the dance, the older folks left for home.

"Come for a drive with me?" Danny asked.

"I think I can steal away without anyone noticing," she said. Her man knew the music might be too much for her to resist, and dancing tonight would not be good for her. Besides, the prospect of sliding across the Ford's bench seat close to Danny appealed. And the cleanup crew had already been briefed, assuring her the museum grounds would be immaculate for her first guided tour of the season tomorrow. No one would expect her to stay.

They parked alongside a fence where a grove of wild chokecherry bushes laden with blossoms waved in the evening breeze, promising a good crop this year. Paige opened her door and listened. Yes, they were far enough from the museum that she could barely hear the man-made din over the buzz of dusk-time insects and the rustling of leaves. And the fragrance! The breeze carried the sweet scent like a blanket and wrapped her up in it. Frilly clusters of tiny flowers coated each bough, white petals surrounding yellow, pollen-dusty centers. She leaned out and broke a few twigs off to tuck into her Victorian apron pockets. If the blooms didn't brown too quickly, she'd press them to glue onto her baby announcements.

And Danny loved his homemade jelly. He'd spent his childhood outside and was used to the seasonal task of berry and cherry picking. This was new to Paige, whose city-bred mother—though a wonderful cook—always bought preserves. Danny's parents made a family event every summer of strapping buckets to their waists with a belt, or a scarf from the hat-and-mitt drawer, slathering themselves with bug repellent, and finding the most productive groves on their land or out along the byways of Pembina County. Last season buffalo berries, elderberries, and gooseberries all made their way into her heavy-bottomed stainless steel pot.

But chokecherry season was Danny's favorite and, by extension, Paige's as well. From him she'd learned that the Plains Cree and Blackfeet used the bark and roots for medicinal purposes and crushed the fruit, stones and all, to flavor stews and pemmican. Of course, she added lots of sugar to the small cherries—purple-black and bitter even when ripe—to cut the astringency. The jars of jam and syrup and jelly stocking Paige's pantry gave her a sense of accomplishment and brought a memory of high-summer days during snowy winter.

She and Danny lounged on the new grass under the trees until the festival fireworks burst and whistled overhead.

"What was the best part of your day?" Danny asked, and she could see his irises glimmer with the lights in the sky.

"The morning service, I think, with our folks beside me in the pew for the early Mother's Day tribute."

"Sorry I couldn't make that." Danny draped his jean jacket around her.

"We all understood. I'm glad you finished seeding." She nestled up under his arm. "The chapel is on its last legs, of course. But the volunteers decorated it with tulips and brought the harmonium in from the museum's music parlor for the singsong, and we all belted out MDM's favorite hymn."

How fitting that she and MDM shared a love for this same song long before she knew his name or the anthem of the Laird dynasty. The regal words and melody, sung at top volume by all filling the tiny sanctuary—and those outside, too—had rung on in Paige's spirit all day. She'd memorized its lyrics in childhood and, as Danny drove home, she sang it for him, sang it out again so that Baby could hear and start memorizing it himself:

> *Come, Thou Almighty King,*
> *Help us Thy name to sing,*
> *Help us to praise.*
> *Father, all glorious,*
> *O'er all victorious,*
> *Come, and reign over us,*
> *Ancient of Days.*

CHAPTER TWENTY-EIGHT

Today

"*Faith quenches the violence of fire and out of weakness makes strength.*"

Libby jumps at the somber young voice interrupting her scrutiny of the art on the museum library walls.

"Sorry. Didn't mean to startle you." It's one of the girls standing near her, in front of a painting of a prairie fire with great flames filling the horizon and, in the foreground, women bending to soak gunnysacks. "I was reading the saying underneath." She meanders off to join her friends.

MDM's comment—script brushed on a plank this time—is a reiteration in different words of Gram's admonition: "What doesn't kill you, girl, will make you stronger."

It's as though Gram and MDM are speaking in unison to her, truisms crossing eras and sifting down from one generation to another.

Libby shakes the impression out of her head. The mansion is playing tricks on her, blending together the past and the present in a warping of time, her recent and sharp bereavement of Gram and her long-ago and half-forgotten revelation in this very house. Her rejection of Elsa on Friday and her mother's estrangement all those years ago. Her looming homelessness and yet the abiding sense of home that won't leave her. Financial insecurity and the wealth ensconcing her here, now, in this palatial mansion. They all bubble together in a confusing new soup that isn't, to use Virgil Oxenbury's philosophy, retaining its integrity. Libby can't differentiate the base note from the dominant flavor, and her grasp of reality at the moment is not pure and nuanced and complex, either. Rather, her life is a complicated hodgepodge—one hot mess.

But standing before the leftovers of MDM's life in his well-planned abode, Libby sees order, design. Since childhood she's been looking for something to believe in, to hope for, to belong to. Perhaps—no, certainly—down the next hallway or around the next corner lies the answer to the restlessness in her beleaguered soul.

So why is she wasting time in this room of questions when the room of her answers is within reach?

Libby elbows her way past the clutch of students congregating around the door, almost tripping on the area rug as she darts out of the library.

"What's your problem?" Sybil calls it out to Libby as she dashes in front of even Paige, taking the lead in the tour. But Libby has no problem—not now that she's finally catching on to the enigma of this house.

So she doesn't answer Sybil but slows down on her rampage through the dining room, where Paige is commenting on the Chippendale table and the oak highchair with the cane-bottom seat, long enough to read MDM's thematic statement inscribed on the face of the squat fireplace: *Taste of the heavenly gift*. And Gram's words echo: "Who has never tasted sour knows not sweet." Tasting is not on Libby's mind. Rather, she wants to gulp down a great bellyful of the time-twisting atmosphere of the mansion. She strides through the butler's pantry, with its soapstone sink and bottle-glass window and smell of cinnamon, to reach the kitchen.

She passes beneath the lineup of copper pots dangling from the brick arch above the gaping hearth. Out of the corner of her eye she catches its sooty engraving: *Let no root of bitterness spring up to trouble you.* The many cooks in this kitchen would have labored together beneath that guidance all day, beneath Gram's constant remonstrance against spoiling the broth. But Libby doesn't slacken her pace—as Paige, behind her, talks about the wooden icebox and the marble pastry counter and the dumbwaiter—until she reaches another wainscoted hallway.

Sybil catches up and positions herself against the wall, blocking Libby's way and tapping at the baseboard with the heel of her cowboy boot. The beads in her fake, teal-colored hair bounce in time.

"What's your rush? Not that I want to linger in homemaker purgatory any longer than necessary, but you're sure in a hurry."

What's her rush? Libby knows what's ahead—or, at any rate, she feels it calling out to her from her dreams, her hazy recollection of the details clarifying bit by bit. At every point in this tour, she rounds another corner of her memory. Each room in its turn takes her into the chambers of her past, ever closer to a growing but unnamed presence.

"I'm remembering," Libby says. The water fountain on the wall by her side gave sweet coolness to a little girl in the darkness of a summer night.

Sybil snorts. "What did you forget?"

Libby forgot the sound of a fatherly voice, for one thing, hearing only her own inner entreaties to a faceless, nameless parent. She forgot what a granddaddy hug and a scratchy beard feel like. But she doesn't say so, and Sybil moans out a yawn and looks at her phone. "Has it only been an hour since we began this interminable tour?"

The teacher enters the hallway from the kitchen amidst his adolescent gaggle, and Sybil wiggles her fingers in a coquettish greeting as though tickling the air between them.

While Sybil is distracted, Libby squeezes past her to continue down the hall. Which door is she looking for? She checks the whereabouts of the grand staircase to get perspective and then focuses on the brass doorknob halfway down the corridor. But Paige's commentary to the chattering tour group in the hallway catches her attention.

"These framed floor plans hanging on the wall were only recently discovered in a secret cubbyhole," Paige is saying. "If you press just the right spot . . . *voilà*." At the school kids' exclamations, Libby retraces her steps to find the guide demonstrating a small, spring-loaded door hidden in the wood paneling. But it's not the nook that interests Libby. She sticks her nose up close to the framed blueprints on the wall. How could she have blasted right past them?

Paige watches the quiet woman, Libby, shoulder her way back through the group clogging the hallway and make a beeline for the floor plans. Seizing the teachable moment, Paige lets the curious teens poke around in the hidden wall cupboard and steps close to Libby for a chance to expound on the blueprint and maybe glean information herself.

"Do you recall," Paige begins, ostensibly addressing the general group but observing Libby, "that earlier I suggested you keep your eyes peeled inside the mansion for the pattern of enclosure—a repetition of the square-within-square motif we saw when we looked out over the grounds from the third-floor terrace?" In Paige's peripheral field of vision a few heads nod. But she's watching Libby's remarkable eyes—almost black with golden flecks, like the polished agate she picked up one summer along the river. "This original drawing by MDM's draftsman clarifies the design of the house as a miniaturized version of the outside plan."

The Australian woman asks, "What do you mean by miniaturized?"

"You can see here the circuitous path we've been taking since we entered the mansion via the third floor." Paige traces their route on the glass of the blueprint, outlining the concentric configuration of right-angle walls and connecting hallways and stairwells of increasingly tighter squares. "Inside the home, I've drawn your attention to particular objects for a reason." How can she explain this simply? Libby is gawking at the floor plans, her jaw flexing. Paige wants to get this right in case she's listening. "The main elements in the outer rim of the larger farm—livestock corral, lake, gas lantern, and the vegetable plots—are echoed in the domestic yard's gazebo, water pump, lamppost, and potager garden. This pattern, compressed, is again replicated in the house itself; you saw it in the great hall's receiving desk, lily pond, floor lamp, and sideboard set for tea."

"It reminds me of the art of M.C. Escher." Mr. Nelson has edged his way up to Paige and now clears his throat theatrically to draw the attention of his students—and maybe to impress the woman clinging to his arm, too. "Think about our unit on tessellation and Escher's mathematical repetition of architectural and organic shapes."

"We scored an 'A' on our group project for that," one boy says, fist-bumping a buddy. Several other pupils gather closer, grinning over what was evidently a fun assignment. But beside Paige, Libby is chewing her bottom lip.

"Right," the teacher replies. "We applied the visual arts aspect of repetition in our cultural studies class by looking at parody and caricature through YouTube iterations of some early, rather historical memes."

"Yeah, my favorite was the Doge meme," one teen says.

"No—Socially Awkward Penguin rules," another declares.

The class erupts in an argument about Grumpy Cat versus Overly Attached Girlfriend, all terms foreign to Paige. Not to the woman with the leggings, though, who's cheering the kids on with her own contributions. How did Paige's tour get hijacked so quickly?

Mr. Nelson regains control, shushing his students and explaining to Paige, "We saw how ideas generate and morph over the Internet. It's the same as what you're talking about here." Several teenagers nod.

"Well, maybe." Paige doesn't really see the application in the same light as Mr. Nelson and his students seem to. She explains to the wider group, "A meme in the general sense is the repetition or imitation of a central cultural idea through such media as videos or literary text. Memetics is a minor field of sociological and mind-thought study." And that's about all Paige knows about it.

"What has that got to do with lampposts and water wells?" It's one of the old gals this time. "I think you're talking about symbolism, aren't you?"

"Exactly." Paige inhales and lets the air out slowly. Finally they're back to an established subject area. "I, like you, would call it symbolism. The Victorian take on it was known as 'typology.' As an architectural style, it fused Neo-Classicism and Romanticism. During this time period, artists—who were considered society's conscience—often viewed art as a means to an end."

The students blink blank stares at Paige, but the sisters twinkle, their matching cameo brooches suggesting they have a penchant for the era. Libby is still contemplating the framed plans on the wall.

"The Victorians were earnest," Paige says, "and art wasn't always appreciated for beauty alone but often held an underlying message. So we see designs incorporated into jewelry and household decorations intended to convey a certain significance. For example, the armrests of the library chair were carved in the shape of a dog, an emblem that stood for loyalty." Earlier a couple of the girls had sketched those dogs into their notepads. "On Valentine cards we see cherubs of love and fertility, or the clasped hands of friendship, or the swooping swallow signifying a return home—all classic Victorian imagery."

"And don't pearls stand for tears?" one sister asks, and she touches her earrings.

"And the peacock for immortality? I've seen that on headstones." It's Libby's friend this time.

"Yes." Paige loves the enthusiasm of some of her audience. "In fact, although MDM died long after the Victorian period ended, his wishes regarding his gravestone were respected and the Victorian dove of peace was carved above a laurel wreath of victory along with his epitaph: *He hath obtained a better resurrection, consecrated forevermore.*" MDM's voice comes through loud and clear in everything he wrote, in everything Paige has read.

She'd spent several afternoons last year making rubbings in the cemetery. She should have suggested to the school group that they bring charcoal and paper to make souvenirs; maybe she'd suggest that to Ophelia for future tours. "I'd encourage you all, before leaving the grounds, to walk through Kirkton Cemetery to view the older sculptures from the turn of the century, representative of MDM's extended 'family'—the Native Americans he adopted. Watch for the knot signifying unity on the double grave of a married couple, the scalloped shell of rebirth for babies overcome by influenza. The oak leaf, corn cob, and rooster memorialize Algonquian lives."

"So are you saying," the second sister asks, "that MDM meant to convey a message through his architecture and décor? Is he speaking to us across time to get our attention?"

Paige can't go quite so far. "Of course, we don't know for sure what MDM's intentions were. He doesn't tell us directly." Maybe he would have, if evidence hadn't been destroyed. Disappointment over lost research still nips at Paige. "But given the established Victorian custom of such practices as, say, sending secret messages in bouquets of flowers, I suspect this was MDM's way of communicating his meaning."

A girl asks, "What messages in flowers?"

"A young man might court his sweetheart by bringing a nosegay of asters to compliment her on her daintiness." Last spring, Danny had picked a bunch of wild asters for Paige from the ditches around home. "The magnolia meant dignity and the mimosa chastity, and roses—depending on color—could refer to purity or passion."

"Texting is easier," a boy says, and his buddies guffaw.

And then Libby speaks above the fracas in a voice crisp and loud and sure: "I think MDM was deliberately *pointing* at something."

All eyes turn to Libby, and Paige holds her breath. Throughout the tour, the woman's agitation has increased—Paige has seen the way she zones out and fondles her necklace and strains to get into the next room, and the next one after that. And now her statement confirms she's not just a random tourist with polite interest in a local site.

Paige happens to agree with Libby. She, too, believes MDM had a purpose to his design. But then again, she's been leading the tour for a couple of seasons and knows it ends with the grand wingback and its attendant footstool. She's taken many groups from the outside yard through the layers of the mansion to the room at the center. So maybe it's her hindsight that convinces her MDM, throughout the entirety of his estate, was pointing to the handmade ottoman—that single furnishing indicating more of his personality and purpose than any other item in the whole estate.

If indeed Libby is referring to the footstool—if she believes the "something" MDM was pointing at was the ottoman—then she must have been in the mansion before now! The mystery of the footstool isn't disclosed on the website, and the tour always ends with a request that the participants not spoil the surprise for others by posting about it.

"The Victorians were fond of miniatures, weren't they?" the

Australian woman asks. And Libby is nodding as though she's putting the puzzle together herself.

"Yes," Paige says, "this pattern of well, lamp, desk, and food repeats itself over and again, ever smaller, and we see a version of it once more in the den—starting with the vestibule, the front part of the den screened off from the back third." She checks out Libby again; the woman is nearly vibrating. "Well, come along and I'll show you what I mean." Paige sets off down the hall to the last room of the tour, to that final and most sacred place. She turns the brass knob and opens the door.

Tunnel vision takes over and concentrates all Libby's attention, her consciousness, her memory, onto the floor-length, purple-blue drape hanging by golden rings, wall to wall and closer to the back of the room, where the light once glowed around its edges and through the slit between the two panels. And she wants to push everyone aside and run to it and fling it open—like a hospital curtain—to expose the room-within-a-room behind it.

Libby's dream floods back, of when she was five and moonlight had lain in a ribbon over her linen garden of forget-me-nots. All alone she climbed down from the strange bed and went seeking the source of the faraway surging, the fierce and familiar rhythm of her mother's voice. More than that, she was searching for the deep, low voice that earlier had said, "Elizabeth? Is that you?" She'd been standing in the hallway with Gram's pink train case, waiting for Mommy and the lady to finish arguing so she could go to bed.

"We have no money for you or the child." The matron's face flushed. "Go away."

"You gotta recognize his writing." Mommy spat the words from between her teeth. "These letters prove it."

And the lady tried to snatch them from Mommy but couldn't, and giving up she said, "For the child's sake, then, stay the night. It's almost gone anyway. But you can't see *him*. Not in his condition." The house matron scowled at the curtain and muttered, "He can't seem to keep that cursed drape closed. He's too weak for this nonsense."

And when the grown-ups tramped off up the stairs expecting her to follow, Libby heard him again, croaking out to her from behind the curtain, "Meet me here. Come back later without them, after they are sleeping."

And she did. She crept down the darkened hallway, sliding her hand along the polished wooden railing, toes tickling on carpeted stairs all the way to the bottom. She strained to sip water from the fountain, dribbling on the front of her nightie, and the door was open, and the light was glowing, and she thought maybe it wasn't a dog after all but was Mommy breathing behind that curtain. But no, it couldn't be. It wasn't her sound. Libby was afraid of what was breathing there, raspy and ragged, but she was more afraid to go back upstairs alone. And so she entered the room and smelled the sweetest perfume, and she stretched to get her nose closer but bumped the pedestal, almost upsetting the flowers in the glass vase.

And then Paige's words filter back through Libby's fog, along with a luscious aroma wafting towards her in the present moment from the same vase on the same pedestal across the room in front of the same rugged drapery room divider.

What lies behind that curtain today?

As she speaks, Paige caresses the cool lacquered surface of the antique Chinese piece in the den's vestibule. "This cherry-wood secretary—look at the lovely Star of David inset—is where MDM answered his personal mail and kept his stack of Legal Tender Notes at the ready to make payment for delivery of furs and hides."

She unlocks and folds down the front panel to expose its writing surface and the filing slots inside, the quavering of her voice disclosing to even herself once again her fascination with the research. At this very desk MDM would have penned the letters to Father Laird and read his return mail, by the light of the oil lamp he preferred in this room and would carry with him when he entered behind the curtain. If only she could have unearthed more than those few faxed letters from the Manitoba museum archive.

She goes on. "I believe this desk is meant to represent the larger, walnut desk in the great hall, which corresponds to the receiving gazebo outside in the yard, where MDM traded in wild animal skins. That, in turn, references the corral within the stone-fenced periphery, and perhaps his livestock grazing in the pastures beyond. Do you see what I mean?"

The facial expressions of most of the guests suggest to Paige that she should give up on postulating about her scholarly breakthrough. After all, even for her the concepts had been difficult initially, and her academic advisors tried to dissuade her when she pitched her theory as a thesis project to them.

But then Libby speaks up again, her strange eyes shining. "I think I get it. The outside lake and the yard's well are copied again in the foyer's lily pond and here in the vase?" She nods towards the wild pink blossoms spilling over the squat crystal vase on the pedestal.

"Yes, that's it." Paige has finally found someone in the public who gets her theory. She has the whole group's attention again, even the students'—except for Libby's friend, who sidles up even closer to the teacher, Mr. Nelson, and straightens his collar for him. "This fruit bowl is a mini version of—"

"The tea tray," one girl bursts out, entering into the spirit of the riddle, "and the gardens."

Goosebumps dance over Paige's arms and she pushes her explanation further. "We walked clockwise through the attic around the elevator shaft and storage space; then we moved down to the second story to trace a similar path around the rooms bordering the upper great hall. And now we've made it around the first-floor rooms to the final stop, other than the gift shop, before our tour is over. You won't want to rush through this room. Good things come in small packages. This den is the physical center of the entire house."

"And that heady perfume?" The Australian woman treads towards the pedestal, nose protruding a bit more with every step, until she bends over the mass of flowers.

"Wild prairie roses." The two sisters sing it out in unison and then laugh at each other. One finishes the thought: "They grow all over the state, but maybe you don't have them down under?"

"Not on the streets of Sydney, anyway."

Paige explains, "MDM insisted that fresh bunches of flowers grace his most private of spaces—wild roses in season and lilies otherwise." What an extravagance during the winter, to be sure—the lilies gathered for the vase from the bronze pool in the foyer, where they were kept alive until a springtime batch could again be collected from the waterways and ponds of North Dakota. "It was all part of his ceremonial approach to the sanctity of the den."

"Sounds like the rituals of the goddess Ishtar's temple and her fertility cult," the flirt in cowboy boots says to Mr. Nelson. Several students titter. He turns a raw shade as his seductress presses up closer. She adds, "You see it all the time in sacred sites around the globe. Nothing really new here."

Paige bites her tongue. To compare MDM's inner room to a prostitute's shrine is beyond ridiculous. She doesn't honor the comment with a response.

At this part of the tour, Paige often reads an excerpt from the 1967 obituary, which pinpoints MDM's locus of death to be the massive leather chair behind the curtain. But—she checks the time—she's running a bit late. She won't bring up the formal statement or the unsubstantiated report suggesting robbery played a part in his demise.

"In a sense," Paige says, "the mansion pivots around this hub of the den, like the house is the hub of the yard, and the yard is the hub of the farmstead, and the farmstead is the hub of the greater universe. Each step has taken us farther down and closer in, drawing us towards the center of the structure."

And right on cue, Libby, eyes narrowed at Paige and dandling that ring at the end of her necklace, demands in her resonant voice, "So, what is at the center of the center?"

Paige has been waiting for this, of course. It's usually a child who asks. She pauses to heighten suspense before answering. "Why, the hidden treasure, of course."

The teens, most of them fitting in the den while some overflow into the hallway, immediately yammer.

"Hidden treasure? This is cool!"

"Look at the message above the curtain: *Greater riches than the treasures of Egypt.*"

"Riches? C'mon, let's see it."

"Hold on." Paige shows them her palm as the kids start pushing. "I'm sorry, but you can't actually enter the back segment; it's cordoned off for protection. When I open the curtain, I'll step inside and demonstrate."

Paige expects this sort of response, but she ignores the tumult as she stands before the drapery curtain and takes hold of the inner edge, preparing for the effort of the pull. She's watching the odd expression on Libby's face.

That woman must know about the footstool.

Exhilaration courses through Paige. Libby *has* been here before! And then, amongst the continuing exclamations of the school kids, she overhears Libby whisper to herself, almost as a prayer, "Thank you, Gram."

Gram? The room swims in front of Paige. That was it, for goodness's sake! "Gram" was the word Libby used earlier that had been picking at Paige's brain. Libby is Gramsgirl! She's the anonymous e-mailer who asked about the dark brown, buttoned leather cushion—not a porch swing cushion after all but, in actuality, the ottoman in front of the great chair. Both footstool and chair are behind this curtain, so far unseen on the tour by anyone, least of all Libby. Didn't Libby and her unlikely friend say they were from the Twin Cities? It should have been obvious to Paige all along. Her aggressive e-mail questions hadn't scared Gramsgirl off after all.

How can Paige get Libby into a corner and quiz her about what she might know, and about who she really is?

CHAPTER TWENTY-NINE

Today

Sybil is squished up against the wall by the mass of teens jamming into the den. She can't even smell the wild roses anymore—just boy stink and some girl's idea of cologne. Her left arm is glued to the cute, if awkward, teacher's, and she fishes for his hand at her side. Their fingers intertwine, unseen by his charges—not that she cares. She stifles a smirk. He's such a pushover.

Libby is on her right, closest to the curtain, and Sybil cranks her head around to chat with her but ends up looking into her ear. Libby's been pretty well snubbing her for the whole tour. She'd been locked up inside herself from the moment they climbed the metal stairwell outside the museum and entered the musty attic, muttering to herself periodically but not being at all entertaining. It's a good thing Sybil can entertain herself. She nuzzles Mr. Nelson's bicep. Libby isn't usually so tight lipped. She hasn't spoken a dozen sentences in total—though she's been nervy since they entered the den, asking histrionic questions that make no sense at all.

Sybil scratches the teacher's palm lightly with her nails and he squeezes back. Yeah, he's hooked. She nudges Libby's arm with her other elbow, but Libby is fixated on the guide posturing in front of the curtain like a magician with a vanishing act about to snatch away the scarf of disclosure. Why doesn't she yank the stupid curtain open already? Her attempt at building tension is infantile. Sybil elbow-jabs Libby this time and, as if in slow motion, her friend turns her head until, just inches away, she gazes full on into Sybil's eyes for the first time since they were overlooking the great hall from the balcony.

Sybil jerks back from the electric jolt of those two-toned jewel eyes. She shrinks into the teacher, away from Libby's intensity that burns into her while registering no recognition. Libby is looking beyond her—looking *through* her—but what does she see? It's creepy.

And yet Sybil knows this facial expression from somewhere... yes, from that time years ago when she stared death in the face. At least, she assumed it was death at the time, before she understood the process of spirit crossing. It happened while her mother lay in the hospice bed, emaciated and almost transparent with the cancer, one foot in the other world as she exited off the stage of this one. Doing her own vanishing act.

No, Libby's facial expression comes out of neither death nor fear. It's her own mother's double emotion that Sybil sees again in the living and fearless Libby—that same *joy* opening wide her mother's eyes just before she left Sybil behind, and that same *pity* flickering out at Sybil in the seconds before the light left her mother's eyes. Libby's eyes, too, are full of joy for something unnamed and full of pity for, it seems, Sybil herself.

How dare Libby be so judgmental?

Anger washes over Sybil. Libby could have no idea about how Charlotte Tansey invited her own fate. She doesn't understand the law of attraction dictating that a person brings about positive or negative experiences by centering on positive or negative thoughts. Like attracts like, after all. Ask and you shall receive, right? Mom evidently sent a request to the universe, perhaps subconsciously, and the universe complied by taking her away, thank you very much.

Sybil slows her breathing to wrestle her anger under control, glad that at least she hasn't verbalized her rage aloud. The universe is subject to the spoken word. Her mother is at fault for manipulating the faith-force and gypping Sybil out of relationship—she needs to place blame where blame is due—and her useless father did nothing to stop it. Mom brought about the end of the mother-daughter relationship through her choices, and Dad threw Sybil under the bus with his own form of abandonment in remarriage.

To ground her senses, she focuses on the floor-length curtain bunching in the guide's hand, breathing out her angst and breathing in self-control.

As a little god, Sybil has chosen to access the power of faith through positive confession for her own successes. She speaks goodness into existence, words being containers of power that unfold upon utterance. It's up to Sybil to release faith and defeat unbelief, to reclaim the atmosphere she lives in.

Then why is she so resentful of that joy and pity in Libby's eyes?

And at this moment, in the moldering room of this deserted house, Sybil takes her emotional leave of Libby. She physically turns and burrows her face into the sleeve of Mr. Nelson's shirt, close to his armpit, inhaling to fill her olfactory senses with the aura of his essence. The visceral inundation sweeps away conscious thought.

Libby feels again the texture of the curtain, though it's Paige who's gripping it. In her mind, Libby strokes the twisted yarns, purple and blue and magenta with slender threads of gold worked in almost invisibly. And she knows again that the impenetrable barrier blocks her way to warmth and light and love. And she shivers again as though in her thin nightgown, damp at the front. And she's back again into her waking-dream, the past merging with the present without leaving her any choice in the matter. She is time traveling.

"Can you hear my voice?" The hoarse rumble had come from behind the curtain. "Press forward, child. Come boldly."

She'd tugged, but the curtain moved only enough to show her the split between the two panels, a sliver of light shimmering through. She was too little. Maybe if she sort of bumped it?

"Lift your foot, woman," the female voice had barked out behind her in the hallway. It was that grumpy lady with the apron who at first said there was no room for them when they arrived in the borrowed car earlier tonight—until Mommy stuck those letters into her face. After that, the lady hushed them and took them up to the pretty forget-me-not blue room and told them not to come out. She even brought them a tray of food to eat in bed—egg salad sandwiches on soft white bread, and apple juice and cookies.

"Some welcome home we get." It had been Mommy's voice from the hallway this time. She was slurring. Libby heard a thump, and then her mother swore.

"For pity's sake," the lady had said, "don't make me drag you back up to bed."

Was she hurting her mom? Little Libby had let go of the fabric and padded silently past the table and the fruit bowl to the open door. In the darkness of the hallway, the lady's arm was around Mommy's waist. Mommy's head was flopping, and she wasn't yelling anymore like she had when Libby was upstairs in bed all alone. And then the elevator door closed on Mommy and the lady, and Libby scuttled back to the curtain and shouted to the rumbly, invisible voice, "I'm here!"

"For many years, this curtain was kept closed whenever MDM sat in residence, ruling *ex cathedra*, so to speak," Paige says, picturing to herself the wingback chair still hidden from their view. She glances again at Libby, who looks almost catatonic, no emotion playing over her ashen face. Was she about to faint? "The drape acted as a privacy indicator, like a hotel's 'Do Not Disturb' sign hanging on the doorknob against the interference of the staff—in this case, the original housekeeper and then her daughter, both named Henrietta, along with their underlings. Seeing that curtain closed, they knew their employer—their benefactor—was alone with his thoughts, perhaps recording in his accounting books or reading communication from Father Laird or penning a letter himself."

Paige would give anything for those lost letters, the personal missives in which MDM would have recounted the building of the mansion, his roaming throughout the western states, his thoughts and feelings.

"A closed curtain? Rather off-putting." The tall traveler from across the ocean flares his oversized nostrils, and his wife nods in agreement. "Who was welcomed in, then?"

"During the early days, MDM made business transactions with passing hunters out in the yard at the gazebo, bringing them into the great hall to collect their payment. Some of these people entered into the outer den where we're standing now, if they were intimate enough with MDM. Few were given access to the area behind this curtain." She pets the weighty weave. "Later—from what I can tell—when MDM's work life was done and he'd retired, the curtain was open to all. He received visitors from far and wide. However, my reading indicates that eventually his caretakers used the curtain almost as a prison door, with the idea of keeping him in place and others out." She shakes the weighty drapery and the metal rings at the top jangle against the rod, startling the students whose attention is lagging. But Libby doesn't even flinch, her eyes burning coals as though she can see right through the curtain.

It's time to disclose the secret, if only for the poor woman's sake.

*

"There you are," the old man had said as little Libby fell through the curtain at his feet. "I've been awaiting you a long time, Elizabeth. I knew you would return."

His confusing words were creaky as a screen door. Sprawled upon the hardwood floor, Libby saw the feet of the chair, and then the hem of a housecoat, and farther up the outline of pajama pants ending in plaid slippers propped on a leather footstool. The old man's veiny hands clung to the arms of the dark brown throne, his fingertips blue.

He'd coughed and she was afraid to look into his face. Then he reached down his hand for hers, a heavy gold ring sagging onto the knuckle of his papery skin, and both metal and flesh were cold to her touch. She peeked up into a face as wrinkled as crinkled blankets, with eyes as soothing as Gram's.

"Let me examine you, child. Draw near." So she'd clambered up and stood tall in front of him in her dampened nightie, shy eyes cast downward, and he placed his old, old hand on her head gently. "How you bear her image, Elizabeth."

Whose image? Her mind, trapped in long ago, asks it now.

"I'm Libby," she'd said to her bare feet.

"I know who you are." With his hands he'd dragged his legs down, one at a time, to plant his slippers on the floor. And then he grasped her under her arms, and his bony hands hurt her a bit. He grunted as he lifted her up onto his knee, and he wrapped his arms around her in a hug bigger than any Gram ever gave her, and his beard was wiry and scratchy, and she didn't pull away because his robe was cuddly, and he smelled of soap and leather and tobacco.

"You've come to take possession of your inheritance." His words had been solemn. "It is finished."

Libby didn't get what he was talking about—not then.

A part of her knows now, in this day and this hour, that her mind is caught in an eddy, but she could swear she's sitting on his knee right at this moment.

He'd shifted her to the edge of his lap and then reached deep into a pocket of his robe to withdraw a brass key. He stretched out his hand to insert the key into a hole on the front edge of the buttoned leather ottoman, but his hand shook and Libby wanted to help him. Finally the key went in and it turned with a click. Then his vein-mapped hands grabbed hold of the two front corners. Very slowly, he lifted up the lid as he said to her, his short and shallow breaths puffing warmth into her hair, "Let us consider together the gift I fashioned of my own hands for you, and which I vowed so long ago to have ready upon your return home."

Paige eyes the tour group members lined up in front of her, taller ones in the back except for Libby, everyone effectively positioned for the moment of unveiling. She'll be able to observe their reactions, her greatest pleasure of the tour. She slips her hand into her apron pocket for the key ring and isolates the one with a looped end and deeply notched blade.

And then she wrenches the curtain asunder and her audience collectively gasps, except for the teacher's pet—otherwise occupied—and Libby.

Libby's eyes are screwed tightly shut.

Paige steps into the intimate, windowless chamber, snaps the velvet rope into place, and moves towards the back to allow everyone a full view of these final furnishings at the heart of the Laird Mansion Museum.

"This wingback chair and matching ottoman were handcrafted by MDM himself, after the house was completely built, as his crowning achievement." She stoops over the rectangular, padded box that's about eighteen inches in height, its length and width measuring roughly two-and-a-half by three-and-a-half feet. She inserts the key and turns against the resistance until it gives way with a soft tick.

As she straightens again to a fully standing posture, she raises the front of the lid along with her—carefully so that nothing inside is upset with the unfolding. Now every eye is on the contents and every mouth hangs open, including Libby's.

"It's magic." Five-year-old Libby had watched the dollhouse come into full view inside the footstool that first time. It opened out beneath the old man's hands in stages—like Gram's sewing basket when she was looking for a needle and thread to mend Libby's stockings.

"This is a model of our home," the old had man told her. "The top level is the attic. See, here, the stove and the laundry tub and the door to the elevator?"

Libby curled over on his knee, bent forward to see the tiny windowpanes that looked as thin as fingernails. What was an attic, anyway? She wanted to press the teeny dot of the elevator button, but the old man coughed again, and this time Libby saw a smear of blood on the back of his hand.

In the here-and-now, halfway between two times, Libby stares through the crowded den, past the tourists' heads craning towards the cordoned-off sanctuary where she had once taken refuge. Paige is demonstrating the clever machinery of the collapsible dollhouse, just as Libby remembers it. From the lid, the attic floor drops down a few inches, a tray hanging in midair by jointed arms. The second level, stacked atop the bottom one, lifts up and out on its own hinges to expose the main floor. The whole three-story construction cantilevers open like a 3-D greeting card, a paraphrase of the mansion's blueprints replete with miniature furnishings made to scale.

Libby scrunches her eyes closed again to re-enter her *déjà vu*, and Paige's commentary morphs into MDM's, yet she can't tell if it's now or then.

"The upper stairs fold down, so," he said, "leading to the bedrooms on the second story."

She scooted off his lap and knelt before the enchanting dollhouse with its bitsy bronze basin, matchstick pantry cupboards, and enameled bathtubs.

The old man explained, "I cut up scraps of your mother's dress goods—leftovers of her white lawn blouse for these pillows, her blue floral frock for the wallpaper." Just like the bedroom upstairs that Libby fell asleep in. But Mommy had no white blouse, and her blue dress was shiny, full of sequins.

"See the pebble fireplaces, Elizabeth, and the rugs I braided from yarn, and the wooden billiards table covered in green felt? I whittled the banisters," he told her as his old fingers ran down along the tiny, curved handrail, "and the beds, and your cradle."

When had Libby had a cradle—as a baby fifty years ago? Babette once told her that Elsa kept her in a cardboard box until they found a crib at a garage sale. And why does he—did he—keep calling her Elizabeth? But she thinks about the letter from Gram, stuffed into the pink train case in the back seat of Sybil's Prius, parked outside the mansion's yard. Elizabeth was Babette's mother, Elsa's grandmother, Libby's great-grandmother. Time is so fluid . . .

She blinks her eyes fully open. Paige is talking about the miniscule books set on balsa wood library shelves, the minute copper cooking pots imported from Germany, the door halfway down the hall on the main floor opening into the dollhouse room with the purple-blue curtain where the tour group, life sized, stands at this very moment.

"He upholstered the mini-wingback chair with softest deerskin, dyed as red as highbush cranberries." Had he used the Old World madder root he'd imported for his kitchen potager? Paige arranges the miniature chair but doesn't pick up the tiny footstool.

Why doesn't she pick it up? The ottoman inside the ottoman,

two-and-a-half by three-and-a-half inches, has for buttons red glass seed beads from Libby's mother's moccasins. Her mother? What is Paige saying? No, the old man had been the one to say that—had referred to the moccasins of her mother.

But Elsa wore beat-out running shoes the last time Libby saw her. She groans inwardly as she pictures again the crumpled figure in the parking lot of her condemned apartment block, the prone figure on the stretcher being whisked off to the hospital. What has she done to her own mother? Fiercely Libby's other side answers the question: What she has done to Elsa is exactly what Elsa did to her. When Libby was a helpless child, Elsa threw her away, abandoned family, surrendered to addiction. Now neither of them can atone.

"Let's move on to the gift shop." Paige is shooing the group out. "We've got a great selection of fine bone china in thistle and tartan patterns, as well as local crafts."

Sybil is first out of the den, dragging Mr. Nelson by the hand, followed by the students. Libby stays behind, in her bi-temporal daze. The adult tourists make appreciative comments, as though they are satisfied over the stunning finale of the miniature house within a house, but Libby knows there's more to the revelation than this.

Oh yes, there's so much more.

Paige turns to face Libby, who longs to fall on her knees before the altar of the footstool. Pausing with hand on brass doorknob, Paige says not one word. She fixes her eyes on Libby and pokes her chin towards the dollhouse and then nods at her and closes the door firmly behind her.

Libby is alone with MDM. She steps forward from the wall

of the den, unhooks the rope, and enters into the epicenter of the mansion—and maybe, at the same time, into the inner chamber of her own soul.

Sybil waits for Libby in the gift shop amidst the clamor and clatter of intemperate kids buying teacups for Mother's Day or replica hunting knives for themselves. She's still simmering over the look in Libby's eyes that is so like her dying mother's. She solaces herself by purchasing an extravagant, wide-brimmed Edwardian hat heaped high with silk roses and black netting—likely meant as a wall hanging, but she'll wear it on sunny days. Or perhaps she'll model it for the teacher tonight, along with her new lingerie.

That's a good idea, she decides. So she tugs at his arm while he's trying to herd the mass of his charges outside, and she whispers a few words about following him and the bus back into Grand Forks.

Now regarding Libby . . . Where is that woman, anyway?

Sybil might have considered a stroll through the Kirkton boneyard as the tour guide had suggested, if not for her brainwave. The gift shop has emptied except for the Aussie couple asking Paige for directions, and Sybil pounces.

"Hey, you two are heading to the Twin Cities, aren't you?"

The man rubs the back of his sunburned neck, but the wife chirps, "Yes, the airport. We're on our way home."

"Would you give my friend a lift back?"

"Couldn't do that." The husband shakes his head.

"Why not, Frank?" his wife asks.

Sybil smiles at the wife and removes a wad of cash from

her purse. That gets Frank's attention, and she peels off several twenties.

"You can drop her anywhere in the city. She'll take transit from there." Sybil folds the money into Frank's hand and gives an extra squeeze for good measure.

That takes care of one problem. The teacher, meanwhile, is overseeing the boarding of the student group as Sybil fetches Libby's pink case from her car. She saunters back into the gift shop and—feeling Mr. Nelson's unteacherly eyes on her—makes sure to let her hips swing before the screen door closes behind her.

"Give this to Libby, will you?" she asks the girl at the till. "She's the only one left on this tour. I think she's still in the last room. Got a pen?"

She dashes off a note of explanation to Libby, almost illegible with eagerness over her upcoming rendezvous. That she hasn't learned Mr. Nelson's first name adds to the intrigue. At least this trip hasn't been a total bust.

Libby kneels before the open footstool and the intricacies of MDM's handiwork. How could she ever have doubted his existence, forgotten her meeting there with him the first time, drifted away from his words and into denial? The exposure of the dollhouse inside the ottoman would delight any onlooker discovering it. Yet something more waits for Libby. She can't quite put pictures to it yet, but it isn't all pleasant.

She tucks her long hair behind one ear and reaches down, around the staircase, and past the barrier of the curtain that, in the miniature, is permanently fastened wide open, welcoming and even beckoning. She touches the tiny ottoman, jiggles it to be sure it isn't glued down as well. And when she picks it up, it doesn't rattle. She won't shake it as she'd done last time.

"No, don't shake it." MDM had said it with a chortle in his voice." The child Libby tried to pry up the lid but it wouldn't budge. "You can't open it that way."

"How, then?"

Today, kneeling as then, she hears her own artlessness, her babyish inflection.

"Opening it follows certain principles." He'd enclosed her hands—holding the box—in his own, and his fingers guided hers. "A twist of the leg to the right, and now push it in." The tiny chest sprang open. The inside was lined in deep blue velvet like a king's robe. But it wasn't empty.

Oh no, it wasn't empty at all.

For inside the jewel box lay one perfect circlet of gold, and the old man—MDM, as she knows now—said, "Go ahead, take it out." So she had, her chubby fingers clumsy in the taking, and she saw that the gold of the surface formed a lacy cage encasing strands of flaming red hair. He removed the larger band from his own finger and it matched the smaller ring but for the narrow twist of hair, black and coarse as her dolly's.

"You see the numbers on the inside of the smaller ring?"

Libby'd nodded. "One, nine, four. And I see letters."

"That's right—very important numbers and letters. I have them in mine as well. Let us put them away together." And so she put the smaller band back into the casket, and he fit his larger band down around it—two concentric halos gleaming up at her.

"And where is yours, child?"

She had no answer. Not then.

So he'd closed the lid, shutting the rings into a tight secret once again, and instructed her to reposition the tiny ottoman in front of the wingback chair in the den of the dollhouse.

At the moment Libby had set the toy furniture back in place, the old man sputtered out a cough, and droplets of red bloomed on his snow-white beard. He didn't appear to notice, and so she thought maybe it was okay, maybe he didn't hurt himself like when she skinned her knee last week.

Of course it wasn't okay.

And suddenly the speckles of blood didn't matter because the old man took her face in his bony hands so that she looked into his wonderful, happy eyes and—it seems to her now, nearly five decades later—he looked right into her heart, sad and broken as it is today. And then he uttered ten words she didn't believe at the time she could ever forget, not in her whole life. Ten words, clear and simple and completely understood by her then but today forgotten.

And today, half a century later, she's holding the spring-loaded coffer with the two rings still nested, smaller within larger, brilliant against the royal blue velvet. She doesn't touch the sacred things yet, but only drags the chain off her neck and dangles before her eyes the dirty, worn, child-sized ring Gram had bequeathed to her.

And then, at that moment in the long-ago past, he'd started hacking again—deep, wracking, horrible sounds—splattering her in a shower of warm, wet blood. He'd leaned back on the chair, his head thrown heavenward, his eyes wide open.

And that was when her little-girl self had begun to scream.

CHAPTER THIRTY

Today

"Ms. Paulsson?"

For the moment, Paige ignores the youthful tentativeness of Jamie Farris's voice as the teen stands behind the gift shop counter. Paige waves goodbye to the two sisters making their way out to a jalopy in the parking lot. The garishly dressed woman climbs into her car and spins off after the school bus. Wasn't she Libby's ride?

Paige turns to the till. "Yes, Jamie. You needed me?" But her mind isn't with the girl and any potential sales problems. Rather, she's second-guessing her impulse to leave Libby alone in the den against all protocol. What was she thinking?

"That weird lady took this old case out of her car and left it here. Said to give it to her friend, who's catching a ride back to Minneapolis with the Australians?"

"That's fine," Paige says. Had Libby been consulted? She hustles to the den, suppressing her haste in order to knock softly on the door before opening it.

Libby hasn't heard her. She's sitting on the floor, her back against the footstool and her legs ragdoll splayed. She's gaping in open-mouthed horror at the empty leather chair. Paige jumps to her side.

"Libby?" She shakes the woman. "What's wrong? Can you hear me?" Libby's eyes are unfocused. Is she going to faint after all? "Bend over." Paige places her hand on the back of Libby's head and presses down so that the woman's forehead almost reaches the floor between her knees. Libby comes around and pushes herself back into an upright sitting position.

"He died right in front of me!"

Paige's heartbeat stutters, and Baby jumps, too. She sinks to the floor beside Libby. "Who died?" She can't believe what she's hearing.

"The old man. He coughed again, and the blood spurted at me and I screamed." Libby turns burning eyes on Paige. "I couldn't stop. I just kept on screaming and then that lady came running in. Henrietta, you called her."

"You were here when MDM Laird *died*?" Adrenaline surges through Paige.

Libby closes her eyes again. "I could hear my mother sort of falling down the stairs and she came stumbling in, swaying and swearing. I was bawling, but they both just pushed me aside."

"They let you watch a man die?"

"That Henrietta was yelling 'Mr. Laird!' and my mother was shrieking at her and even at the old man—at MDM—about how they couldn't do this to her. Finally the police came with their flashing lights and sirens, and Henrietta accused my mother of stealing the ring right off his hand. But I hid in the folds of the curtain until the officers took the body away and my mother passed out on the couch in the library."

Paige reaches out automatically, pats Libby's arm.

"I sat on the floor of the den wrapped in the curtain until the sun came up and we left for home." Libby opens her brimming, pleading eyes. "But I felt as though I was leaving home back here."

She's crying now, quiet tears swelling up out of those amber-speckled eyes and spilling down over high cheekbones. Paige wraps her arms around the woman, her own belly in the way. And just then Baby kicks, and Libby's body goes rigid.

"I felt that." It shocks Libby away from the edge of her childhood and the moment death coughed in her face. It brings up pictures of her own baby kicking to come out into the world of the living and breathing, but denied life and breath.

And the ten words MDM spoke to her before that old-man gush of blood—the words she can't recall even now—mingle with the blood of her miscarried baby. And it dawns on Libby that she, who couldn't bring life from her own body, was given another life while in the womb of this den, in this mansion, by the words from that bloody man.

If only she could recall all that he'd said.

"What is this? What are you holding?" Paige's voice quivers. Libby looks down at her fist tightly clasped around the miniature footstool, its spring-loaded lid still open. Her hand is shaking, but the three rings don't rattle as the single ring had, and Libby knows why. They fit three-in-one together, nesting within the velvet interior.

Paige strokes Libby's hand and then peels away her fingers from the box. Her voice is full of wonder. "With all my research, my cleaning out the dollhouse and repositioning the furniture for a more accurate representation, how in the world did I miss finding this?"

"I remembered how to open it," Libby says. "He put it away with only two rings in it, but I brought the smallest one with me today." She's gripping the empty chain and lifts it for Paige to see. Libby can hardly believe it herself. "I was wearing it—the smallest one. It fits perfectly inside the other two."

"But where did you get it to begin with? A garage sale?" Paige doesn't wait for an answer. "They're obviously a set. Where did they all come from?"

"Us."

The short word of identification—of demarcation and relationship—feels so right in Libby's mouth, though she's not sure she understands the extent of what's she's saying, of what she's intuiting. And she's not sure Paige has even heard her.

Forehead furrowed, Paige turns the jewelry box over to let the matching rings fall into her palm. She picks up the largest one between pointer and thumb, bringing it close to eyeball the inner surface. Her eyes fly open wide at Libby. With spasmodic movements she checks the other two bands.

"The engraving on this one is unreadable." She peers at the baby ring. "Wait here. Don't move."

Moving is the last thing Libby intends to do. Her legs wouldn't hold her if she tried to stand, and the inner quaking hasn't abated, either. She wants to examine the rings herself. Dropping that innermost circlet inside the other two had been like placing a final jigsaw piece. But Paige has taken them all with her, leaving Libby alone to process the wave of memories engulfing her.

As deftly as her bulk allows, Paige bounds up the stairwell of the great hall, dashes through the second-floor hallway, and fairly flies up the attic steps. Elation fuels her, and Baby leaps inside as though he's as astonished as she. Could Libby be giving her the missing piece of evidence, the linchpin to her whole academic argument? How did she come by this baby ring?

She taps on her desk light and rifles through the drawers. She slams them shut. She roots around in her supply basket of pens and glue, scissors and flashlight, and slips the magnifying glass into her pocket. She's got a jar of jewelry cleaner here somewhere—although, come to think of it, she doesn't want to damage the organic material. A toothbrush and a bit of dish detergent will have to suffice for the moment.

She's panting hard by the time she gets back to the kitchen, but it takes only a few minutes to scrub the interior of the smallest ring and gently suds the outside. She rinses and dabs it dry and then holds it up in direct sunlight, inspecting the filaments as well as the inscription within.

Yes, it's as she suspected. She can barely contain the bliss mounting up inside as she rushes past Jamie, who's standing in a doorway with her mouth hanging open, to Libby in the den.

Libby is pacing when Paige erupts back into the den.

"Look at them." Paige's command further rouses Libby's own tumultuous emotions, the throbbing in her throat, the pounding in her chest.

"What am I looking for?" Libby marches to the window.

"Didn't you see the hair in the smallest ring—the colors of the hair?"

"Hair?" Libby plucks her ring from Paige's moving hand—the one she's worn on her neck for the past day and a half. "I thought it was just badly scratched." But why wouldn't it be hair, considering the other two rings in the trio?

"Not scratches. Look at it closely."

Yes, she can see now that the battered ring cages fine strands beneath gold filigree.

Paige dumps the other two into Libby's palm. Her tone

sharpens. "Look at the initials inside, the dates." Before Libby can do that, Paige seizes them all again.

Libby runs her hands through her own hair. "Slow down," she says in her best motherly impression. She forces Paige gently onto the wing chair. It isn't good for her, in her state, to get so agitated. Paige gulps air, and Libby touches her back. "That's it, relax. Now begin again, please. I'm totally lost."

Lost, yes, but she's being found.

"Right." Paige nods and motions for Libby to sit down herself, so she does, plopping onto the floor with the ottoman at her back. It's Paige's turn to shut her eyes for a moment. She exhales and then starts in. "This is classic Victorian hair jewelry, fashioned in the late aesthetic style, circa 1880 to 1900, and worn by mourners or lovers to commemorate a special union. A woman would sometimes have a whole bracelet or brooch constructed out of the hair of her deceased husband, to carry a bit of him around with her."

"But these rings are made mostly of gold."

"Yes, but"—Paige opens her hand and holds the medium-sized ring out for Libby to take—"look at the hair encased in this one, caught and held in place beneath the mesh."

"Red. Like, from a ginger." She remembers it from the first time.

"MDM was known for his vibrant red hair."

"It was pure white when I saw him," Libby says. White as clouds.

"A red lock worn as a token by his sweetheart." Paige holds out the largest ring. "And this one?"

"Black." As black and coarse as her dolly's hair; as black as a

Native maid's. She opens her hand to receive back her own ring—Gram's worn ring—but Paige keeps it clenched in her folded-up fingers.

"Now check the inscriptions inside those two."

Libby reads the largest one aloud. "*M.D.M.L. w. 04.04.91. Within.*" She looks at Paige. "Shouldn't it say 'd' if this were the date of death? For mourning?"

Paige nods and urges her, "Now the second one." Her eyes glisten.

"*N.L. w. 04.04.91. My Heart.*"

"You see?" Paige asks, turtling her head forward. "Initials and a 'w' and the same year, same day of the same month." Libby studies the inscriptions again. Paige goes on. "This pair of rings symbolizes the *wedding* day—April 4, 1891—of MDM Laird and a woman whose first name begins with the letter 'N.'"

Libby N. Walker stares at Paige but doesn't mention aloud her middle initial shared with Elsa N. Walker and Babette N. Walker. Can it be coincidence? It must be coincidence.

Paige is bouncing up and down on her chair. "Look again at the ring you brought." She thrusts it onto Libby. It's much brighter and cleaner now. "The hair." Paige stabs at it.

"I can hardly see it." Libby squints at the threads. "They're not all one color and they appear almost . . . braided."

"Yes!" Paige is shouting. "Black and red and a sort of auburn or, well, a blend of the other two." She pulls a magnifying glass out of her apron pocket for Libby.

"I can make it out," Libby says. "Yes, three colors."

"And the inscription?" Paige prods. "It's worn, but use the glass."

Libby reads it aloud, slowly, realization seeping in. "*E.N.L. b. 09.10.93. God's Oath.*"

"That was two years after the wedding." Paige's face is glowing, triumphant. "Using a 'b' indicates this is the birth date of the child, E.N. Laird, legitimate offspring of MDM and his official wife!"

"I think—"

Paige cuts her off. "As far as the full words go, we often see sentiments engraved on jewelry from this era—fragments of poetry, personally meaningful phrases. We'll have to do some research, figure out how this baby ring showed up at a garage sale."

"No, there wasn't any garage—"

"More importantly," Paige interrupts again, "this type of engraving was used to set dates as a way to track the family in lieu of photos or other documentation systems. Obviously the larger two rings were wedding bands and the smallest a birth memento."

"Whose birth?" Libby asks, but she knows. It's coming together for her.

"And who was 'N'?" Paige is musing to herself, not really asking Libby. "Nancy? Nora? Nora is an old-fashioned name."

But neither "Babette Nancy Walker" nor "Elsa Nora Walker" sounds right to Libby. And the thoughts are whirling in her head, but words are not making their way through the jumble.

Then Paige frowns at the inside lid of the footstool, sticking her nose closer. "What if I missed something else?" She scoots forward in the wingchair, pushes her bulk off the edge to kneel on the floor, and then flicks with her nail at the inner corner of the dollhouse ceiling. "I've always thought this didn't look secure."

Libby crouches down to Paige's level as the girl digs into the loosened lining, fishes around behind it, and slowly extracts a slim book the color of the doll furniture—bright blood red.

"It's the softest leather, like fine gloves," Paige whispers. She opens the cover as though it's a holy thing and reads aloud the first few lines:

> *November 23, 1898. My Beloved, My Very Heart, At sundry times and in divers manners over the past months I have attempted correspondence with you. Now I must confess that, in all likelihood, you will never set eyes upon this script . . .*

Paige can't believe her find—a dated, hand-written journal from the pen of MDM himself! The slim volume of onionskin paper is delicate, and a pang zaps her for not donning her archival gloves. She flips through the entries spanning seven decades, the first page putting MDM at thirty-three and the last one written on the day before his death in 1967. Letting her eyes skip and bounce over a script that degenerates from a sturdy cursive to a cribbed and wavering scrawl, the few phrases she picks up here and there hold their note of confidence throughout in language reminiscent of the epigraphs appearing throughout the mansion: . . . *prevailing testament of my love for you . . . matrimony delivered us both . . . persuaded of better things . . . foundations will never vanish . . . law of love . . . enduring substance . . . we do not fear*. More than that, they promise answers to the questions plaguing Paige since the beginning of her studies—the issue of MDM's personal life, missing from all other extant sources.

"What does it say?"

Paige jumps. She's forgotten Libby is still here in the room with her, and she lowers the journal and lifts her chin to scrutinize the other woman with a new perspective that brings its own rash of questions.

"It's a diary. This journal could be the bridge from the past I've been pursuing." And a few weeks too late for her thesis. But in her heart she's doing cartwheels.

Libby has latched onto her with her eyes, and Paige senses an unexpected bond with this stranger who's been catapulted into her research.

"I have another letter," Libby blurts.

"What do you mean?" Paige's heart leaps again.

Libby's answer comes in staccato bursts. "In the car. In my overnight bag. The letter Gram wrote. About my ring—*this* ring." She extends the tiny circlet towards Paige.

A bag from the car?

"Ms. Paulsson?" Jamie is at the door of the den with the Australian couple lurking behind. "Sorry to interrupt."

Paige shoots a command at her: "Bring that pink overnight case to me immediately." While the girl scurries off to the gift shop, the couple fills Libby in on the new travel arrangements. Libby seems perplexed, but it turns out she's not upset at being summarily dumped by her ride home.

"May I?" she asks, and slips the journal off Paige's lap. From her custodial perspective, Paige shouldn't really let her handle it. But she's broken rules today already. Libby examines the inside flap of the front cover, where leather meets glued-down paper. Then she runs her finger along the seam of the back flap. "You never know if you've found it all unless you double check, as you said. Better safe than sorry . . ."

And, sure enough, Libby extracts from the loosened lining a small, tattered sheet of paper, creased and worn yellow.

The paper is brittle, and an edge crumbles off. Libby's stomach makes its nervous noise, a grinding and burbling telling her she's way more excited than she can verbally express.

The script is barely legible. It appears to be an official document, labeled with fancy print from the Office of the Synod of North Dakota, Pembina County, stamped on April 4, 1891. She reads the first line to herself and her scalp tingles.

"I think it's a marriage certificate," she says aloud, but her hand is unsteady and the print blurs before her. She doesn't resist when Paige takes the sheet from her and reads:

Given under the hand and seal of the officiating minister . . .

Paige pauses to lift the paper higher towards the dim light of the oil lamp.

. . . declaring joined in holy matrimony Moses David Melchizedek Laird and . . .

She stumbles here, falls silent.

Libby is nauseated with tension. She swallows hard. "And who?"

"I can't believe this." Paige lowers the paper and the two women gawk at each other. Libby slides closer to read the rest herself.

. . . declaring joined in holy matrimony Moses David Melchizedek Laird and Nuttah of the Plains Cree Tribe.

Libby leaps to her feet and cries out, "Nuttah? Not Nancy or Nora. The 'N' stands for Nuttah!"

Her chest is pounding with the powerful thudding of her heart, chanting silently to her mind, My name is Nuttah! My name is Nuttah!

Paige pushes herself up to a standing position with the help of the footstool. "There was something else there." She picks up the magnifying glass from the arm of the wingback and holds it over the paper.

Libby gawps with Paige at a scrawled notation inserted after the bride's name, penciled in different script, faded more than the ink: *My Heart*.

"That must be the English translation for 'Nuttah,'" Paige says. "'My Heart'—same as on the middle ring. Same as in the journal, in MDM's salutations." It's Paige's turn to hyperventilate. "Look here." She flicks open the journal again. "He addresses all the entries to 'My Heart.'"

Jamie comes back in with the pink case, and Libby retrieves Gram's last letter. She would read it aloud to Paige but the Australians, still standing in the doorway of the den, are insisting they need to leave in order to return their rental car in time.

"I suppose I should go." Libby is reluctant. She doesn't want to be anywhere else.

With a nod of apology, Paige says, "Just a minute." She plucks the envelope from Libby's hand and whips Gram's letter free from it without asking. Her gaze flickers across the text at amazing speed and flips to Libby and back again. She folds the pages and draws a deep breath.

"Leave this with me, and the ring, too, please. I'll give you a receipt for them." Her voice is tremulous. "I need to do some cross-referencing with the journal and my other documents. This find could have far-reaching historical consequences."

"But when can I read the journal to figure out how I fit into the whole scheme?" Libby can't think this fast. She has more she needs to tell Paige.

"We're going to have to speed as it is." The Australian's accent is intimidating. His wife is doing an anxious jig as she taps her wristwatch.

"Don't worry, we'll be in touch." Paige gives Libby a quick, surprising hug. "I'll put the journal and letter and rings into the mansion safe for now." She leads the way back to the gift shop, with Libby and the couple following close behind, and she asks them to wait for her as she writes up a receipt.

Libby's mind is racing. She has so much to figure out. Her restless eyes spot a stack of cookbooks on the gift shop counter by the till, titled *Historical Laird Museum Recipes*, and—out of absentminded habit more than deliberation—she lifts the top copy to check if there's a chapter on soups. Jamie, maybe smelling a purchase, pitches right in.

"This is a wonderful souvenir and costs less than ten dollars," she says. Libby reaches for her wallet. Jamie upsells her: "Maybe you'd also be interested in our selection of wild herbs and spices, gathered and dried right here on the Laird property by the descendants of the first Great Plains people MDM welcomed into his estate." The girl's patter sounds canned—she's young and maybe this is her first job—but Libby takes note of the rack full of bags with labels indicating the contents: field garlic and wild celery, sorrel and mint, prairie turnip and lambsquarters.

Then her eyes alight on a package of dried chokeberries, shriveled and almost black, and her mind tumbles back to an Indian summer day, after the first frost, when Gram came by to get her from elementary school with a picnic basket of supper sandwiches and a blanket to sit on. That was their ritual during the season Gram called the "Black-Cherry Moon." They caught a bus out of the city as far as the line took them and then walked in the golden haze a fair bit farther down a dusty country road until they hit a creek. And Gram, looking into Libby's eyes, said, "Still waters run deep," and Libby knew she wasn't talking about the stream but about the depth of a soul. After they ate together in the shade that buzzed with bumblebees, they picked from a loaded chokecherry tree to fill up the basket with cups and cups of the fruit, staining their hands. Libby stuffed her mouth with the tart cherries and spat out the pits until Gram warned she'd have a bellyache if she kept it up. And they went home for Gram to boil up a pot of chokecherry syrup for their pancakes.

Then—Libby recalls this now with a sense of wonder that she'd not thought of it despite wringing her brain for such a detail—hadn't Gram, with her waste not, want not attitude, dried some of the cherries at home to use during the winter?

Despite her horrible luck with Sybil's powdered Goji berries, or maybe because of it, Libby tosses the bag of dried chokecherries on top of the cookbook, if only that it reminds her so of Gram. Who knows? Maybe a subconscious taste for those chokecherries in Babette's Bowl was what drew her to Sybil's soup suggestion of Goji in the first place. And hadn't Chef Virgil recommended experimentation with the flavors of one's culture? What could be more essential to Gram's wild-tasting soup than the distinctive astringency of wild chokecherries?

Jamie rings up the sale of book and berries. "Oh, I forgot to give you this." She hands Libby a note from Sybil: *Sorry for ditching but knew you wouldn't mind.* Wouldn't she? Sybil always assumes what suits her own interests—that being, as usual, another man and a better proposal than Libby can offer.

> *I've promised the teacher a nice evening and thought you'd rather spend the night in your own bed than stuck in Grand Forks waiting for me. Don't worry, I paid for gas.*

How completely consistent with Sybil's inconstant friendship. Rather than negotiate a problem, she just throws money at it. Well, Libby's actually glad to be spared Sybil's drama right now. She needs to untangle all that's happened in the past couple of hours.

※

Paige dials in the combination for the Victor floor safe kept in the small office behind the gift shop counter and then depresses the cylindrical lever to swing the heavy door open. She can't believe her incredible discovery. She'd never have put the story together without Libby's presence, and even yet plenty of research remains to substantiate the familial bond tying the Walker women to MDM. With shaking hands, Paige places the papers and jewelry into the safe. She'll scrutinize them as soon as her afternoon tour is completed.

The grandmother's letter needs careful rereading, but Paige's cursory scan convinces her of uninterrupted lineage from MDM straight down to Libby. And the marriage certificate—what a find! Doubtless it will have a place in the Farris-Yeast litigation, should that continue. But it's the journal that will likely afford the completion of revelation she's been seeking—that full and personal and final record MDM left behind as evidence of his life. The windfall is pure manna, a gift beyond anything she could have hoped for, and it might well be the basis for her eventual doctoral studies. Perhaps her graduate committee will allow a supplement to her formal thesis, once she shows them the remarkable documentation Libby has brought to her attention.

On her haunches before the safe, Paige closes her eyes in appreciation. What amazing providence that Libby—who wouldn't know the academic implications for Paige—came to the museum and showed *her* the way. After Paige analyzes and merges all the information, she'll give Libby a comprehensive history of her family tree. Paige has a funny feeling this is just the beginning of an interesting friendship.

She stands up and moves to the till beside Jamie, who's bagging Libby's purchase, and writes up a receipt for Gram's letter. But she stops dead in the middle of her pen stroke and stares downward. Warmth is flooding her thighs and then wetting her ankles and then running over her shoes.

Libby is at her side in a moment. "What is it?" Following Paige's gaze, she, too, looks down at the floor, where a puddle of fluid is pooling at Paige's feet.

"My water broke." Paige whispers it the first time and then yells with exhilaration, "My water broke!"

Pandemonium lets loose in the gift shop of the Laird Mansion Museum. Libby turns white, which isn't very comforting to Paige. The Australian, Frank, gapes at his wife, his fish mouth opening and closing. Jamie screams about the baby coming and should she phone for the ambulance?

Paige is the calmest of all.

"Listen," she says, turning to Jamie, "call Danny at home. It will take the ambulance too long to get from the hospital." He'll make it here in few minutes. But why is Baby coming now, so early? "Then phone Ophelia to take the afternoon tour, whether she's ready or not."

Jamie dials, hopping from one foot to another. "Your husband's not answering."

Paige's eyebrows pull together. "I forgot. He went into town for machinery parts this afternoon." A contraction doubles her over.

"Come with us," Frank's wife says. "We can get you there. It's a good excuse to speed."

"I'm not due for over a month." Paige is getting scared now. Another gush issues forth between her legs.

"It's okay," Libby says. "I took a first-aid course a couple of years ago. I'll be there to help."

They make it out to the parking lot and into Frank's rental car, Paige tearing the bonnet off her hair and glad for all the absorbent bulk of the cotton costume she's wearing, which she bunches up to protect the back seat as her abdomen hardens in a violent spasm.

Libby holds Paige's head on her lap in the back seat of the car. What on earth possessed her to offer medical help? Taking a first-aid course in case her grandmother choked on dinner was one thing, but what does she know about birthing a live baby? This is a nightmare. But she's got no time to dither as Paige writhes.

"Breathe," she says, smoothing Paige's hair away from her forehead. "Deep, slow breaths." Gram had coached her this way when she labored through the miscarriage. "How much farther?" she demands of Frank in the driver's seat, as if an Australian tourist would know better than she the distance to the hospital. He's got the wheel in a death grip, and his wife, with the map open, navigates.

Between pains, Paige begs Libby for her mobile so she can call her husband's cell.

"Danny?" she squeaks. "Danny, get over to the hospital as fast as possible." She crunches up as another cramp hits, and Libby can hear Danny on the other end in an absolute panic. Before Libby can take the phone, Paige declares between gulps of air, "Danny, today you're going to become a father."

Her words send Libby into a slow tailspin.

✒

Paige's contractions are heavy and hard, and nothing she and Danny learned in prenatal classes is coming back to her. This is supposed to be a natural process? Every ounce of her mind is concentrated on weathering the cyclone battering her, breakers of pain increasingly intense and finally so close together that she's drowning. When they reach the city limits of Grand Forks, she really has to push. So she's blowing and panting by the time they pull up to the hospital, and then Danny's there and it's so much better because he'll make sure she's okay. Their beloved Baby is coming into the world and she'll have him in her arms so soon.

✒

Libby's been mulling over her insight ever since Paige's declaration to Danny on the phone an hour ago. It's been a day of discovery, for sure.

After off-loading the frantic Paige into the care of husband and nurses, Frank herded his wife and Libby back into the car, fretting about getting to Minneapolis on time. He darted out onto the I-29 southward for the four-hour leg, and now his dear little wife is chiding him to slow down because they're going to have an accident and end up back in the hospital themselves. They leave Libby to her thoughts in the back seat.

Paige's announcement to soon-to-be father Danny had snapped its fingers at Libby's memory. For almost half a century now, she's been chanting her childish rhymes to the beat of ten words while stirring her soup or taking a stroll: *Step on a crack and you'll break your mother's back* and *Once upon a time in a land far, far away* . . . Finally, when Paige had pronounced her wonderful news of Danny's impending fatherhood, Libby recalled the ten words MDM said to her just before he died. And it was wonderful news to her, as well.

For when she'd knelt there before the old man, having replaced the miniature doll furniture enclosing the two rings, and when he'd stroked her face with his paternal hands, he pronounced ten words that had gone clean out of her head. For almost fifty years—for her whole lifetime—she'd forgotten that decalogue.

But no longer.

No, now she remembers as if hearing those words for the first time, and they proclaim to her orphaned soul as though chiseled in stone:

"*You are my daughter. Today I have become your father.*"

So there in the back of a speeding rental car driven by virtual strangers, and even though she's returning to a mess of a life with no surety about where she'll live and how she'll survive, with no financial or personal security whatsoever—yes, then and there the curtain of her heart is rent in two as she finally enters into the rest that comes from truly belonging.

Libby Nuttah Walker has a father.

THE RED JOURNAL

Red Journal entry, dated July 7, 1967:

Nuttah, My Heart,

Can a decade have passed since last I wrote? Finding strength to retrieve this journal from its hiding place was miraculous, but exhilaration fuels me to pen what will surely be my final words, for, earlier this evening, I heard Elizabeth outside the veil. I caught a glimpse of the wee thing between the panels, that confounded housekeeper ever trying to close the curtain against guests. Now, for all my struggling, my faith shall have great recompense of reward, for faith is the substance of things hoped for and the evidence of things not seen.

The vixen Henrietta—along with her undeserving litter that out of sheer mercy I have so long kept on in spite of their treading underfoot my gracious forbearance—Henrietta, I say, has argued tonight in my hearing, on the other side of the curtain, selling hospitality like some commodity to sojourners needing shelter. Since when has my compassion cost others? No, she and hers will not see my inheritance, for only we who have believed do enter into rest. And, yet, her offense awoke me from slumber to the presence of our child, to whom our wealth belongs—my Scots and your Cree blood mingling within the bonds of holy matrimony.

I tremble as I write, my eyes barely seeing, but my prophecy cannot be muted.

Nuttah, My Heart, you have returned in Elizabeth. What you have begun with me, let her complete by her entrance. Would that I could call more loudly so that today she might hear my voice and, mixing that with faith, enter herein.

Come to me, my child.

CHAPTER THIRTY-ONE

A month later

The scarlet yarn tied around Sybil's wrist to ward off evil is soggy from her soak in the outdoor hot tub. Not that she feels any evil threat with such a good-looking, half-naked man lying beside the pool with her at the hotel in Lhasa. Tibet has exceeded her expectations. She came here looking for the land of Shambhala, and indeed she's finding it.

Isn't she?

Sybil reaches up with her right hand to massage the sudden spasm in her neck. Why does achievement of a goal always fall flat after the anticipation of pursuit? She shrugs her shoulder to loosen the stiffness and chase away the doubt. She reviews the past week's itinerary as proof of her contentment.

On the first day in Lhasa—the "place of the gods"—Sybil indulged in a luxurious treatment in the hotel's traditional herbal spa, sipped champagne from a sabered bottle in the five-star restaurant, and meditated in the ground's consecrated gardens. Then she began her journey in earnest.

She toured the Potala Palace housing the mummified remains of its builder, the Fifth Dalai Lama, in his funeral stupa studded with pearls and jewels. She ascended the palace's celestial staircases and descended below its ramparts to the seventh-century Dharma Cave, where an inscription above the entrance declared Buddhism to be *A Blessed Field of Wonderful Fruit*. She circumambulated the famed Jokhang Temple clockwise in company with throngs of crimson-clad lamas and acolytes accruing virtue. And she shopped the markets for sacred artifacts: a spinning prayer wheel, a religious scroll. And she came upon a set of cloth flags in blue, white, red, green, and yellow—symbolizing the five elements—that spur her on towards the rainbow-body level of realization.

Yes, her spirituality has so far been greatly enriched. Sybil sticks her chewed gum to the bottom of the poolside teakwood table and tips up the bottle of local beer made with Himalayan spring water. She runs her palm over her prickly nape. She's digging her new vacation 'do chosen in solidarity with Tibet's monks, so closely cropped it's basically shaved.

But maybe the greatest indulgence has been wandering the warren of alleys and courtyards hand in hand with the latest man of her karmic dreams—an American this time and one she brought with her. She smiles over at the lounge chair beside her, never having fully appreciated back home that such a gorgeous physique existed beneath his jeans and sports jacket.

"What's up, cupcake?" Clive asks.

"Just admiring the scenery." She winks at him. How superior he is to Mr. Nelson, her last conquest. Or for that matter to Clive's cousin Iggy, who of course is way too stodgy to leave his wifey for a week of blissful contemplation on the rooftop of the world. Sybil might be finished and done with Iggy. And with Libby, too, for that matter. Neither of them brings her the *tashi deleg* everyone here wishes on her, and good luck—in the form of excellent food, accommodations, and loving—is the underpinning of all her metaphysical growth.

As if reading her thoughts, Clive props himself up on one elbow. His six-pack ripples. He says, "I could get used to this lifestyle."

She laughs and says, "Sure, on my dime. You owe me."

"That's not what you said last night." He wiggles his eyebrows at her, and she titters like a schoolgirl.

It takes a lot to bring a blush to her cheeks these days. But in their almost-too-intimate encounter last night, they'd utilized material purchased on a whim at a nearby bookstore. It instructed them in weaving together the physical and spiritual through breathing techniques that channeled divine energy and linked them to the macrocosm of the godhead. This morning Sybil checked out yoga classes on the 'Net facilitated by an authentic Tibetan yogi back home. She registered for one titled "Surrendering the Self through Mantra, Yantra, and Tantra."

Everything is finally coming together for Sybil, her beliefs merging into a holistic structure. This finding of the tantric in Tibet parallels what she learned in the Arabic souvenir book brought home from Bahar's bedside and what she took with her from the Bahamian voodoo cave, the Parisian graveyard, the Native American buffalo jump—what she's taken from each of her encounters with the sacred. Whether embodying Krishna or Confucius, Bailey or Blavatsky, this great amalgamation is the solution to her inner conflict—the fullness of peace, compassion, and love that connects the cosmos.

And yet . . . What about the look in Mom's eyes? What about the sensation that Libby sees something just beyond Sybil's own grasp?

Sybil clears away the unbidden thoughts with a sharp shake of her head. After all, a whole new world is opening up to her, and Clive seems more than willing to come along on her geo-psychic-amorous expeditions.

"So you're happy now that you didn't follow through with your offer of shelter to Libby?" Sybil makes her tone neutral, as though the question isn't a test. She finds herself listening for innuendo in his answer.

"Libby? Who's she?" They both laugh. "To be honest, I might have stuck around to see whether she'd bite and move in with me, if those interfering people owning the property she wanted hadn't cut me out of the equation."

"'Interfering' as in they wouldn't sign your realty contract after you pressured them to open their place for Libby's viewing?" Sybil lets a sneer creep into her voice. How dare he intimate she's second choice, and to Libby of all people? "They were totally within their rights to pursue a private sale, Clive. It was a long shot that Libby would have bought the house for the price you wanted. Anyway, you and I agreed you were going to convince her to buy a condo in my complex." Not that she'd enjoy living anywhere near Libby at this point.

Clive lies back down again and closes his eyes as if parsing his answer. His salesmanship rises to the surface and he says, "Kitten, it's all about comparisons, all about the best deal."

"I hope you're talking real estate and not women."

"There's no contest over which woman I'd have picked from the beginning if I'd known I had a chance with you."

She smirks to herself. This serves Libby right for her addiction to security. After all, which one of them got the man in the end? Sybil arches her back to show her cleavage to best advantage, but Clive is already snoozing.

"I'm bored," she says, letting the petulance raise her volume. "Talk to me."

He opens one eye. "What about?"

"Spirituality."

"I don't know anything about spirituality." He locks his hands behind his head and wiggles his toes. "I just know about real estate."

Apparently Libby isn't the only one who needs instruction regarding deeper issues. Sybil doesn't mind beginning over with the clean slate of Clive's ignorance—and she can speak his language, use his terminology, to steer him towards subjects of her interest. She says, "Okay, real estate, then. Let's talk realty." She sucks up more beer. "I had a tour of a historical mansion museum in North Dakota last month."

"You, in a museum?" The cleft in Clive's chin deepens.

His humor is offensive. Clive should open his eyes to the sacred history she's been showing him here in Tibet for the past week. Men can be so freaking stupid. Sybil takes a cleansing breath, letting go of the negativity. There's teaching to be done.

"Yes, the Laird Mansion," she says. "It had the strangest layout I've ever seen in a house."

"For sale?"

"Not at all. It's state owned." She's about to launch into a description of the museum, from which she might branch into discussion about Wednesday's inspired tour of Jokhang Temple. But Clive interrupts.

"Not interesting to me, then." She should have seen that coming. He is, after all, into *realty* and not *reality*. He turns onto his side away from her. "Order me another brewski, will you, cupcake?"

She maintains her equilibrium despite his macho demand. She'll have lots of time to teach him all he needs to learn. But to herself she follows up on the comparison between the Laird Mansion Museum and the main temple in Lhasa, though it might be unfair of her to evaluate a century-old house against the Buddhist landmark that's had fifteen centuries to accumulate holiness.

The ambience alone of the monastery sets it apart, the interior obscured by aromatic smoke from burning incense, flames from the yak-butter candles flickering against silken hangings and gilded carvings of gods and bodhisattvas. It's a riot of sensuality unlike the stark functionality of the residence in the ghost town of Kirkton on the banks of the Red River of the North. But the layout of both temple and mansion bear similarities. Both are labyrinths—aren't they?—with a path to walk to the center.

Sybil and Clive had made their way through the mass of supplicating pilgrims crawling on hands and knees or wriggling along on their bellies. Many worshipers hummed prayers. The circuitous route through the complex took them past chapels devoted to various deities, monks, and kings. Their favorite was the one full of *yab-yum* statues of male and female entwined in the embrace of primordial union. They finally reached the core of the Jokhang Temple, built over the heart of a slumbering giant female demon subdued beneath it. There they'd found Tibet's most venerated relic—the life-sized, gem-encrusted statue of young Buddha enshrined in the house built just for him.

What did the North Dakota museum have to offer at its heart but a childish toy dollhouse and a chair covered in the skins of a poor beast butchered unnecessarily?

But Libby's eyes . . .

Sybil squirts too much sun lotion into her hand, then grinds it onto her face and décolletage. With Clive paying her no attention for the moment, Sybil calms her spirit by letting her mind skip back to the day preceding their departure for Tibet. That afternoon in Minneapolis, Sybil out of curiosity paid a visit to Hearsay after buttoning up her own shop across the street. Libby's old boss Terence had a few choice words about his former employee.

"She stopped in last week for her final paycheck." He snorted. "I offered her old job back to her, and she turned me down. What an ingrate." He glowered, but Sybil had to give grudging respect to Libby for standing up to the lout. "Said something about working in the food industry now. What, is she a barmaid? She's not going to make much in tips at her age."

Libby phoned Sybil to let her know she'd bought the Craftsman-style house in the Longfellow neighborhood after all, maybe expecting congratulations or a housewarming gift. Her purchase put the lid on any chance of reformation and sealed her fate against future travel with Sybil. It confirmed Libby's closed attitude towards change. She was dedicated to the banality of domesticity and the inevitable slide into old age that would follow.

Libby once had the audacity to say to her, "We're all going to die eventually."

What a slap to Sybil's whole worldview! As if death wasn't an illusion. As if only one's first go-round counted, the first cycle of consciousness on this lowest plane of the material world. In this city teeming with afterlife, the truth surrounds her. So no, Libby isn't the sort of people she wants to hang around, anyway. She's an inflexible and tedious drudge who can't go with the flow, who doesn't even realize there *is* a flow to life, to the universe, to the All. Libby has consigned herself to death.

Well, that's not ever going to be Sybil's fate. She's too much of a glutton for living. She picks up her current reading from the teak table, *Tibetan Book of the Dead,* and checks out that phrase she found last night. Yes, here it is: *Fear not the Lord of Death . . . You are incapable of dying.*

Incapable of dying. That's the whole secret to living.

Sybil relaxes on her lounger and begins chanting her favorite breath prayer—"From the unreal lead me to the real, from the dark lead me to the light, from death lead me to immortality"—until her mind empties and she falls into thought-obliterating sleep.

Paige Paulsson snuggles her newborn in his cozy flannelette cocoon, his milk-drunk cooing honey to her soul. She's almost forgotten the manic rush to the hospital, the fierce labor, the premature appearance that put Baby on supplemental oxygen for several days. But look at him now, flushed and pink and getting chubby already. They'd named him Martin Daniel Myles after father and grandfathers, not so coincidentally forming the initials "MDM" for Paige's hero. In fact, the Kirkton Preservation Society allowed her to borrow MDM's monogrammed christening gown for the ceremony, so fitting for the child of a historian. Paige lifts the blanket away from his button nose to adore his rosy cheeks and then burrows more snugly into the easy chair in the farmhouse living room.

Life's been a whirlwind in the month since Marty was born. Paige retrieved the treasures from the Laird Mansion Museum's safe as soon as she got home from the hospital. She sent the three rings and marriage license to experts for historical assessment. She studied MDM's red journal in conjunction with Babette Walker's letter, yielding groundbreaking information. She then put together a hasty addendum that had wowed her academic advisors. Finally, last week while Mom kept the baby ready for nursing in an adjacent office, Paige stood before the university panel to defend her thesis and to engage her judges in details that finally fit together. She earned a resounding academic endorsement with recommendation that future articles be submitted to top-tier journals for publication. But, perhaps most important, the unfolding of MDM's personal story still leaves Paige reeling with that "eureka" feeling, not to mention the joy of giving Libby a new name.

MDM Laird met Nuttah and Hokoma on a bison hunt in the mid-1880s, when she was only ten or eleven. Eight years later, the girl and her older brother were the first Native Americans to respond to their patron's sociological proposal—an alternative to the reservation life MDM never saw as offering the People a place to settle emotionally. The siblings broke away from their nomadic wanderings and convinced many in their starving community to join them in finding a better life and health and home by pitching their tents with MDM.

Within a year he married Nuttah, who in due course birthed a daughter, Elizabeth. When the child was about five and not yet fluent in English, Nuttah and her brother Hokoma set off with Elizabeth to introduce the girl to some full-blood Cree relatives on a reservation in southeastern Minnesota near the Iowa border. During their absence, MDM worked on a pet project for his darling little girl—a dollhouse mimicking the grand home the family had recently inhabited.

But here the documentation becomes sketchy so that Paige

has to speculate. It seems the young mother Nuttah contracted a virus and died with her beloved People. The unanswered letters and wedding ring made their way back to her widower, but Hokoma—commissioned to return his niece to her father in Pembina—never brought the girl back to MDM. When Hokoma, like his sister, succumbed to disease, the girl Elizabeth, wearing the third ring, disappeared, arresting the official family history. Until Libby came along, that is.

The story chokes Paige up as she tells it to herself again, holding in her arms her own child so ensconced in a family with father and mother and grandparents all at hand. How could MDM—how could any parent—face such tragedy and go on?

Elizabeth, lost to her family on both sides, eventually bore a child of rape. This daughter, Babette, in turn gave birth to Elsa, Libby's mother. But though the tale is heart wrenching, Paige's part in solving the Laird heritage riddle gives her deepest gratification. She's closed the family loop. Or, rather, she's found the one—Libby—who closes the loop.

There is one entry in MDM's diary she didn't bring up to the thesis committee—she who'd so recently gone through the learning experience of childbirth to suffer her way into motherhood. She pulls Marty closer to her breast as she thinks about it again. MDM's study of Greek had been no surprise to her, but his exposition in the journal of those two words in relation to his marriage—he "suffered" (*epathen*) and he "learned" (*emathen*)—showed both his humanity and his humility. That is, MDM took on the afflictions of Nuttah's race and bent his neck in submission to the situation, his suffering teaching him what he could never have learned otherwise.

As a white man, MDM willingly identified with Native Americans, loving them and loving Nuttah as one of them. So he dignified her vulnerability with the stamp of official wedlock in a day when Victorian prejudice saw interracial marriage as an audacious act. Nuttah in turn dignified his immersion into her community by legally marrying into the Laird line in a day when most indigenous wives were unwelcome within the Euro-American social classes. MDM came alongside Nuttah in spite of both their cultures, creating something new in trusting the nuptial tie to bind them as one.

Had MDM been influenced by his meeting with the Black-Bearded Barbarian, his Scottish shirttail relative with the Formosan wife? Paige would jump up and check her notes if not for Marty in her arms, but she must trust her memory here. The literature surrounding the era of European colonialism—not so comprehensively negative as the term is used nowadays—turned up a quote she'd included in her thesis without really understanding its full application: "The simplicity of a marriage certificate carries deep religious, cultural, and social meaning; it has the potential to profoundly change a person's destiny." Marriage between disparate groups globally had brought peace between warring lands throughout the ages, the mixing of blood in progeny proof of armistice and often the genesis of new nationality. Why would this connubial arrangement between MDM and Nuttah be so different? Besides, this was more about the love between individuals than any sort of cultural revolution.

And to top it off, Paige has secured a formal statement from the Kirkton Preservation Society reinstating MDM Laird's impeccable reputation, resulting in local media coverage and the termination of the Farris-Yeast lawsuit once and for all. The troublemakers dropped the case when threatened with DNA paternity testing involving the hair in the family rings and the tooth of MDM's mother's brooch. Libby, last in the line of the Laird household, has been invited by the KPS as featured speaker at next spring's museum opening and festival celebrations. Of course, there's no direct money in it for Libby, although the red journal proves her ownership of the heirloom rings and perhaps other holdings of the museum. But it's likely Libby will receive some remuneration in the future. MDM's journal puts everything into perspective, and its immaculate condition makes it an exhibit that museums around the country—and up in Canada—have already been clamoring after. The journal's blood-flecked final entry is the written record verifying to Paige, just when she was starting to believe no family existed, the irrefutable truth of Moses David Melchizedek Laird's legacy and character.

Just then Danny edges into the room on tiptoe. His hand is warm on her shoulder. "You are one good mother," he whispers, and he bends down lower to kiss the top of his son's head.

Paige's own little MDM shrugs and stretches and opens his blue, blue eyes. Yes, she's ready for this next phase of her life as a mommy. Her self-identity as scholar has given birth itself to the whole new sphere of motherhood, and she's up for the challenge.

Libby stands in her kitchen at Seven Canaan Lane—*her* kitchen—savoring the rich aroma of Babette's Bowl simmering on the stove. She surveys the glass-fronted cabinets and open shelving, and the farm sink with its backsplash of subway tiles. The finances came together quickly after her return home from North Dakota. The previous homeowners—Gloria and her husband, now on their way to retirement in Palm Springs—approached her with a more-than-fair asking price. Mr. Jordan at the bank was impressed with the compensation due her over the apartment eviction—and her two new jobs, of course.

Gram's soup kettle was the first item Libby took out of the moving boxes last month. Today she had cranked up the heat beneath the seasoned cast iron so that, when she dropped in the chunks of smoky bacon, they danced in the pot and gave off fat to sear the other meat—the mystery meat she should have guessed at long ago—and sautéed the grated carrot, onion, and turnip. She added water, salt, pepper, and then her second secret ingredient tied up in a muslin bag and immersed to stew in the broth.

"Halloo? Anybody home?"

"Come on through to the kitchen," Libby calls out, stirring up the wild rice clumping on the bottom. The porch screen door to the front room meows open and claps shut. Her friend shuffles across the hardwood floor, puffing and wheezing. She pops her shiny face around the corner.

"That there's a long walk from the bus stop." Zinnia mops at her forehead with a cotton hanky.

"Is that ingratitude I hear?" Libby asks it with a giggle as she hugs the portly woman. She smothers a further urge to tease her about the "long walk" between bus stop and front door being less than a block, hardly worth the sweat even in this early summer heat. A leisurely stroll gets Libby over to the Haven from here in less time than Zinnia takes to ride the public transit route. Not that Libby walks alone these days to volunteer at the Haven, what with her new companion and tenant taking Gram's place. At least

Zinnia is mobile enough to come for dinner now and then.

The elderly lady peers into Gram's soup kettle and inhales so that her ample bosom swells. "Mmm, smells good." Zinnia picks up the wooden spoon and prods at the partially submerged cloth bag, stained purple. "What you got in here?"

"You'll have to guess when you eat," Libby says, and she flips closed her newest cookbook to forestall further hints.

"You thought any more about using my family recipe at the restaurant? The one for *egusi* soup with spinach, tomatoes, and shrimp?" Zinnia sticks her pink tongue out and licks her lips as though she's tasting it.

"West Africa, right?" Zinnia nods and Libby continues. "I think I can convince Phil that our regulars will go for it."

Libby's new boss is becoming more amenable every day to her trying out dishes on his customers, such as her personalized variations of Italian minestrone, Hungarian goulash, and Scottish Cullen skink—consecutively renamed, to pacify Phil's patriotism, New York Bean and Veggie Soup, Hungry Cowboy Beef Stew, and Smoky East Coast Haddock Chowder. She's been working part time at Phil 'Er Up for almost a month now. She dreams up concoctions here at home and tests them first on her housemate and then on the restaurant clientele. Next she sends the recipes off to Folkways Nutrition Group for ratification by Quentin Hardy—her second employer. This dual position as Phil's chef and Quentin's culinary contractor is a marriage made in heaven, as far as she's concerned.

Libby takes out three place settings of flatware and fills a jug with tap water.

"That there's a pretty baby," Zinnia says of the picture on the refrigerator.

She pauses in her dinner preparations to stand beside Zinnia and admire the cutie in the photo. "Marty is the little boy I helped deliver," she says. Not that she actively saw him into this world, but she did attend the laboring Paige on the harrowing ride to the hospital. Entering into Paige's agonizing ecstasy turned out to be a gift to Libby in fully expunging the pain of her long-ago miscarriage.

Since the birth, Libby's had several telephone conversations with Paige that have helped clarify the historical and genealogical links between MDM Laird and the Walker women. Along with the photo of the baby, Paige sent a bound photocopy of MDM's journal that Libby has already read three times, front to back. Many of MDM's lines echo the inscriptions he carved all over the Laird Mansion Museum, his voice sounding like Gram's spouting of commonsensical slogans that got Libby through her formative years. But Gram's clichés tended to be, well, elementary—not shallow per se, but preliminary. It's as though Gram hinted but MDM proclaims, as though Gram showed the way but MDM *is* the way. As with her room-by-room tour of the museum, Libby's perusal of the journal has, page by page, imbued her with a whole new sense of home and belonging and legitimacy.

Paige also provided Libby with a copy of the marriage license, proving the legal union between a Scottish-Canadian immigrant and the full-blood Plains Cree bride for whom he built his grand house. Their daughter's footstool dollhouse along with its miniature footstool jewelry box and the rings within it are Libby's most prized physical possessions. Of course, she doesn't physically possess them, having agreed to leave all exhibits and original documentation at the museum on loan in perpetuity. Paige explained to her the complicated mediation process she launched on Libby's behalf, an ethical matter of acquisition and de-accession that will eventually declare these personal items officially belonging to Libby.

Libby is not the only one benefiting from this relationship with the new mother, for Paige also has needed information Libby holds. The flow goes both ways. For example, Libby riveted Paige with a narrative of Babette's memories surrounding Gram's mother, Elizabeth, and her daughter, Elsa. Then Paige contributed the fact that many of MDM's foremothers, too, bore names from the same root: Liza, Bella, Elspeth. That the Walker women were called by the same name as the Laird women is an anecdotal indication of a family tradition carried on and further corroboration of common bloodline. So says Paige, anyway.

Their conversation has taken Libby and Paige back to the sentiments engraved on the inside surface of the gold rings. Each ring follows the same pattern: date of marriage or birth, name initials, and then a word or two of commentary or definition. That is, next to Libby's great-great-grandfather's dated initials of M.D.M.L. is the word "Within." Next to her great-great-grandmother's dated initials of N.L. for Nuttah appears the transliteration of the Cree name, "My Heart." Finally, beside their child's dated initials of E.N.L. for Elizabeth is inscribed the meaning of her name, "God's Oath."

Libby had been the one to figure out this conundrum. As she takes hot cheese scones from the oven, she flushes again with the thrill of discovery. The three rings, nesting one within the other, successively spell out the phrase *Within My Heart God's Oath*.

Elizabeth—Libby—is "God's Oath" held safe inside the hearts of her forebears.

But is it God's oath or MDM's promise? Maybe they are the same. From habit Libby reaches for the chain around her neck, but it's empty now, her ring with the others on display at the museum. No matter—she carries it in her own heart.

The child of MDM and Nuttah reposed within their joint love, three nested rings, three interlocked lives. Elizabeth by name and blood bequeathed this blessing to Libby Nuttah Walker Laird. "You are my daughter," the centenarian MDM had said to her. "Today I have become your father." The ten words are engraved on her soul. She has a father and a name, and she is no longer walking away. Her quest has been satisfied. The dollhouse made for Elizabeth was made for Libby, as well. In the same way, Elsa belongs to Libby as much as Libby belongs to MDM, co-heirs of the Laird name, reinstating the circle of family.

Libby lifts each scone with a spatula onto a serving plate. Given the meaning of her name, it might be worth paying closer attention to what "God's oath" is. Can she really be the heiress of MDM's covenant—the promise of love made between father and that first daughter, her great-great grandmother? Is MDM the father she herself has been invoking all these years, inaccessible for so long and now brought near? The one she's been imploring without knowing his name? The only true end to every quest—whom, even today, she would entreat on behalf of Sybil, beseeching him to warm her cold heart at the hearth of his love?

Zinnia, sitting at the table and having caught her breath, breaks into Libby's thoughts as though reading them. "And what about that friend you had coming over to the apartment at all hours of the night?"

"Sybil? Oh, I think she's fallen into another adventure somewhere." Maybe she'll find what she's looking for, though the cure for her restlessness isn't a journey to the East. Aren't Sybil's world travels just another version of Elsa's drunken, homeless drifting between Minneapolis and Los Angeles? But there's no call for Libby to place blame—she herself has done her own internal wandering in looking for home and rest. Father, she exhales silently, give Sybil a vision of home.

Libby hasn't heard from Sybil since their trip to North Dakota. On returning to the Twin Cities, Libby went straight to the hospital where the ambulance had delivered Elsa after their tussle in the dark parking lot. Mom was sitting up in bed as though awaiting her. The doctor's opinion was that, although Elsa's injuries were not life threatening, she exhibited early dementia due to decades of alcohol abuse. Her mental confusion and apathy were already responding to the medication, he said, though some brain damage was irreversible. She'd need care and would spend the last part of her life institutionalized as a ward of the state unless—and here the physician paused and fixed Libby with a meaningful look—unless a family member stepped up to the plate.

After he left the room, Elsa blubbered "I'm sorry" over and over for causing Libby pain. Tears of regret coursed down over the corrugated cheeks, and Libby couldn't stop her own from swelling up over her lids and pouring out and dripping from her chin. They sat on the bed for a long while and talked, but not about every detail. Elsa has no recollection of her past fits of rage, and maybe that's just as well.

Now in her new kitchen, Libby scoops out servings of steaming soup—her first pot of Babette's Bowl since finding a butcher specializing in wild meat.

"You want me to holler 'supper'?" Zinnia asks.

"No, thanks. I hear her moving around up there now. You just sit and I'll get her." Libby doesn't need the trauma of two old ladies falling down the stairway. She counts her steps out the kitchen and through the front room—*peyak, niso, nisto, newo, niyanan*—practicing the Cree studies she's taken up lately in celebration of her heritage.

"What's that I smell?" Elsa teeters at the head of the stairs, and Libby leaps up them two at a time to steady her. Tidy gray hair frames her mother's lined face, but her eyes are clear and pleasant and peaceful, perhaps her forgetfulness dousing her sorrow.

"I made a special treat. Let's join Zinnia at the table." Libby ushers Elsa to her chair in the kitchen, and Zinnia hugs her in welcome.

"I could have came down earlier to help," Elsa says.

"You needed that nap, Mom." Saying "Mom" rather than "Gram" would take getting used to, but Libby enjoys the feel of the word in her mouth. If a reorganized family is her inheritance, then it is Elsa's, too. Elsa is her mother, and Libby is again becoming her daughter.

"Anyway, I never learned to cook." Elsa hangs her head.

"No problem. I did." Libby watches her mother's expression. Will this first taste bring a memory? Her hand shaking, Elsa dips her spoon into the thick, wine-brown broth and touches it to her lips. Her eyebrows leap up, but she keeps her focus on the bowl.

Swallowing, she stirs the soup and examines the vegetables and shreds of meat that rise in the bowl.

Libby can't keep from grinning. "Do you like it?" Elsa, head wobbly on her neck at the best of moments, nods with vigor. "Is it familiar to you, Mom? Do you recognize it?"

"Yep, but I'm not sure where . . ." Her voice drops off. She takes another healthy spoonful and then, smacking and swallowing, says, "It's the one *she* used to make, isn't it?" Elsa is still overcome by tears whenever she says Babette's name, but now her eyes are sparking in recognition. It's the expression Libby unsuccessfully tried, with so many batches of soup, to elicit from Gram over the last few years of her life.

"So this is the soup you kept talking about?" Zinnia licks her lips, poking her pink tongue out between brilliant dentures. "I thought you gave up on it, thought you couldn't find Babette's recipe in the end."

"I was looking in the wrong place." Libby dabs her mouth with the napkin. She'd only needed the proper resource, the source of truth. She rises to fetch the museum cookbook from the counter containing favorite recipes of the Laird household. Today Libby used the one for "Mum's Red River Colony Scottish Scones," dated 1881, a decade before the mansion was built. But the desktop publication is much more than a recipe book, filled as it is with stories and quotes attributed to homemakers in and around Kirkton. It's a neighborhood collection of traditional family dishes that made their way into the Laird kitchen.

Libby pages past "Aunt Frieda's Kuchen" and "Habitant Maple Syrup Baked Beans," stopping to read one of many anonymous sayings. This one she doesn't quite agree with: *Between soup and love, the first is the better.* She reaches the page that stupefied her when she first came across it and that made Paige laugh out loud when Libby directed her attention to it.

"Right under our noses?" Paige had shaken her head. "All through my research, I never thought to look for evidence in the museum gift shop."

Libby now shows the page to Elsa and Zinnia: "Bison and Chokecherry Soup" attributed to Nuttah L., circa 1892, with attending comment:

> *A typical dish of my People, taught to me as a child by the fireside in my parents' teepee, passed along to our wee daughter at the hearth in the mansion's kitchen.*

Zinnia scrapes up the last of her bowl and holds it out for more. But Elsa is dallying over every bite, her eyes closed and that smile—Gram's smile—playing around the edges of her mouth.

Dear Reader,

Everyone is looking for home—for inner peace, a place of rest for the soul. Maybe you're suffering the conflict of alienation or financial insecurity or the death of a loved one. Maybe you feel "homeless." In *The Red Journal*, Libby Walker has been seeking something lost generations ago: her heritage and the legitimacy only a Father can give. Perhaps her story of homecoming—the return of the restless wayfarer to hearth, heart, and spiritual health—will be yours as well.

Exalt ye the Lord our God and worship at his footstool; for he is holy . . . (Psalm 99:5)

Let us therefore come boldly unto the throne of grace, that we may obtain mercy, and find grace to help in time of need . . . (Hebrews 4:16)

Having therefore, brethren, boldness to enter into the holiest by the blood of Jesus, by a new and living way, which he hath consecrated for us, through the veil. (Hebrews 10:19-20)

ABOUT THE AUTHOR

Deb Elkink lives in a cottage beside a babbling creek in rural Alberta, Canada. She grew up in Winnipeg, Manitoba, and attended college in Minneapolis-Saint Paul (B.A. Communications, Bethel) before publishing her first short stories and articles. She married and spent twenty years as a Saskatchewan ranch wife and homeschooling mom (during this time earning her private pilot's license, learning to round up cattle on horseback, and cooking for huge branding crews). Graduate studies (M.A. Theology, Briercrest) then prepared her to edit doctoral dissertations, a professional quarterly magazine, and an online expository Bible study. Today she writes and speaks to women's groups about Christian faith. Her debut novel, *The Third Grace* (2011), received Canada's prestigious Grace Irwin Award. This was followed by her 2015 literary study on the fiction of a late-Victorian British writer, *Roots and Branches: The Symbol of the Tree in the Imagination of G.K. Chesterton*.

Other Books by
DEB ELKINK

The Third Grace

Roots and Branches: The Symbol of the Tree in the Imagination of G.K. Chesterton.

LET'S CONNECT!

Find Deb online at www.debelkink.com, and on Facebook and Goodreads.

For news and encouragement about upcoming books, contests, giveaways, and other activities, sign up for Deb's monthly newsletter.

If you've enjoyed *The Red Journal,* please consider leaving a review on Amazon and Goodreads. Your words bring hope and encouragement to the author as well as to other readers.

ACKNOWLEDGEMENTS

A special thanks to The Mosaic Collection, who found my voice amongst the cacophony and honored me with an invitation. This vital group of women has given breath to my story!

During the writing and publishing process, my spiritual life has been bolstered especially by Elma, Cal, Rod, Lori, Derrick (and spouses) and also by Marj and Dallas, Pearl, Wayne, Grant, Russ—and untold family and friends. Thank you.

With love, I dedicate *The Red Journal* to Gerrit, Tyler, Meghan, and Challis.

Coming soon to
THE MOSAIC COLLECTION

A single mother's journey from bitterness to forgiveness.

Three years ago, Erin Belden's happy life became a shattered mess. After her husband admitted to an affair and that a child had been conceived, he left her and their young daughter for his new family. Now, she's finally ready to put the pieces of her life together. She's set to launch her own business and even thinks her heart might be open to romance—should the right man come along.

But just when everything seems to be lining up, she receives a devastating call: her ex-husband and his wife have been killed in a car accident, and Erin is listed in their will as their daughter's legal guardian.

How can she be a mother to the child—let alone *love* the child—who broke up her marriage? Does she have the courage to start over yet again and turn this mess into a mosaic of beauty?

About Brenda S. Anderson

Brenda S. Anderson writes gritty and authentic, life-affirming fiction. She is a member of the American Christian Fiction Writers, and is Past-President of the ACFW Minnesota chapter, MN-NICE, the 2016 ACFW Chapter of the Year. When not reading or writing, she enjoys music, theater, roller coasters, and baseball (Go Twins!), and she loves watching movies with her family. She resides in the Minneapolis, Minnesota area with her husband of 30-plus years and one sassy cat.

www.ingramcontent.com/pod-product-compliance
Lightning Source LLC
LaVergne TN
LVHW040036080526
838202LV00045B/3357